CLOSE-HAULED

A SIM GREENE/*FIGARO* MYSTERY

Keep Sailing!

ROB AVERY

Jack Tar Publishing

Provo, Utah

Published by Jack Tar Publishing, LLC
1979 North 1120 West, Provo, Utah 84604, U.S.A.

Close-Hauled / Rob Avery -- 1st ed.
www.robavery.com
ISBN 978-1-945809-01-9
Library of Congress Control Number: 2016913481

Author's Note: This is a work of fiction. Names, characters, places, and incidents are a
product of the author's imagination. Some locales, businesses, organizations, and public
places or names are used for atmospheric purposes. Any resemblance to actual people,
living or dead, or to businesses, companies, events, institutions, or locales is completely
coincidental.

*To Emily who shares my love
of sailing and enjoys my writing.*

You can't sail a boat straight into the wind but you can nudge up next to it. You trim your sails hard, winching the sheets in tight, and bear off the wind barely enough to keep them full and hauling. It isn't a comfortable point of sail, though. A fifteen-knot wind feels like twenty or more and the boat pounds into oncoming swells. Spray comes over the bow and soaks the helmsman. The boat heels over more than usual and the wind wails a mournful song through the rigging. Being close-hauled is hard on the boat and it beats up the crew but you endure it when you must because it either gets you where you need to be or, sometimes more importantly, takes you away from where you shouldn't.

PROLOGUE

A man sat in a wooden chair and listened to the Anacapa foghorn eleven miles away. Shipping crates obscured the warehouse doorway but sunlight reflected off the building's metal roof and a few rays crept in under the large doors of the loading dock. Gulls screeched as they fought over something on the other side of the loading dock doors. The place smelled of damp wood and rusted metal, the scent of ocean-going commerce. The foghorn sounded again. The man loved the smells of the sea and the sounds of the foghorn and the gulls.

Shadows moved across the inside of the metal roof as two men entered the building. The man in the chair heard their footsteps, soft at first. The blond guy, the one in charge, had brought a tall, young Asian fellow with him.

"Who's he?"

"He's the guy who's gonna make you tell me where it is," said the blond man.

"Prepare to be disappointed."

The blond man pulled out a pair of red-handled wire cutters and snipped the plastic ties that bound his victim's right arm to the chair. He grabbed the man's wrist and placed his hand palm down on the wooden table in front of him. The second man produced a short roll of blue cloth, untied it, and laid it on the table revealing a collection of straight blades, hooked picks, and long serrated knives. He selected a thin blade of surgical steel and quickly pushed it through the bound man's hand, anchoring it to the wooden table. The man in the chair winced, knowing that he should feel excruciating pain. Instead, he only felt the discomfort of not being able to move his hand. A thin stream of blood pooled near the blade and rolled down his hand to the table.

The foghorn on Anacapa blew its maritime warning again and the man in the chair smiled at his captors. The young Asian selected another tool.

1

THERE were six of us aboard that night. Al had dropped *In Depth*'s anchor into a sweet spot of flat water behind the north end of the breakwater where we were protected from the waves but could still see the sunset. It was one of his favorite places in the world to host a barbecue.

An endless chain of ocean swells, born of a storm boiling somewhere between Southern California and Hawaii, rolled in from the southwest. It wasn't quite high tide but as each new swell arrived, a wave crashed onto the seaward side of the breakwater sixty yards away, throwing spray into the air. Its unmolested brother to the north would roll on toward the beach, rise up, and form a waist-high wall of water for the surfers to ride into shore.

I sat on a padded bench on the bridge deck explaining to Ashley Barringer how the sunset, on clear days, would cast a momentary "green flash." Ashley was the fine blonde marketing director I'd been dating for the last six months. She was smart—she'd fought her way up through the ranks of a high-tech startup—and she was also fun, athletic, and believed that a smile was a woman's best makeup. Most importantly, she liked to sail.

"So we won't see the green flash tonight?" she said.

"Only on clear evenings," I said. "We've got too many clouds to the west."

"It'll probably rain tonight," said Al.

He was the old salt firmly planted in his deck chair, cigar somewhere in mid-career, arms folded over a bare chest. His short muscular legs jutted from faded red canvas shorts. The shorts almost covered a wide scar on his right leg.

He propped his worn leather boat shoes onto the starboard bulkhead.

"It'll blow out, though," I said. "We'll still have plenty of good weather through the fall."

"You sailors are such romantics," said Monica. "Talking about rain on a beautiful evening like this."

She leaned in close to Al and he put his arm around her. Theirs appeared to be a happy and uncomplicated relationship with no discernible commitments. I felt a mild tinge of envy.

"So who's the new girl?" asked Monica.

"Jessica?" I said. "That's Reid's girlfriend."

"I thought his girlfriend was a redhead."

"That was three weeks ago," said Al.

"Reid's girlfriends seem to have a short shelf-life," said Monica.

We heard the door from the main cabin open and changed the subject. Jessica, a junior at the local university and probably half Reid's age, popped her head out and climbed the stairs up to the bridge deck.

"Do you guys have dinner out here every Wednesday night?" she asked.

"When the weather's nice," said Al. "And when Sim wins the Point Mugu Surf Contest."

"Second place this year," I said. "That Coastie from Bodega Bay won."

"Second place means you were the first loser," said Al.

"Well," said Ashley, "he is my first loser."

She patted my arm. Al shook his head.

"That fish was so awesome," said Jessica. "Awesome" was the most valuable adjective in her personal lexicon. "What kind is it and where do you get fish so fresh?"

"It's yellowtail," said Al. "I speared it this morning right over there."

He pointed west toward Santa Cruz Island.

Reid came up to the bridge deck with two six-packs of ice-cold Corona Extras. He was tall, almost my height, and lanky, with a short chinstrap beard mildly reminiscent of a modern-day Ahab. He put some of the bottles in the deck cooler and wielded a church key on the remaining six. He sat down next to Jessica and handed each of us an open bottle.

"Hey Reid, how come we never hold The Midweek Dinner on your boat?" asked Monica.

"My bank account shivers every time I fire up those twin diesels. I'd rather just bring the beer. It's a lot cheaper."

Reid had made a small fortune on Wall Street in his younger years and then, in early middle-age, brought his Ph.D. and *Dances With Fish* to Ventura County to teach economics, live in the marina, and chase college girls. Not always in that order. He had at least one redeeming quality, though; two field box season tickets between home plate and first base at Dodger Stadium.

"Here's to tall ships and small ships and all the ships at sea," Reid toasted. "But the best ships are friendships. Here's to you and me."

He raised his beer in the air and smiled as he put his arm around Jessica.

"The meek shall inherit the earth," said Al as he raised his bottle. "The brave will get the oceans."

We drank to the toasts and I realized how happy a man can be with a marvelous sunset before him, a cool ocean breeze whispering across the deck of a capable boat, and a beautiful blonde to put his arm around. A beautiful blonde who smiled.

A small flying fish launched into the air off our starboard bow. It veered to the right, inches from the water, and plunged into the sea fifty yards away. You rarely saw them in the harbor mouth. Something bigger must be chasing it. From the north came a formation as tight and precise as the Blue Angels; brown pelicans flying low over the waves, wingtips barely touching the water. Poor little fish. Predators above, below, and all around.

Nothing dies of old age in the sea.

"Sim, are you still planning on taking *Figaro* over to the islands this weekend?" asked Monica.

"No, it'll probably be next weekend if the weather's any good," I said. "Labor Day is coming up and the islands will be packed so I've arranged with my boss to take that holiday the weekend before. Ashley's conference ends Saturday morning so we'll probably leave then and come back Monday evening. You two want to join us?"

Al shook his head. "Pass," he said. "I gotta clean this boat up."

A variety of other vessels—cabin cruisers, fishing skiffs, sailboats returning from the local Wednesday afternoon races, and a couple of brightly painted and annoyingly loud ocean-racing speedboats—passed behind us on their way to or from the blue Pacific. The eternal train of harbor traffic. Some of the skippers recognized Al and waved as they passed.

"It seems wrong for you to sell this beautiful old boat," said Monica.

"She's a good boat," said Al. "But I can't take her to the Caribbean with me."

He paused to drink more of his beer.

"Warm water, blue skies, fine rum," he continued.

"That sounds awesome," said Jessica. "Sign me up for that."

"And the occasional hurricane," I added.

"Never mind," said Jessica.

The boat rolled slightly with the passing, close astern, of a large commercial sport fishing boat. Amateur fishermen crowded the rail and drank beer while the crew bagged the fillets they'd sliced from the unlucky fish. Dozens of gulls followed the boat and cried for remnants of the catch. Some of them flew over us toward the breakwater with fins, heads, or other castoffs in their beaks. More gulls waited on the rocks to fight over the spoils.

"Let's toss the leftovers to the birds," said Jessica. "Would that be okay, Al?"

"Sure. Do it off the stern, though. That'll keep the birds downwind and the guano off the boat."

"I'm sure glad that cigar is downwind," said Reid. "What are you smoking these days, Al? Old boxer shorts?"

"Every man should have a few vices, albeit carefully chosen ones," said Al.

Reid smiled, fully aware of his own chosen vices.

Ashley and Jessica carried the leftover bits of barbecued yellowtail down to the main deck and tossed pieces into the air. The birds responded with characteristic enthusiasm and soon the area behind the boat featured more flapping wings and screeching gulls than a Hitchcock movie.

Jessica shrieked loud enough to frighten some of the birds and all eyes turned to her.

"My glasses!" she said.

"What's the matter, sweetheart?" asked Reid.

"I just threw a piece of fish at a seagull and my lousy sunglasses fell off," she said. "There goes a hundred and fifty bucks."

"Don't sweat it," said Reid. "I'll buy you some new ones."

"But those matched this outfit perfectly."

A smarter fellow would have let it end there. Another pair of sunglasses sacrificed to Poseidon.

"You want to do it this time, Al?" I asked.

"And put down this fine cigar?"

"Okay. I'll give it a shot, I guess. Depth?"

"About twelve feet," said Al. "The sun's going down so it'll be getting dark at the bottom. And the water's murky here by the breakwater. Better take that flashlight under the console."

I grabbed the rubber-coated underwater light from its mount under the helm and fished a pair of goggles out of the tackle tray. I peeled off my T-shirt, kicked off my Nikes, and stepped up onto the starboard bulkhead.

"There goes the manly hero," said Monica.

Gauging the distance and the need to clear the deck rail below, I pushed outward as I dove. I put my left hand over the goggles to keep them from being torn off my face and broke the surface. The water closed in behind me and I felt that strange but familiar feeling of being at home. A creature of the sea.

The dive gave me more than enough momentum to reach the bottom and I dry-swallowed to equalize the pressure in my ears. I found a good-sized rock and held it in my left hand to counteract my natural buoyancy so I wouldn't have to spend a lot of energy staying down.

I moved deliberately and took my time panning the beam of the powerful flashlight back and forth under the boat in an effort to find the prized sunglasses. The beam caught a piece of anchor chain off to the left, an empty soda can off to the right. Ahead was a golf ball.

How does a golf ball find its way to a harbor mouth?

Forward and to the left again I saw more of the same anchor chain, a man's brown loafer, and a market crab the size of a dinner plate. To the right, a rigger's knife too corroded to be of further use. No sunglasses here, either. Forward again.

When I panned the light to the left a third time, I realized that the shoe I'd seen before held a foot. A leg and more anchor chain stretched forward out of the flashlight's beam. Another crab ran across the ankle. My heartbeat raced and I suddenly felt the need to surface. I moved forward again. I didn't get much time to look at the man but I saw the tattoo on his left forearm and instantly knew he was one of us.

2

I forgot about the sunglasses, dropped the rock, and headed back up. I surfaced near the boat and pulled myself up onto the swim step.

"Hey, Al. Get down here."

He heard the tone in my voice and hopped down from the bridge deck.

"What's up?" he asked.

"Better call 911. There's a body down there."

Reid wandered over.

"A drowning?" asked Reid.

"Not unless the guy was trying to swim away with somebody's anchor chain," I said.

Reid shook his head and closed his eyes. Al let out a low whistle.

I stepped onto the small aft deck and reached into the plastic bin where Al kept his diving gear. I grabbed some fins, a mask, and a weight belt.

"Can I borrow your underwater camera?" I asked.

"What for? It's not your job."

"I think the guy's a squid," I said. "About your age, I'd guess. If it turns out that he's Navy, I might wind up working the case."

Al walked into the aft cabin of the boat and returned with a digital camera in a waterproof case, an underwater flash, and a small compressed-air bottle with an attached regulator.

"My other tanks are empty," he said. "This pony bottle will give you about ten minutes."

"That's all I need. I just want to get some good shots before anybody disturbs the body."

Jessica walked aft toward us.

"Did you find my sunglasses?" she asked.

She looked at the camera and diving gear and her brow wrinkled. Reid took her arm and walked her away from the stern.

"Hey, what's going on?" she said.

Al went forward to find his cell phone and I went back down.

The body lay in twelve feet of water at mid-tide. Two fathoms. I examined the scene while taking photographs. I'd recovered a few drowning victims in the past—part of my job—and this one looked like he hadn't been in the water long, a day or two at most. He was, or had been, a Caucasian male, early to mid-fifties, of medium build, with a thin blond mustache and longish hair that flowed behind him in the slight current. His open eyes stared directly at me but not with the vacant, disinterested look that belongs to the dead. They implored me to release him. The rest of his face had frozen in that moment of terror when death became a reality.

He wore a white button-down business shirt with the sleeves rolled up to the elbows. The faded blue fouled-anchor tattoo on his left forearm was typical of sailors who'd served overseas thirty or more years ago. The shirt itself had faint blood stains over the chest but I couldn't see any bullet holes or other signs of obvious trauma without moving the body. And I knew better than to do that. He wore tan slacks, penny loafers sans socks, and about fifty feet of 3/8" anchor chain. It's hard to swim in an outfit like that.

I tied a marker buoy to a rock and placed it a few feet from his head so the Sheriff's department wouldn't have any trouble locating him. Then I took about sixty photos of the body, the chain, and everything nearby. I also found Jessica's sunglasses.

We heard the whine of the Harbor Patrol boat's engine well before the boat rounded the jetty. I handed the camera back to Al.

"Can you copy these pictures for me before Jerry grabs the memory card?" I asked.

"Done."

Al took the camera below and I put away the diving gear. Jerry tossed me a line as he pulled the boat up to *In Depth*'s port side.

"Who's been injured, Sim?"

Jerry was the classic California beach boy turned water cop. He stayed in shape and surfed every morning he could find a decent break off our part of the coast. When there wasn't a good swell running, he'd swim a mile in the open ocean for exercise. He didn't care much for liveaboards but he treated me pretty well since I was the guy who got him onto the base to surf Point Mugu when the big winter swells came in.

"The body's down below," I said. "Looks like a murder. I dropped a buoy near the victim and snapped some photos."

"Are you sure it's a murder?" Jerry asked.

"Your call, Jerry"

He thought for a minute.

"Okay."

Jerry called it in to the Ventura County Sheriff's Department and told us that the Search-And-Rescue unit was on the way. He worked his way around the boat, getting names and phone numbers and taking notes. It was predictably unproductive as I was the only one who had actually seen anything, but it was the usual police legwork and it needed to be done.

I grabbed a towel, dried off, and watched as Jerry questioned the others. Ashley and Monica appeared to be shocked at news of my discovery. Jessica was overwrought. Reid talked a lot and tried to comfort the women. Al showed no reaction.

Jerry finally turned to me. He asked me about how I found the body and I told him the whole story from seagulls to sunglasses.

"Why'd you go back down there?" he asked.

"To take some photos," I said. "Basic preliminary police work."

"It's not your jurisdiction, Sim."

"I'm pretty sure the guy is Navy and it just might wind up in our office."

"Have you got the photos?" he asked.

Al produced the memory card from his underwater camera and handed it to Jerry. The SAR unit arrived moments later in their giant inflatable quick-response boat. By that time, the beautiful sunset had been replaced with a pitch-dark night lit only by the buildings ashore and the sporadic flashing of the red and green harbor entrance lights. Al pointed out the marker buoy to them and they dropped their anchor north of the body. The two rescue divers worked rapidly to get their equipment ready.

"You guys need any help?" Al offered.

A uniformed Sheriff's deputy stood up.

"Who are these people, Jerry?" he said. "And why are they here?"

"Just some liveaboards partying," said Jerry. "These two guys," pointing at Al and me, "are Navy. They found the victim."

"Well, get them the hell outta here so we can do our job," said the deputy.

A little fire showed in Al's eyes. His voice lowered.

"That guy couldn't find his ass with both hands and a flashlight," he said.

"You know, Al," said Jerry. "One of the problems with growing old is that people no longer look at you as being much of a threat."

You couldn't really blame Jerry for being wrong. He didn't know Al as well as I did. He didn't know how Al had gotten that scar on his leg. Al smiled at Jerry the way an alligator might smile right before taking your arm off.

We weighed anchor and motored back into the harbor.

3

MONICA, Ashley and I stayed on the flying bridge with Al as he piloted *In Depth* down the main channel. Reid and Jessica joined us as we entered the main harbor. I tried to remember who it was that had suggested we anchor off the north end of the breakwater and then decided it probably didn't matter. Reid tried to buoy our spirits by suggesting we tie up at Tugs for a nightcap, but the mood was considerably less than festive. Jessica just wanted to get off the boat as quickly as possible.

"How come everybody seems to hate you guys so much?" asked Ashley.

"They don't hate us," said Monica. "The harbor management and the patrol just think that those of us who choose to live on our boats are more trouble than we're worth. So the people who run the marinas stop accepting liveaboard applications and then hope we'll eventually go away."

"We get blamed for everything," said Al. "Some weekend warrior's kid flushes a turd into the harbor and the patrol points at us. Like we'd crap in our own backyard?"

"The five of us are the last ones at Vintage Marina," I said. "When Al sells his boat and leaves, he won't be replaced."

"Five?" asked Jessica. "I only count four of you."

"Judith lives on that old wooden cabin cruiser a couple slips down from me," said Reid. "But she's a bit of a loner and doesn't hang out with us very much."

We motored past Channel Islands' small but brightly-lit commercial dock and watched the jib crane unload plastic crates of sea urchins from a gray utilitarian work boat. A bare-chested diver watched as the crane operator moved the crates into a refrigerated truck and made entries in his load book.

"I can't believe people actually eat those nasty things," said Monica.

"I tried it once in a place outside Yokosuka," said Al. "It looks like a poodle's tongue."

A few groans followed Al's description.

"They give you two pieces of the stuff stacked on little rice cakes," continued Al. "I only ate the second because everybody else was watching me."

The groans turned to chuckles.

As we got closer to J-dock, Reid and I hopped down to the deck and hung the boat fenders from the ship's bulwarks. Al expertly maneuvered the large trawler into its slip and we made her mooring lines fast to the dock cleats. Al handed me a thumb drive as I stepped off the boat.

"Your pictures," he said.

"Thanks."

Reid and Jessica hopped off the boat and walked over to Reid's sport fisher, Monica volunteered to stay and help Al finish cleaning *In Depth*, and I left to walk Ashley back to the parking lot. There wasn't a lot of small talk; no 'See you next week' or 'Great dinner, Al.' It wasn't the usual conclusion to The Midweek Dinner. But it wasn't normal for us to discover a murder victim, either.

The low clouds closed in on Vintage Marina. Thick moisture hung in the air. You couldn't really call it rain and it hadn't thickened to a true fog. Amber-hued dock lights glowed in the haze.

"Do you really think the guy you found was murdered?" asked Ashley.

I nodded.

"Couldn't it have been an accident?"

"No," I said. "Somebody wrapped him up in that chain."

The metal hinges connecting the floating docks of Vintage Marina creaked and groaned as we walked toward the card-key gate that separates the 'yachties' from the general public. We walked up the ramp to the parking lot.

"Are you going to be okay?" Ashley asked.

"I'm a little shaken, I guess. It's not like I haven't seen a dead body before in my line of work. It's just that I've never seen anything quite this cold and calculating. So deliberate."

I didn't share any more details. She didn't need to know about the moment in time—the moment of death—frozen in the victim's face. I opened the car door for her and she stood there and held my hand. She didn't let go.

"It's all so dreadful," she said.

She put her arms around my waist and buried her head in my chest.

"I need you to drive me home," she said.

She lived only a couple of miles away in a rented duplex a hundred yards from the beach. I drove her home, parked on the street, and walked her to the front door. She took my hand and led me inside. She cried and shivered and, eventually, fell asleep in my arms.

The vision of a drowned man looking at me in horror from the other side of death kept me awake for some time.

4

I woke before sunrise to a gray and drizzly Thursday morning that was unusually cool for August. Ashley was still asleep and I tucked the comforter around her as I got out of bed. I tugged on my shorts, strapped on my running shoes, and picked my gray University of Washington T-shirt up off the floor.

I've never attended the University of Washington or, for that matter, any other college. The T-shirt had been sent to me by a fabulous redhead who, for a few wonderful months, had shared the close confines of my boat with me before returning to the Evergreen state for another dose of higher education.

I slipped out Ashley's front door and jogged down to the beach for an early morning run. I headed south, running along the hard sand left by the receding tide, passed the Mandalay Bay resort, and continued toward the north jetty.

The sun tried to grind its way through the clouds to the beach but could only force a gray light through the low overcast. A thick fogbank shrouded the channel, daring unwary vessels to venture forth. I figured the edge of the fog to be just a little over three miles offshore as I could barely see *Gina*, the oil drilling platform that sits between Channel Islands Harbor and Anacapa Island, poking its nose through the mist.

The fog obscured the lighthouse on Anacapa but the foghorn, eleven nautical miles away, blew its low warning to the commercial vessels sailing these waters. A good percentage of the coastal shipping bound for Los Angeles passed through the strong currents and occasional thick fog that hides the steep cliffs and sharp rocks of the Channel Islands. Well over a hundred large ships have foundered on the islands' shores over the years but GPS and modern communications have all but eliminated the problems of current and fog.

Strong winds came with the night's rain and an above average amount of sea junk had washed ashore. Plastic soda bottles, a busted life preserver, a dead harbor seal covered with fat blue flies and sand fleas, and lots of kelp lay on the beach. I bent down to pick up some old Styrofoam coffee cups. It wasn't much in terms of total trash reduction but I like to think that it adds up over time. And there isn't a whole lot of room in a shorts pocket anyway.

"Whatcha got there, boy?"

I looked up to see Old Jed, king of the local beach bums, sitting on an improvised throne of seaweed and sand. He smiled as he sipped from a small bottle in a brown bag. He wore faded army fatigue pants, Converse All-Stars from a previous decade, a stained windbreaker, and an L.A. Kings bill cap. His wardrobe rarely varied. With a change of clothes and a longer beard he could have been mistaken for the bass player from that little old band from Texas. But you couldn't quite guess his age. He could have been forty or seventy.

"It's just an old cup, Jed. Nothing worth anything."

"Yeah," he said. "There's just junk on the beach today. Nuthin' worth nuthin' here."

He sat back a little farther on his seaweed mound and took another sip from the bag.

"Didn't see nothing wash ashore up north, did you?" he asked.

"No," I said. "Should I have?"

"Big package," he said. "Never saw it up close but I seen it fall, I did. Fell off a boat right out there. I been watchin' for it but it ain't washed up here on the beach."

A spray of mist on the wind sent a shiver down my spine.

"When was this?" I asked.

"Night a'fore last, boy. Late."

Another shiver.

"Where?" I asked. I'd already guessed the answer.

"Out there off the north end of the breakwater," he said. "Right at the edge of the harbor mouth."

He pointed at the exact spot Al had anchored his boat yesterday.

"Did you see the boat?" I asked.

"Sorta," he said.

"What kind of boat was it?"

"It wasn't so as I could tell you which boat," he said. "It was too dark. But I seen a shadow over the moonlight moving real slow and I heard a boat out there growling a little. The light from the moon was just right so's I could see the splash on the water."

"Was it a fishing boat?" I asked. "Cruiser? A sailboat, maybe?"

"Real low down kinda boat but sorta long," he said. "Thirty foot or so, maybe more. No navigation lights, neither. I figured they lost a package and I could find it and sell it. You know, finders keepers and all that."

He looked at the bottle in the bag and made a frown.

"I sure as hell need the money," he said.

"Do you remember what time it was?" I asked.

"Couldn't really say, son. It was late. After the Mart closes."

The Harbor Mart stayed open until eleven on weekdays. Old Jed might have been drinking — he usually was — and he'd have been pretty tight by midnight. There was probably nothing to his story.

"Well, it's always good to talk with you, Jed, but I'd better get running again. Got to keep in shape, you know."

"You do that, boy. You'll let me know if you see anything good on the beach, okay?"

I left Old Jed perched on his seaweed throne, thought about his observations, and paid special attention to the flotsam on the beach as I continued my run south to the jetty. A piece of paper, a business card, a shred of a shirt, anything like that could be evidence but there was nothing promising; nothing worth picking up. I turned back at the jetty and retraced my run north. Jed had moved on by the time I reached his seaweed sofa. I continued north to the lifeguard station at the end of Ashley's street and walked the last hundred yards to her apartment. She kept a spare key in a fake hollow rock in the garden by her front door. I let myself in.

I found her still asleep somewhere under her jumble of fluffy pillows and down comforter so I slipped into the shower as quietly as I could and washed off the running grime and salt. When I finished, I wrapped one of her thick white cotton towels around my waist and launched an attack on the kitchen.

Ashley didn't keep a lot of food in her house as she was, in her own words, "not much for cooking." But I dug through the fridge and found half a dozen eggs, some sharp Irish cheese with a green rind on it, a half package of mushrooms, and some sliced ham. A couple of leftover baked potatoes and an onion sat in the bottom of the vegetable drawer. I couldn't find any bread worth toasting but I figured I could transform the balance into a decent breakfast for two. I sliced and sautéed the onion, mushrooms, and potatoes and shredded some of the cheese. Ashley interrupted me before I could crack the eggs.

"Do you always cook breakfast naked?"

She stood in the doorway in her robe, wiping the sleep from her eyes.

"I always wear a towel whenever I fry something," I said. "Safety first, you know."

She grinned as she walked up and grabbed the towel where I'd tied it.

"And what comes second?"

Breakfast, obviously, had to wait.

We made omelets, later, and ate them by the gas fire in her small living room.

"Are you still coming to dinner Sunday night?" she asked.

"Sure," I said. "At your folks' house."

"Pick me up at five?"

Meeting the parents. A milestone in a relationship. Or is it a crucible?

"Sounds great," I said. "Are you gonna eat those potatoes?"

We finished breakfast and dressed and she drove me back to Vintage Marina so I could get ready for work. She dropped me off near the gate and a light rain began to fall the second she drove away. I opened the gate, walked down the ramp, and headed toward *Figaro*. She is such a pretty boat and I marvel at her every time I see her. I unlocked the hatch and stepped down the companionway into the cabin. The patter of rain on the deck increased as I pulled the thumb drive from my windbreaker, attached it to my laptop, and transferred the crime scene photos to a new folder on the hard drive.

I changed into the dark pants and khaki short-sleeved shirt of my service uniform, locked up *Figaro*'s companionway, and made my way back up the dock to my Jeep. A small folded piece of paper sat tucked under the windshield wiper; a note from Ashley thanking me for breakfast. She had drawn a little Valentine's heart at the bottom next to her name. I felt like I was back in high school. It wasn't a bad feeling.

My Jeep started on the first tick and all was right with the world. I called Jerry.

"Those photos turn out all right?" I said.

"Yeah," he said. "Absolutely. The Homicide unit says you did a good job."

"Glad to hear it. I ran into Old Jed during my run this morning."

"He give you some sort of trouble?" he asked.

"No, no. He said he saw somebody dump something into the water out where we found the body last night."

"Out where you found the body, you mean," he said.

There was something wrong in the tone of his voice.

"Yeah," I said. "Jed told me he saw it go in."

"That old bum's a crank," said Jerry. "I don't know if it's booze or meth or something else but the guy's brain is scrambled like an omelet."

I thought about the mixed metaphor for a moment and decided to let it pass.

"Well, it's what he told me and I thought it best to let you know. You could pass it on to Homicide. They'd want to know about it and maybe talk to him."

"Yeah, thanks," he said. "By the way, they want to ask you a few questions."

"Sure," I said. "Anytime."

I ended the call, drove through the North Mugu Road gate at Naval Base Ventura County, and began Another Fine Navy Day.

5

MY office door opened and Master Chief Joe Richardson walked in with two foam cups and a box of donuts. He put the box on my DoD-issue metal desk, handed me one of the cups, and sat down in the poorly-padded metal chair opposite me.

"You trying to poison me?" I asked.

"Only if I thought it'd work," he said.

He fished around in the box and pulled out a packet of sugar and a small round plastic tub of regulation U.S. Navy creamer.

"Cream?" he asked. "Sugar?"

"I like my coffee black," I said. "Just like my boss."

He smiled and his white teeth gleamed past his ebony skin.

"That is so damned funny," he said. "I just never tire of hearing racial slurs from my underlings."

Joe was the rarest of bosses. He appreciated hard work, had a sense of humor, and protected the men who reported to him. He had a wife and five children but, as far as any of us could tell, he was all Navy all the time. He pulled the tab off the creamer, poured it into his coffee, and stirred in a half packet of sugar.

"Do you still want to get into the Chief Warrant Officer program, Sim?"

I nodded as I grabbed a donut.

"And you're hoping to land a billet with NCIS, too, right?"

"That is A-ffirmative, Master Chief," I said.

He smiled again and drank some of his coffee. I ate some of my donut. Probably the best thing the Base Mess ever baked. The cake was light and crumbly and the maple frosting was airy and not overly sweet. Joe had something on his mind, something that bothered him, but I knew there'd be no point in asking about it. He'd tell me when he was ready.

"You're the best detective I've seen come through this office, Sim. The absolute best by any measure and I'll be sad to see you go."

"Are you telling me the CO has approved my application?" I asked.

Joe leaned back and folded his right leg over his left knee.

"No, Sim. He hasn't. He called me this morning," he said. "He wants to talk to you."

I drank some of my coffee and took another bite of donut.

"I'm not sure I like the sound of that," I said.

"There is no reason you should."

He reached into the box and tore a chunk out of an old fashioned.

"You got any idea why he wants to talk to you?" he asked.

I shook my head.

"Neither do I," he said. "Usually, he'd sign the lousy application and send it in. But he hasn't signed it and didn't offer any reason why not. All he'd tell me was that he has an assignment for you that will require me to redistribute your entire case load."

"I'm not sure I like the sound of that, either."

"He also said that you will report directly to him," said Joe. "I am not to inquire into your actions or supervise you in any way."

I drank some more coffee.

"That seems pretty unusual, Joe."

"That's because it is unusual," he said. "Pretty damned unusual. And I don't like it one bit."

He thought for a minute.

"He did *not*, however, tell me that I couldn't give you any advice, Sim. So I'm going to do that right now. Be very careful when you talk to him. Listen closely to what he asks you to do and don't over-promise results based on what you think he wants. Don't even let him think you over-promised. And you damned sure better not under-deliver."

He finished his coffee and tossed the empty foam cup into my trashcan.

"Either way, I'm sure gonna miss you, Sim."

"How's that?"

"If you make Captain Overson a happy man, he'll approve your application and you'll be on your way to Officer Training Command Newport. Screw it up, though, and you'll go from Chief Petty Officer to E-Nothin' in no time at all. And you'll be humpin' your duffels all the way to the Black Hole."

The reference to the Naval base at Norfolk, Virginia, the place where sailors' careers go to die long and painful deaths, was not lost on me.

"What if I need some help?" I asked.

He stood up to leave.

"Beats me. You can ask Gil if you need something done but don't ask me." He threw up his hands as he walked out. "Love you like a brother, Sim, but I don't want to know anything about this."

6

"I understand you found a body last night."

"Yes, sir," I said.

"Was it murder?" he asked.

"The circumstances point in that direction, sir."

The roar of an F-18 during takeoff filled the room and the Captain held up a hand, palm forward. Captain William Overson was the Commander of Naval Base Ventura County and it was the first time I'd ever been to his office. It seemed understated and sparse given the size of his command. No mahogany on the walls, no opulent furnishings. DoD grade carpet.

The Captain sat in a leather chair behind a simple wooden desk. A long window to the left, the top half obscured by venetian blinds, allowed him a view of the base's two runways. He watched for the approaching fighter. I looked around the office.

A plain wooden bookcase covered the wall on the right. The lower shelves contained tactical treatises and history books regarding naval aviation and sea power; all Government Printing Office publications. The upper shelves held framed commendations and citations, a picture of the Captain in a flight suit on the deck of an aircraft carrier, and three more of him receiving promotions from superior officers.

A picture of the current commander-in-chief, flanked by smaller pictures of the USS *Enterprise*, USS *Abraham Lincoln*, USS *Nimitz*, and USS *John C. Stennis*, hung in the center of the wall behind the desk. I wondered how many captains had flown fighters off four different carriers.

Captain Overson himself appeared to be somewhere around fifty, probably only a dozen years my senior. He was probably three inches shorter and forty pounds lighter. A jet jockey. But he carried four bars and a star on his sleeve and that made all the difference. A single inch-thick manila folder sat to his left on the desk's top; a single blue pen to his right. Every detail of the office radiated function over form. The sound of the F-18 faded.

"Sorry, Chief," he said. "But no man who has ever flown can keep his eyes out of the sky."

"Yes, sir."

"Tell me about last night," he said.

I told him how I had discovered the body, taken the photos, and interacted with the Sheriff's department. I described the victim. Captain Overson listened intently and asked only a few specific questions. When I finished, he stood up from his chair and walked around it toward me. He picked up the manila folder, handed it to me, and leaned his backside against the front of the desk.

"The man you found was Lieutenant Barry St. James, U.S. Navy, now retired," he said. "Barry and I were shipmates years ago. He was a good man and a good friend. A very good friend."

"I'm sorry, sir."

The Captain looked at me in silence for a moment.

"I want you to find out who killed him and why," he said.

"With all due respect, sir, do we have jurisdiction over this case?" I asked. I already knew the answer.

The Captain shook his head, walked back behind the desk and sat down in his chair.

"No, Chief, we do not have jurisdiction," he said. "And NCIS isn't the slightest bit interested. Barry retired ten years ago. He was not on active duty and it appears he was killed off base. So, everybody around here tells me it's a civilian matter and that Ventura County has complete jurisdiction."

"The county's Major Crimes Unit seems quite capable, sir."

"I don't give a rat's ass how capable they are," he said. "They aren't Navy. This man was a good friend of mine and I want to know who did this to him. Your boss says you're the best he's got and I want you on the case."

I sat without speaking.

"Barry may also have had some sensitive documents in his possession. Letters, we think, that could embarrass the Navy if the wrong people obtained them and made them public."

I nodded.

"I understand you have a CWO application pending and that you'd like a chance at getting a slot in NCIS," he said.

"Yes, sir."

"I also understand that your previous commanding officer did not share Master Chief Richardson's favorable opinion of you," he said. "I've been informed of the circumstances surrounding that assessment."

I felt the blood in my neck getting hot and suppressed the urge to tell my version of the story.

"We had our professional differences, sir."

"I don't care," he said. "I don't care in the least. I understand that you don't have the greatest appreciation for accepted military procedure and that you can be difficult to deal with sometimes. But Joe says you're the best he's got and I trust his judgment."

"Thank you, sir," I said.

My teeth unclenched a bit.

"I'll be straight to the point," he said. "If you find out what I want to know about Barry's murder and locate those documents then I will directly recommend you for Chief Warrant Officer School. I will also write a letter to NCIS in your behalf and mention it to my superiors. That could be very helpful to you."

"Thank you, sir."

"That folder you are holding contains every non-classified piece of information I could gather on Barry given the short no-tice. His apartment, friends, ex-wife, family; most of it is in there."

I opened the folder and began to read it.

"None of that information is official, Chief Greene, and, for the record, I never gave it to you."

I looked up at him.

"If you decide to do this for me, it is not on my order," he said. "It is entirely voluntary, it is entirely unofficial, and it is completely quiet. Completely. You will have minimal support from my staff and, just so you know, even they don't know anything about this assignment."

I thought about my obligation to obey the lawful order of a superior officer and the possible penalties for refusing. It was a weird order but not unlawful. Still, I had to wonder why this investigation required so much secrecy.

Captain Overson leaned back in his chair and studied me for a moment. He cocked his head to the right and squinted his eyes.

"How did you break your nose, Chief?" he asked.

"Organized bar fight in Pearl City, sir."

"Organized?"

"They had a ring and gloves and a guy who held the clock and rang the bell," I said.

He smiled.

"So, you lost that one, eh?" he asked.

"No, sir," I said. "It made me angry and I finished it."

He chuckled and nodded.

"I'm glad to hear that," he said. "I'm glad to see a sailor who gets it done."

He thought for a moment.

"This assignment is to be kept entirely between you and me, Chief. If I am repeating myself it is because I want to stress this in the strongest possible way. You will not discuss this case with Master Chief Richardson, with your coworkers, with anyone from

JAG, with your girlfriend, with anyone. You will report your findings directly to me and to no one else. Is that understood?"

"Yes, sir."

"Any questions, Chief?"

"Can you give me any information about these missing documents, sir? Anything that will help me know that I've found them?"

"Only that they are extremely sensitive and that they were last seen with Barry. The contents are not your concern. If you find anything that he has written or received on Navy letterhead, any letter or document he may have received from anybody, or anything that looks the least bit unusual at all, you will bring it directly to me. Immediately. Is that understood?"

"Yes, sir."

"Master Chief Richardson knows that I have informally asked you to handle a special project for me and that you will not be working regular office hours until such project is completed. He and I have a good relationship and he is okay with this arrangement. He will be temporarily re-assigning your current case load to your co-workers."

He put his hands together and made a tent of his fingers. He rested his chin on his fingertips.

"How long will it take you to wrap this up?" he asked.

"It is hard to say, sir. Most homicides are fairly straightforward and the perpetrator is easily identified. This one is, well, unusual."

"We have two weeks until the Labor Day weekend," he said. "I'd like to see some definitive results by then."

"Yes, sir," I said.

He picked up a pen and made a notation in his desk calendar.

"I want you in my office with a status report on Monday afternoon," he said.

So it would be like that.

"Yes, sir."

7

IT was after quitting time when I finally got out of the Base Commander's office and the usual line of cars formed to drive out the Mugu gate. The cool morning fog had given way to a hot afternoon sun that baked large swaths of military asphalt to that hellish temperature where the blacktop softens and the simple act of turning a steering wheel digs a hole in the parking lot. The soles of my leather shoes warmed as I walked to my Jeep but it started quickly and the air conditioning kicked in with welcome enthusiasm.

Ashley had to work late preparing for some important corporate retreat so I had to eat alone. I detoured into Silver Strand and picked up a burrito from a local place with lousy parking but great food. I ate it in *Figaro*'s cockpit under her dark blue bimini top. I held the burrito in my left hand and a new book in my right. It was one of the books that Hemingway didn't quite finish before swallowing a shotgun.

Thomas Hudson's friend Roger had upset a big man on a nearby yacht in the Bahamas and the argument turned into a fistfight about the same time that I finished my burrito. Hemingway knew a thing or two about bare-knuckle fighting. Only a former boxer could write with that perfect sense of timing and the awful realism of facial injuries inflicted by bare fists. I instinctively raised a hand and felt my nose. But as much as I love Hemingway and get lost in his writing, a few nagging questions kept breaking into my train of thought. Why had the Base Commander picked me to investi-

gate the murder of a retired sailor in a case where we had no jurisdiction? Why the personal interest? Why was it such a big secret?

Someone tapped a foot against *Figaro*'s hull and I looked up to
see an all-too-familiar female face.

"Judith, how are you?"

"Hungry," she said. "I could eat a horse. You need to take me
out to dinner tonight and woo me over a piece of rare steak and a
bottle of wine."

"I'd love to but I have a very sensitive survival reflex and I've
developed a healthy fear of venomous fire-breathing female jour-
nalists," I said.

Judith Norton smiled. Younger than me by only a few years,
she was news editor for the regional paper. She lived aboard *Norton's Ark,* an old wooden cabin cruiser that had, years ago, passed
over to the other side of seaworthy. She didn't hang out with the
rest of us liveaboards but it was just as well. Most of us felt uncomfortable around her, like we couldn't let down our guard.

Her figure caused happily married men to sigh from a distance.
In closer proximity, it could rob a man of any excess reason. We'd
had a fine time together years ago for several months but I eventually realized that a military cop and an ambitious journalist get
along like oil and water. As I remembered it, the mix produced
something more like napalm.

"And it is journalism that brings me here, Simba."

"I hate it when you call me that," I said.

She climbed the three-step fiberglass dock box to deck level,
stepped aboard, and sat across from me in *Figaro*'s cockpit. She
wore gray slacks and a white long-sleeved shirt with deep violet
stripes. Probably on her way to work that evening. From my experience she was always on her way to work.

"Tell me about this murder last night," she said.

"I don't know anything about any murder last night."

"You found the body."

"I found a body," I said. "But I don't think he was murdered last night. In fact, I have no idea when he was murdered. Come to think of it, I'm not even sure that he was murdered."

"Some folks are suggesting that it was a mob hit," said Judith. "That he was wrapped in a heavy chain and thrown overboard alive as an example."

"The classic organized crime conundrum. How do you kill somebody and make an example of them without having witnesses around to talk about it?"

She cocked her head to the side.

"I honestly have no information about this," I said. "If you want details, you'll have to get them from the cops or the coroner."

She leaned in close and whispered conspiratorially.

"Who was he, Sim? Give me something I can write about for tomorrow's paper."

"You were probably up all night badgering the police for information," I said. "I'd bet you know more about him than I do."

She sat there with a look of pure annoyance.

"They're withholding the victim's name pending notification of next of kin."

"Standard operating procedure," I said.

"I want to write about this tonight, Sim. I want something good for the morning paper. I'll keep you as an unnamed source."

"I barely saw the guy," I lied. "It was dark and the water was murky and I never really got a good look at him."

"Monica and Reid told me you went back down with SCUBA gear and an underwater camera."

Those rats.

"I gave all the pictures to Jerry and I didn't keep any copies."

"You're lying," she said.

She leaned over and brushed a finger against my cheek.

"Give me an hour on my boat, Sim, and I'll drag it all out of you. It'll be an hour you'll remember for the rest of your life."

"Can I just go back to my book, instead?" I asked.

"Even with that broken nose, you're a handsome bastard," she said. "But you're still a bastard."

She smiled, stood up, and turned around to step off the boat. I admired her best side as she walked away and up the dock ramp to the parking lot and her old Mercedes.

Al passed her on the dock ramp on his way back from an errand ashore and stopped at *Figaro*. He sat on the fiberglass dock steps.

"You're not taking up with that one again, are you?" he asked.

"No, Al."

"If you ask me, she's a constant bearing, decreasing range target," said Al. "You should alter course and get her off your radar entirely."

"Unrequested advice duly noted."

"You really scared the hell out of us when you started hanging out with her."

"I'm glad to hear of your collective concerns."

Like it's any of their business.

"That Ashley's a pretty nice girl, though."

"I think so," I said.

"A keeper?"

"Do all old sailors get this nosy as they advance toward senility?"

He laughed.

"If you must know, I'm going to her folks' house for dinner Sunday night."

He shook his head.

"Meeting the parents," he said. "It's the first in a series of bad steps, my boy. I suppose you'll be selling your boat, too, eh?"

"No," I said. "I don't think so."

"I'm going to make a prediction, Sim. Sunday evening, over a fine dinner of glazed spiral-cut ham and mashed potatoes, green beans and dinner rolls, you'll get the traditional 'my daughter won't be marrying a sailor' speech. It comes about fifteen seconds after you turn down a job at daddy's firm and about three seconds before you tell him to shove it up his aft scuppers."

"No, Al, you got it dead wrong. Ashley and I like things just as they are. She lives ashore and I live on a boat. I'm not selling *Figaro* and I'm not quitting the Navy."

He laughed and shook his head again.

"Good luck with that, Sim."

He walked back to his boat two slips farther down J-dock, climbed the stairs and disappeared into the pilothouse.

8

I awoke to a Friday so bright that it hurt my eyes and a sky so clear the Ventura Hills popped out in stark detail from ten miles to the north. A few wispy clouds floated off to the west. The day promised to be a scorcher.

I made breakfast thinking about Captain Overson's special off-the-books assignment and wondering what I had gotten myself into. No matter how many times I mentally tossed that coin, it always landed heads down as a murder investigation that was outside my jurisdiction and unsupervised by my direct command. I started to feel jealous of Al who'd left the Navy when, as he'd once put it, it had "ceased to be fun."

My boss didn't expect me in the office so I opted against the normal service uniform in favor of more comfortable civilian clothes. I wasn't exactly sure how the U.S. Navy would look at it but from the Base Commander's point of view I was executing this assignment undercover and on my own time. Civvies were, therefore, acceptable attire. I ate my breakfast in *Figaro*'s small salon, pulled the victim's folder out of my briefcase, and began to read.

The basic info was all there. Barry St. James grew up in a small farm town near Pocatello, Idaho, and entered the Navy ROTC during his freshman year in college a little over thirty years ago. He'd graduated with a degree in accounting and went to the Navy's Supply Corps School in Georgia, then completed several assignments on surface ships. He was promoted to Lieutenant early in his career, earned his NASO warfare qualification pin, and finished his career after serving on the USS *Enterprise* as a Naval Aviation Supply Officer.

His career followed a positive trajectory until about ten years ago when, for no apparent reason, he retired from the Navy, took the state CPA exam, moved to an apartment in Ventura, and hung out an accountant's shingle in Oxnard.

The file offered little information about his family. His parents still lived on the family farm south of Pocatello and his ex-wife worked at a small restaurant a couple of hours up the coast in Oceano. No kids.

I turned on my laptop and opened up the pictures I'd taken Wednesday night. They weren't very different from what I remembered. The clothes, the chain, the look of open-mouthed horror on the victim's face. But things always look a little skewed and distorted underwater at night through a diving mask. There were several details I hadn't picked up that night.

The first things I noticed were rectangular bruises and marked indentations in the tissues of the wrists. Barry had been handcuffed, probably with plastic zip ties. But whoever had done it had taken off the ties before they'd tossed him in the channel. Why bother?

There was also a puncture wound through the back of the right hand. It was thin and about an inch long. I couldn't really tell from the pictures but it looked like a clean knife wound. The third finger on the right hand bore a distinct line indicating that Barry routinely wore a half-inch wide ring, now missing, on that hand.

The last thing I noticed was a set of thin, parallel scratches on the side of his face leading from below his right eye straight down to the corner of his mouth. It looked as if he'd annoyed the family house cat one too many times.

I spent a lot of time looking at the chain segments in each picture trying, with no luck, to find a maker's mark or an identifying stamp. As best as I could tell it was old, galvanized, proof coil. It wasn't the good stuff a yacht or a commercial vessel would use for anchoring but it was heavy enough to take Barry to the bottom and keep him there. And it was heavy enough that it would have taken at least two strong guys to get the chain and Barry over the side of a boat.

I turned off the laptop and did the breakfast dishes while thinking of Barry's last moments. Were the wounds on his hand and face evidence of a fight or had his killers just wanted to hurt him badly before sending him over the side? Given the murkiness of the water at the harbor mouth, they had probably thought it would be months—well after the crabs had their fill—before anybody found what was left of him.

Barry had once had a home, an office, an ex-wife, and a mom and a dad. Not knowing where to start, I hit the closest one first. I grabbed my briefcase, locked up *Figaro*, and made the short trek up the dock to the parking lot.

He'd kept his office in an older two-story building not far from the Oxnard airport. It was a tan stucco affair with timbers framing the windows and old overgrown landscaping. The design was supposed to give visitors the impression that Father Junipero Serra had built it over two centuries ago. To me, it looked like nobody had bothered to clip the hedges in fifteen years.

A law firm occupied the entire first floor. The firm screamed of shysters gathered from the bottom ranks of their respective graduating classes. The top floor was broken up into five single office suites. Barry's was the second office down the hall and on the right.

A nice wooden sign on the door read "Barry St. James, CPA." The door wasn't locked. It was a small but efficient suite with a conference room and an adjoining private office. The furniture, filing cabinets, and a small copier were still there and intact but it looked like somebody had removed nearly everything else.

Not a single file or shred of paper lay in the two filing cabinets. Dust patterns showed that there had been, until recently, books in the bookcase. A monitor, keyboard, and a few cables on the floor indicated where an office computer had once sat. I went back to the door, locked it, and began the process of thoroughly examining the small suite.

It only took me ten minutes to find the key that was taped under the bottom of one of the filing cabinet drawers. It was a small brass key with no markings. Either the people who had emptied the office didn't look as thoroughly as I had or they didn't care. I put the key in one of the small plastic evidence bags I carry around on the off chance that I might stumble over something that could possibly be evidence. I put the bag in my pocket.

There was nothing else of interest in Barry's private office.

A leather couch lined the long wall of the conference room and two leather chairs sat against adjacent walls. A steel and glass coffee table squatted between them. It didn't look as if the couch had been moved so I played a hunch and tipped it over. Under the couch was a business card for an insurance agent. That, too, went into a plastic evidence bag.

I walked downstairs and went into the attorney's office. The receptionist had blonde hair extensions, a fine figure, and a black mini-dress that barely covered a pair of dangerously long and well-proportioned legs. She was rather proud of her cleavage. Mid-twenties, I guessed. I wondered if her name might have been Roxy or Savannah and I looked around for a brass pole.

"May I help you?" she asked.

Her voice had that squeaky-toy quality that some girls think is attractive. She smiled at me and threw in a generous hair flip.

"Did Mr. St. James move?" I asked. "He's supposed to be helping me with a tax problem and I had an appointment to meet him this morning."

Her winning smile vanished immediately.

"Move?" she said, "He couldn't have moved."

"He was supposed to be here ten minutes ago," I said, "but his office is empty."

She picked up the phone, punched a few numbers, and relayed what was, apparently, bad news. A blond guy with a pointy nose and a nearly invisible mustache shot out of a back room and up the stairs like it was an Olympic sport. He wore gray slacks, a blue shirt, and a yellow tie. He ran like he was wearing Lycra.

He came back down the stairs a minute later spouting language most lawyers wouldn't use in the office. No, Barry didn't leave a forwarding address. Yes, he owed them two month's back rent.

I walked out and got into my Jeep. I looked at the business card in its plastic bag and grabbed my cell phone. A deep voice answered.

"Ray Jackson Insurance, this is Ray. How can I help you?"

"My name is Sim Greene. I am with the United States Navy and I am assisting in an investigation regarding Lieutenant Barry St. James. I would like to ask you a few questions."

"I thought Barry retired from the Navy years ago," said Ray.

"We still show him as active reserve," I lied.

"He's not in any trouble, I hope."

"It's a routine investigation that we conduct regarding active reserve personnel. It has no bearing on Lieutenant St. James' character. It is strictly routine, sir."

"Oh, yeah," he said. "Sure. Anything to help the Navy. I could meet you at, say, two o'clock this afternoon."

"Sounds good."

"You want to come to my office in Camarillo?" he said.

I agreed and he gave me directions to the address printed on his card. The news reports had not identified the murder victim but that bit of info would certainly be out later this evening. I wouldn't be able to lie about Barry after that.

A couple of hours stood between me and my appointment with Ray Jackson and I had nothing useful with which to fill them. I decided to visit Dr. Craven.

9

THE Ventura County Coroner's office was in a new building adjacent to a residential neighborhood up the hill from the county medical center. I drove past the phalanx of twenty-foot tall California Fan palm trees hiding it from public view and turned into the small parking lot. The building is a white and beige concoction of square cement columns and beams with glass and skylights and other elements of a modern environmentally-friendly building. A large hedge surrounds the property to shield the neighbors from the sight of body bags being trundled into the facility and the grounds are pleasantly interspersed with small drought-tolerant bushes planted among gravel and rock beds.

I walked the twelve steps up from the parking lot and through an open atrium into the office lobby. It was at least twenty degrees cooler in the lobby than it had been outside. A pleasant-looking lady with a winning smile sat behind an oval countertop set into the wall. She looked comfortable in the cool air wearing one of those headset/microphone devices designed to give the impression of being both busy and efficient.

"How may I help you?" she asked.

"Is Dr. Craven available?"

I showed her my military ID. She punched a button and spoke quietly.

"He's in his office, Mr. Greene. Go down that hallway and turn left at the second door."

Dr. Kenneth Craven, the county's CME, stood a few inches taller than me but he was a lot heavier. Not that he was over-weight. He was just built bigger than most guys, with broader shoulders and a thicker chest. Even his hands were massive; the size of dinner plates. I guessed he was in his mid-sixties and I ima-gined that he could have been a formidable boxer in his youth had his disposition urged him in that direction. His head was about a third longer than it was wide and topped with thinning hair. A pair of half-glasses threatened to jump off the end of his nose onto his prominent gently-rounded jaw. His voice was low enough and loud enough to rattle windows and pierce walls. Tony the Tiger with intensity. He had an uncanny memory for detail and that made him good at his profession. He'd been Chief Medical Exa-miner for as long as anyone could remember and the county was lucky to have him.

"Greene," he said, thinking. "Greene."

He looked over the half glasses at me and tilted his head about twenty degrees to the left as if I were one of his expired customers.

"Weren't you in here about six months ago?" he asked.

"March," I said. "A suicide."

"Yes, yes. A young lady. Pills. Damned shame. And you were al-so here about two years ago for that redheaded sailor that passed on in Simi Valley, weren't you? Drug overdose, as I recall."

I nodded.

"Did you catch the guy who sold him the stuff?" he asked.

I nodded again. He smiled.

"That's right," he said. "I remember you. You're with NCIS."

"No, sir. I only work with them in a support role on specific lo-cal cases."

"Well, I'm always glad to work with the military. Did my first twenty-five years as an Army doctor in Japan."

A short white cardboard box containing what looked like brown and white segments of some sort of organ tissue sat on a porcelain tray in front of him. He picked at and explored the contents with a tined surgical instrument.

"Doing examinations at your desk?" I asked.

He grimaced.

"This, Mr. Greene, is my lunch," he said. "And it is still too hot for me to eat. It is amazing how one can remove something as solid as granite from the freezer, place it in a microwave oven, and, a few minutes later, be presented with something hotter than the surface of the sun. Absolutely untouchable. But it is only 240 calories, a metric I am now carefully counting these days, and it is almost satisfying."

"Well, I'm sorry to interrupt your lunch, Doctor."

He pushed the tray away.

"You're probably doing me a favor," he said. "What can I do for you, Mr. Greene?"

"I'd like to talk to you about Barry St. James. His body would have arrived here early yesterday or the night before."

"He's on the table now," he said. "Our pathologist and I are going to examine him this afternoon. Would you like to have a look yourself?"

I followed him out of his office and down a brightly lit hallway to a wide door labeled "Autopsy." That door opened into a space slightly larger than a fair-sized living room. It was kept another twenty degrees cooler than the offices. Skylights, augmented by fluorescent fixtures, provided plenty of light for the white-tiled facility. A large low sink stood on one side of the room. A stainless steel scale that could have been stolen from the produce section of a neighborhood supermarket hung over the sink. To the right of the sink was a flat work area lit by a large round surgical lamp. A heavy mechanics tool cabinet and two small rolling work tables stood near the work area. On the other side of the room were two doors that led to twin storage areas. Each room could hold thirty-five bodies. I'd visited those rooms several times before and knew they were colder still; not far above freezing.

Two rolling stainless steel examination tables shared the autopsy room, each supporting the body of a deceased person. Both were naked. Television shows and movies depict autopsy rooms as being populated with bodies covered in light blue paper; FCC restrictions and good taste require such departures from reality. Nobody ever covers them up in an autopsy room. Neither the coroners nor the deceased embarrass easily.

Dr. Craven walked to one of the rolling work tables, retrieved a pair of blue latex gloves and stretched them over his huge hands.

A small rolling cart with a flat top held a number of odd tools including a pair of red long-handled pruning shears. I knew that those shears, made for cutting heavy tree limbs, were the doctors' favorite tool for cutting through the bones of the chest cavity.

The doctor walked back toward the table on the left, examined a paper tag attached to a toe of the occupant's right foot, and stepped toward the head.

"Barry St. James," he said.

The chains were gone along with his clothes. Other than that, he was as I had remembered him. White, middle-aged, and dead.

"I am told that he was found underwater wrapped in steel chains," said Dr. Craven.

"That's what I understand," I said.

He began a quick review of the body looking at the fingernails and eyes and feeling the stiffness in the tissues.

"I won't be able to give you a time of death, yet, but I can't imagine he spent more than a full day in the ocean."

"No decomposition?"

"A body in relatively cold water like ours won't decompose very rapidly. I'm basing that preliminary assessment—and it is very preliminary—on the apparent lack of predation. You see, he still has his eyes and lips. Those are the first things to go when the crabs and fishes start snacking in earnest."

He continued the exterior examination.

"None of this is official," he mumbled. "I'm just waiting for my lunch to cool."

I nodded and he continued.

"Puncture wound on the right hand. Thin blade. I'll look more closely at this later."

He moved up the arm feeling the tissues and examining the joints. He gave a cursory glance at the head and face.

"Parallel scratches on the face; superficial in nature."

He moved down from the face to the chin and then to the chest.

"Wait a minute." he said. "What the hell is this?"

He adjusted his glasses and looked closely at St. James' chest. He ran his gloved fingers over a set of long thin lines that curved across the left breast. Then he went back and looked at the facial scratches.

"Something unusual?" I asked.

He ignored my question and continued examining the lines on the chest. He used his gloved fingers to spread them apart revealing thin deep fissures in the flesh of St. James' left breast.

"I've never seen anything like this," he said.

He walked over to the tool chest and replaced his prescription glasses with a nylon headband that held a pair of magnifying glasses. He dug into one of the smaller drawers and pulled out a small thin metal ruler. He came back, clicked on the glasses' illuminating lights and studied the cuts on St. James' chest. He pulled the flesh apart to reveal the depth of the cut and measured it with the metal ruler.

"Two millimeters."

He checked the skin on the right breast quickly and shook his head slightly then checked the scratches on St. James' face. He turned off the small lights, walked back to the tool chest, and took off his headband.

"Consistent," he said. "All those cuts are two millimeters deep."

"What does that mean?"

"Hell if I know," he said. "But all of those cuts are down into the dermis; they don't go into the flesh at all. These would have been very painful."

"Are you saying that this man was tortured?" I asked.

"I have said nothing of the sort. I am observing that the deceased has sustained superficial cuts down to the hypodermis in the face and on the left breast. There are about a thousand nerve endings in every square inch of skin and cuts such as these would be extremely painful. You will need to draw your own conclusions after you read my final report, Mr. Greene."

He paused for a minute to review the information on the toe tag. His brow furrowed.

"Mr. Greene, it says here that the Sheriff's Department retains jurisdiction over this case as a possible homicide. I don't see the Naval Criminal Investigative Service listed as an investigating party."

"That is because NCIS isn't working the case, Doctor."

"Then why are you here?" he asked. "And why am I talking to you?"

I pointed at the fouled-anchor tattoo on St. James' forearm.

"That's why," I said.

I handed him my card and he looked at the fouled-anchor imprint in the background. A flash of recognition crossed his face. With twenty-five years in the military he understood. He took off the magnifying glasses, put them back on the tool chest, and removed the latex gloves. He led me through the door and back toward his office.

"I'll send you a copy of my report," he said. "But it won't be official and if anybody asks if I sent it to you, I'll deny it."

He wished me luck and I thanked him. He turned back to his lunch as I walked out the lobby and down the concrete steps to the parking lot.

10

RAY Jackson looked to be somewhere north of sixty with thin arms, a thin neck, and thinning brown hair. He probably had to stand up twice to cast a shadow but he had a nice smile and soft blue eyes that made you want to trust him. The eyes probably sold the insurance.

He seemed to be doing well at it, too. His office looked new with gray carpet thick enough to swallow your dropped car keys. A beautiful wooden desk dominated the space. Expensive-looking fountain pens stood vigil in a dark hardwood rack on the left side of the desk and a large wooden display case on the adjacent wall held a collection of golf balls from various country clubs. Condensation dripped down the sides of a bottle of mineral water onto a round leather coaster and cool air poured out of an overhead vent, rustling the few papers lying on the desk. It was a nice place to be on a hot summer afternoon.

Ray sat in a large leather office chair and continuously flipped one of the fountain pens around his right thumb. The debate club pen flip that I never mastered.

"Did you say you were in the Navy, Mr. Greene?"

"Yes, sir," I said. "You can call me Sim, if you like."

"You're not in uniform."

I looked down at my comfortable shorts, polo shirt, and beach sandals.

"My other assignments today require me to maintain a much less military profile, Mr. Jackson."

I pulled out my military identification and a business card and handed them to him. He studied them. There aren't a lot of secrets afforded to military personnel. He could see my picture, name, rank, and pay grade. At least it didn't show my social security number or mother's maiden name.

"Chief Petty Officer," he said.

I nodded. He handed me back my military I.D.

"Undercover work of some sort?" he asked.

"I'm not at liberty to say. I'm sure you understand."

"I got ya. Loose lips and all that," he said. "I was in during 'Nam. At eighteen, I fired five-inch guns into rice paddies and jungle. Sometimes, we fired those guns all day long and into the night. I got tired of the sound and worked a transfer to a flattop. There was lots of crap we couldn't talk about back then."

"Were they good years?" I asked.

"I got seasick the first two days of every tour. Had to make my sacrifice to Poseidon, don't you know. But I also visited Pearl Harbor, Subic Bay, Taiwan, Australia, and Pago Pago. It was the best time of my life."

"Join the Navy and see the world, eh?" I said.

His smile was broad. "You got that right, brother. How can I help you?" he asked.

"Did you meet Lieutenant St. James in the Navy?"

"Yeah, sort of," he said. "We were on Three-Quarter-Mile Island together."

"The *Enterprise*?"

"Yep. But we served in different parts of the ship and barely knew each other. I recognized him when he joined my Rotary club about five or six years ago. I handle his professional liability insurance and he does my taxes. It's a good arrangement and he's a dang good fellow. Real squared away guy."

I watched his eyes as we talked. An investigator learns to read eyes. Windows to the soul. Jackson's soul was lying.

I spent the next half-hour asking benign questions about Barry St. James. Foundational stuff. Basic data. He was more cooperative than most; the poster-boy for a helpful pro-military citizenry. He tightened up as the questions moved toward Barry's accounting practice.

"What sort of information do you gather for your underwriters before you can submit a professional liability policy?" I asked.

"It depends on the insurance company. We usually have to attach two years of income statements and a breakdown of gross revenues by type of practice. Straight tax work for an accountant has a substantially different risk profile than audit work, you understand, and the risks for both vary widely by the type of client you serve."

I swallowed hard and licked my lips.

"You wouldn't have a glass of water, would you?" I asked.

"Better 'n that," he said.

He reached under a credenza behind his desk and opened up a door revealing a small built-in refrigerator. He pulled out another cold bottle of mineral water and handed it to me.

"Thanks," I said as I twisted open the cap and took a swallow.

"Anything for a fellow sailor," he said.

"That information you mentioned, Mr. Jackson. The two years of income statements and gross revenue breakdown for Lieutenant St. James. Can I get a copy of that for our files?" I asked.

"I don't think I'd be comfortable giving that out," he said. "There might be some references to specific clients of his in there and I'd have to consider that privileged information."

"Are you his lawyer?" I asked.

"No."

"Doctor?"

"No," he said.

"His clergyman?"

He laughed slightly.

"No."

"Then I'm having a hard time following your privilege argument," I said. "But it doesn't matter to me. I'm just here to interview you and write things down. I'll note that you withheld information and the Base Commander or JAG can deal with it as they see fit. They might request an NCIS inquiry and get it from you that way, I suppose."

I made a few notes on my yellow pad. Ray stopped laughing. He pulled at the collar of his shirt and rubbed his thin neck.

"Look," he said. "I don't want to get in trouble with the Navy but I don't want to get sideways with Barry, either."

I took another sip of mineral water.

"This file will be sealed and its contents will be kept confidential, Mr. Jackson. Barry will never see the information in this folder," I said.

Not much threat of that.

"I can assure you that the information you provide will be held in strict confidentiality," I said.

Ray twisted the corner of his mouth for a moment, stood up, and walked into a back room of his office suite. I heard a filing cabinet open and a copy machine squeak some pages out. I slipped the bottle of water into my briefcase. He returned with a sealed manila envelope.

"You never got this from me," he said.

"Your country thanks you."

We shook hands and I walked out to the parking lot. I put the water bottle into another plastic evidence bag. I drove back to the base and gave the three plastic bags to a young sailor named Gil who worked as one of the office assistants.

"What case are these for?" he asked.

"They're not for any open case at the moment, Gil. General research only. There should be two sets of prints on the bottle; one of the sets is mine. I want to know who the other guy is. Check the key and business card, too."

"Roger that."

"And I need you to contact BUPERS/NPC and get the detailed personnel records for a guy named Ray Jackson."

The Bureau of Naval Personnel/Navy Personnel Command maintains nearly sixty million military personnel records for every sailor enlisted since 1885. They are much more thorough than the on-line access we have in the office and they are reasonably quick.

"There's probably a fair number of Ray Jacksons in their records, Chief."

"He's a white guy, fifty-five to sixty-five, discharged, and claims to have served on the USS *Enterprise*. Try both Ray and Raymond and leave the results on my desk."

"And none of this is assigned to a case?" asked Gil.

"Correct."

He shot me a puzzled look but didn't comment on the unusual practice of requesting lab work and personnel records in the absence of an active case.

I left the base and drove up South Ventura Road to Highway 101 and then headed north. The afternoon traffic on the freeway was slow enough that I was able to tear open Ray's sealed manila envelope and read the contents en route.

The financial statements indicated that Barry's was a relatively small CPA practice that provided a modest living at best. His client list detailed a lot of individuals and a few small to medium-sized businesses. Two larger firms, neither of which I recognized, accounted for nearly a third of his billings.

I got off the freeway at South Mills Road and drove to Barry's apartment, barely a half-mile from the freeway. As I turned onto Barry's street, I noticed three unmarked police cars, a police lab van, and two squad cars parked near the apartment complex where he had lived. My eyes strained sideways out of their sockets as I drove past.

Policemen, detectives, and lab technicians swarmed through Barry's first floor apartment. It didn't look like the best time to drop in if I wanted to keep a low profile.

11

YOU could toss a grenade into the Anacapa Fitness Center at four o'clock on a Friday afternoon without hurting a soul. It was the best time to enjoy unchallenged access to the facility's machines and equipment. Any other time and you'll find the place packed with the sweating bodies of white-collar middle management types and their personal assistants.

The Center housed their free weights in a half-hidden half-basement that was, at minimum, psychologically isolated from the more popular weight machines, treadmills, ellipticals, and stair climbers. I suspected that this was meant to keep the steroid and beefcake boys a safe distance from the Spandex and iPod crowd.

A heavy bag hung from the ceiling in one corner of the half-basement and a speed bag dangled from its mount on the wall nearby. It gave the impression that boxers routinely worked out there but, as far as I could tell, the two bags got little use. I'd never had to wait for anyone to finish a workout with them.

I was doing a mixed routine of circle and straight punches on the speed bag while waiting for Al to show up. We worked out together a couple times a week because we both hated to lift free weights without a spotter.

"Sorry I'm late," said Al. "Had to show the boat to a potential buyer."

"No worries," I said. "Serious buyer?"

"Just a tire kicker."

Al started a workout on the heavy bag. It danced and jumped disproportionately at the end of his fists. A dozen years after leaving active SEAL duty status, he still had the moves. I finished my speed routine and loaded up some plates on the bench press. Al came over to spot me.

"You getting sick of the Navy, yet?" said Al.

"Not really. Why do you ask?"

"You left the dock in civvies this morning. I figured you were quitting. I mean you've almost twenty years in the service and that's when a lot of sailors get antsy and start looking for their DD-214."

"Well, I certainly get frustrated at times. My boss likes me but doesn't want me to transfer because I solve cases and make him look good. I like my work but most of the assignments are lightweight stuff. The good cases, the serious stuff, go to NCIS and I only get to work with those guys when they ask for me."

"But you like your work?"

"Sure," I said. "Mostly."

"And your boss gives you good reviews?"

"Yeah."

"Then you're in the very slimmest minority of the human population," said Al. "Enjoy it while it lasts."

I did four sets of ten reps and then switched places with Al. He removed a single thin plate from each side of the bar. Nobody would expect a guy his age to bench that much.

"I still can't believe you're actually retiring," I said. "Again."

"Cause it's my second shot at it?" Al said.

"Uh-huh."

He put up the bar for ten slow reps with no visible effort. Showoff.

"I did twenty full years in the Navy and seven more teaching," he said. "What more do you want from a guy?"

"I thought you liked teaching."

"I love it. The kids are great."

The "kids" were all students at Cal State Northridge learning history from a Navy SEAL turned Ph.D. I'd often wondered if any of them knew of his former life, his Purple Heart, or his Silver Star. Or if they had the slightest inkling of how he'd earned them and how dangerous a man he'd once been.

"I just can't stand the bureaucracy anymore," said Al. "Too many reports, too many cutbacks, too many bosses. They've taken all the fun out of it."

"And when it ceases to be fun..." I said.

"...it ceases," finished Al.

"But the Caribbean," I said. "I don't get it. Are you going down there to just swim and live off your retirement check? Do you really get that much?"

"Two retirement checks. And I'll do all right with them. But what I really want to do, Sim, is run a dive shop. I've always wanted to do that. I figure I'll get a job with one of the shops down there and use the money from *In Depth* to buy in as a partner when the time is right."

We finished our workouts, showered and dressed, and walked out to the parking lot.

"You can't believe how beautiful it is there," he said.

"What?"

"The Caribbean. The water is warm and clean and as clear as the air on a windy day. Better than Hawaii. The locals are nice, too. Tourists fly in and drop thousands of American dollars on folks who do nothing but try their damnedest to help the visitors have a good time."

"I'll have to come visit you," I said.

But I didn't really think so. I was in the Navy to stay and, with any luck, would get a shot at officer training and a job with NCIS. We both knew that our friendship would probably end with the sale of his boat. Al got in his truck and headed south to the harbor.

I walked back to my Jeep and drove up Victoria toward Ventura. I had one more thing to do that day but it was a task more suited for darkness. I figured I could spend an hour or so in the bookstore north of the freeway. Ashley called as I drove onto the bridge that crosses the Santa Clara River.

"Miss me?" she asked.

"Always."

"Just another week or so," she said. "We can spend more time together once this retreat is over."

"Can't I just meet you at the office? You've got a couch there, right?"

"And some too curious coworkers," she said. "One more week."

"Another one of the many sacrifices made by America's men in uniform."

She laughed and it brightened my day. We talked for a few more minutes and she hung up to get back to preparing her presentation. I continued north to the bookstore.

Two hours later, I drove over to Barry's apartment complex. The police cars and evidence vans had left so I parked two blocks away, pulled a pair of cotton gardening gloves out of the Jeep's center console, and put them on.

A sign claimed that the building's lobby door would be locked after ten o'clock but my credit card fooled the latch. I walked into the lobby, found the hallway to Barry's apartment, and rang the bell. Nobody came. I rang it again and waited a few minutes. The lock on the apartment door also surrendered to my plastic money. It was the easiest B&E I'd ever committed.

Barry's apartment was as clean as his office. A few pieces of modest furniture, a flat-screen television, two chairs, and a coffee table filled the small front room. Two antique travel posters and a half-dozen framed photographs of Barry hung on the walls. Barry with a friend posing by a canyon in some National Park; Barry standing at the stern of a sport fishing boat with a couple of friends all holding up their catch of albacore; Barry sailing on a small boat with some other friends; Barry with his arms around a pair of show girls inside a large casino. Barry seemed to have a lot of friends.

The kitchen featured a toaster, refrigerator, coffee maker, and the usual utensils in the usual drawers and cabinets. A small dining table and a few chairs occupied a corner by a window.

I walked down the short hallway toward the bedroom. As I passed the bathroom, I heard a Spanish word I didn't recognize and a slight whooshing sound like a small bird flying past my right ear. I thought I glimpsed a brown cowboy hat right before the fireworks went off inside my head and I felt my knees buckle.

A moment later, I had the odd sensation of standing up straight with my face against the floor. It made no sense. You can't stand up and still have your face on the floor. But the flat surface I stood against was linoleum and nobody covers a wall in linoleum.

The world rotated ninety degrees as I regained more of my consciousness. My face was definitely pressed against a white linoleum floor. My ears rang and pulsed with every heartbeat and a sharp pain radiated from somewhere inside my skull. I moved my right hand around to the back of my head and my fingers found the soft puffy spot where I'd been hit. I felt like throwing up but suppressed the urge and stayed prone until I could recover more of my senses.

It seemed like I'd been on the floor for an hour or more, but when I finally thought to turn my wrist and look at my watch, I realized that only forty minutes had passed since I'd parked the Jeep. I took a few deep breaths and got up on my hands and knees.

Somebody had hit me on the head, pushed me into the bathroom, and turned off the lights. A faint glow from the front room reflected through the space at the bottom of the bathroom door. My eyes adjusted to the dark and I could see that the bathroom drawers had been emptied onto the floor. I sat there waiting for the ringing in my head to subside and listening for anybody who might still be in the apartment. Anybody who might want to finish the job they'd started. Anybody I could get even with.

After a few minutes, I realized that whoever had attacked me was gone. I reached up and turned on the lights to find an empty beer bottle and my wallet lying on the floor next to me. My cash and credit cards were still there but my military I.D. was now behind my gym card. Whoever had hit me was more interested in who I was than in how much he could steal.

I checked out the rest of Barry's apartment. Somebody had turned his bed and frame upright and leaned them against one of the walls. The closets were empty. A small desk in the corner held a computer monitor, printer, and keyboard. All of the computer's peripheral wiring was there, but as I'd seen in his office, the computer itself was gone. There were no papers, no correspondence, no files, nothing. Bare nails in the walls showed where pictures had once hung.

Something looked odd when I walked back out to the front room. It took me a minute but I soon realized that whoever had conked me had taken the framed pictures that Barry had kept on the walls. But the travel posters were still there. They'd only taken the photographs.

I sat down in one of the chairs by the coffee table and thought about the pictures. A picturesque canyon, sailing with some friends, a couple of Las Vegas show girls, and a sport fishing trip. Pictures of Barry with a few of his friends.

Why would anybody take those?

I locked up the apartment before I left and walked out to my Jeep. I drove back to my boat with a pounding head, shucked off my clothes, and crawled into *Figaro's* cozy quarter berth wondering what sort of nonsense I'd wandered into.

12

SLEEP tempered the previous night's concussion and I woke to nothing more than a sore neck and an empty stomach. But I needed cold water more than food so I pulled on my sweats and a T-shirt and locked up *Figaro*.

I don't keep my surfboards on my boat. They are big and clumsy and fragile. The marina office rents me a small storage unit—more like a closet—where I keep tools, tackle, dive gear, wetsuits, and surfboards.

Out of the closet came my old wetsuit with the cut-off sleeves and the rail-fin fish that had extra foam in it for the small crumbly days of summer surf. I managed to change into the suit without mooning the dog-walking dawn patrol and jogged across Harbor Boulevard and down two blocks to the beach. A late summer south swell, mixed with a slight north-west bump, combined to set up a series of scattered A-frame peaks that spanned the entire beach. Another hundred yards across the sand and I was in the water.

The ocean helps me think. Swimming, sailing, and surfing. The paced rhythm of paddling out to the breaking waves calms me and organizes my thoughts. The perfect timing needed to catch the right wave at the right spot and then slice it to shreds focuses my mind. My most important decisions are usually made in the water. Sometimes it's the only opportunity for peaceful introspection.

What had I done with my life so far? Two days after graduating from Bakersfield High School I'd ridden my motorcycle to the recruiting office and joined the Navy to see the world. I'd seen a good chunk of it in almost twenty years.

Twenty years. Half a life. A marriage, a divorce, a few good girlfriends. Too many bad ones. The only constants were the sea and the U.S. Navy. But now my career was like a stalled car in traffic with drivers behind me laying on their horns. I felt a need for something more.

I sat in the water and caught a few waves, but not many. Mostly, I just thought. A trio of dolphins appeared out of nowhere and stole a few waves. Most people don't know that dolphins surf. Most people don't know that dolphins are truly great at it. Most people don't know all that much.

I knew a lot. I knew about surfing dolphins. I knew where to get the best Mexican food. I knew about tides and currents, wind and weather, sailing and surfing. But I didn't know anybody who wore a cowboy hat and the only people I knew that might want to hit me over the head knew better than to try it.

I paddled parallel to shore, caught a wave, and threw some spray in the air in the turns. I'm a big guy and I throw a lot of spray. I kicked out and paddled long strokes back past the breakers.

Ashley. At some point she would want a permanent relationship; a land-based relationship. It was inevitable. The image of a beige stucco home with a red tile roof shoehorned into a large tract of identical beige stucco homes with red tile roofs came to mind. The thought of a life ashore in such a place was enough to scare the tan off me. I stuck my face in the water to cool it off. No use worrying about that right now. Stay in the moment.

Sufficient unto the day is the evil thereof.

I caught a fair-sized wave and rode it almost all the way in to shore. As I dug my toes into the hard wet sand and started my jog back to *Figaro*, I decided that the Navy wasn't perfect by any stretch but that it still suited me and that my boat was nearly ideal and infinitely superior to a tract house in the suburbs.

The newspaper box in front of the Harbor Mart displayed the front page of the local Saturday morning paper. Staring out through the glass above the fold was the picture of a living, breathing, happy Barry St. James.

Local Accountant Drowned – Foul Play Suspected.

Well, that news was out. I showered the salt water off and walked down J-dock to *Figaro's* slip.

It was a Saturday and I was technically off-duty but Ashley wasn't available for fun and games and the surf, though good, was getting crowded. It would be crowded all up and down the coast today. I wanted to complete Captain Overson's special assignment quickly so I decided to make the drive north to visit Lieutenant St. James' ex-wife. It was official Navy business. I wore the uniform.

13

SATURDAY morning traffic on the 101 was light once I got past Ventura, and the ride up the coast by the ocean was pleasant. The sun shone through scattered high clouds, the wind was absent, and the sea was calm. Even Rincon, the Queen of the Coast, one of California's best point breaks, was little more than a sheet of disappointing flat water. Still, there were a dozen surfers waiting in the lineup for something big enough to ride.

August in Santa Barbara isn't April in Paris or Springtime in the Rockies or any other hit tune from my grandparents' generation but it's not bad. Highway 101 follows the ocean west of Santa Barbara and then leaves the Pacific behind as it turns north through a few tight canyons toward Santa Maria. It is a pleasant drive past old cattle ranches and new vineyards; old wooden barns held up by history and new mansions standing behind black Mercedes. I'd come up this far last fall on my way to surf Jalama beach but hadn't driven farther north in some time.

Suzanne St. James lived in Oceano, a small town tucked between the Pacific Ocean and hundreds of acres of melon and vegetable farms. It was a blue-collar town that either hadn't been discovered by the developers or had been affirmatively ignored by them. Her place wasn't hard to find. I parked in front. A beige minivan that had seen better days sat on nearly flat tires to one side of the dirt brown duplex's wide concrete driveway. A dual-axle trailer cradling the remains of a losing demolition derby car squatted next to it.

I rang the bell on Suzanne's front door and a thin little girl hopped out of the neighboring unit.

"Suzie isn't home, mister."

"Thank you," I said.

"She's at work."

"Where does she work?"

"She works over at Frank's Lunch on Grand," she said. "Are you a soldier?"

A gruff female voice told the girl to come back in and mind her own business. A meaty arm pulled her back into the unit and the door slammed shut.

"Thanks," I said.

I drove back to Grand Avenue and found Frank's Lunch nestled between a used book store and a motorcycle repair shop. I parked on the street behind a couple of older choppers. They weren't the nice shiny Harleys you see ridden by lawyers and accountants on weekends. These were the rough kind driven by guys who live in their leathers and cut their steaks with a sheath knife.

Frank's was an old-style single-waitress diner with space for maybe a dozen customers around a U-shaped counter. The choppers' owners sat at the far end with a couple of burgers.

One of the bikers was a tall guy with a horseshoe mustache that dripped over the corners of his mouth. He wore a tight T-shirt that might have been white in a previous decade. It set off a collection of tattoos decorating his arms down to the wrists. I couldn't tell if it was the mustache or his temperament that gave his face a natural, perhaps permanent sneer.

The other guy wasn't overly tall but he was big. Big arms, big legs, and a big neck. He had the look of hard fat; the gristle of a football player or wrestler gone to seed. He had a Van Dyke beard that I had previously thought was the exclusive province of trendy artists and poets. He didn't have as many tats as his companion but he still probably looked pretty badass draped over the sides of his chopper.

I picked a seat in the middle of the U-shaped counter. The menu was written in chalk on a blackboard hanging from the wall and it listed a wide variety of sandwiches, several burger options, and the usual beverages.

An older attractive woman came out from the small kitchen in back. She wore khaki cargo shorts paired with a blue- and white-striped cotton top that had an oval embroidered badge that read "Suze."

"What can I get you?" she asked.

"Reuben and a Coke, please."

"Do you want that on rye bread?"

"I didn't know they came any other way," I said.

She gave a half-smile.

"Reuben on rye," she yelled back to the kitchen. "Can I get you anything else besides the Coke?" she asked.

"Are you Suzanne St. James?" I asked.

Her eyes fluttered.

"Yes, I am," she said. "Have we met?"

"Were you married to Barry St. James?"

She nodded. Her brow furrowed.

"There's no easy way to say this," I said. "Barry was killed earlier this week. I'm investigating his death and I'd like to ask you a few questions about him."

She looked confused for a brief moment. The confusion turned to shock and she sat down on a stool behind the counter and cried quietly into a napkin. This drew the bikers' attention.

"Is that overgrown Boy Scout buggin' you?" asked Horseshoe.

"We could fix him for you, Suze," said Van Dyke.

I turned to look at them.

"Hardly," I said. "There's only two of you. Even if you count the stupid ones."

Horseshoe started to get off his stool and I balled up a fist.

Suzanne picked up a carving knife and pointed it at the two bikers.

"You two can either shut your pie-holes or get the hell out of here," she said. "You say one more word and I'll turn you both into geldings."

Silence is a great mediator. I wasn't about to break it. The bikers gave me some stink eye but went back to their burgers and fries with no more complaint. Suzanne put the knife down and went back to the kitchen.

She returned a few minutes later with a wrapped sandwich and a large covered styrofoam cup.

"I turned this into a to-go order for you," she said. "I take a break at two. Come back then and we can talk."

I paid for the food, walked out to my Jeep, and drove north to Avila Beach. I ate the sandwich in the parking lot and watched a trio of young kids paddling around on foam body boards south of the pier. The little spongers were probably hoping that nature would toss them a wave or two but the water was flat as glass.

Circumstance had granted me another hour to kill so I dug around in the plastic tub I keep in the back of the Jeep, found a pair of old swim trunks, and swam out to the end of the pier and back. The water was colder than I was used to so I increased my pace to keep warm.

A young lifeguard in the obligatory red shorts approached me as I walked out of the sea and onto the sand.

"We don't encourage folks to swim that far out anymore," he said. "A lady was killed here a few years ago by a Great White and we've had some sightings lately."

"The finned type don't bother me much." I ran my left hand over the back of my head where it was still a little tender. "I worry more about the two-legged variety."

He gave me a funny look and shook his head. I walked past him up to the showers and changed back into my uniform.

Suzanne was waiting on a bench near the road when I got back to Frank's Lunch. She climbed into the Jeep and I drove down the street to a parking lot overlooking the dunes and the ocean.

"Barry was really a great guy but once he joined the Navy I rarely saw him," she said. "He was always aboard ship on a tour of duty somewhere and they always turned out to be long tours."

She sniffled into some tissue.

"It was great when he was home, though. It was the best. He just wasn't home enough. We split up fifteen years ago."

"Did you hear from him much after your divorce?" I asked.

"He'd call maybe three or four times a year," she said. "He always called on my birthday and on our wedding anniversary. He never missed either one."

She went back to the tissue and gave it a good workout.

"Sounds like he treated you well for an ex-husband," I said.

"Yeah," she said. "He even started sending me money a few years ago. Almost every month."

"Alimony?" I asked.

"No," she said. "I didn't ask for that in the divorce."

"Why then?"

"I don't know. I guess he was making a lot as a CPA."

"Do you mind if I ask how much he sent you?" I asked. "I know it's none of my business but it might help me find out why he was killed."

"It was a lot. A couple thousand a month, sometimes. I never asked for it or anything but it really helped and I guess Barry felt bad or something. "

"Did he ever come up here to see you?" I asked.

"No," she said. "I'd invite him when he called but he was always too busy. Always working on his boat or finishing up some accounting project. I would've liked to have seen him. I would have liked it a lot."

"His boat? What kind of a boat did he have?"

"It was a sailboat," she said. "He loved sailing and he spent a lot of time cruising the islands down there. The boat had a clever name. He told me once, but I don't remember it."

A group of three dune buggies blasted down the street and on-to the sand.

"I got the feeling that he might have wanted to get back to-gether," she said. "He texted me a little over a month ago and said he wanted to take me sailing away on a long trip."

"Where to?" I asked.

She shook her head.

"I don't know. I deleted the text and didn't dare text him back."

"Why?"

She laughed a little.

"My boyfriend would have gotten really pissed."

"What's your boyfriend's name?" I asked.

The laughter stopped. She told me his name and I wrote it down.

"Did Barry ever mention any enemies? Anyone who might want to hurt him?"

Her eyebrows reached for the sky.

"Are you saying he was murdered?" she asked.

"I can't share any details, ma'am, but that is a possibility."

"Oh, God," she said. She shook her head slowly for a minute, saying nothing. "I don't know anyone who didn't like Barry."

"Except maybe your boyfriend?" I said. "Where is he now?"

"Bob didn't know anything about this," She laughed. "And he wouldn't hurt a flea. Anyway, he's on a ride with some friends. They went to Sturgis this year and then down to Texas to visit somebody. He's supposed to be back before Labor Day."

She sat there quietly. I had no more questions.

"I never should have left him," she said. "He was the nicest, most caring person I've ever met. I don't think he could have had an enemy in the world."

14

I dropped Suzanne off at Frank's Lunch and thought about calling in the information about biker boyfriend Bob Carter. Except it was the weekend and I had no official office support for this assignment. So I headed back up Grand toward the highway. Al called shortly after I reached freeway speed.

"Where are you?" he asked.

"Classified. Who wants to know?" I asked.

"Classified my ass," said Al. "Local law enforcement is down here beating the bushes and asking around about you."

"Tell me more."

"Jerry rolled up to the dock late this morning with a couple of detectives from the Major Crimes Unit," said Al.

"So what?"

"So they're grilling Reid, Monica and *moi* about you. They even walked around and asked some of the weekend warriors."

"Asked them what?" I said.

"Oh," said Al, "things like, 'did I know where Mr. Greene is right now?' and, 'does Mr. Greene have any enemies?' and, 'does Mr. Greene spend an unusual amount of money or engage in any suspicious behavior?' That sort of thing."

"Are they trying to make a case against me?" I asked.

"It sure looks like it."

"So I snuck out in my little sailboat the other night with a prisoner, wrapped the guy in a couple hundred pounds of chain, and heaved him overboard?" I said. "Then I talked you into anchoring directly over him the next night so I could find the body? Is that their theory? Seriously?"

"I'm not saying it makes any sense, Sim. I just wanted to give you a heads up."

I was quiet for a few moments. There wasn't much to say. Al broke the silence.

"You want me to find you a good lawyer?" he asked.

My reply didn't reflect either my sense of professionalism or accepted Naval protocol.

"Hey," said Al. "Don't shoot the messenger."

"Sorry," I said. "No lawyer needed right now. Thanks for the info."

"It's no big deal," he said.

"I'm on my way back. Probably two hours away. Call me if something else shakes loose."

"Will do."

I hung up, picked *American Beauty* from my CD case, and slipped it into the stereo. Driving music. Great stuff. I sang along with the first track as I drove south even though I had no idea what a box of rain was supposed to be. The second track was much more easily understood. Garcia's acoustic guitar sets the pace and you can almost see him running from the cops and their twenty hounds as Weir joins in.

I checked the rear-view mirror and slipped into the fast lane as I sang with Jerry and crossed the long bridge over the Santa Maria River.

And then I spotted the tail.

15

IT was a black car with tinted windows and no front plate. It kept even with the flow of the late Saturday afternoon traffic—two or three hundred yards back; a quarter-mile, at most—and always stayed in sight. When I slowed by five miles per hour and let a few cars pass, it slowed too. When I sped up another ten, it stayed with me.

It followed me off the 101 when I took the turnoff to San Marcos Pass. A few miles later, I pulled in at Mattei's Tavern, parked near the large white wooden water tower, and walked in to get a soda. The black car passed me and continued down the road. It made a left turn at the next intersection.

Through the tavern window I watched the tail return and park on the side of the road where he or she or they could keep an eye on my Jeep. I thought briefly about walking over and asking if one of them knew how to swing a beer bottle. I decided against it as there was a better than even chance that I was either outnumbered or outgunned or both.

I ordered a local micro-brewed root beer. I sipped it and wondered whether my tail had the air conditioning on or not. If so, they risked overheating their big V-8 engine. If not, then they were slowly baking in a black car that took the full force of the hot late-afternoon sun. The thought made the root beer even more satisfying. I smiled to myself and ordered another. Twenty minutes later, I ordered some buffalo wings.

By the time I was down to nothing but ice in the bottom of the glass for a third time, I had the pieces of a plan forming in the back of my softened head. I paid the bill, left a tip, and walked out into the parking lot. The big car's exhaust belched as it started and I smiled to myself.

I got back onto the 154 and headed south toward San Marcos Pass. The acres of grape vines on both sides of the highway gave way to brown grazing land and gnarled old oak trees as we climbed up toward Lake Cachuma. I checked the mirror. My tail was still back there.

The road was arrow straight for a mile or two as we dropped into a wide river bed but it curved back and forth around some small ridges as we approached the Cachuma dam and climbed higher into the mountains. The tail was nearly a half-mile behind when I reached the first of several sharp corners. I punched the throttle as soon as I rounded the first and escaped their view. The Jeep's tires squealed at each bend in the road but after three more turns, I saw a welcome sight.

The sign indicated that the road on the right led to a Boy Scout camp. I braked hard to make the turnoff in time and the Jeep bounded up the tree-lined dirt road like a buck on the opening day of deer season.

I continued up the road about two hundred yards, parked under a large oak, and grabbed my Navy-issue Beretta M9 out of the glove compartment. I checked the magazine and chambered a round. I walked down to the highway under green leafy oak trees filled with acorns while holding the pistol down by my right leg. There was a tree near the entrance with thick brush just outside the drip line and I sat down under it with my back against the trunk and my eyes peering over the vegetation.

Cars, RV's, pickup trucks, and small fishing boats on trailers passed both ways on Highway 154. The tail must have already passed me because it returned from the east about fifteen minutes later. It didn't slow down at the dirt road but continued back toward the way we'd come. I waited another half-hour but the black car did not return. I walked back up to the Jeep and put the pistol in the console between the seats.

The drive through San Marcos Pass and down into Santa Barbara was uneventful. The sky was crystal clear and the reddish light from the setting sun was glorious and bright on Santa Cruz, Santa Rosa, and San Miguel islands. No postcard could ever do that view justice.

The three islands are almost entirely uninhabited, have no tourist facilities to speak of, and are largely ignored by the tens of millions of people who live within an hour of the coast. There are dozens of quiet coves out there that will firmly hold a small boat's anchor and the fish grow fat in the cold, nutrient-rich water. It is one of the most beautiful unnoticed places on Earth.

I turned back onto the 101 when I reached Santa Barbara and headed south toward Ventura. The tail picked me up again as I passed Carpinteria. It was time to call in reinforcements.

16

THE sun had slipped off to bed by the time I exited the 101 onto Victoria Avenue and headed south toward Channel Islands Harbor. I couldn't see him but I knew Al was somewhere behind the black car tailing the tail. Crossing the bridge that spans the mostly dry Santa Clara River, we passed by dark strawberry fields, a large commercial nursery, and several brightly lit greenhouses. It is always comforting to see a few spots of agriculture still thriving in crowded southern California.

I passed the single runway of the Oxnard airport, pulled into the parking lot of a small strip mall, and turned left to drive behind the long building. I drove about halfway down past two small loading docks and several stacks of wooden pallets. I parked next to a dumpster, grabbed my pistol as I hopped out, and crouched low by the left-rear tire waiting to see if the tail would follow.

They did not disappoint.

The black car pulled into the area behind the building with its lights off and drove slowly toward the Jeep, stopping about twenty feet away. Two suits got out and approached on foot. They took slow steps and made little noise. They were both of medium height and medium build. They could have been brothers. Importantly, their hands were empty.

Al drove his lifted pickup truck in behind them and gunned the engine. The two men turned toward the noise and Al turned on his bright off-road lights, temporarily blinding them.

"Keep your hands where I can see them," I said.

They turned to see my Beretta leveled at them from close range. Al took his truck out of gear, left the engine running and the lights on, and climbed out. He pulled a short-barreled shotgun from behind the seat.

The younger of the two suits turned around to look at Al.

"Who the hell are you?" he asked.

"I'm the guy with the shotgun," said Al.

"And I'm the guy you've been following all afternoon," I said. "Now it's your turn."

The suits were quiet.

"Speak up, fellows, and don't be shy," said Al.

Al racked a shell into the chamber of his shotgun. There is nothing like that sound. It is a highly effective icebreaker.

"We're Officers Jensen and Bartholomew with U.S. Immigration and Customs Enforcement," said the older suit.

"That's a great start to a good story if it's true," I said. "Keep talking."

"We understand that you've been asking questions about Mr. Barry St. James," he said.

"It's a free country," I said.

"We'd like to know why," said the younger suit.

"Because soldiers, sailors, airmen, and Marines keep it that way," I said.

Al smiled.

The older suit shook his head.

"No," he said. "We want to know why you're asking about Barry St. James."

"That's classified," I said.

"You can tell us," said the younger suit.

"But then we'd have to kill you," I said.

They weren't amused.

"Now there's an idea," said Al.

The suits stood there with their hands at their sides.

"Which one of you hit me on the head last night with that beer bottle?" I asked.

"What are you talking about?" said the young suit.

"Somebody conked me on the head last night in Ventura," I said. "I figured it could have been one of you fellows."

"We're part of Homeland Security," said the older one. "We don't 'conk' people, we waterboard them."

He wasn't smiling. It still wasn't a convincing argument.

"This isn't getting us anywhere," said the older suit.

He reached into his shirt pocket and tossed a business card on the ground.

"Give us a call," he said, "if you ever think of anything interesting to say."

He walked back to the car and sat in the passenger seat. The younger one got behind the wheel and they pulled forward around my car and past the far side of the building at a measured and unworried pace. The guns in our hands were as intimidating as prom flowers.

"Well, that worked out nicely," said Al.

He bent down to pick up the business card.

"Were those the guys that were nosing around the marina with Jerry?" I asked.

"Nope," said Al as he looked at the card. "Jerry had Sheriff's detectives with him. These two jokers are ICE."

He handed me the card and turned to walk back to his truck. He ejected the unused shell from his shotgun, caught it midflight, and slipped the gun back into the scabbard behind the seat of his truck.

"Showoff," I said.

Al shrugged and pulled himself up into the cab.

"At some point, Sim, you might want to tell me just exactly what it is that you have gotten yourself into."

"I wish I knew," I said.

He put the truck in gear, drove around me, and headed back down toward Channel Islands Harbor.

17

THREE California yellowtails—nature's own little torpedoes—gave me the eye as they cruised past well out of range. Two of them were at least 20 pounds. Both of the larger fish turned around and wandered back to get a better look at me and figure out what I was. *Is it big enough to eat me? Can I eat it?* Questions animals ask about other animals.

We'd anchored in sixty feet of clear blue water at a spot that Al swore was a treasure trove of pelagic fish. I hovered about halfway between the surface and the bottom and held my breath. The two yellowtail circled me. One turned in and swam within range. I pulled the trigger; the fight was short but vigorous. I swam back to the boat with the fish and tossed my gear onto the deck.

"Success," said Reid.

He sat under the bimini on the flying bridge of his boat with a book in one hand and a beer in the other. From what I could tell, he hadn't moved in over an hour.

"Enough for me," I said. "You want any?"

"Al's got me covered," he said.

I dragged the inert yellowtail toward the refrigerated hold, opened the hatch, and slid my fish in next to the two Al had already taken. He certainly had Reid covered. I looked east and saw Al hunting a couple hundred yards away. He had a regular and predictable style. A minute and a half on the surface to breathe; a minute and a half below to hunt. I climbed up to the flying bridge to talk with Reid and he handed me a beer.

"I don't understand why you guys go to so much trouble and spend so much time and effort actually getting in the water to kill a fish," said Reid. "I can get all the fish I can eat with a rod and reel in one hand and a beer in the other."

"As far as I can tell, Reid, you spend more time catching co-eds than fish."

He laughed and went back to his book.

"Catch and release, baby."

"What are you reading?" I asked.

"*Economic Sophisms* by Bastiat," said Reid.

"Good book?"

"Excellent. Bastiat sets forth some very compelling arguments for free market economic theory emphasizing the foolishness of national trade protection schema. Good arguments."

"I'm not big into politics," I said. "It seems that most of the world's problems would be solved if people would just mind their own business and keep their hands to themselves."

"Yeah, well, keep hoping for that," he said.

A Coast Guard cutter rounded the West Point of Santa Cruz Island and turned south a mile or so away. A flash of sunlight reflected from the bridge. I reached over and grabbed Reid's binoculars. Sure enough, a boatswain's mate was taking a good long look at *Dances With Fish* through his own high-powered binoculars. I waved. He didn't wave back. The cutter continued south.

The beer was delicious and ice cold. It perfectly and completely washed away the salt that always finds its way down my throat during an ocean swim. The sound of something thrashing on the surface reached us and we watched Al fight another fish on the end of his spear. He swam to the boat, handed me the fish and his gun, and crawled over the transom.

"That's more than enough to fill the freezer," he said.

He dragged the fish across the deck, opened the hold, and admired the day's catch.

"Nice," he said.

Reid started the twin diesels and we weighed anchor as Al set up the cleaning table and filleted the four fish. I joined Reid on the flying bridge as we got underway.

"How long you been single, Reid?" I asked.

"I was divorced almost ten years ago. Why?"

"I dunno," I said.

He smiled.

"You're getting serious about Ashley."

I shrugged. It was a shrug meant to suggest that I didn't know. And I didn't.

"It happens," said Reid. "A lot of guys, younger guys like you, meet a fine lady and decide to live ashore and raise a family. Some of them actually seem happy."

I couldn't think of anything to say to that.

"The cops figure out who killed that guy you found Wednesday night?" asked Reid.

I was grateful for the change in subject.

"From what I've heard there aren't any witnesses or solid clues," I said. "It seems that everybody loved the guy. Even his ex-wife."

"Not everybody," said Reid. "Somebody wanted him dead bad enough to spend a lot of time and effort in doing it."

He looked at me closely.

"Why are you investigating this murder, Sim?"

"What are you talking about?" I said. "It's a local case. The Navy has no jurisdiction."

"I made a small fortune in my younger days watching for patterns and picking up anomalies in the marketplace. You're serious about your career Monday to Friday but your weekends are always yours. Sacrosanct. You work on your boat, you sail, you surf, or you spear some fish. Or you hang out with some cute girl. Your weekends are yours and you always do whatever it is that you want to do."

He chugged down a little more of his beer.

"The last few days, however, have been atypical," he continued. "You didn't wear the uniform on Friday but you carried your briefcase. So you were on the job while trying to look like you were not working. Then you left yesterday morning, one of your sacred Saturdays, in uniform and you were gone all day. Another major anomaly. I don't know what to make of the local cops hanging around and asking about you but when I add it all together it tells me that you are investigating this guy's death."

I thought for a moment about how far I could trust Reid and decided I could.

"I am," I said. "The guy was Navy and I was asked to quietly investigate. I'd appreciate it if you didn't mention it to anybody."

"One thing a fellow learns in the stock market is how to keep his mouth shut."

The diesels droned on as we approached Santa Cruz Island's west end.

"So, if you don't mind my asking, how is your 'quiet' investigation progressing?"

"Not great," I said. "I haven't found a shred of hard evidence pointing to a decent suspect. There are little ghosts of clues out there—a drunk having visions of a boat late at night, the victim's office and apartment being cleaned out, some federal agents following me because I'm asking about the victim—but nothing concrete. Nothing I can put a finger on. Nothing normal; nothing usual; nothing that fits the pattern."

"Well, there's nothing usual about finding a dead guy wrapped in chains at the bottom of the harbor mouth," said Reid.

I took another pull from my beer and thought a few minutes.

"You know, Reid, there might be a way you could help me."

"How's that?" he asked.

I went below, opened my bag, and fished out the client list and financial statements that Ray Jackson had given me. I climbed back up onto the flying bridge and handed it to Reid.

"You've examined a few financial statements in the past," I said. "How would you characterize this accountant's practice?"

Reid reviewed the information carefully and clucked to himself in disapproval as he turned the pages of the report. He handed the list back and shook his head.

"This guy's kids are starving," he said.

"Not married. No kids."

"Okay, well, it's a modest practice at best," he said. "A small-time accountant making a little money doing some tax work and a bit of corporate advisement here and there. I'd guess that he lives in a cheap apartment, operates out of a one-room office, and drives a ten-year old Toyota."

"Could he afford to send his ex-wife a couple thousand bucks a month?" I asked.

"Maybe a hundred every other month if he ate nothing but ramen."

"Own a sailboat?"

"Not a chance."

I pondered how a nice-guy accountant could make a few thousand "off the books" dollars per month. None of the alternatives I could think of were legal.

Al brought a plate full of yellowtail sashimi up to the flying bridge.

"The sea gives up her bounty for the mere price of effort and cunning," said Al.

Reid laughed.

"That and about six hundred dollars in diesel fuel."

18

A guy who lives on a 39-foot sailboat does not, without major alterations to both natural law and the space-time continuum, have a lot of wardrobe options. It's a sacrifice but one I can live with. I grabbed my ditty bag and my nice clothes, locked up *Figaro*, and trotted up to the showers.

The shower and shave invigorated me, the creases in my khaki chinos stood proud, the long-sleeved blue oxford cloth shirt tucked in nicely, and my good leather boat shoes gleamed. I felt like a new man. I picked up Ashley and we drove east to Camarillo, stopped at a fruit stand to buy some flowers, and then entered the 101 southbound toward Thousand Oaks.

"You," said Ashley, "are a total suckup."

"I don't know what you mean."

"Buying flowers for my mom? You don't even know her."

"You know what they say about first impressions," I said.

Ashley wagged her head.

"Complete and total suckup," she said.

Thoughts of yesterday's tail returned and I kept an eye in the mirror as we drove through Camarillo and up the Conejo grade. I saw only one vehicle that could have been following us, one of those lifted four-wheel drive pickup trucks that always seem out of place in sunny Southern California. An unlikely choice for a tail but I watched it anyway. It was a hot Sunday afternoon and the traffic slowed as thousands of vehicles returned home to L.A. at the end of a summer weekend. Two cars sat in the emergency lane halfway up the grade with their hoods propped open. I checked the Jeep's temperature gauge.

"Your folks won't be upset if we're a little late because of the traffic, will they?"

"Worried?" said Ashley. "Don't be. Traffic is always the best excuse around here."

We topped the grade and dropped into the Conejo Valley, a relatively small depression in the coastal mountains north of Malibu. It's an upper middle-class area with nice weather, a low crime rate, excellent schools, and predictably high real estate prices.

We exited the freeway and the tall pickup I'd been watching continued east. I turned north on the four-lane feeder road toward one of the valley's many golf course communities and discarded the notion of being followed. I focused my attention on Ashley. She was worth it.

Her folks lived in a gated community in an expensive area of an already upper-crust valley. A uniformed fellow frowned slightly at my vehicle as we rolled up to the guard house. Once he recognized Ashley in the passenger side, however, he quickly tipped his hat and flicked a little switch that opened the gate. It was that kind of place.

The Barringer house was huge, probably four times the size of the home I grew up in, and surrounded by palm trees and manicured lawns. The property backed up against the golf course. Ashley showed me where to park without blocking the garage. One of the doors was open and I saw a golf cart flanking a trio of late-model German cars. The home's thick wood entry doors, decorated with iron bands and studs to make them look a thousand years old, were tall enough and wide enough for André the Giant and Hulk Hogan to walk through simultaneously. While carrying Sasquatch. A tall blond man in his fifties opened the door, hugged Ashley, and shook my hand.

"I'm Philip," he said to me. "Come on in."

The entry hall was bigger than *Figaro*. A wide staircase led to an upper floor. A dark green wooden sideboard opposite the staircase displayed a pair of Japanese bamboo fighting sticks and a large mask with blue quilted fabric to cover the head and horizontal steel bars to protect the face.

"It's good to meet you, Dr. Barringer," I said. "Sim Greene."

"That 'doctor' nonsense goes right out the window when I get home, Sim. Call me Philip."

A slender blonde woman who looked very much like a slightly older version of Ashley with shorter hair walked in. Philip introduced us.

"Sim, this is Ashley's mother, Florence."

She leaned in and gave me a kiss on the cheek.

"So good to meet you, Sim."

Ashley excused herself to freshen up and she and her mother disappeared down a hallway. Philip led me to his private study. Dark paneling covered the walls and a thick, rough wooden mantel topped a gas fireplace. Two stuffed ring-neck pheasants stood on opposite ends of the mantel with an antique flintlock rifle hanging on the wall between them. A pair of very expensive Austrian binoculars stood near the pheasant on the left. Any idiot could have pointed out that one does not shoot pheasants with a rifle and binoculars but I didn't really want to come off as an idiot.

An imposing oak roll-top desk with a computer keyboard and two large monitors stood against one of the shorter walls adjacent to the fireplace. A picture of Philip and a well-known professional basketball player standing in front of a golf cart hung from the wall to the immediate right of the desk. Another picture of a smiling Philip, clad in a red and white flight suit and standing on a grass strip next to a red and white aerobatic biplane, hung on the other side.

"Golf is great fun, Sim, but that's my real passion."

He pointed at the airplane.

"There is nothing like boring holes in the sky in a Pitts," he said.

"Mine is sailing, I guess."

"The slowest form of travel versus the fastest, eh?"

"Tortoise and the hare," I said.

I was already running out of clever things to say and didn't feel the least bit comfortable in the huge house. He took a seat in an overstuffed chair and motioned for me to sit on a large dark brown leather couch across from the fireplace. The leather seemed to have been intentionally distressed. It had scars and brands all over it, more than any cow I had ever seen, but the couch itself was very comfortable. I imagined lying down on the thing after a big Sunday brunch and taking a long nap. The way my dad used to.

We reached the point in our discussion where the interested parent asks the inevitable questions about parents and siblings but those questions didn't come. I realized that Ashley must have already told both of them to avoid embarrassment on their part. It was a good call.

"So how long have you been in the Navy?" asked Philip.

"Almost twenty years."

"You must have joined right out of high school."

"Three days after graduation I rode my Yamaha down to the recruiting office, looked at the posters, and said 'Get me out of Bakersfield, Uncle Sam.' And he did."

I looked out the large windows through a covered veranda past the swimming pool to the golf course. A couple in their sixties stopped their cart to take a shot on the fairway. The woman wore a red and white striped polo shirt over a red golf skirt that was shorter than it should have been. She selected a club and sent the ball well over two hundred yards closer to the green. Impressive.

A small flash of reflected sunlight reached the room from across the fairway and a little voice deep inside me spoke up about the boatswain's mate I'd seen on the Coast Guard cutter that morning. I stood up and reached for the binoculars on the mantel.

"May I?" I asked.

"Sure," said Philip. He seemed mildly amused.

I walked to the window and trained the binoculars in the direction of the flash. I turned the focus wheel until I had a clear view of the area across the fairway. It took a while to find the source of the reflection, but I eventually focused on a man leaning against the wall of the golf course's clubhouse. He was a little over four hundred yards away and he was looking directly at the Barringer home with his own binoculars.

He stood behind a tall hedge and I couldn't get a good look at him. His face was covered in binoculars and there was little to see other than an abundance of yellow hair. I guessed that he couldn't see me through the window.

"See anything interesting?" asked Philip.

"I've never seen such a view," I said. "It's truly marvelous."

"Well, you hardly need binoculars to appreciate it."

Florence and Ashley entered the study and interrupted my reconnaissance.

"Checking out the legs on the lady golfers?" asked Ashley.

"Funny," I said. "Actually, I'm thinking of upgrading the optics on *Figaro* and thought I'd give these a try. They're quite good."

I put the binoculars back on the mantel where they sort of belonged. I felt the strong urge to jump into my car, drive over to the clubhouse, and have a long talk with a blond guy but that would have been somewhat difficult to explain to the Barringers.

"Ashley tells me that you enjoy spicy food so Wendy has prepared a meal of Indian dishes," said Florence. "I believe we're having lamb bhuna, chicken kurma, lemon rice, and naan tonight. I'm hoping that's not too exotic for you."

We walked toward the dining room and I thought of the cuisine I had seen served over the years in foreign ports. I remembered watching a big guy in Guam eat a monkey's brain from the head. On a street in Hong Kong I'd seen a skinny cook slice up live snakes, the headless bodies coiling around his wrists as he drained their blood. I thought of the teriyaki dogmeat-on-a-stick offered by smiling little girls in Olongapo City.

"Indian sounds delicious," I said.

Wendy was an excellent cook and Al a poor prophet. There was neither ham nor mashed potatoes on the table and the curry was at that perfect heat where the spice is apparent without overwhelming the other flavors of the meal. The conversation ranged between Ashley's marketing campaign, my travels in the Navy, and Philip's career as the orthopedic surgeon who gets emergency calls from professional basketball teams. It was a pleasant meal with pleasant company.

We walked out onto the patio after dinner and sat in heavy wicker chairs under a massive wooden grape arbor to watch the last of the golfers and to listen to the thwack of the stricken ball. The setting sun reflected off the swimming pool.

"So you live on a sailboat in Channel Islands Harbor," said Florence. "How do you like that?"

"I love it," I said. "Every day is a little different. The sun, the wind, and the birds. The fish in the harbor. I surf when the waves are nice, swim in the ocean when they aren't, and sail to the islands whenever I get a few days off. It's a decent life.

"But you grew up in Bakersfield," said Philip. "How did you ever become a fan of the ocean?"

"My folks took us kids to a small town on the beach near San Luis Obispo for summer vacations and by the time I was a teenager, I was hooked on salt water. My uncle had a sailboat in the Bay area and I went up there to stay with him on it for a couple of weeks. After that, living on the ocean became sort of a lifetime goal."

"Are you an officer in the Navy?" asked Florence.

"No, ma'am, I'm enlisted. I'm a Chief Petty Officer."

She seemed a little confused when I used the words 'enlisted' and 'officer' in the same sentence but I felt no need to clear it up.

"So, do you have any tattoos?" she asked.

She seemed almost excited at the prospect.

"Mom," said Ashley.

"Don't all sailors have tattoos?" asked Florence.

"A lot of sailors do," I said. "But when I told my folks that I'd joined the Navy, my mother made me promise that I wouldn't get any. So, I haven't."

"She must be a good woman," said Florence.

She paused and almost corrected herself.

"She was," I said.

The four of us sat and watched the sun set and talked of golf and flying and Ashley's job and, to a much smaller extent, of sailing. I wasn't offered a job in daddy's firm—I wasn't even sure if orthopedic surgeons could do that—and I felt no pressure to conform to a land-based lifestyle, to marry, or to get a different job. There was nothing but unmitigated happiness in the back yard that evening.

As we said our goodbyes, I looked around at the house and the pool and the fine German automobiles. I weighed that lifestyle against my CPO pay rate and realized that my entire monthly check wouldn't even cover the Barringer's property taxes. The realization didn't leave me with any envy or sadness; only a single puzzling question.

Why was this beautiful rich girl wasting her time with me?

19

I helped Ashley into the Jeep and we drove toward the gate, the darkness of the evening interrupted only by the lights from the large homes we passed. The ornate steel gate blocking the road leading out of the community opened automatically as the car rolled over some unseen sensor and we drove on. Streetlights became more common after we left the gated community and I watched a little more intently for vehicles following us. I didn't see any.

"I think my folks like you," said Ashley.

"What's not to like?"

"Lack of humility comes to mind."

"They seem like wonderful people," I said.

"You seemed a little quiet tonight. Were you nervous or something?"

I thought of the guy with the binoculars.

"No," I said. "I got handed a priority case last week and I have to work it solo. Not much in the way of staff support, either, and nothing is really falling into place."

"What kind of case is it?"

I could have told her that it was the case that started Wednesday night when Jessica dropped her sunglasses but the little voice suggested I keep it to myself.

"Nothing I can talk about, really," I said.

"Is there any way I can help you?" she said.

She smiled and put her hand on my arm.

"I'm sure you could," I said. "But not right here. We'd get into an accident."

She slapped my arm but didn't stop smiling.

Only a few streetlights illuminated the four-lane feeder road leading toward the 101 but the major intersections were well lit with their orange glow. I kept an eye in the mirror as we passed through those intersections. One set of headlights stayed close to us; a Chevrolet sedan, gray under the orange glow of the streetlights. I kept an eye on it and watched it follow me onto the northbound freeway onramp.

"My conference in Santa Barbara got extended until late Saturday evening," she said. "Bill wants me to make a special presentation to the Executive Committee on the Hopkins project and I won't be able to get away until pretty late that night."

Bummer.

"We can leave Sunday morning, if you like," I said.

"Can we just go out for the day, maybe just for lunch?" she asked.

"Sure. Come out Saturday night and stay on *Figaro* with me. We'll get an early start in the morning."

"That sounds marvelous," she said.

Yes, it did.

I thought about the gray Chevy and decided that if it were following me, I didn't want to lead it to Ashley's place. I watched the rear-view mirror quite a bit and, at one point, was sure I'd lost them. To be on the safe side, I drove down Mandalay Beach Road and parked a half-mile south of Ashley's duplex.

"Walk on the beach?" I asked.

"Absolutely."

She hopped out the passenger side and walked toward the beach. I grabbed the Beretta and slipped it into my pants pocket as I got out of the Jeep and locked its doors. Ashley took off her sandals when she hit the sand and carried them in her right hand. I kicked off my boat shoes. She waited for me and handed me her purse when I caught up to her. I can be pretty comfortable with my masculinity when I have a Beretta in my pocket.

The soft white sand near the road, still warm from the day, felt good on the soles of my feet and we walked down to the hard cool wet stuff along the water's edge. The twin beams of headlights played across the beach and I turned to see a car park on the road south of my Jeep. I wondered if it was the gray Chevy and, if so, how they had followed me.

"We're having a company dinner at the hotel Friday night and I get to invite a guest."

"Who's the lucky guy?" I asked.

"I was thinking that I might invite you but it is black tie," she said. "Do you have a tuxedo?"

"A tuxedo? In the vast wardrobe I keep on my sailboat?"

"I thought so," she said. "Can you rent one?"

"I'll think of something, Ashley. I won't disappoint you."

"Promise?" she said.

"Scout's honor."

We reached her street around eleven. I looked around and saw no gray Chevys or black Fords or any other strange cars. Ashley dug around in her purse for her key, opened the door, and invited me in for a drink by the gas fire. We made it as far as the couch.

I left her place a little after one in the morning and started walking back to where I'd parked. It was low tide and walking on the hard sand at the edge of the water kept me out of sight of anybody on the street. A couple hundred yards south of where I'd parked I turned back to the road near a lifeguard station.

A gray Chevy sedan sat in a no parking zone about eighty yards south of the Jeep. It was parked so anybody inside could watch my car. I sat on a bench near the road and watched the Chevy. After a few minutes, the telltale glow of a cell phone screen indicated that the car was occupied. I decided to find out by whom and why. I crossed the street at an unlit area.

When I got closer, I noticed that both front windows were down. I pulled out my Beretta and moved toward the passenger side crouching low and avoiding the side mirror. A talk show was playing on the radio. The moderator was interviewing a guest about crop circles and Bigfoot. I held my pistol below the window.

"What are you doing here, Jerry?" I asked.

The happy surfing Harbor Patrolman froze with his hands on the steering wheel. His fingers turned white, almost luminescent in the darkness.

"Man, you sure know how to scare a guy," he said.

I stuck the Beretta back in my pocket, opened the passenger door, and slid in.

"You think you might want to tell me just what the hell you are doing?" I asked.

"Hargrave asked me to keep an eye on you," he said.

"You've been following me all night," I said. "I want to know why. And who the hell is Hargrave?"

Jerry's grip on the wheel loosened.

"He's the new guy they brought in last spring to run the Major Crimes Unit," said Jerry. "And he takes his job seriously. He's got his crew working overtime on the Barry St. James murder and now he's even dragged me into it."

"What's all that got to do with me?" I asked.

"You're the guy who found him, Sim. Hargrave thinks you know something."

"You guys are pathetic," I said. "Truly pathetic second-class hacks."

I got out of the car, pulled out my wallet, and fished out one of my business cards. I handed it to Jerry.

"Give this to Detective Hargrave," I said. "And stop following me around. If he wants to talk to me, he can call me and make a damned appointment."

I walked back to my car, started it up, and drove home to my boat.

20

I stepped up into *Figaro*'s cockpit the next morning to see Al crouched on *In Depth*'s flying bridge sanding some teak. He never used a power sander. He didn't believe in them. He was careful and exacting. Any wood that Al sanded and varnished looked better than when it left the factory. He looked over at me as I stepped onto the dock.

"Going to work?" he asked.

"The uniform is a bit of a giveaway, isn't it?" I said.

"You're sounding angry this morning."

"What are you all of a sudden? The Dalai Lama?"

He laughed as I walked up the dock to the parking lot. I thought of Jerry as I drove to the base and wished I'd punched the guy in the mouth. The guard waved me into the base and I parked next to our unit's building. A single flight of steps led to my office. It was small, no bigger than a college dorm bedroom, but it was mine and it had a door that closed. Much better than my former cubicle.

Somebody had cleaned off the top of my desk. The files and paperwork that usually hid every square inch of steel were gone. Captain Overson had been true to his word. Joe and my co-workers had absorbed all my active cases. The only things left were my computer, the lab results I'd requested, a note from Gil, and the medical examiner's preliminary report for Barry St. James.

The report was unopened. Nobody had made a copy for the office files or scanned it to the network server. The word was out.

Don't bother Sim, don't ask about his case, and don't tick off the Base Commander. I tore off the report's seal.

The summary gave the usual "preliminary in nature" and "results are not final" warnings. It stated that specimens from the stomach, liver, brain, kidney, vitreous humor, blood, and urine had been taken for forensic toxicology testing and that results would be received and provided within thirty days. But the preliminary findings were revealing.

The vast majority of homicides are solved quickly because they are spontaneous and driven by anger. Network television notwithstanding, most murders aren't meticulously planned by devious criminal masterminds. A jealous spouse or angry family member kills a sailor in the family home. Or somebody gets white-hot mad at words said in a bar, fists fly, a bottle breaks, and one of the U.S. Navy's finest bleeds out on the floor. Horrified onlookers tell you what happened and who did it. The evidence is typically obvious and hastily crafted alibis crumble under questioning.

According to Dr. Craven's preliminary findings, however, Barry's murder was carefully planned. He'd found salt water in Barry's lungs; blood-tinged foam in the nose, mouth and trachea; and evidence of clawing on the fingers consistent with trying to escape the chains. Barry hadn't been beaten or shot in unplanned rage and then dumped overboard as an afterthought. The killers meant for him to drown.

The report also detailed fifty-eight cuts made to the chest and face with surgically sharp instruments. While not the cause of death, they were "consistent with the initial stages of Lingchi; also known as 'Death by a Thousand Cuts.'" The truly unexpected wild card, however, was the discovery of a large mass deep in the thalamus of Barry's brain.

I called Dr. Craven's office and left a message thanking him for the report.

Gil's note said that the BUPERS/NPC search returned records for a lot of Raymond, Ray, and Ramon Jacksons. Several had served on the USS *Enterprise* but none were of the insurance agent's race and approximate age. So the Ray Jackson I'd spoken with had either lied about his service or had changed his name. It didn't matter. I had his fingerprints and he couldn't change those.

I opened the lab results.

The only readable print on the brass key was the victim's. No surprise there. The water bottle was more problematic. The lab found a very distinct right thumb print and two partial finger prints on the bottle but hadn't received a match from the FBI's automated fingerprint database. They were, however, identical to prints found on the business card.

Military personnel have been fingerprinted for decades but a lot of older records aren't yet electronically accessible. Jackson was an older record and some staff member in a warehouse somewhere was probably doing a physical search for his prints.

I called the California Department of Insurance. After twenty minutes on hold and five transfers, I was told that there was no Ray Jackson Insurance in Camarillo and no licensed agent named Ray or Raymond Jackson in all of Ventura County.

So there I sat at my desk with no witnesses, no angry family members, no obvious identifiable suspects, and a very good friend of Barry's who didn't actually exist.

Gil walked in, knocking on the door as he opened it.

"You see the lab results?" he asked.

I nodded.

"You want me to press them for the fingerprints?" he asked.

I thought of being tailed twice in as many days.

"Yeah," I said, "and take the Fly Swatter downstairs and give my Jeep a once over."

"Some crazy girl stalking you again?"

"No comment," I said.

"Or is it a guy this time?" he asked.

"Don't ask, don't tell, Gil."

He laughed and walked out.

Detective work starts with looking closely at lovers, family, friends, business associates, and acquaintances. In that order. I initiated background searches on Suzanne, her biker boyfriend, and Barry's family. I didn't have bupkis on Ray Jackson—not even the right name, apparently—so I decided to pay him a visit and ask some rather detailed questions.

All that extra cash he'd been giving away made me certain that Barry was into something illegal. Nobody tortures a CPA, wraps him in a couple hundred pounds of chain, and dumps him alive into the blue Pacific for a late tax filing. And why would Homeland Security, with all their irons spread among numerous fires, show any interest in a retired sailor's murder? It didn't fit.

I opened a new window in my browser and checked the state DMV records to see if Barry or the other ten persons on my list had ever owned a boat. No sailboats, no powerboats, not even a canoe. More dead ends.

Gil knocked on the door and entered. He had a large black briefcase in his left hand. The Fly Swatter. Gil opened his right hand and tossed a small black box onto my desk. An attached magnetic strip clung to the metal top. It was half the size of an old-school pager; the kind doctors used back in the Dark Ages before cell phones.

"Unmarked," he said. "And it's not a cheapie. Transmits GPS coordinates every thirty seconds." He smiled. "This girl must be pretty serious about you, Sim."

I pried it off the top of my desk and wondered who was tracking me. Local cops? Military Police? Somebody else? There was no comfort in the question.

"Where was it?" I asked.

"Stuck to the bottom of the rear bumper."

We walked downstairs and Gil showed me the spot forward of the trailer hitch where nobody, even the guy in the lube pit changing oil, would ever spot it. I stuck the transponder to the back of a parking sign and went back to my office.

A pop-up window on the computer display prompted me to download preliminary results from the ten background searches. Multiple green status lines filled in from left to right as they arrived. Ten new files.

Barry's parents and six siblings were clean. Four traffic tickets between them. Nothing else. Suzanne St. James was even cleaner. Not a single traffic stop in over six years. Nothing serious ever. Everybody I'd looked at so far was law-abiding, boring, and bland. Right until the moment I clicked on the results for Suzanne's biker boyfriend.

Bob Carter had been arrested three times in five years. The first two were for misdemeanor battery; impromptu bar fights where nobody was seriously hurt. He pled both down to assault with suspended jail sentences, community service, fines, and informal probation.

The third arrest was a different animal; felony assault with a deadly weapon. Apparently he'd brandished a knife during another barroom altercation. The prosecutor, probably worried about the poor quality of his witnesses, let Bob plea to a misdemeanor. He could have had a year in jail to think about intimidating folks with a knife but the prosecutor, the public defender, and the judge agreed to send him away for a thirty-day timeout with another 330 days suspended. He was still on supervised probation. I called the San Luis Obispo County Probation office and was transferred to his probation officer.

"How can I help you, Mr. Greene?"

"I'm investigating a crime in Ventura County and Bob Carter's name came up. I'd like to ask you a few questions about him."

"You're a sheriff's detective?" she asked.

"No, ma'am. I'm a U.S. Navy Master-at-Arms," I said. "Military police."

"Oh, did this happen when Robert was in the Navy? That would have been some time ago."

"I wasn't aware that he'd served in the Navy."

"Oh, yes," she said. "Robert was a Navy SEAL during the invasion of Panama. His team blew up Noriega's yacht during the first strike."

The needle on my BS meter shot into the red zone. Nothing I'd read about Carter meshed with SEAL team training or service. It was more likely that he claimed to be a SEAL merely to gain favors or respect or free drinks. Or to impress a probation officer.

"How is he doing with his probation?" I asked.

"Very well," she said. "Not a problem. He's a model citizen."

"Do you know where he is right now?"

There was a pause on the line.

"Actually, he is somewhat delinquent in reporting," she said. "He told me he'd be attending a motorcycle rally, something related to his work, but he was supposed to report in Thursday. And he hasn't."

"Is it usual for him to report late?" I asked.

"No."

There was a note of resignation in her voice.

21

THE outer door to Ray's office had been open the first time I visited but now it was locked. A button for a door bell had been screwed to the right hand side of the outside wall but nobody answered the chime. I knocked on the door with the same result. Knocking louder didn't change things.

A brass plate, hinged at the top, covered a mail slot cut into the door about waist-high. I lifted the brass plate and looked inside. All I saw in the darkened room was a small collection of letters and junk mail that had been shoved through the slot. Probably a day's worth. I called his office number on my cell phone and it rang straight to voice mail.

Maybe he was out huckstering insurance. Maybe his Rotary Club met on Mondays. Maybe he was out having lunch with the wife. The possibilities were endless.

The drive to the base was uneventful and I made it back with plenty of time to check my computer for any follow-up information from my background requests. There wasn't anything new. I walked across the parking lot to the Base Command center.

Captain Overson's yeoman saw me walk in and immediately notified the Captain of my presence. I didn't have to wait long.

"What have you got for me, Chief?"

"Nothing of any substance so far, sir."

I told him about Barry's office and home being cleaned out, about his ex-wife and the money that Barry sent her, and about the ex-wife's current boyfriend and his criminal record. I shared the contents of the coroner's report with him.

"Why would anybody want to torture him?" he asked.

"I have no idea at this point," I said. "But it is still very early in the investigation, sir."

"Where is this Bob Carter fellow?"

"Nobody seems to know. Not even his probation officer."

The Captain rested his elbows on his desk chair and made a tent of his fingers. He looked down at the tent.

"Do you know of anybody named Ray Jackson?" I asked.

"Not off the top of my head," he said. "Why?"

"He claims to have served on the *Enterprise* with you and Lieutenant St. James, sir."

"There were a lot of guys on the Big E," said the Captain. "I don't remember anybody named Ray Jackson. Doesn't mean he wasn't there, though."

He thought for a few moments. I looked at the commendations and citations on his bookcase. I looked at the pictures of the Captain in his flight suit and the four carriers he'd served on. I looked at his clean and uncluttered office desk.

"I received an inquiry from Rear Admiral Peters today," he said. "He was asking about you. Can you tell me why?"

"I have no idea, sir."

"He wanted to know if you were trustworthy," he said. "He told me that this inquiry was initiated farther up the chain of command. He did not tell me how far."

I couldn't imagine why an Admiral would even hear my name, much less ask about my trustworthiness.

"I am getting the distinct impression that this homicide investigation has somehow acquired federal interest," he said. "Do you have any idea why that would be?"

I thought of the black car that had followed me from Oceano.

"No, sir."

"I am not pleased with this development, Mr. Greene. This was to be a perfectly quiet assignment and I have half a mind to reassign the investigation, to lose your CWO application, and to get you transferred."

He was quiet and I had nothing to say. So I kept my mouth shut.

"However," he continued, "I would still very much like to see your assignment completed and I would very much like to recover the documents I mentioned to you."

"I intend to do so, sir," I said.

"That is good," he said. "That is very good."

He stood up and walked to the window.

"There are times, Chief, when a man's entire career is laid on the line," he said. "Times where one critical mistake can cost him everything he has worked for."

"Yes, sir," I said.

He turned around and stared at me.

"You are right in the middle of it, Chief. If you foul this up, I will make damned sure that you spend the rest of your career cleaning latrines at Lemoore or scraping paint in Norfolk."

He paused for dramatic emphasis. I wondered if it was really *his* career on the line.

"Do you understand the seriousness of this situation?" he asked.

"Yes, sir," I said.

"Then get the hell out of my office and find those documents."

"Yes, sir."

I left his office, went back to mine, and grabbed my briefcase and the other things I needed for tomorrow's trip. I retrieved the little GPS transponder and considered sticking it to something else. Maybe the underside of Captain Overson's Buick or the cockpit of an F-18. The latter could be stupidly dangerous; the former just plain stupid. I stuck it onto the metal dash of the Jeep deciding that I could use it later to mess with whoever was tracking me.

22

THE Anacapa Fitness Center was as quiet as a boat on a windless sea when I stepped down into the free weight and boxing room. Al was there completing a strength routine on the large speed bag. He had let some air out of the bag to slow it down and was working a left jab, right cross, left hook combination punching the bag hard and counting the rebounds.

I grabbed some dumbbells and did a few sets of bench flys.

"How's your little investigation going?" asked Al.

"I'm not talking," I said.

"Those ICE guys got you spooked?"

"No," I said. "Captain Overson has."

I worked quietly on my weight routine and Al continued pounding on the speed bag.

"You need a partner in your little Caribbean dive shop?" I asked.

Al laughed. "Thinking of punching out of the Navy, eh?" he asked.

"I'm open to the possibility."

"I don't know what I'm going to do, Sim. A dive shop is the big dream but it'll take a lot of money. Money I haven't got right now. I'll get a good chunk of dough when my boat sells but it might not be enough. You got anything to chip in?"

I looked at him like he'd asked me to wrestle an alligator. Naked.

"That much, eh?" he laughed.

We continued our workouts and spotted free weights for each other just as we had for the last eight years. I realized how much my life would change with Al gone and I didn't like it. We finished up and walked to the parking lot.

"Jerry is still snooping around," said Al.

It was almost an afterthought.

"Asking about me?" I said.

"Yep."

"He was following me last night," I said. "That is just plain weird. He knows where I live. Why doesn't he just drive that damned patrol boat over to J-dock and ask me directly?"

"Can't say."

"I wish he'd just show up with this Hargrave guy, ask me his stupid questions, and run off to go surfing or something."

Al nodded. "I'm going spearfishing in the morning," he said. "Leaving early. You want to come?"

"Thanks but no thanks. It's a work day and I'm going up to Idaho to talk to the dead guy's family."

"You think they killed him?" Al asked.

"No. They're just the next link in my well-crafted investigative chain."

He smiled, stepped up into his truck, and drove off. I tossed my gym bag into the car, sat down behind the wheel, and felt alone. When I turned the key, however, a Beach Boys tune filled the cab with good vibrations and I suddenly felt better. And hungry. But I'd eaten too much restaurant food in the last few days and couldn't bear to look at another sandwich. I turned away from Channel Islands Harbor and drove into Oxnard. I didn't see anybody following me but why should they bother? They had a GPS transmitter on the dashboard of my Jeep. I pulled into the parking lot of my favorite Hispanic Super Mercado. Let them think that one over for a while.

I speak no Spanish besides *Mas cerveza, por favor* and *Donde esta la playa nudista* but I like most Hispanic people and I love their food. I walked into the store, grabbed one of those red plastic baskets you carry around when you don't quite need a cart, and walked straight to the fresh meat counter at the back of the store.

I asked for a pound of thinly-sliced marinated skirt steak and a half-pound of *queso blanco*. The fellow behind the counter knew me by sight and always filled my order correctly even though neither of us spoke the other guy's language. But I could still point at what I wanted while saying *uno* or *dos* and he always figured it out. Our simple communications, with smiles on both sides, filled my basket.

The corn tortillas were fresh enough to steam the insides of their plastic bags. The smallest bag held thirty. It was more than I needed but extra tortillas somehow always get eaten. A few large tomatoes, an onion, an avocado, and a small jalapeno rounded out what I needed to make the world's freshest salsa and guacamole. I added two cold Mexican Cokes, the ones they make with real cane sugar, at the cash register.

I drank one of the Cokes as I drove back to Vintage Marina and looked for Jerry and the other cops who, apparently, quietly suspected me of evil deeds. Would they eventually arrest me? Somebody was pushing it in that direction.

My boat didn't look right as I carried my groceries down J-dock. I looked carefully at her as I approached. A small amount of greenery grew at the waterline; a loose main halyard slapped against the mast in the wind; a slack mainsheet allowed the boom to slip to port and starboard as the boat rolled. Small signs of neglect shouted at me and I felt the need to apologize to her as I brought my groceries aboard.

"Don't worry, *Figaro*. I'll get you shipshape and we'll be sailing this weekend."

I unlocked the companionway, slipped a John Lee Hooker CD into the stereo, and stepped over to the galley to dice tomatoes, slice onions, peel an avocado, and seed the jalapeno. The scents elicited Pavlovian responses before I could even get *Figaro*'s grill lit and roaring from its station on the stern pushpit.

The beef grilled up nicely and the tortillas bubbled up and browned over the hot fire. I consumed more than my fair share of *carne asada* tacos and drank one-and-a-half ice-cold Coronas while the sun slipped down below the horizon in a fiery display of persistence.

"Got any leftovers?"

"Come aboard, Judith. I'll cook you up some street tacos you'll never forget," I said.

"You're on a boat," she said.

"Okay, then. Fleet tacos."

She navigated the dock box, sat in the cockpit and finished my beer. I went below and retrieved some more skirt steak, a few more tortillas, and the rest of the white cheese. I grabbed another beer for her on my way back up to the cockpit.

"That guy you found was a former sailor, wasn't he?" she asked.

"Yep."

I handed her the beer and fired up the grill again.

"But you couldn't tell me about him, could you?"

"Nope," I said.

The skirt steak made that wonderful sizzling sound as it hit the hot grill.

"Are you investigating the murder?" she asked.

I felt my guard going down.

"Uh-huh."

"The coroner's report says he was tortured."

"How'd you get that so soon?" I asked. "Oh, never mind."

"Was he tortured?"

"Could be," I said. "I wasn't there."

"Some of the local investigators seem to think you were."

"Hogwash. They are grasping at straws. Thin, weak, imaginary straws."

Judith was quiet as she drank her beer.

"I'll tell you more about this case when I know more, Judith. You'll get the whole story after I catch the guys who did it."

"There were two of them?" she asked.

"Are we off the record?"

"Unless you give me something so good that I have to print it."

"There were at least two," I said. "Maybe more. But I have no idea who they are or why they did it. Not yet, anyway."

I moved the cooked beef off to one side of the grill to keep it hot and warmed a few tortillas for her. A small fish jumped behind *Figaro's* stern and a gull swooped down low to check it out before calling off the attack. Judith crossed her legs and looked over her beer at me when I handed her the plate of tacos.

"Why didn't we get married six years ago when we had the chance, Sim?"

It wasn't a threatening question.

"I can only count it as one of the lost opportunities of a tarnished youth, Judith."

She smiled at my answer but volleyed no follow-up questions. We talked about the marina and local news as she ate her tacos and drank my beer. Then she thanked me and walked back down the dock toward her own boat.

Captain Overson's threat of a career-ending mistake rang in my ears as I cleaned up the dinner dishes. I'd spent nearly twenty years kissing officer ass and working to become the best at what I do and suddenly my entire career rested on a single unofficial case and a set of unidentified, possibly non-existent papers.

I thought of the next day's travel plans and decided to turn in early. My book was there on my bunk when I crawled between the sheets.

I read about Thomas Hudson's three boys visiting and their memories of growing up in Paris and I wondered how much of it was fiction and how much was Hemingway slipping in a bit of autobiographical reminiscence. I wondered how different my life would have been had I grown up in Paris rather than pruning grape vines in the San Joaquin Valley.

23

THE flight to Salt Lake City was as uneventful and predictable as a British government workers' strike. Modern airlines do their jobs so well that the act of flying over four hundred miles an hour at thirty-five thousand feet has actually become an exercise in averting boredom.

We landed a little before noon local time. The plane's Captain stood at the front and thanked deplaning passengers for flying with his airline. He scanned my uniform and smiled.

"Nice landing, Captain," I said.

"Thanks, Chief," he said.

A lot of civilian pilots earned their wings in a Navy flight suit.

I picked up a rental car, drove east, and turned north on I-15 for the two-hour drive to the farming town where Barry St. James grew up. The billboards, smokestacks, and business districts of the city gave way to more open spaces as I drove. Glimpses of the Great Salt Lake gave the impression of a huge inland sea stretching fifty miles away to the west and north. If it weren't for a couple of ranges of craggy mountains getting in the way, the casual observer might think the big lake stretched all the way to San Francisco.

I continued past large tracts of undeveloped land that had been overlooked during past residential expansions and four lanes of highway merged into three. Majestic mountains to the east gazed across the towns, interstate, and lake as if they were protectors shielding the citizenry from outsiders. Three lanes merged into two as I passed into a region of hay fields, grazing land, and small farming towns.

The towns became smaller and less frequent as I drove into Idaho. I found my exit and turned south along the railroad tracks. I crossed the tracks and drove east past fields of alfalfa so bright and green that they almost hurt the eyes. Large pole barns and small metal silos marked the few farmhouses in the area.

The St. James' family farm lay tucked up against some low brush-covered foothills a few miles south and east of town. A modest home that looked like it had been built during the Coolidge administration and remodeled during the good Reagan years stood a hundred yards from the county road. Red brick wainscoting supported newer aluminum siding. Half-hidden basement windows peeked over well-tended flower beds.

A man twice my age tinkered on a bright red Farmall tractor in the shade of a huge sycamore at the side of the house. He looked up and squinted as I parked in the driveway. He spotted the uniform when I stepped out of the car. He set down his socket wrench, wiped his hands on an old towel, and walked down the drive to meet me.

"I'm Barry's father," he said.

He shook my hand with a gnarled claw that had worked hard through too many hot summers and freezing winters. He motioned toward the front door of the house.

"Please come on in," he said.

He opened the front door and led me to a comfortable brown leather chair in the front room. A swamp cooler hummed in the attic and pumped cool, moist air into the house. A cat lay curled up on the carpet near a brick fireplace. The smells of home canning and the muffled hiss of a pressure cooker reached us from the kitchen.

"Mother," he said. "Please bring us some lemonade, will you?"

He sat down on a worn brown sofa and a woman entered the room with a white pitcher and three glasses filled with ice. She wasn't much younger than Barry's father but she was fit, looked strong, and had a face that carried laugh lines instead of crow's feet.

She poured the lemonade and served it and smoothed the wrinkles out of her apron as she sat on the sofa next to the man. She smiled broadly and patted her husband's knee. I was immediately impressed with a sense of warm satisfaction and joy in the old home. I hoped my visit wouldn't put an end to that.

"Thank you for allowing me into your home, Mr. St. James."

"You call me Darren," he said. "And I'm sorry I don't remember your name, son."

"Sim Greene," I said. "As I mentioned on the phone, I'd like to talk to you about your son."

"We already heard about what happened to Barry, Mr. Greene. They said it was murder but we just can't believe that." His brow furrowed. "Barry was our fourth child, Mr. Greene. It's an awful thing to lose a child but we'll see him again in God's heaven. And probably not all that long from now, either. "

He looked at his wife. She knotted her hands in her apron and stiffened noticeably.

"Out of seven kids, Carol and I knew from the first there was something special about Barry. He was the kindest boy, never had a problem with the law, never got in any fights. I don't think he ever spoke a cross word to anyone. Everybody 'round here just loved that boy."

Mrs. St. James stood up quickly and hurried back to the kitchen. Darren excused himself and followed her.

The room was humble but clean. Everything in its place. I stood up to examine the family pictures that hung from the walls and stood in wooden frames on the mantelpiece and on the bookshelves. The cat yawned and threw me a look of bitter disapproval.

Barry's siblings had all married and given their parents numerous grandchildren and, apparently, some great-grandchildren. I didn't count them. There were two pictures of Barry. One was a high school photo with his arm around a much younger Suzanne and the other was of him in dress whites being promoted to Lieutenant. There were a few family portraits with him, too. None appeared to be recent.

Darren and Carol returned and sat down.

"I'm sorry if this is a bad time," I said. "But I do have some questions and your answers could help me solve this case."

"Please sit down, Mr. Greene," said Darren. "This whole thing has caught us a little by surprise."

I sat back down in the leather chair and eased into the questions I needed to ask. Most of the answers confirmed what I already knew. Barry had joined the Navy ROTC during college and had, over time, advanced to the rank of Lieutenant. He married his high school sweetheart while they were both in college but the long tours of duty after graduating kept them apart. Barry and Suzanne had no children and were divorced. Barry retired ten years ago. He had no enemies that they knew of.

"Do you know what he did for a living after he left the Navy, Darren?"

"Oh, he was an accountant. It's what he studied in college and he was real good at it," he answered.

"Do you know if he had money problems?" I asked.

"Oh, no," said Carol. "He was very successful. He had his own firm and did quite well. He even sent us on a cruise two years ago."

"That was real nice of him," said Darren. "It must have cost him a pretty penny, too. He flew us out to Ft. Lauderdale in the middle of winter and we saw the most beautiful islands and the darndest most pretty water I ever seen. Two whole weeks on the biggest ship ever. Thousands of people on that ship. And swimming pools and huge tables of food."

"I'd seen pictures of the Caribbean before," said Carol, "but I never thought I'd actually ever see it in person. Or swim in it, neither."

There was a pause while Carol fumbled with a tissue.

"Nobody ever done nothin' like that for us before," she said. "I just can't believe anybody would want to hurt Barry."

"Do you have any more pictures of Barry?" I asked. "Or of his friends?"

Carol got up and walked down the hall toward the bedrooms. I heard her sliding a closet door to the side and fumbling around in some boxes. She returned with a thick manila envelope. She opened it and laid out pictures on the coffee table for me to see. There were a few shots of him in his Boy Scout uniform, participating in a church activity, and playing basketball on the high school team with four other short white guys.

One of the pictures immediately caught my eye. It was a print of Barry standing on the deck of an aircraft carrier with three other officers. Four shipmates posing for the camera. A much younger Captain Overson stood with his arm around Barry's neck and grinned at the camera. On the back of the picture was written "Bill O., Barry, Glenn, and Steve – USS *Enterprise*, South China Sea."

"May I take this picture?" I asked. "It could be helpful to my investigation. I'll return it when I'm done."

"Of course, Mr. Greene," said Darren. "We don't really need this picture to remember Barry, anyway."

Another picture caught my attention and they let me have that one, too. It was a photograph of Barry sitting in the cockpit of a sailboat with a pretty blonde. I couldn't tell much about either the boat or the harbor from that photo but I instantly recognized the blonde.

She worked downstairs in the lawyer's office.

24

I thought about Darren and Carol and the family photos on the mantelpiece for a good chunk of the two-hour drive south. My folks should have had pictures like that. My sisters would have given them some photogenic grandchildren by now. How long had it been? Sixteen years? Seventeen?

A sleepy trucker.

A sleepy trucker late at night on a two-lane road in rural Kern County who drifted across the center line and converted an old Pontiac into a pile of unrecognizable scrap metal. I thought of the four closed caskets in the small church ceremony that I couldn't attend because I was aboard ship a thousand miles south of India when it happened. I tried to hold back feelings I'd kept down for nearly two decades but it didn't work and it was only me in the car anyway.

The late summer sun stood about fifteen minutes off the horizon when I drove into the rental return lot at Salt Lake International. I passed through TSA with the rest of the lemmings and headed toward my gate searching for an airport lounge. I didn't really need a drink but I knew I was going to have one. I justified the second by deciding that the first had been a light load. I stopped at three when they announced that my flight was boarding.

It was dark and hot in Los Angeles when I walked out of the terminal to find my Jeep in the central parking area. I tossed my bag in the passenger seat, paid the exorbitant daily parking rate, and headed down Century Boulevard toward the 405. I spotted a liquor store near the freeway, gave it some thought, and quickly decided that a prudent sailor would wait until he got back to his own boat before he crawled into a bottle for the night.

25

MY head throbbed as I lay in *Figaro*'s quarterberth. The throbbing turned into a steady thumping and I woke to the sound of somebody pounding on the side of the hull. I pulled on a pair of shorts, opened up the companionway hatch, and squinted from the late-morning sunlight.

"Where the hell have you been?" asked Jerry.

He was flanked by a guy who, based on the suit he was wearing, was either an FBI agent or a mortician.

"Idaho," I said. "Who's your friend?"

"I'm Detective Hargrave, Mr. Greene. Ventura County Sheriff's Department. We'd like to speak with you."

Settles that question.

"Gimme a minute," I said.

I ducked back down into the cabin, splashed a little water in my face over the sink, and fished a cold bottle of spring water out of the icebox. I'd learned years ago that my hangovers tended to yield quickly to a course of rehydration. I found my bill cap and sunglasses, put them on, and climbed up into the cockpit.

"Okay," I said. "What can I do for you guys?"

"May we come aboard?" asked Hargrave.

"Not unless you have a warrant, Detective." I took a slug from the spring water. "You're wearing the wrong shoes. I hate shoes like that. They're awful shoes. Those things will leave black streaks all over my pretty fiberglass boat and I'd rather not clean up after you."

Hargrave said something unpleasant indicating his distaste for my assessment of his footwear. I didn't care. I sat next to the helm with my head under the bimini and my back exposed to the morning sun. It felt good on my bare skin. Jerry and Hargrave stood on the dock eight feet away. They could stand there as long as they wanted, they could get a warrant, or they could leave. Their choice. I drank more spring water.

"What's the matter with you?" asked Jerry.

I looked at Jerry and said nothing. It was nobody's business if I had stepped off the wagon for a night. Nobody's damned business at all. Sure, a guy tries to stay sober when he knows he's got a weakness for the hard stuff, but so what if he drops off once in a while. It's no skin off the law's nose. Then again, it's no reason to be uncivil.

"Take your shoes off and come aboard," I said.

They took off their shoes, climbed the three steps to deck height, and joined me in the cockpit.

"Didn't Al tell you we didn't want you to leave town?" asked Jerry.

"He did and I ignored it." Jerry looked at me like I'd sprouted horns. "Am I under arrest, Jerry? If so, then speak the poetry that is Miranda and give me some government-issue bracelets. If not, then I'll go wherever the hell I please."

I drank more of the cold spring water.

"No, you're not under arrest. We just need to talk to you about this murder," said Jerry.

"You've got the statement I gave you on Al's boat when I found the body," I said. "Nothing about my observations has changed."

"We're not talking about that murder, Mr. Greene," said Hargrave.

"I'm not tracking you," I said.

"We want to know what you can tell us about Jedediah Wayton," he said.

"Who's that?" I said.

"Old Jed," said Jerry. "Our own friendly beach bum. Somebody killed him. When did you last see him?"

It took only a few minutes to retell the story of finding Jed on a lonely and cold Thursday morning. Jerry, like any good cop, listened carefully for any inconsistencies with the story I'd told him days ago. Hargrave asked a few pointed questions.

"How was he killed?" I asked.

"Two surfers found Jed's body Saturday morning in a dumpster near the south jetty," said Jerry. "He'd been shot behind the left ear with a small caliber gun."

"Suicide?" I asked.

"No gun," said Jerry.

"Somebody could have stolen it," I said. "One of those surfers might have wanted a popgun."

Hargrave shook his head.

"The surfers are fourteen-year-old kids," he said. "They were scared into next week."

I couldn't think of anything to say.

"From what we can tell, Mr. Greene, you may be the last person to see him alive," said Hargrave.

I finished the bottle of spring water.

"Nope," I said. "Not true, Detective. The last person who saw him alive was the person who shot him."

Hargrave shrugged.

"You got a time of death?" I asked.

"Friday night between 8:00 and 11:00 p.m.," said Hargrave. "You got an alibi?"

Of course I had an alibi. A really good one, too. I was nearly ten miles away breaking into Barry St. James apartment and getting whacked on the back of the head. But it didn't seem like a great idea to share that with them.

"I worked out with Al at the Anacapa Fitness Center then drove up to Ventura. Got back to my boat around eleven."

"Why'd you go to Ventura?" asked Hargrave.

"I was looking for a book," I lied. *"Islands in the Stream"* by Hemingway."

"Long way to go for a book with gas prices being what they are these days," said Hargrave.

"It's a pretty good book."

Hargrave did not look happy or amused. Jerry looked as if he'd swallowed a lemon.

"I can answer your next three questions, Detective," I said.

"What are those?" he said.

"I paid cash, threw away the receipt, and didn't run into anybody I knew at the bookstore."

Hargrave looked me over without saying anything. It's the pregnant pause, the intended silence meant to induce the suspect into talking more, into saying something incriminating. I didn't bite.

"Do you mind if I ask you a few questions, Detective?" I said.

He shrugged. I went back down the companionway into *Figaro*'s cabin, dug around in my briefcase, and brought the little black GPS tracker back up into the cockpit. I held it between my right thumb and forefinger.

"You guys want this back?" I asked.

"I don't know what you're talking about," said Hargrave.

"Don't lie to me. You've been using this thing to follow me around since Sunday."

Hargrave shook his head. Jerry looked stupid. He excelled at that.

"Either of you ever hear of *U.S. v. Jones?*" I asked.

Blank stares.

"The Supreme Court? Ever hear of them?" I asked. "They decided that sticking one of these on my Jeep constitutes a search under the Fourth Amendment."

"What are you, a lawyer?" said Hargrave. "You thinking of suing us?"

"No. But I might just walk over to *Norton's Ark* and hand this thing to Judith. She's always looking for a story. Do you think the Sheriff wants to deal with another scandal in the department?"

"Be my guest," said Hargrave. "That thing isn't even one of ours."

He didn't seem concerned but he could have been bluffing. If he was, then he was one of those guys I don't want to play poker with. I drank some more cold water.

"Have you gotten anywhere on the Barry St. James murder?" I asked.

"We're still investigating," he said.

"Any kind of forensic evidence? DNA samples, hair follicles, somebody else's skin or blood under the fingernails?"

"Nothing and everything," he said. "The ocean washes a lot of stuff away from a body. And it washes a lot of stuff back onto it. We haven't found a single useful piece of evidence."

"How about the chain?" I asked.

"Stolen off the docks at Hueneme."

He was quiet for a few moments. Thinking.

"It's almost like the killer knew the best way to hide the body and cover up forensic evidence," he said. "Like they were in law enforcement and knew our procedures."

It was his turn to be aggressive and my turn to shrug.

"Don't disappear on us, Mr. Greene. I'm sure we'll have a few more questions for you," he said.

"I only go where the Navy tells me, Detective."

"Like a bookstore?" he asked.

They stepped off the boat, put their shoes back on, and walked up J-dock to the parking lot. I gave them a few minutes to drive away and then threw the little black box into the channel.

26

WHAT I'd planned for the day required a low-profile look so I left my uniform in *Figaro's* hanging locker, dug out a clean T-shirt, and slipped on my boat shoes. Judith's old Mercedes pulled into the parking lot as I walked up the dock ramp. She rolled down her window as she drove up to my Jeep.

"Sim, can you hang on a minute?" she asked.

"Sure. What's up, sweetheart?"

She smiled.

"Not good news, Simba. You are officially the 'primary person of interest' for the St. James murder."

"Great," I said.

"I think they're trying to set you up for a Grand Jury indictment. My cop sources are talking about it like you're toast. One of them told me early this morning that the case they're building against you will be," she paused a moment to look at her electronic notebook, "and I quote, 'tighter than a frog's ass stretched over a rain barrel.' Seriously, some of these guys actually talk like this."

"Elegant," I said. "They think I killed Old Jed, too."

"I know a guy we need to call," she said. "Emmanuel Goldsmith. The guy is amazing."

I recognized the name. As a younger man, working as an Assistant U.S. Attorney in New Jersey, he'd prosecuted a sizable number of strong family men. Men with Sicilian names who headed strong families. A dozen years ago, he switched sides, moved west, bought a big house in Ojai, and made another name for himself as a defense lawyer who loved the camera as much as the courtroom.

"I don't need a lawyer, Judith."

"Yes, you do."

She grabbed a yellow sticky note and wrote a phone number on it.

"Please call this guy, Sim. For me, okay?"

"Thanks," I said.

I got into my Jeep wondering why the local cops were so convinced that I had something to do with either the St. James murder or Jed's death or both. Were they that bereft of any actual clues? And why was Judith so friendly to me all of a sudden? Then it occurred to me that I didn't have any answers or any clues, either. Except, maybe one.

I drove across town to Barry's old office and walked into the law firm's first floor lobby. The receptionist recognized me.

"Did you hear about Mr. St. James?" she asked.

"I did," I said.

"We're all very sorry to hear of his, uh, passing," she said.

"It must have been much harder for you."

Her brow furrowed in puzzlement for a minute. I pulled out the picture of her lounging with Barry on his boat and showed it to her. Her eyes went wide.

"Where did you get that?" she asked.

She wasn't angry or defensive.

"From his parents in Idaho."

The furrows in her brow deepened.

"But aren't you one of his clients?" she asked.

"No," I said. "I'm actually a policeman with the United States Navy. Mr. St. James was a retired officer and I'm investigating his death. I'd like to talk with you about him."

She looked at me blankly for the few moments it took to sink in. Once it did, she threw a quick look at the clock on the wall.

"I get a lunch break in fifteen minutes," she said. "There's a sandwich shop about a half-mile east on Fifth Street."

She wrote the name of the restaurant on a piece of scratch paper and drew a crude map under the name. I agreed to meet her there and walked out.

Twenty minutes later, she walked into the little shop and tossed her hair back. Her figure, the hair, and her dress created a truly stunning package. Pheromones permeated the air and every male eye followed her to my table. I sensed a healthy portion of envy in the room.

"Do you have any identification?" she asked. "I'm not really sure who you are. And you're not in any kind of uniform."

"My name is Sim Greene," I said.

I pulled out my military I.D. card and showed it to her.

"I'm Erica DeYoung," she said.

"What are you hungry for?" I asked.

"I'll just have a salad and a Diet Coke."

I nodded at the waitress and she came and took our orders.

"You knew Barry St. James pretty well," I said.

"He was the guy upstairs and he paid his rent to our office. We got to know each other a little."

"It was considerably more serious than that," I said as I handed her the photograph.

She looked at the picture again and started to cry softly. I kept my mouth shut. She stopped crying and wiped her eyes with a handkerchief.

"Barry was the nicest man I've ever known," she said. "I can't tell you how shocked I was to hear he was murdered."

"How did the two of you meet?" I asked.

"Like I said before. We met in the office one day when he came down to pay his rent. He was so nice and understanding."

She gave a little snort into the handkerchief. It was as ladylike and refined as a snort could be.

"He was quite a bit older than you," I said. "I'm guessing nearly twice your age."

"He was so funny, though," she said. "After a while, I never even thought of his age."

"How serious was your relationship?"

"We were really just good friends at first," she said. "Like I said, he was very funny. He always made me laugh."

"And?"

"I was dating Dustin—he's one of the lawyers in the office—but I was going through a difficult time with him. And then Barry came along and..."

"Swept you off your feet?" I asked.

"Well, we started dating," she said. "For a little while, anyway."

"How long did the two of you date?"

"About three months or so," she said. "I think I pushed him too hard, though. I told him that I wanted to move in with him and he backed off."

She stopped for a minute to wipe her eyes again.

"I mean, I thought we were, like, both serious," she said. "I guess only I was."

I thought about how many single guys in their fifties would refuse her offer to move in. I didn't think there would be more than a couple. Maybe a Cardinal or a Bishop somewhere. Or a eunuch.

"Did he take you on his boat very often?" I asked.

"That's where we...that's where we spent most of our time together."

"Where does he keep the boat?"

"In the harbor," she said. "The one in Ventura. He's got a slip for it near the fish and chips place. We ate there a lot."

"Did the boat have a name?" I asked. "It's usually printed on the back."

"I don't remember it."

"Could you take me to it? Show me where it is?"

She shook her head.

"I tried to find Barry a couple of weeks ago. He wasn't answering his phone so I went down to the harbor to find him but all those boats look alike and I didn't see him."

She stuck her nose back into the handkerchief.

The waitress brought her salad and my sandwich and our soft drinks. She asked if we needed anything else and I briefly considered asking for a box of tissues. I decided not to.

Erica calmed down and foraged through her greens taking only the small bits and pieces that appealed to her.

"Can you tell me about his work?" I asked. "His clients? Did he like to fish? Who were his friends? Did he have any enemies?"

"We didn't talk much about those things," she said.

"What did you talk about?"

She went back to the handkerchief. Her crying grew in intensity and volume and a couple of the guys who had seen her walk in rolled their eyes. Any envy that might have been in the air evaporated.

"He trusted me," she said.

"Okay," I said.

I went back to my sandwich and let Erica cool down.

"When did you stop seeing each other?" I asked.

"Three weeks ago, I guess."

"What happened?"

"Dustin stopped Barry and me in the lobby as we were leaving the building for lunch," she said. "And he created a bit of a scene."

"What do you mean?"

"Dustin is a bit demanding and possessive and he tries to come off like a tough guy sometimes. He thinks it adds something to his lawyer image."

"What happened?" I asked.

"Dustin grabbed Barry by the shoulder and spun him around and said some very rude things. Then he accused me of being a tramp and he threatened to hit Barry. It was very embarrassing."

"What did Barry do?"

"He did something that scared me to death," she said.

She pulled the handkerchief away from her nose and swallowed hard.

"He pulled a knife out of nowhere and stuck it against Dustin's throat," she said. "I've never seen anybody move that fast in my life. He told Dustin that if he ever saw his face again, he'd dice it up into little squares and feed it to him one piece at a time."

She gave a little shudder.

"It was horrible," she said.

"What did Dustin do?" I asked.

"He...um...he wet himself. Barry laughed and walked away. I just sorta followed Barry out the door."

"And Barry was the nicest man you've ever known?" I asked.

"Yeah," she said. "I try to forget the knife, I guess."

"So who broke off the relationship?"

"I guess we both sort of drifted apart," she said. "We just didn't see each other much after that. He didn't call me anymore and I didn't call him."

It sounded like he broke it off and she'd never experienced that before.

"Are you seeing anybody now?" I asked.

It wasn't a pick-up line. I swear it wasn't.

"Dustin," she said.

Oh, well. No accounting for taste.

"It isn't what you think it was with Barry," she said. "It was much more than that. He really trusted me. He even asked me to keep some things safe for him."

Oh ho.

"Like jewelry or money or his complete Beatles collection on original vinyl?" I asked.

"He came by the office a week ago or so and gave me a box of stuff to hold for him. He told me to give it to a cop if anything bad happened to him."

Bells rang and lights flashed.

"Do you still have it?"

She nodded. I motioned to the waitress for a to-go box and dropped some cash on the table.

"Erica, I am a cop. Let's go get this box."

We walked out to my Jeep and drove to her apartment. During the drive she talked about a detox diet that some actress was using. It may have been the longest ten minutes of my life.

The apartment was definitely all girl. It screamed of fashion and brightness and texture and color. A bright red sofa and chair sat on a pure white carpet. I thought about how stupid it would be to have a carpet like that if you had little kids with muddy shoes. Then I realized that little kids would never be a part of this equation.

Erica returned a few minutes later with a white box with red and blue lettering. It was a medium sized, unstamped box from an overnight delivery service. There was no shipping label.

I drove her back to her car at the sandwich shop and gave her my cell number.

"If you remember anything about Barry that seems unusual or important, anything at all, please give me a call," I said.

"Okay," she said.

She pointed toward the package in the back of my car.

"Can I trust you with that?" she asked. "I don't really want to get involved with the police."

"I'll take care of it," I said.

She threw her arms around me and kissed me on the cheek.

"You're such a dear," she said. "Thanks for listening to me."

She got in her car and drove back to work. I reached into the back of my Jeep and picked up the box. I considered taking it directly to Captain Overson. I'd tell him that I'd found the documents he was looking for and that Barry St. James had been caught in a love triangle between Dustin and Erica. I'd call it a day and look forward to a new slot at NCIS.

But it didn't feel right. The facts didn't line up in a nice neat row. At least two guys were involved in killing Barry St. James and torture didn't fit well with the theory of a jealous lover. And there were still questions to ask Bob Carter. The little voice inside told me that the package wasn't what the Captain wanted and that the jealous attorney didn't do the deed.

Instinct won out.

I drove back to the marina, walked down J-dock to *Figaro*, and grabbed a cold Corona out of the fridge. Barry's little box opened easily with the aid of my pocket knife but the contents were more than a bit confusing. No jewelry or bonds or money. No insurance policy. No important Navy documents.

There was a handwritten single sheet of paper indicating that it was Barry St. James' last will and testament, a business card from Frank Bartholomew with the ICE logo on the front and three Chinese characters drawn on the back, a gray ballistic nylon CD wallet with seven compact discs in it, a gold ring, and an envelope addressed to Suzanne St. James.

The handwriting on the will wasn't the easiest to read but it appeared that Barry wanted most of his earthly possessions to be sold and the proceeds to go to his parents. There was also a specific instruction to mail the envelope and ring to Suzanne. There was no mention of the business card or the CD's.

The ring was a plain gold band with the inscription *All My Love* engraved inside. I decided to violate any expectation of privacy and slit the top of the envelope with my pocket knife. Inside was an unlabeled brass key and a short handwritten note to Suzanne.

I'M SORRY, SUZE. I NEVER DID DO RIGHT BY YOU. YOU DESERVED MUCH BETTER. MAYBE THE MONEY HELPED A BIT. I HOPE SO.

THE DOCTORS SAY I'VE GOT THE BIG "C" AND THAT THERE'S NO WAY OUT BUT THE SLOW WAY. I

DON'T WANT THAT SO I'VE SET IT ALL UP FOR YOU
AT OUR PLACE IN VENTURA.

THERE'S SOME CASH AND A SMALL INSURANCE
POLICY IN THERE. THAT'S FOR YOU. GIVE THE REST
OF THE STUFF TO THE COPS AND TAKE A LONG
VACATION. DON'T EVER TELL ANYONE ABOUT ANY
OF THIS. TRUST ME. IT'S THE LAST THING I CAN DO
TO MAKE THINGS RIGHT FOR YOU.

LOVE YA, BABE.

BARRY.

There wasn't any cash or any insurance policy in the envelope
or in the package. Nothing indicated what the brass key was for. I
compared it to the brass key I'd found hidden in his office. They
were close but not identical. So now I had two brass keys that fit
unknown locks. Wonderful.

I'd already been through his place in Ventura and had nearly
been killed for my trouble. Anything that had been set up there for
Suzanne was gone by now.

The whole exercise left me wondering why St. James would
put an envelope containing his last love letter and a brass key in a
package that was intended to be given to police.

*Why not just tell Erica to mail the letter to Suzanne? Was he afraid
Bob Carter would get his hands on it?*

I picked up the business card, grabbed my cell phone, and
punched in the numbers.

"Speak," said a voice.

27

"MR. Bartholomew? This is Sim Greene."

"The sailor, right?" he asked.

"Uh-huh."

"Where did you get this number, Greene?"

"You gave me your card the other night, remember? It was dark. You were standing by your big black car with your boyfriend. I was holding a pistol. You asked me to call you if I had anything interesting to say. Is any of this coming back to you?"

"You're very funny," he said. "A smartass, but funny. You should be on late-night television. But this phone number wasn't on the card I gave you."

I opened up my chart table and checked the business card he'd given me the other night behind the strip mall against the one I'd found in Barry's little box. Sure enough, the numbers were a couple digits off.

"Well, I have something interesting to tell you if you're still interested," I said. "And I threw away your little GPS transponder."

"Are you still looking into the St. James murder?" he asked.

"Yes," I said. "And I'd like to meet with you."

"Friday at noon," he said. "What's that place near your boat that has those delicious tri-tip sandwiches? The place where you and your buddy have dinner all the time? The Harbor Mart or something, right?"

That he knew so much about my boat and my dinner habits was more than a little disturbing.

"Yeah," I said. "That's the place."

"Friday at noon, then. And be prepared to tell me where you got this number, Greene."

"No problem," I said. "But I'd like to meet earlier, say in half an hour?"

"Oh, are you in Portland?" he asked.

"No."

"Well, I am," he said. "So, I'll see you at the Harbor Mart on Friday at noon."

I told him that would be okay.

"Oh, one more thing," he said. "I don't know what you're talking about in regards to any GPS transponder."

28

I picked up the picture of Barry and Erica happily snuggling in the cockpit of Barry's sailboat and gave it a thorough examination. There weren't a lot of clues. The boat had tiller steering instead of a wheel so it was probably on the small side. A boat in the background had a canoe stern; a relatively rare feature. Another boat behind Barry's flew the distinctive burgee—a white seagull on a blue triangular background—of the Pierpont Bay Yacht Club.

It wasn't a long drive to Ventura Harbor and I spotted a good candidate within a few minutes of getting there. I waited by the card-key gate to the docks and watched a father-son duo unload their gear from a sportfisherman into a wheeled cart. I waited for them to open the gate and then held it open for them. Security.

Rum Runner was one of those mass-produced fiberglass boats that sold well in the late 1960s and early 1970s. I'd seen plenty of them for sale when I was shopping the market before I found *Figaro*. They were cheap on the used boat market; cheap for a reason. I wouldn't consider taking such a boat on a long trip.

Barry had used a brass padlock to secure the companionway hatch but the padlock, its shackle snapped in half by a bolt cutter, lay on the cockpit sole. I slid the companionway hatch open and stepped below. The cabin had been stripped with the same efficiency displayed in his office and apartment. Every piece of paper was gone. The VHF radio and marine stereo had been ripped out of the cabinetry. The cushions in the salon and mattress in the V-berth had been torn and searched. The storage area below the chart table, usually a catchall area in a sailboat, was empty, as were the bookshelves, kitchen drawers, and hanging lockers.

There was nothing to see. I climbed the companionway, closed the hatch behind me, and put the remains of the brass padlock into a plastic bag. *Rum Runner* was just another hole in a case full of holes. I walked back to my Jeep and tested the brass keys on the broken padlock. One of them opened it.

I drove to the base to play my usual game of turning a difficult case into a jigsaw puzzle. It was late in the afternoon and waves of heat lifted off the asphalt like ghosts rising from the dead. I climbed the stairs to my office, nodded at Gil, and sat down at my desk. It was still uncharacteristically clean and uncluttered. I felt a little out of place.

I pulled the coroner's preliminary report out of my briefcase, thumbed through it, and called Dr. Craven's number. His assistant answered on the third ring and transferred me to Craven's extension.

"I've got a few questions about your preliminary report on Barry St. James," I said.

"And I probably have very few useful answers," he said.

His voice betrayed a sense of fatigue as if he'd had this conversation too many times with too many detectives regarding too many deaths.

"You say he had a tumor in his brain," I said. "Do you have any idea what that could be?"

"I have all kinds of ideas, Mr. Greene, but I don't have the final pathology reports."

"Was it cancer?" I asked.

"Probably," he said. "I don't know for certain, yet."

"And it was near the thalamus."

"You are a thorough reader, Mr. Greene."

"How would that affect him?" I asked. "Would that mess up his cognitive abilities? His speech? His judgment? I'm trying to find out more about the victim."

He sighed and took in a deep breath.

"It probably wouldn't affect those parts of his life," he said. "The thalamus is between the brain stem and the cerebrum. It acts as an interface regarding issues of muscle coordination, fine touch, pain and temperature sensation, and a host of other neural issues. I'm not an oncologist but I've seen more than a few of these things. If this mass was a malignant cancer, it would have been inoperable. The guy was toast. If somebody hadn't drowned him, he'd only have six or eight months left at the most."

"You reported that you thought he'd been tortured," I said.

"Lingchi. Very painful. There isn't any way to know for sure but I would say, given the nature of the cuts, that he was almost certainly tortured."

"Could his cancer have cut off sensations of pain; made him resistant to it?" I asked.

He was quiet for a minute. I was about to ask if we'd been cut off when he broke the silence.

"I hadn't considered that," he said. "But I suppose it could have. There's no way I can tell, of course, but it is a possibility."

"Thanks for your time, Doctor."

He paused again for a moment.

"Mr. Greene?"

"Yes," I said.

"What has the Navy gotten itself into?" he asked.

"I have no idea, Doctor."

I hung up the phone and emptied my briefcase on the desktop in front of me. It was time to assemble the puzzle. There were the two pictures of Barry I'd picked up in Idaho the day before, the contents of the box I'd just received from Erica, the brass key and business card I'd found in his office, and the file I'd received from Capt. Overson.

I pulled a pair of scissors out of my desk drawer and cut some three-by-five index cards in half. I wrote the names of the people I'd interviewed or met or read something about onto the little squares. Old Jed, Suzanne, Barry, Ray, Erica, and Dustin. I wrote ICE on another piece of card and, almost as an afterthought, Capt. Overson on another. I added squares for Barry's parents and siblings and wrote the words *"Rum Runner"* and "chain" on two more. Bob Carter got a card.

Barry's card went into the center of the desktop and all the other names and items that I considered to be directly related to Barry went in a loose circle around him. I placed some of the other pieces, the ones that seemed far removed from the victim, outside that first circle. Moving pieces of paper allowed me to categorize the people, events, and circumstances together into different groups. Barry's high school years; his Navy years; the years since his retirement. I moved the cards around and tried different groupings but nothing seemed to make sense.

I heard the sounds of people leaving their offices and starting their cars and heading toward the main gate. Quitting time. I studied the little square cards again. Nothing jumped out at me. Pieces of the puzzle were missing. I picked up the phone and called Suzanne.

"This is Sim Greene," I said. "We spoke on Saturday about Barry St. James."

"Yes."

"I found a letter that Lieutenant St. James…"

"Please call him 'Barry'," she said.

"Yes, ma'am. I found a letter that Barry wanted you to have."

I read the letter to her and told her about the brass key and the ring. It was his wedding ring.

"Do you have any idea what that key could be for?" I asked.

"Not the slightest," she said. "He had cancer?"

"I don't know for sure, ma'am, but that is what he said in his letter."

"Oh, heavens," she said. "He never told me. I would have helped him."

"Are you aware of any insurance policies he could have or of any letters he might be holding for the United States Navy?"

"No."

"Do you know if he had any disagreements with his brothers or sisters or their families?" I asked. "Any kind of strife or family tension at all?"

She sighed.

"You don't have any idea who killed Barry, do you?" she asked.

"I'm still working on getting background information, ma'am."

I wasn't about to admit that she was right.

"Okay," she said.

She took a deep breath and let out another long sigh.

"He never had any problems with his family, Mr. Greene. None at all. They might have been a little disappointed in some of the choices he made—you know, marrying me and joining the Navy and such—but his family loved him dearly. Everybody did. He was the nicest boy and, later, the nicest man."

I thanked her and we hung up. I stared at the card pieces on my desk and asked myself who would torture and drown such a charitable, wonderful, model citizen as Barry St. James. Then I rang Gil's extension. He was still in.

"Have we got a positive ID on those fingerprints from the water bottle yet?" I asked.

"No, sir."

"Did we get a 'No Record' response?"

"No, sir," he said.

"It's been four days, Gil. What's going on?"

"I called this morning and they say they are still searching for a valid military record."

"Thanks," I said. "Keep on it for me, okay?"

I hung up and looked at the clock. It was a quarter to six. I looked at my desk. None of the pieces of paper had moved. There weren't many tag ends of thread left to pull. But there were a couple. I flipped over the picture of Barry and his three buddies on the deck of the *Enterprise* and read the description again.

Bill O., Barry, Glenn, and Steve – USS Enterprise, South China Sea.

Barry was dead and Bill O. was my very own Captain Overson and a known quantity. Glenn and Steve, however, were unknowns. It would have been easy to take a shortcut and ask Captain Overson if he'd kept up with either of his former buddies but he wasn't in the best of moods and I decided that it would be better to see how far I could get without annoying him.

The information offered by the Navy's on-line personnel search program was not very deep but it was exceptionally wide. I found fourteen Glenns, sixteen Glens, and seventy-two Steves, Stephens, and Estebans who had served on the USS *Enterprise* the same years Barry had. Just over a hundred files to examine. Gratefully, the on-line files contained photos. In two hours, I'd found Lt. Cmdr. Glenn Alvarez and Lt. (JG) Steve Holdsworth who, respectively, looked a lot like the Glenn and the Steve in the picture with Barry.

Glenn Alvarez hadn't risen in the ranks as quickly as Captain Overson. He was now a Lieutenant Commander at the Naval Reserve Center in Bangor, Washington. Steve Holdsworth hadn't gotten past his Jay-Gee, and retired the same year Barry had. I wrote the names Glenn and Steve on two more small card pieces and set them on the desk near Barry. It didn't fill in much more of the puzzle.

I rang Gil's extension again and found he'd left for the day. I left a message on his voicemail asking him to order up the complete personnel files for both Glenn and Steve. As I hung up, I thought of the apparent non-existence of Ray Jackson and decided to do something about it. It was dark when I left my office. Traffic was light for a Wednesday night and it didn't take long to get to Ray Jackson's office in Camarillo.

The lights were off and the door was locked when I got there. Not a surprise given the late hour. Nobody answered the doorbell.

That was fine with me. I stuck my flashlight into the mail slot and peeked in to find that the stack of mail on the other side of the door had grown taller. I called the office number again. No answer; voice mailbox full.

I examined the door locks carefully and found the deadbolt latched. My credit card wasn't going to get past that one. I looked into the mail slot again, realized my good fortune, and walked down the street a half-block to a small locally-owned hardware store. The kind of store that is disappearing at an alarming rate. The kind that stays open late, stocks a little bit of everything, and is run by an old guy who can tell you anything you need to know about fixing nearly anything on the planet.

I bought a package of light-gauge welding rod and a folding mirror with an extendable handle. I'd always wanted to have one of those mirrors aboard *Figaro* but had never made it a point to buy one.

Back at Jackson's door, I bent one end of the welding rod into a small u-shape and poked it and the mirror into the mail slot. I stuck the flashlight in my mouth to keep it from being a three-handed job. In less than a minute, I hooked the handle of the dead bolt and pulled it back. My credit card made short work of the knob's door lock and I was inside.

It didn't take long to find out why my bell ringing and door knocking had gone unanswered. The office was empty. Every stick of furniture, every filing cabinet, the beautiful wood desk, the pictures on the wall, and Ray's fine leather executive chair were gone. But the office wasn't just empty; it had been thoroughly cleaned. The blinds had been washed. The nails that held the pictures in the walls had been removed and the holes filled with putty. The window sills had been dusted and the carpets professionally cleaned.

I locked up the office, got back into my Jeep, and pointed it back toward Vintage Marina. I thought about all the tracks I'd found that disappeared into the dust and the dark back alleys that seemed to end in brick walls. And I thought about a nice, tidy, clean office. The word "sanitized" came to mind.

29

DONOVAN'S Irish Pub fairly breathed old-world comfort and tradition. A stainless steel shield guarded a heavy dark brown wooden door with black metal bands across it. A green snake coiled around an upraised sword in the heraldic crest painted on the shield. Once you got past the snake and the door you found homey rooms with gas fireplaces, warm lighting, a lot of polished wood in the ceilings and walls, and twenty or more brass taps dispensing various forms of the brewer's art.

Donovan kept his boat about fifty yards from *Figaro*. He'd played six seasons as middle linebacker for the Vikings and, at 6'3" and 250 pounds, was still an imposing figure five years later. He used the money he'd saved during his NFL years to open the restaurant. It was one of the rare places where you could find a good rib-eye steak, lamb shank, steak and kidney pie, and 20-year single malt Scotch on the same menu. Irish music filled the place and those who loved Irish dancing would find it there on Saturday nights. It was a popular spot with local families.

Al sat at the bar with a half-empty pint of Guinness. It could have been his second pint. Probably not his third, though. Still, it was hard to tell with Al.

"How's the investigation going?" he asked.

"Strangely," I said.

Donovan walked over.

"Usual, Sim?" he asked.

I nodded and he placed a drawn Smithwick's Ale in front of me. Al finished his beer and ordered another. It arrived and he tasted it.

"There is absolutely nothing like that first taste of a new pint," he said. "So, what is so strange about this case?"

"The victim was the nicest guy ever. Everybody liked him. And he knew he was going to die. He put a box together with a note to his ex-wife and he may have gotten an insurance policy in her name."

I tasted my ale. It was smooth and creamy and had a bit of caramel flavor to it. It was exactly what I needed at the moment.

"And the guy was tortured before somebody wrapped him in chains and tossed him into the drink," I said. "Weirder still, the torture may have failed. The guy had a form of cancer that could have blocked the pain."

Al said nothing. He seemed to focus all of his powers of concentration on his Guinness.

"And his insurance agent has disappeared," I said.

Al looked up and smiled.

"You think his insurance agent killed him?" he asked.

"I don't know what to think," I said. "The agent should be nothing. Probably is nothing. But his office is empty and the guy has disappeared."

I drank some more ale.

"It's just weird," I said.

The heavy wooden door opened and three bikers in riding boots and full black leathers stomped in. The first two were the fellows I'd seen at Frank's Lunch in Oceano. I only knew them by their mustaches. Horseshoe and Van Dyke were joined by a guy who looked like he'd been born sour and got worse. Horseshoe nodded toward me and the sour guy approached.

"I hear you've been bothering my girlfriend, sailor," he said.

The room fell silent. Donovan heard the remark and saw the bikers. He approached us from his side of the bar. A few of the locals, three guys who knew my face if not my name, got up and formed a loose semi-circle behind the bikers. A tinge of concern passed across Van Dyke's face.

"We reserve the right to refuse service to anyone," said Donovan. "This is a family place and I think you three boys need to leave."

Horseshoe looked as if he were about to argue the point when Donovan pulled his fish billy from its hiding place behind the bar.

"Nothing to worry about, Donovan," I said. "These two guys are old friends of mine and I think they're just a little thirsty."

I tossed a twenty on the bar.

"Give these fellows something to drink while Mr. Carter and I take our conversation outside," I said.

Donovan gave me a weird look as he laid down the fish billy. The locals wandered back to their seats. Al moved over to make room for Horseshoe and Van Dyke who, confused by the warm welcome, sat down to two newly drawn Harps.

Bob and I walked through the heavy wooden door and out onto the sidewalk. Three choppers were parked at the curb, angled out toward the street. He lost some of his aggression when he realized how big I was and that he was now alone.

"So your probation officer tells me that you blew up Noriega's yacht when you were a SEAL," I said.

"Yeah," he said. "So what?"

"So what's your BUD/S class number?" I asked.

No Navy SEAL forgets his Basic Underwater Demolition/SEAL class number. Hell is not easily forgotten. Carter gave me a number that, if true, would have required him to complete BUD/S training at about age twelve.

"You were talking to my probation officer?" he said.

"Yeah, but I didn't tell her you were lying about your military record."

He balled up a fist.

"Did you see that short middle-aged guy sitting next to me at the bar?" I said. "He was a SEAL. A real one. He even trained SEALs down in Coronado. He'd love to come out and talk to a poser like you. Man to man."

He stared at me with hot eyes.

"It would be a short conversation," I said.

The fist relaxed and his face adopted a more compliant look.

"Suzanne has been pretty upset ever since you saw her last weekend," he said. "I want to know what the hell is going on with you two."

"There is nothing 'going on' between your girlfriend and me. Her ex-husband died last week and I drove up there to give her the news. And to ask her a few questions."

"Barry is dead?" he asked. "Awesome. That guy was a royal pain in the ass."

"How so?"

"He was always sending her money and a card for their anniversary and calling her on her birthday. It was like they were still married or somethin' and every time it happened she would get all cow-eyed and tear up and act like she missed him. Pissed me off."

"You didn't like the extra money?"

"I make plenty and don't need any of his."

"Where were you a week ago?" I asked.

His eyes narrowed and his neck straightened a little.

"Who wants to know?" he said. "And why?"

"I'm a cop," I said. "And I'm investigating his death. Boyfriends who hate the ex-husband fall directly into to the 'suspect' category."

A grin wrapped across his face. I felt a little like wiping it off with a fist.

"I was in Mineral Wells, Texas all last week on business," he said. "And I got a dozen people who will back me up on that."

"Where is Mineral Wells?"

"West of Dallas," he said. "An hour away, maybe."

"What kind of business?"

"I'm a machinist. I make parts for old Harleys. I met these guys up at Sturgis and they said they might want to buy my stuff and resell it. So I took an extra week off and rode down to their shop. I was there until Friday night."

I asked a few other questions. Background stuff. We walked back into Donovan's and I collected Al before Bob could start cadging free drinks with lies about his non-existent military record. And before Al could respond by cleaning the floor with him.

30

TOM Nguyen picked up the phone on the second ring. We'd worked together in Guam half a career ago and now he was my counterpart at NAS Ft. Worth.

"Pretty early for you to be in the office, isn't it?" he asked.

"I wanted to catch you before you started drinking for the weekend," I said. "I seem to remember you had a habit of starting on Thursday."

"Funny," he said. "Except I got married three years ago and have a kid now. Drinking had to go."

"Congratulations," I said. "I think."

"You didn't roll into the office at seven a.m. Pacific to congratulate me, Sim. What can I do for you?" he asked.

"How close is the town of Mineral Wells to you?"

"I dunno. Hour west of here, I guess."

I told him the name of the company and the names of the people Bob Carter had supposedly been visiting when Barry St. James was killed and asked Tom if he could check out Bob's alibi. He said he had some time that afternoon and that he'd call me back.

Gil brought in the personnel files for Lieutenant Commander Glenn Alvarez and Lt. (JG) Steve Holdsworth (Ret.) after I hung up, and laid them on my desk. Neither of them contained anything interesting, suspicious, redacted, or noteworthy. From what I could tell, these were two fairly boring guys. Alvarez was active duty at the Naval Base Kitsap-Bangor so I figured I'd call him first.

The United States Navy is a huge organization with almost a half million personnel; about three-quarters of them serving active duty. But, like any organization, there is always the friend-of-a-friend-of-a-friend connection. I remembered that a fellow CPO I'd worked with on an accidental death investigation in Vallejo had been transferred to Bangor about four years ago. I called him. He didn't know anybody named Alvarez but he knew a guy who might know the guy and, within a half hour, the way had been smoothed for me to call a superior officer outside my chain of command to ask some informal questions.

"Freddie said you had some questions for me," he said. "He says you're squared away. How can I help you, Chief?"

I didn't know Freddie and he didn't know me but I was squared away. Straight up. A guy you could talk to.

"I'm investigating the death of Lieutenant Barry St. James and I understand you served together," I said.

"Barry's dead? I had no idea."

"Yes, sir."

"Wow, I haven't seen him in, what's it been, nine years? Ten? How'd he die?" he asked.

"Suspicious circumstances, sir. That is why I am asking questions."

"Are you with NCIS or something?" he asked. "You're just a CPO, right?"

"I'm not with NCIS, sir. The local police are investigating his death. I'm just asking a few questions for the family," I lied.

"Okay," he said. "Shoot. Anything to help."

"How well did you know Lieutenant St. James?" I asked.

"We were good friends on the *Enterprise*. Didn't keep in touch with him, though, after he left. Haven't seen him since."

"You also knew Bill Overson and Steve Holdsworth," I said.

"Oh, yeah. The four of us hung out a lot and had some great times together. Younger days, you know. I read somewhere that Bill is now a Captain and the CO of Naval Base Ventura. We all figured he'd go pretty far. He knew how to work the system even way back then. I'll probably read about his bump to Rear Admiral in a couple of years."

"Do you have any idea why Lieutenant St. James left the Navy?" I asked.

There was a small quiet patch in the conversation. One of those low spots in volume where the other guy is thinking hard about what to say. And maybe a lot harder about what not to.

"I dunno," he said. "Did his twenty and got out, I guess."

"He retired about the same time as Lieutenant Holdsworth."

"Could be," he said. "I don't know anything about it."

He was quiet and I was thinking about my next set of questions.

"Shouldn't that all be in their personnel files?" he asked. "If not, I suppose you could ask Admiral Harker about it. He drove the Big E back in those days. He'd have signed their paperwork."

I made a note to look up Admiral Harker and give him a call.

"Sir, what can you tell me about Lieutenant Holdsworth?" I asked.

"The Senator?" he said. "What's to talk about? The guy was connected. Got everything he wanted."

"You called him the 'Senator,' sir. Was that his nickname or something?" I said.

Glenn chuckled a little.

"Okay, maybe you're too young to remember," he said, "but Steve's daddy was a four-term Senator from California. The guy had big mojo with the DoD. A serious mover and shaker and one of the guys that controlled the money that bought the bullets and the boats and the jet fuel."

"Are you saying Lieutenant Holdsworth got special treatment?" I asked.

"Are you kidding me?" he said. "If Steve hinted that he might want a cake for his birthday, the Navy would fly out two pastry chefs on a Greyhound."

"Well," I said. "It wouldn't be the first time a politician's kid got special treatment, I suppose. "

"Not at all."

There was another lull in the conversation.

"I hear Steve now runs some big outfit in Southern California," he said. "Alavont or Illevan or something like that. I read in the paper that he was getting grants from the Department of Energy for solar energy research or some such nonsense. The guy's gotta be rolling in dough."

I made a few notes on my paper squares.

"You said Barry's death was suspicious," he said. "What did you mean by that?"

"He drowned, sir."

"It happens, I guess. Isn't that usually an accident?" he said.

"It hasn't been confirmed as such, sir," I said.

"So, are we done?" he asked. "I've got a meeting in about fifteen minutes and it's a ten minute drive."

"Thanks for your time, Commander."

"No problem, Chief."

I heard the relief in his voice. We hung up and I opened an internet search engine on my computer. I typed in "Holdsworth" and "solar energy" and "California" and got back over two million results. The third item down on the first page was a link to a web page for Solavon, Inc. I clicked on it and cruised around on their website until I found the bio pages for the corporate executive team.

Steve Holdsworth, President, CEO, and Chairman of the Board, was listed right there at the top. He'd aged since the picture taken on the deck of the *Enterprise* but it was definitely the same guy. His bio touched on his service in the United States Navy, an MBA from Wharton, and some "breakthrough work in Chinese manufacturing relationships" whatever that was supposed to mean. I cruised a little more and discovered that the corporate headquarters was in Santa Paula, California; barely half an hour from where I sat.

The little voice murmured and I picked up Barry's file. Neither Alvarez nor Holdsworth were mentioned. No reason they should be, I supposed. I reviewed the list of Barry's accounting clients and immediately noticed something. I'd seen it before but it hadn't been noteworthy until after my call with Lieutenant Commander Alvarez.

I reached over and picked up the phone.

31

"MR. Holdsworth will be with you shortly."

I suppose every CEO deserves a leggy personal secretary. She smiled at me as she crossed them. She had light blue eyes, slightly wavy hair, and a narrow aquiline nose. I guessed she was of Nordic descent. There was no way to gauge the sincerity in her smile but it gave a guy something to think about while waiting.

We sat in the executive lobby on the fourth floor of the Solavon building at the west edge of Santa Paula. The property had been farmland a few years earlier and I remembered when the company first proposed building a shipping and manufacturing business, albeit a "green" one, in a decidedly rural area. The local paper had groused more than a little about urban sprawl creeping into the citrus orchards and destroying the agricultural flavor of the county. They had even gone so far as to question Solavon's environmentally-friendly intentions, as expressed in their press release, "to create a more verdant world by leveraging technology to capture and use sustainable, renewable solar energy alternatives."

Yeah, well, this part of California actually talks like that.

A low hum buzzed at the receptionist's desk. The Norse goddess picked up her telephone, listened intently for a moment, and leveled her blue eyes onto me.

"Mr. Holdsworth can see you now," she said.

She rose from her desk and I realized just how long her legs were. She led me down a short hallway and opened a door that opened into an extraordinarily large corner office. A tall man sat in a massive leather chair behind a wooden desk that couldn't have been much larger than a tennis court. The office's two adjacent exterior walls were expansive, tinted floor-to-ceiling windows. Impressive.

From Steve Holdsworth's office you could see brown hills to the north and hundreds of acres of lemon groves to the west. It wasn't a bad view but you couldn't see the ocean from the top of a four-story building in Santa Paula and that was a pity. Too far away. Reason enough to have built it in Ventura.

"How can I help you, Mr. Greene?"

We shook hands and I noticed something instantly familiar about the guy. I couldn't place it. Might have seen him on TV once. Except I never watch TV.

"I appreciate you meeting with me this afternoon, Mr. Holdsworth."

"Always willing to help out the Navy," he said. "It gave me some of the best experiences in life and a focus for the future."

I didn't know what that meant but it sounded like a positive thing.

"I mentioned to your assistant that this was in regards to Lieutenant Barry St. James," I said.

Holdsworth nodded and motioned for me to sit down in a chair opposite him.

"Barry and I were buddies on the Big E. We had a lot of fun back then. I was more than a little shocked when I read that he'd been killed."

"When was the last time you saw Lieutenant St. James?" I asked.

"Oh, goodness," he said. "I guess it was when I left the Navy. How long ago was that? Ten years?"

"He retired three weeks after you did," I said. "Did he mention why he was leaving?"

"Well, that was a long time ago and I don't recall hearing about him getting out. I always thought he'd be a 'lifer,' you know. Like you, I guess."

I didn't like the way he said the word 'lifer.' It was denigrating. It made me want to punch him.

"You haven't seen him since you were in the Navy together?" I asked.

He nodded. He was lying and I knew he was lying. And he knew I knew.

I opened up my briefcase and pulled out a copy of Barry's client list. The one where I'd highlighted the name of his company. I looked at it carefully and then handed it to him.

"Your firm hired him several years ago," I said. "And he worked for you right up to the time of his death."

"You're kidding me, right?"

He looked at the page carefully.

"I haven't seen Barry since I left the Navy," he said. "Honest. I didn't even know he lived around here. He must have been hired by one of my division managers."

32

I left Santa Paula and headed to my regular appointment with Al. He rarely talked much during a workout but this time I could tell that something was on his mind.

"The whole harbor seems to think you killed that guy, Sim."

"The evidence of which is?" I asked.

"I didn't say I agreed with 'em."

I continued lifting and he continued spotting.

"Cindy over at Tugs has it all worked out," he said. "She thinks he tried to lure Ashley away from you and you aced him."

"And I wrapped him in a chain and dumped him off *Figaro* and then, less than 24 hours later, I decided to discover him."

"I never said she was Stephen Hawking, okay?" said Al.

"Al, you're repeating the theory of a waitress who slings hash at a waterfront eatery," I said. "I cannot describe the depth of my disappointment in you."

He laughed.

"So, who is spreading all this pungent fertilizer?" I asked.

"I think it's Jerry. He's trying to be the big shot Harbor Patrolman."

"What do you think?"

"I think somebody is under some serious pressure to solve this case," he said. "And that somebody is running into a lot of dead-ends so he keeps coming back to you. Jerry picks up on it and blabs it around to look big and connected."

"Hargrave is the new guy in the department," I said. "He's probably feeling some pressure."

Al nodded.

"I'll have a talk with him," I said.

We finished our workouts and I drove back to the harbor. The sun had nearly set as I parked near the marina office and the diffused orange glow of dying sunlight cast long shadows across the docks and the boats and the water. I grabbed my small duffel of workout clothes, locked the Jeep, and walked down J-dock toward my boat. Detective Hargrave walked out from behind the big Sea Ray that sits in the slip across from *Figaro* and held his right hand up palm towards me. He wore a dark suit that looked painfully uncomfortable in the late August heat.

"We'd like to bring you in for questioning," he said.

"Am I under arrest?" I asked.

"Not yet."

Another dark-suited fellow, a guy closer to my height, came in behind me.

"Then let me put my clothes away down below and I'll come with you," I said.

I unlocked my boat, took my stuff below, and grabbed my book. I knew the routine. I'd been in his position many times. At least they weren't arresting me. Yet.

We walked up the dock to their big unmarked sedan and the three of us rode the six miles up Victoria Avenue to the big Sheriff's station in the County Government Center. They led me to an interview room. It was nicer than the one we had at the base. Two wooden chairs faced a comfortable faux-leather couch that sat against one wall. The wall across from the couch had alternating tiles of brown wood and dark stone. Some cheap art hung from the other walls. I was sure that one of the stone tiles was actually a piece of darkened glass with a video camera mounted behind it. I sat on the couch so the camera could get a good look at me.

"I'll be back in a minute," said Hargrave.

I figured he needed to make sure the camera was rolling.

"You want anything to drink?" asked the taller guy. "Coffee? Soda?"

"Dom Perignon, 1956, with Beluga caviar, please. Extra toast."

Then I stared directly into the dark glass tile.

"They never give you enough toast," I said.

The cop smiled. If there was a good cop/bad cop play tonight, he'd be the good one.

"Coffee it is," he said.

He left the room and I opened my book and read quietly. Hargrave walked in a few minutes later, carrying a small briefcase, and sat in one of the wooden chairs. I closed the book.

"How do you know Barry St. James?" he asked.

"I don't, Detective. I never met the man. Never saw him before the night I found him dead at the bottom of the harbor mouth."

"You got a better answer than that?"

"Nope," I said.

He thought for a minute and pulled a small plastic bag out of his briefcase. He handed it to me. It had one of my Navy business cards in it.

"We found this in his office," he said. "One of yours, isn't it?"

I nodded.

"We also found your fingerprints on his filing cabinet and desk drawer handles. Would you care to modify your previous answer?"

"Not at all," I said.

"So you've never met the guy before but he has your business card and you were in his office looking around his files and in his desk."

I shrugged. And I wondered about the business card. How did it find its way into Barry St. James' office? How many had I handed out in the last week? I took a mental inventory: Jerry, Homeland Security, Dr. Craven, and Ray Jackson.

"The lawyer downstairs from St. James' office tells me that a guy your height, your build, and with your broken nose was one of the victim's clients," continued Hargrave. "Does that little bit of information make you want to change your story at all?"

"No, sir. As I told you, I had never met the man."

"So the lawyer downstairs is lying?" asked Hargrave. "Don't try to sell me that. I'm not buying."

I thought about Captain Overson's injunction to keep the investigation quiet and decided that Hargrave needed to know. After all, he was a fellow cop.

"No, Detective, I was in the process of invest…"

The door opened before I could finish telling Hargrave and a tall, thin, middle-aged guy in jeans and a blue L.A. Dodgers warm-up jacket walked in. His black shoulder-length hair had more than a few streaks of gray. The hair flowed out from under an L.A. Dodgers bill cap. He looked at Hargrave and smiled broadly.

"Hi, officer," he said. "My, this is a cozy interrogation room."

He winked at the dark tile of glass and turned to look at me.

"And this must be Mr. Sim Greene," he continued.

I nodded.

The taller detective walked in with a white foam coffee cup. The man in the Dodger's jacket took it from him, drank about half of the cup, and handed it back.

"That's actually pretty good for station coffee," he said. "But I can't spend all night gabbing with you fellows, can I? Let's go, Sim. I'm late for a game."

"Excuse me," said Hargrave. "But who the hell are you and how did you get in here?"

"I am M. Emmanuel Goldsmith, Attorney-at-Law," he said. "You've heard of me. Everybody has heard of me. As to your second question, I spent several years in the Orient learning the power to cloud the minds of men and to walk into police interrogation rooms unbidden."

Hargrave looked like he'd suddenly caught the flu.

"Mr. Greene is my client and I understand that he is not under arrest. My guess is that you haven't even read him his Miranda rights. None of this surprises me since my client is innocent of whatever you are trying to pin on him."

Hargrave tried to recover.

"Who the hell do you think you..."

"This interview is over, Detective. Unless, of course, you have enough evidence for a prosecutor to charge Mr. Greene within 48 hours. Do you?"

Hargrave was silent.

"I didn't think so," said the lawyer. "Come with me, Sim. We got things to do."

I grabbed my book, stood up, and followed my newfound attorney out of the room. The detectives could have been hotel bellhops for all he cared. We walked out of the building and into the parking lot toward a dark red Mercedes.

"Get in," he said

He pushed a button on the dash and the engine thrummed with nearly-silent power as he pulled out of the parking lot and turned south onto Victoria.

"I know who you are, Mr. Goldsmith, and I can't afford to pay you," I said.

"Judy has taken care of it."

"She can afford to pay you?"

He smiled.

"We have what you could call an 'arrangement,' Mr. Greene. Can I call you 'Sim'?"

I nodded.

"Then you call me 'Mel', okay? My friends call me Mel. Judy Norton calls me Mel. She phoned me and said she saw them grab you off the docks. I was on my way to a Dodger game and decided to make a little stop for Judy. So here I am."

I couldn't think of anything to say.

"You're single, right?" he asked. "No kids?"

"Um, yeah."

"So it's Thursday night and you got nothin' to do, Sim. No wife, no kids, no worries. You like baseball?" he asked.

"Absolutely," I said.

He turned south onto the 101. Toward Los Angeles.

"There you go, Sim. I got an extra ticket and you're coming with me. It means I don't have to waste any time driving you back to the harbor and it means we get to use the diamond lanes. Double bonus, my friend."

I learned quickly that nobody argues with M. Emmanuel Goldsmith. And nobody drives like him, either. Traffic opened up before the big Mercedes like the Red Sea before Moses. I figured it was the byproduct of some closely-held religious secret. We got to the game in the bottom of the third inning and I never had such a good time.

Mel never even asked me if I'd killed Barry St. James.

33

IT was Friday morning. I was supposed to meet Frank Bartholomew for lunch at the Harbor Mart, barely a hundred yards from my slip, and I couldn't see any sense in driving to the office, turning around, and driving back home for lunch. I slept in.

Figaro's cabin glowed as the morning sun reflected off the polished teak of her interior cabinetry. I lay in my berth for a while and enjoyed the warmth and the light and entertained plea-sant thoughts of seeing Ashley that evening. When I finally got up, I realized that it had, once again, been too long since I'd been in the water. I knew the waves would be crowded this late in the morning so I pulled on my swim trunks, jogged to the beach, and dove into the surf. It was a Friday morning and the summer break was ending. Hordes of teenage surfers sat on their boards and waited for the big wave of the next set to come in. I swam past them in an unbroken rhythm of steady strokes.

There weren't any dolphins to disrupt my thinking and I thought long and hard about Barry St. James and who could have killed him. The obvious problem was that I couldn't identify anybody with a reasonable motive for torturing *and* killing him.

Barry had a great family, an ex-wife who still loved him, and an insurance agent who didn't exist but still managed to disappear. He had a pretty girlfriend who certainly liked him but who had a boyfriend who tended toward violent jealousy. The ex-wife also had a boyfriend who was both jealous and violent. Was jealousy a motive for murder? Sure it was, but the boyfriends were both rash actors who would have left fingerprints and witnesses and messy evidence all over the place. And they would have had to act together. It had taken at least two people to chain Barry and drop him in the ocean.

My mind kept coming back to Ray Jackson, Steve Holdsworth, and the boys at ICE. So there were still a few threads I could pull on. Ray Jackson was an unknown and Steven Holdsworth was lying about something. Who could say what ICE was up to?

A large pile of seaweed lay on the beach south of the lifeguard tower. I saw it as I walked out of the surf and it reminded me of what Old Jed had told me. It made me wonder if Jed's death was related to Barry's. I jogged back to Vintage Marina, showered away the salt and sand, and stepped down the dock ramp back to *Figaro*.

The blinking light on my cell phone indicated that I'd missed a call. I checked my voicemail and learned that Tom Nguyen had driven to Mineral Wells and spoken to the people I'd asked him to visit. Every one of them backed up Bob Carter's story. He was definitely in Texas when Barry St. James was killed. I returned Tom's call and thanked him for doing my legwork. I told him I owed him one. He figured I owed him three.

I grabbed an apple and the box Erica had given me and took both up to the cockpit. I was sitting there eating the apple, enjoying the mid-morning sun, and reexamining the contents of Barry's little shipping box when the lawyer who should have worn Lycra showed up at the card-key dock gate. He tried to open it, then banged on it as if the device would merely sense his anger and willfully submit to his physical superiority. Fat chance.

"Stop that noise, you idiot," yelled Al from his boat. "If you don't have a key to the gate then get the hell outta here."

"I'm looking for Sim Greene," he said.

He threw a lot of attitude into five words.

"Look somewhere else," said Al. He went back to oiling an expansive piece of teakwood on *In Depth*'s topsides.

The lawyer stopped banging and started looking for a way around the gate. At first it was a little fun to watch. Then it became comical. Finally, it dwindled into tiresome annoyance and I stepped off my boat and walked up the dock toward the gate.

"Are you looking for me?" I asked.

He was about six feet tall and somewhere under two hundred pounds. But I could tell that he worked out and was in good shape for a desk slave. He'd traded the tailored business shirt and slacks I'd seen him in last for expensive black workout pants, blue running shoes, and a tight yellow forty-dollar T-shirt. The shirt revealed some well-cared-for biceps and triceps and a six-pack where a lawyer's gut would have normally been. Dustin worked out and he was proud of it. Good for him.

"Yeah," he said. "I'm looking for you. You're trying to steal my girl and I've got half a mind to kick your ass."

"You got the 'half a mind' part right but you're dead wrong on the girl. I have no interest there. As far as 'kicking my ass' goes, you're way out of your league. I've got three inches on you and a thirty pound advantage. Go back to roughing up little kids and flexing for the Girl Scouts."

Al chuckled in the background.

"I've got a black belt in karate, fella. What do you think of that?" he asked.

"I think it's kinda loud and the movies are generally boring and predictable..."

"I'm so gonna kick your ass, funny boy."

"...except that one with Pat Morita," I continued. "It was pretty good, actually. I probably saw it a dozen times as a kid. Very inspiring."

Dustin stared at me with hate in his eyes.

"So are you going to finish me with a 'wax-on' or a 'wax-off'?" I asked.

Al's laughter reverberated throughout the marina.

"I'm going to break both your arms, sailor-boy."

"No, you're not," I said. "You're going to wave your hands at me and shriek a couple of times right before I break your nose and stain your cute little T-shirt."

I turned to walk back down to *Figaro* and he called me a name that I am not fond of. And he kept calling. I turned back.

"You can either shut your cakehole, Dustin, or I will give you a shot at the title," I said.

"How do you know my name?" he asked.

"Erica told me what a possessive and jealous little jackass her boyfriend is and I've managed to connect the dots."

"You talk pretty tough for a guy hiding behind a fence," said Dustin.

I opened the gate and walked past him to the sidewalk near the marina office.

"Okay, Dustin. Let's talk," I said. "No fences."

He followed me to the sidewalk spouting threats and insults. A few of the early weekend boaters gathered to watch. Dustin threw a straight left, palm open and fingers curled inward, toward the center of my face. I bent down and moved to the right and threw my weight into a left jab that connected high in the chest. His open palm brushed my left ear but my jab moved him back a foot. He threw more punches. I have no idea what they call them in a dojo but he couldn't land them effectively. I deflected some and others missed completely. It wasn't his kind of workout.

"I don't want you around my girl," he said.

"I don't want to be around your girl," I said. "Even if she isn't your girl."

He moved around and tried to box me up against the building. I shuffled to my left into the parking lot. He tried to kick me with his right leg like you see in the movies and yelled "YEEeeaaahhhh" like Howard Dean. It was a fine straight kick with good extension but I wasn't there for it. His momentum carried him around counterclockwise and I landed two solid punches into his kidneys.

"I saw you drop her off at her car and kiss her after you..."

He struggled to catch his breath.

"...after you left her apartment," he said.

"You followed us?" I said.

"Yeah."

"And you naturally assumed the worst," I said.

He regained his guard and circled to my left.

"Give it up, Dustin, and go home," I said.

He yelled again, swung again, and missed again. I feinted right and put a solid left into his gut. The punch had follow-through and he stepped back with his eyes wide open. He bent over slightly and put his hands on his upper thighs to steady himself. He gasped for breath for a half-minute and said something unpleasant about my mother. That pushed my "zero tolerance" button. I stepped in and landed a hard left jab on his pointy nose. I felt it shatter beneath my knuckles and watched it bleed all over his expensive yellow T-shirt.

It had been a long time since I'd punched anyone that hard and it felt good. It felt marvelous and wonderful. All the worrying about Barry St. James, Captain Overson, Homeland Security, and Detective Hargrave melted away in the heat of battle.

Dustin's rat-like nose, now misshapen and bubbling, wasn't a pretty sight. It might never be.

"You're done, Dustin. Give it up," I said.

He wasn't breathing well through the broken nose. He backed up and caught his breath. I hoped he'd stop bothering me. I hoped he'd think for a minute and walk away. Beating up a smaller guy was starting to be a little embarrassing. Like I was a kitten killer or something. But the kitten thought it had fangs and charged me. It wasn't elegant and it wasn't karate and it wasn't boxing. It was pure distilled Stone-Age anger with fang and claw.

I shuffled left and put my entire shoulder, chest, and arm into a hook across his jaw. His knees buckled and he fell to the asphalt like a sack of wet sand. His eyes rolled back into his head. I grabbed his wrists, dragged him over to a bench near the marina office, and laid him down on it. He came to in a few minutes gasping like a rockfish pulled from the sea and spitting out blood that ran from his nose to his mouth.

I began to feel a bit sorry for him. He was still an asshat but I felt pity for any guy so devoted to a woman so disloyal. I bought a soda from the vending machine and gave it to him.

"I'll say this for you, Dustin. You're a tough guy and you don't quit easily."

He didn't say anything. He winced as the soda went past his split lip.

"There's no girl on this planet worth the beating I just gave you," I said. "Especially if she's unfaithful."

His right eye began to puff up and close. He mumbled something unintelligible. I wondered how much good he would be as a lawyer for the next week or so.

"Did you know she was sleeping with Barry St. James?" I asked.

He stared at me with red hate from his good eye.

"Yeah," he said. "And he got what was coming to him."

Interesting.

"Did you kill him?" I asked.

"No," he said. "But somebody did and that's fine with me."

"He pulled a knife on you, didn't he?"

"Yeah," he said. "How'd you know that?"

"Doesn't matter," I said. "That's enough motive for murder. Add that to your naturally jealous state over Erica and the prosecutor hits an easy home run."

He thought about that for a minute.

"There's no home run on me," he said. "I was with Erica all that night. She'll back me up."

He tried to touch his nose and moaned loudly. I got him up off the bench and walked him toward his car. Most of the crowd walked away but a few stayed, probably hoping for Round Two.

"Go see a doctor for the nose, Dustin. And go see a shrink for the rest of it."

He got into his car and started it. The sound of the engine gave him new courage.

"I'm coming back. It'll be late at night and I'll bring a gun and I'll shoot you right in the back of your head. So you just keep turning around and looking for me, sailor."

I turned toward the dock gate to see Al only a few feet away.

"Bastard had it coming," he said.

"You're an economist with words, Al."

Other than Al's terse genealogical observation, nobody said anything. The spectators moved slowly back to prepping their boats for the weekend. Peace returned to Vintage Marina.

34

WE were supposed to meet at noon. I got to the Harbor Mart a few minutes early and ordered a pulled pork sandwich with coleslaw and a Coke. Frank Bartholomew walked in at 12:05, took off his black aviator sunglasses, and sat down at my table like he owned the place.

"I've had the tri-tip," he said. "What else is good here?"

"It's all good," I said.

He waved the waitress over and ordered a Black Forest ham sandwich and a non-alcoholic Sangria.

"You don't have a pistol this time," he said as he looked me over. "Or do you?"

"You didn't seem to care all that much the other night," I said.

He laughed but not loud enough to annoy the other customers.

"You don't have the look of a cold-blooded killer, Mr. Greene."

"Did you get a good look at my friend?" I asked.

"Not really."

"It might have altered your assessment of the overall situation," I said.

He shrugged.

The waitress brought his drink and took mine away for a refill. Bartholomew sipped his Sangria and sat back in his chair. He looked me over casually but carefully. I felt like I was being judged for the state fair.

"You're kinda tall," he said. "You must've played basketball."

"You're kinda short," I said. "You must like miniature golf."

He laughed like we were old friends.

"Sim Greene," he said. "Chief Petty Officer, Master-at-Arms, twenty years in the United States Navy. As clean a record as they come but, apparently, not beloved by all of his superiors."

"The word 'superior' is frequently misapplied," I said.

He laughed and picked up his drink.

"You seem to know a lot about me," I said.

"Somebody a few rungs up the ladder from me called a guy he knows who works in the Pentagon. The friend checked you out. He says we can trust you. My boss says we should."

"I'm flattered," I said.

He lifted his glass and took another sip of the Sangria.

"So what do you want to talk about, Mr. Greene?"

"My dad was Mr. Greene," I said. "You can call me Sim."

He nodded.

"And you can call me Frank," he said.

The waitress approached with the refill for my soda. We waited for her to leave.

"So let me have it," he said. "What's the Navy interested in these days?"

I tossed his card on the table.

"My card?" he asked. "It's not that interesting."

He looked at the phone number and frowned.

"It has the wrong number on it," he said.

"You answered it."

He shrugged.

"Different line," he said. "Hardly matters."

"Turn it over."

He turned it over, saw the Chinese characters on the back, and shoved it into his shirt pocket like it was stolen money.

"Where the hell did you get that?" he asked.

"Barry's office. It was under the couch," I lied.

A different waitress brought my pulled pork and Frank's ham sandwich to the table, smiled pleasantly, and asked if we needed anything else. We didn't.

"So why is a mild-mannered CPA like Barry St. James working with the boys at ICE?" I asked.

He thought for a minute.

"Remember, Frank. Guys further up the ladder say you should trust me."

He turned his palms to the ceiling and shrugged.

"One of our junior guys was working a swap meet in Santa Paula last year and caught St. James selling Chinese counterfeit DVD's. It was a routine bust, nothing big or fancy. Small time nonsense. It wouldn't have made page six of the local paper. But Barry offered us information on his supply line and we took the bait."

He took a bite of his sandwich.

"I didn't think it would pan out," he said. "I've never had a lot of faith in informants but the stuff Barry started giving us turned out to be pretty good."

I was eating my sandwich while listening to him and had to swallow before I could ask the obvious follow-up question.

"How good?" I asked.

"Over the last ten months or so we've picked up six decent stashes of counterfeit car parts, fake prescription drugs, copied DVD's, bogus computer software, a little bit of everything China has to offer these days. Oh, and we've snagged a fair amount of cash, too. All of that from Barry's info."

"Sounds like he was a good source," I said.

"The best I've ever seen," he said. "And I've seen a lot."

"Ten months seems like a long time for an informant," I said. "How did he play it out so long?"

"He was careful and thorough," he said. "After the first big find, we took him on as a paid informant."

"How much did you pay him?"

"Enough," he said.

He smiled and took another bite of sandwich. I wasn't going to get many details.

"Anyhow, he was working on getting us the final pieces of the puzzle that would tie it all up," he said. "We figured the stuff originated from a Chinese triad and that it got here commercially through Port Hueneme. But we haven't quite got our arms all the way around this little smuggling operation. We don't know who the wholesaler is or how they distribute the goods. We don't know which boats the stuff comes in on. Barry was working on all of that for us before he died."

"Was murdered," I said.

"Yeah, murdered. Anyway, that's our side of it. You got any questions?" he asked.

"A couple. What do the characters on the back of that card mean?"

"We think it's the name of a Chinese triad, an organized crime syndicate, that supplies the bogus goods," he said. "It doesn't prove anything but I think Barry figured out some details in the last few days. Details that he, unfortunately, took to the grave."

I nodded and thought for a moment.

"Do you always follow people around when one of your snitches dies?" I asked.

"We prefer the word 'informant' to describe our sources of inside information."

"So, do you always follow people around when one of your informants dies?"

"No," said Frank. "But he told us a couple weeks ago that something big was going to happen on the twenty-ninth and we're a little anxious to find out what that is."

"The twenty-ninth of this month?"

Frank nodded.

"That's a week from today," I said.

"So now you understand our sense of urgency," said Frank.

"And you have no idea what it is?"

"Nope," he said. "We think it's a big shipment but our counter-terrorism folk are quite concerned about other possibilities."

That was something to think about.

"How much did you pay him for the information he gave you?"

"Not that much, actually."

He smiled broadly.

"Haven't you heard?" he said. "Crime doesn't pay."

I nodded.

"Now what have you got for me?" he asked.

I told him about Barry's parents in Idaho and how everybody loved him as a kid. I told him about his high school sweetheart and a marriage that slid downhill from having to endure too many months apart. I told him about the girl in the lawyer's office and the sailboat and his CPA practice. I told him what the coroner said about Lingchi and about Bob Carter and Dustin; the two guys who seemed to be the only people on the planet who hated him. I gave him their alibis.

"You're pretty good at this, Sim," said Frank. "You get me to tell you everything I know about Barry St. James and you give me nothing in return that I don't already know. That's a real talent."

I shrugged.

"I can tell you what he did with the money," I said.

"I couldn't care less," he said.

"It went to his ex-wife and his aged parents," I said. "He even sent the folks on a cruise."

"Makes me feel warm all over, brother."

His sandwich took another direct hit and I finished mine.

"Did you ICE guys clean out his apartment and office after he died?" I asked.

"Nope," he said. "Neither did the locals. We thought you might have. That's one of the reasons we were following you."

"That was before you heard about my numerous positive character traits from higher-ups, right?"

"Yeah, before that," he said. "So how'd you know his apartment was cleaned out?"

"I got in there after the cops left. Figured I'd check it out myself."

"Find anything?"

"Somebody snuck up on me and conked me on the head," I said. "All I got out of that visit was a concussion."

"Any idea who gave it to you?" he asked.

"Nope."

Frank finished the sandwich and wiped his mouth with a napkin.

"Ever hear of an outfit called Solavon?" I asked.

"Should I have?" said Frank.

I shrugged.

"What a minute," he said. "Isn't that some sort of clean energy outfit? Owned by a Senator's kid, right? I read somewhere they just got a fat wad of government grants."

He thought for a minute.

"What's the connection, Sim?"

"The Senator's son was a friend of St. James," I said. "The guy hired him to do some work for him and then lied to me about it. Any chance that outfit could be dirty?"

"Squeaky clean as far as I know."

He thought for a minute, took out a pen and another business card, and wrote a number on the back.

"This is my new cell phone," he said. "If you find anything that you think fits in with this case, anything at all, I'd very much like to hear about it." He thought for a minute. "And I'd like to be the first one to hear it, too."

"Don't tell the Sheriff's department?"

"Why bother?" he said. "Most of those guys wouldn't know what to do with a crate of hard evidence if it came with an instruction manual."

I told him I'd keep in touch. I finished my Coke and made ready to leave. Frank leaned in and lowered his voice.

"Barry was the best informant I've ever worked with," he said. "He was straight up all the way and I grew to like the guy. If I can help put away the people who did this to him, well, you can count me in."

"Sounds good to me," I said.

"Oh, there's one more thing, Sim."

"What's that?" I asked.

"You can stop looking for Ray Jackson."

"Who says anybody is looking for him?"

He smiled.

"He's one of ours, Sim. Don't waste your time."

"What do you mean he's 'one of yours'?" I asked.

"He's a fed," he said. "Like me. He's the guy we had running St. James for us. I'm not exactly sure how you got his fingerprints but they won't get you his file."

We stood and shook hands. He left two bucks on the table for a tip and walked out to his black car. I walked across the parking lot back to J-dock while mentally scratching Ray Jackson off my decreasing list of suspects.

35

SO a Chinese gang found out Barry was an informant working for the feds and tortured him before drowning him. Did they torture him to send a message to other gang members? How does dumping him in the Pacific in the dead of night get that message out? Word of mouth? Social media?

There wasn't any logic to it. I wanted to give the Captain some hard facts, anything concrete, that would show him that I was making some progress on the assignment. But I couldn't do it. None of the facts fit a pattern and that bothered me a lot. It meant, among other things, that I wasn't doing my job.

A muted buzz alerted the Captain's yeoman and she picked up the telephone. A few moments later she led me into his office.

The Captain sat at his desk with his back to the Commander-in-Chief. His eyes were cold and hard and the muscles in his jaw bulged like he'd been chewing on leather all day.

"Are you making any headway in your assignment, Chief?" he asked. "Have you found what we are looking for?"

He voice was ice cold.

"I'm still gathering information, Captain."

"Do you have any hard evidence, Chief? Anything at all?" he asked.

"I discovered a box of personal effects Lieutenant St. James left with his girlfriend but I can't really say it's hard evidence. Most of the background information I've reviewed is…"

He held his hand up to cut me off.

"Well, Chief," he said, "If you're having some trouble why don't you give Detective Hargrave a call?"

He stood up from his chair behind the desk and walked around to get closer. It wasn't a casual or friendly approach.

"We had a nice long discussion this morning right here in this office," he said. "He walked in here and sat in that chair and talked to me about Lieutenant St. James for the better part of an hour. And he seems to know all about your involvement in this investigation."

He picked up a piece of paper and looked at it.

"Or maybe you could call Ms. Judith Norton," he continued. "She's a local journalist; seems to know you quite well. She called me yesterday afternoon and, what a coincidence, she also seems to know all about the assignment I gave you."

I knew better than to offer a response.

"Or maybe you could call Admiral Merriwether. He called me on Wednesday and expressed an inordinately high level of interest in both you and your investigation."

I was getting the distinct feeling that my career wouldn't end well.

"Somebody seems to have lied to me, Chief Greene." He walked back to the window behind his desk and looked out over the base. "I specifically asked Master Chief Richardson who could handle this investigation in both a professional and discreet manner. He told me that you were the man for the job. I believed him."

I said nothing. He sat back down in his chair.

"I am seriously disappointed in his assessment of your capabilities," he said. He tapped on his desk with the fingers of his right hand. "I specifically told you last week that this assignment was to be completely quiet and entirely off the record."

He waited for a minute and watched my face. I felt the blood and heat rising up into my neck. I took a deep breath and let it out slowly. Anger wouldn't help the situation.

"From what I have seen, you have FUBAR'ed every aspect of this assignment," he said. "Would you care to explain yourself, Chief Greene?"

I took a deep breath and let it out. Captain Overson stared at me over his desk.

"I have kept the assignment you gave me in the strictest confidence, Captain. Unfortunately, other authorities investigating the matter have observed me and ..."

The Captain held up his hand, palm forward.

"Whoa, Chief. Can you hear that loud ringing noise?" he asked. "Oh, that's my bullshit alarm going off." He leaned back in his chair. "You have gone way too far afield in this assignment, Greene. I wanted some simple answers and some missing documents. I thought you were officer material and maybe even good enough for NCIS but, as far as I'm concerned, you're done."

"I am fairly certain that the documents you want have not been located, sir. We can still..."

He put his hand up again. "Just shut up, Greene." He picked up another sheet of paper and read from it. "I haven't decided what to do with you, Chief. But I see that you have a little over three weeks of accrued leave due. I am of the opinion that you should take it. So consider yourself relieved of this assignment immediately. And consider yourself on leave, Chief."

He put the paper down and leaned forward in his chair.

"I want you out of my office within thirty seconds and off this base within twenty minutes. And you had better be gone for that entire three weeks."

My options being somewhat limited, I stood up and left.

36

THE congestion on Highway 101 out of town and up the coast was typical of a late Friday afternoon. Thousands of folks escaping L.A. for a weekend in Santa Barbara, Solvang, or San Luis Obispo. They sped and braked and merged their way north on the 101 and, on that specific stretch of California coastline, we all drove west into a setting sun.

As always, there were a few Mercedes and Corvettes that took advantage of the rare oases of clear highway to pass and switch lanes and leapfrog through traffic intent on getting to Santa Barbara ninety seconds before I did. Maybe that was what bothered me about living a life ashore. Everybody always in a hurry to make up lost time. Time they'd lost where and doing what?

I, however, had all the time in the world. Three weeks of paid vacation. I toyed with the idea of loading up *Figaro* with some groceries and heading south to Mexico. I could make Cabo San Lucas in less than a week. That would leave me a week to sail around in the lower Sea of Cortez before I had to work my way back home. I thought it over and knew it wouldn't happen. Not enough time to do it right and too much unfinished business in Ventura County. I continued north in the slow traffic.

I got to Santa Barbara about twenty minutes later than I'd planned and hoped that Ashley wouldn't be too upset. She'd stressed that tonight's dinner was a black tie affair and had expressed some mild skepticism as to whether or not I could locate a proper tuxedo so I had taken pains to find suitable attire. It wasn't a tuxedo. It was better.

The hotel sat on about twenty acres of beautifully kept beach-front land. The architects had combined the adobe walls, grape-vine-covered trellises, expansive archways, and red roof tiles of traditional Spanish architecture with modern tennis courts and a driving range. It was as if the builders of the California missions had been preppies hiding in black robes.

I parked my Jeep in the lot next to a fair number of Bimmers, Porsches, and Lexi and texted Ashley to let her know I'd arrived. A gentle breeze blew in off the ocean and wafted the scent of a rose garden into the hotel lobby. I noticed a few brochures touting the health-inducing effects of a dozen different massage therapies available at the resort along with various water-, herb-, and mud-based skin treatments. Everything claimed to be purifying, refining, hydrating, and regenerative. I choked a little when I saw the price tag.

Ashley texted me that the dinner was being held in the Santa Rosa Room and I followed the signs that led me there. More than a few eyes widened when I entered the room in my U.S. Navy Dinner Dress Whites. Ashley saw me and nearly dropped her glass. She walked up and kissed my cheek.

"You certainly like to make an entrance, don't you?" she said.

"Bond," I said. "James Bond."

"More like ham," she replied. "Pressed ham."

"Am I too late?" I asked.

"No, you're right on time."

She led me toward a group of people at the other end of the room.

"So, where's your sword?" she asked.

"Right where you'd expect to find it, my dear."

"Behave yourself."

Ashley took a few minutes to introduce me to her coworkers. The women in the group all were compelled to touch my uniform and decorations. This had happened before and I have never understood it. It was as if they had to verify that I was real.

On prior occasions and in similar circumstances I have almost always run into a former Marine or an ex-soldier, sailor, or airman who greeted me with a different look in the eye and a firmer handshake. There was a shared experience; a mutual respect. But this crowd was the exception. No retired military or current reservists approached me with the confidence that comes from remembering an honorable part of one's past.

Several of the men asked questions about my 'Navy experience' but they all sounded as if they were at the zoo and were curious about the monkey in the cage. It wasn't something I could reasonably complain about, though. After all, I *had* chosen to come in formal military dress. What was most interesting though, was that the men always worked the conversation back to the time that they 'wanted to join the military.' It was something I'd heard many times before and it always reminded me of a quote attributed to Samuel Johnson.

Every man thinks meanly of himself for not having been a soldier.

One of Ashley's female coworkers caught me alone by the punchbowl. She touched the service stripes on my sleeve.

"Is there any significance to these badges being gold?" she asked.

"The gold rating Chevrons and service stripes identify an enlisted man that has met the Good Conduct Service requirements for twelve consecutive years, ma'am."

"So you've been a good boy for twelve whole years?" she asked.

I nodded. I saw it coming.

"I think we need to do something to correct that," she said.

Thankfully, Ashley interceded and led me to one of the ten round dinner tables. I had not hoped for anything exceptional, but the food was at least two rungs up the economic ladder from the usual conference fare. Instead of a gray overcooked chicken breast squatting between a pile of mushy green peas and a lump of gravy-laden mashed potatoes, my plate featured a generous portion of pan-seared Ahi tuna with wild rice, salad greens, and a mango chutney. Nice. There was wine, of course, which I declined.

Some high-level management type, a Senior VP of something or other, spoke while we ate. And he spoke in a tongue that wasn't taught at the DoD's Foreign Language Center in Monterey. He told us that it was *mission critical* that each *team member* adopt *best practices* and a *holistic, client-centric mindset* to achieve *long-term sustainability* of the *enterprise*. He encouraged us to pluck *low-hanging fruit* and develop *core competencies* in each department. He expressed concern over whether or not the team had enough *bandwidth*. Everything needed to be *seamless* and *value-added* and each employee needed to promote something called *co-opetition*. He lost me for good when he suggested *eating your own dog food*.

Interesting thought, but I'll stick with the tuna.

It was nearly ten by the time dinner and the other self-congratulatory festivities finished and various attendees arranged their nightly entertainment. Some discussed hitting local night spots while others merely walked to their hotel rooms.

"We're not far from the pier," said Ashley. "Want to go for a walk?"

We left the hotel and walked west along Cabrillo for a little while and then dropped down to the bike path near the beach. It was a clear night and the ocean was a blanket of smooth rippling silk. The orange light from the gas flares of the offshore oil rigs reflected and danced on the water from five or more miles away. From that distance, they were mere pinpricks that joined the reflections of myriad stars.

"My boss wants me to stay the weekend to discuss our current project with his Senior Vice President," she said.

"That the guy who spoke?"

"Yeah," she said. "He really knows what he's talking about."

"It's good somebody does."

I considered telling her about my experience with Captain Overson but decided against it. No reason to bother her with my problems.

"So we're not going sailing?" I said.

"I'd love to," she said. "But there is no way I can make it. My boss says the Senior VP wants to fast-track this project and I'll be working on it all weekend. Can we go the next weekend, maybe?"

"That works for me. I've got some leave coming and we could go out for as long as you like."

She paused for a moment and we walked a few paces in silence.

"Do you think you'll always live on a boat?" she asked.

"Who can predict the future?" I said.

"It's not about predictions, Sim. It's about choices."

We stepped off the bike path and onto the wooden boards of Stearns Wharf.

"Where are we headed?" asked Ashley.

"Out to sea?" I said.

"No." She thought for a few moments and I waited, keeping my mouth shut but dreading what was coming. "Where are *we* headed? Where does our relationship go from here?"

"Does it really need to go somewhere?" I said. "Aren't you happy where we are?"

"I'm a woman, Sim."

"I've noticed."

She smiled.

"I suppose you would have by now," she said.

We walked past the restaurant and out to the end of the pier where a few old men were fishing and catching nothing. Sometimes it's the fishing that matters.

"I am starting to think in more permanent terms," she said. "Committed terms."

The breeze turned cooler and we sat down on one of the benches near the end of the pier. A few boats came into the harbor, fired up their diesels, and dropped their sails. Probably heading toward their slips after a nice evening on the water.

"We need to have something *more* together," she said.

I thought of Judith and the redhead that went back to the University of Washington. I thought of the art teacher I'd lived with for three years before I bought *Figaro*. There had been others, too. None of them compared with Ashley and I knew it. I hated the thought of losing her.

"Do you ever think of moving ashore, Sim? Maybe to a house."

I thought of a lot of things that I could say that would make her feel better. I could tell her that I wanted to marry her and buy a cozy home in the suburbs to raise a family with 2.4 kids and a dog and a power lawn mower. But lying wouldn't help in the long term.

"Not really," I said. "I like living on my boat. I don't think I could ever afford a house near the beach and I couldn't live far from the water."

A ship's horn blew.

"I think I'm going to need more than that," she said. "Maybe not right away but I need to know we're headed somewhere."

I wasn't going to get out of this discussion. There was no avoiding it. But sometimes the water is cold and you just have to dive in and be done with it. Putting it off doesn't make the water any warmer.

"I don't know how to say this, Ashley. You have all of the qualities I want in a wife and if I woke up tomorrow and wanted to get married and have kids, you'd be the one I'd want to do all of that with."

She folded her arms and dropped her chin.

"I love being with you, Ashley. You are my absolute favorite person to be around."

"But," she said.

"But I'm pretty happy on my boat," I said. "I don't know if I'd ever want a house with a thirty-year mortgage and property taxes and such. I like sailing."

"You can still sail," she said. "A lot of people have a house and a boat."

"I'd find myself mowing a lawn when I'd rather be spearing fish. I'd be miserable," I said. "I think you'd be miserable, too."

It was a conversation I'd had before. The sales pitch I dreaded above all others. There never seemed to be a good way of ending it without tanking the relationship.

"Sometimes I like to go back to my boat and grab a beer and just sit in the cockpit alone. Sometimes I like to throw off the mooring lines and sail out to the islands for a weekend and dive and pry scallops off the rocks and breathe clean ocean air away from noise and people. Sometimes I like to sit quietly in my boat and read."

A pair of gulls flew over and landed a few feet away looking for popcorn or a shred of forgotten fish bait.

"I don't mind working on my boat when it needs attention but I'm not quite ready to trade that for painting a kid's bedroom or cleaning the garage. Maybe I will be someday."

She dropped her eyes to the wooden planks of the wharf. She didn't say anything right away but I could sense the disappointment and the hurt. I felt like crap. She wanted things I couldn't provide. They were things she was probably entitled to but they were too complex for me. I wanted things to be simple.

"I get it, Sim. You don't want to be 'tied down' to just one woman. You don't want to lose your precious freedom."

"I didn't say that," I said.

"Yes," she said. "Yes, you did. Just not in those words."

I'd known this was coming. I'd known it wouldn't be easy. The result was as predictable as the sunrise.

"I suppose I should have seen this a long time ago," she said. "You live on your boat so you can have an excuse to avoid long-term relationships. It's a beautiful boat and it's just large enough to entertain a girl for a night or a weekend but small enough to keep her from staying. You just want to stay somewhere in your twenties even though you're closer to forty."

"What the hell?" I said. "Is it Amateur Psychology night in Santa Barbara? I didn't get the memo."

That plunged us both into silence. The only sounds were the screeches of the gulls, the talk of old men fishing, and the murmurs of the few couples that had strolled this far down the pier.

"I'm sorry, Ash. You deserve more than you're getting from me. Lots more."

She stood up and faced me.

"Well, a wise person recognizes that she just can't have everything. So, I think you'd better drive home to your precious boat tonight. I've got a lot of work to do in the morning."

She turned and walked back down the wharf toward the hotel. And she wasn't slow about it.

37

I walked back to the hotel at a leisurely pace and went straight to my Jeep in the parking lot. It was almost midnight when I turned onto the 101 and drove south out of Santa Barbara. I hadn't counted on driving back to *Figaro* that night, but given the topic of discussion, I wasn't surprised. Still, I felt those first pangs of hurt deep in the gut that hit you somewhere near the beginning of the end of a good relationship.

Most of the speeding sports cars had gone to bed for the night and I was left to make the lonely ride home during what most law enforcement personnel call the DUI hour. I gave that DUI possibility a little thought but the voice told me to give the liquor stores a wide berth. I argued with it for a while. Why shouldn't I? I am a big boy and it had been a lousy day all around. Maybe a touch would make things a little better.

Except I knew it wouldn't. It couldn't fix my relationship with Ashley. It wouldn't change the Captain's mind regarding my career. It would not get me into the CWO program. I'd hit a perfect storm of dead ends.

The lights on the artificial oil island a half-mile from shore blinked as I drove past and I remembered going out there with Al a couple of times last winter to get lobsters. Another couple of months and the bugs would be back in season. But where would I be in two months? Lemoore? Norfolk? Some other hellhole? What would I do with my boat? Lemoore is a hundred and fifty miles inland and Norfolk, where my career could die a slow and painful death, is on the other side of the continent. I couldn't take my boat to either of those spots.

So I decided not to go.

No, if I got transferred to some place where I couldn't take my boat, then I would opt for a twenty-year out. Early retirement. I'd just have to find something else to do. I considered the possibility of getting into local law enforcement with my military police training and then remembered that I was a suspect in a murder investigation. Probably a deal killer.

I turned right onto Channel Islands Boulevard and then left onto Harbor as the futility of my situation sank in. I parked my Jeep next to Al's truck and walked down the dock. Somebody's dog, a strictly forbidden visitor, let out a yelp as I climbed aboard *Figaro*. Thankfully, Detective Hargrave wasn't there to arrest me and I stepped down the companionway, tossed my Dress Whites on the chart table, and slipped between the sheets in my comfortable quarter berth. Alone.

38

TWICE during the last few trips out to the islands *Figaro's* windlass had intermittently refused to do its appointed job of pulling up the anchor. I found such refusal unacceptable and set aside the afternoon for ferreting out the problem. I ran a pair of long cables directly from the batteries to the windlass and found that, once provided with a source of clean electrons, the windlass was more than happy to raise and lower the chain. Within an hour I'd traced the problem to a worn-out master switch on that circuit.

Working on the boat is the price you pay for living on the ocean. It's a fair trade. A quick search of the ship's stores revealed that no spare master switch was aboard so I set off to walk the quarter-mile south to the chandlery. It was time for a cold soda anyway.

As I walked, I reflected on Ashley's words from the previous night. Was living alone on a boat merely a way of avoiding commitment? Was I truly living the life I chose or was I just trying to maintain my status as a young buck free of greater responsibilities?

Maybe it was time to be a grown-up and to settle down in a lasting relationship on a permanent mooring. *Isn't that what adult males are supposed to do eventually?*

I passed the small commercial boat operation where the sea urchin divers sell their catch to the Japanese buyers. The little hoist swung back and forth, quickly unloading one of the low-slung but seaworthy boats that the divers preferred. It seemed like all of those divers had an exact copy of that boat. The boats had small cabins all the way forward, minimal freeboard, and maximum deck space at the stern. They were fast on the water, too.

The boat Old Jed had seen was low-slung too, but longer by his description. Still, allowing for some chemical variance in Jed's observations, it could have been one of them.

The divers laughed and joked as the urchin buyer handed out their payments for the daily catch and I watched a few of them walk back to their big pickup trucks. I wondered how many of them had wives and houses and lawns to mow and I guessed most of them were probably in the same non-committed boat as me. It wasn't a choice-validating observation.

The chandlery was going out of business. The sign didn't say so but it was obvious. One of the larger boat supply chains had opened a store a few miles away and a lot of customers were attracted by the greater selection and the slightly lower prices. It was an inevitable progression. Small boxes get swallowed by bigger boxes.

This small box responded by selling more nautical gifts to the tourists and fewer supplies to the boaters. I walked past the brightly painted gift cards and the small useless brass sextants to find the dwindling electrical parts section. Thankfully, they had a master switch that was a direct replacement for the defunct one aboard *Figaro*. It wasn't cheap but nothing close to the water is.

I took it to the clerk and stood behind a pale man in cargo shorts buying an overpriced ship's clock/barometer set. I imagined that he'd put it on his office wall to show his coworkers what a daring man of the sea he was on the weekends. But no serious sailor would have one of those things on his boat if he had room for ten of them. I bought my switch and a Coke and walked out the door into the hot sunlight.

"Sim," said Judith. "I was just thinking how thirsty I was and here you are with my very wish."

She took the Coke bottle out of my hand, downed a quarter of it, and handed it back smiling.

"Why don't we go somewhere with dim lights where you can buy me a real drink?" she said.

"If I would ever consider punching a woman, Judith, you would be the prime candidate."

A look of genuine shock passed over her face.

"Why? What have I done?" she asked.

"You called Captain Overson and asked him about the St. James murder," I said.

"That's what I do for a living, Sim. I ask questions and I report the answers to the people."

"And your career may have cost me mine," I said.

I drank some of my Coke. I would need another to cool off.

"Well, what am I supposed to do, Sim? I ask questions and I write stories."

I pointed my bottle up the street toward the urchin dock.

"Why don't you report on them?" I said. "Tell your precious readers how, in this lousy economy, there are divers who brave the cold seas of Ventura County to pluck spiny urchins from the bottom and sell them to the Japanese for hundreds of thousands of dollars. Find out where all the money comes from, interview one of those divers as he gets into his big-ass truck, go eat some of the nasty stuff. Do anything but talk to anybody at the Naval base about Barry St. James."

"One would think you'd be grateful to me for arranging to have Mel Goldsmith bust you out of jail," she said.

I drained the Coke. And I softened.

"I am," I said. "Let me buy you a drink."

We walked back into the chandlery and I bought two more Cokes.

39

I locked up *Figaro* about a quarter to six and walked the half-mile to Tugs for dinner. The urchin divers were gone. Only a few broken purple spines lying on the concrete near the hoist bore witness to the day's catch.

The hostess smiled when I entered and nodded toward the back of the restaurant. Al and Monica were in a booth by the window. Al nursed a Budweiser while Monica sipped an ale from a local micro-brewery. I scooted onto the bench across from them.

"I thought you were going sailing," said Monica.

"Something came up. Ashley had to work all weekend."

I didn't feel like telling the whole story.

Our waitress came and brought the ice-cold bottle of Dos Equis I always ordered. She was the friendly busty waitress from Bakersfield. The one who'd graduated from my high school ten years after I had. The one who always put her hand on my arm when she talked to me.

Al and Monica ordered a large seafood platter to share. I ordered the swordfish. The waitress smiled at me before she left.

"That was quite a show," said Al.

"What?" I said.

I was thinking of the waitress.

"Your little boxing match on the dock yesterday," he said.

"It seemed a little one-sided if you ask me," said Monica.

"What am I supposed to do?" I said. "Give him a few free punches to show how fair I am?"

Al grabbed a handful of peanuts and took a sip of his beer.

"What was it all about?" he said.

"Some jealous jerk thinking I was making a move on his girl," I said.

"Were you?" asked Monica.

"No," I said. "I have no interest in her."

"But he does," said Al. "Maybe enough to shoot you in the back of the head."

"An empty threat," I said.

"A lot of men have been killed over a woman," said Al. "Wars have started over women. Ninety percent of history is men trying to impress women."

"Who said that?" I asked. "Socrates?"

"I think it was Woody Allen."

"Well, I have no need to impress her," I said.

"He threatened to kill you," said Al.

I didn't respond.

"What's going on with the cops?" asked Al.

"They're nutbags," I said.

"I saw Jerry and some Sheriff's detective over at your boat Wednesday morning," said Al. "And then I heard the detective grabbed you after our workout. So, what's going on?"

"They think I had something to do with Jed's murder and with that guy we found on the bottom last week."

"You found," Al said.

"Thanks," I said.

The smiling waitress brought our plates and we stopped talking of murder and suspicion. I was glad for the change in subject.

"You get any takers on your boat yet?" I asked.

"A few guys seem interested but everybody says I'm asking too much in this economy," he said.

"Your boat is in perfect shape," I said. "Seaworthy in every respect. The next guy who gets it will have a boat as close to new as I've ever seen."

"There's a lot of inventory on the market right now," said Al. "None as nice as *In Depth*, of course, but it drives down the price."

I thought of telling Al about my increasing level of concern with the Navy and my career but decided it wasn't worth talking about. Not yet, anyway.

"Hey Sim, remember that bet we made in June?" asked Monica.

I nodded. It was a stupid bet on a tennis match and she'd won. I hadn't paid up.

"With Ashley up in Santa Barbara all weekend you'll have time to dive my boat and check the zincs for me," said Monica. "That would be fair payment, I think."

"It would but not tomorrow," I said. "I've got to get out of this harbor and on the water somewhere before I go crazy. I think I'll sail over to Anacapa in the morning."

"Mind if I invite myself along?" asked Al. "I need a break from working on my boat and I suppose I could last a full day on a rag-bagger like yours. Might even be restful."

"Sure," I said.

My cell phone rang. I didn't recognize the number but answered it anyway.

"Sim? This is Erica."

It took a moment to register the name. The law office receptionist. She was crying.

"What's going on?" I asked.

"My place is a mess," she said. "Somebody has thrown everything on the floor and made a huge mess of my apartment. It's horrible, Sim, and….and…"

She cried a little louder. Whatever composure she had left was out the door and running away fast.

"…and Dustin is lying on my living room floor."

She sobbed and took a deep breath.

"There is blood all over my carpet, Sim. I….I think he's dead."

"What happened?"

"I don't know," she said. "I'm so confused."

"Start at the beginning," I said. "Or start somewhere else if you have to. Just tell me what happened."

"I went out this afternoon with a girlfriend to do some shopping. Dustin was going to pick me up at six for dinner and I was running a little late so I tried to call him and he didn't pick up and…"

"Try to calm down, Erica. Take a deep breath. Single sentences, okay?"

She took a breath.

"I got home late and I knew Dustin would be crazy angry at me but when I got to my apartment, the front door was already open. I figured he'd used his key to come in and wait so I put my bags in the kitchen and called out for him. When I walked into the living room, there he was on the floor."

"Where are you right now, Erica?"

"I'm standing in the hallway looking at Dustin."

"Okay, Erica, listen closely. Get out of there right now and get into your car. Right now, Erica."

"He is just lying there, Sim. I think somebody shot him. He's bleeding all over the floor."

The rising tone in her voice told me she wasn't far from losing it.

"Have you called the police?" I asked.

"Not yet."

"Don't, Erica. Don't call them," I said. "Walk out of there right this second. Don't touch anything in your apartment. Don't even close the door. Get out of there right now and get into your car."

"I'm scared, Sim."

"Drive to the harbor, Erica. Right now. I'll call the police. They'll get here about the same time you do."

I gave her directions to Vintage Marina and told her to park next to my yellow Jeep. She told me she was leaving right then and hung up.

Al and Monica could tell something was wrong but they hadn't fully tracked the conversation.

"That guy I fought yesterday morning?" I said. "He's dead. I need to call the police."

I tossed thirty bucks onto the table and stood to walk out.

"Hang on," said Al. "You'll need a witness to tell the cops you were on your boat all afternoon."

He picked up the check and paid it on the way out. The three of us walked back to Vintage Marina as I dialed 911.

40

THE police roared into the parking lot about five minutes before Erica did. There were enough officers and detectives to interview Al, Monica, Erica, and me separately. Standard police procedure. Separate all the suspects and witnesses, compare their stories, and look for inconsistencies. Shoot whatever holes you can into any hastily-prepared alibis. Other officers were, presumably, dispatched to Erica's apartment. Detective Hargrave rolled in to question me directly.

"Another dead guy, Mr. Greene? You're racking up quite the body count."

"If you'd like to ask me some legitimate questions about what I know, then let's do this. Otherwise, I'll call my attorney and the questioning is over. He might even take me to a ballgame."

He stood quietly for a minute and looked at me carefully.

"You want to answer questions?" he said.

"I want you to know everything that I know, Hargrave. Every single damned thing because none of it, not one bit, incriminates me. So let's get going."

"I understand you got into a fist fight with the victim?" he asked.

"Yesterday morning."

"Why?"

"He was being offensive and bellicose," I said.

"Bellicose," he said.

He scribbled in his notebook.

"Yeah," I said. "I read books, remember?"

"Okay, whatever. Tell me about the fight."

I told him roughly what time it started and how it ended. Hargrave left to confer with the other officers to compare notes and see if my story conflicted with the other witnesses being interviewed. I could see a lot of head nodding and then Hargrave returned.

"What condition was this guy in when he left here?" asked Hargrave.

"He had a busted nose, a split lip, and a foul disposition but he was walking and breathing."

"He say anything to you before he left?"

"He said he was going to kill me," I said.

Hargrave raised an eyebrow.

"Where'd you go after the fight?" he asked.

"Back to my boat," I said.

"Reading?" He smiled.

"Not so much," I said. "I had lunch around noon with a Homeland Security officer regarding a case I am investigating. After that, I had a meeting with the Base Commander. I was in Santa Barbara with a lady friend most of the evening, got back this morning around one or so."

He pointed his pen at Erica.

"She the girl you were with last night?" he asked.

"Definitely not."

He asked for Ashley's contact information and I gave it to him. Nothing to lose there.

"And what about today?" he asked.

"I spent it working on my boat, mostly. Fixing the anchor windlass and cleaning up and putting things away so I could take her out sailing tomorrow."

"Her? The blonde?" he asked.

He pointed across the lot at Erica again.

"No. 'Her' the boat," I said.

I pointed at *Figaro*.

"Right, right."

He scribbled another line in his notebook and walked over to talk with the other officers again. This time he came back with his panties in a knot.

"The girl says you told her to leave her apartment tonight," he said.

"I did."

"You think you might want to tell me why you told her to leave the scene of a crime?" he asked.

"I thought there was a good chance that she was in danger, that the killer could still be near her apartment. I was pretty sure you would only want to investigate one murder instead of two."

"Actually, we're investigating three murders at the moment," he said. "Three wonderful new murders all in the last week or so and you seem to have a connection with each and every one of them. You got an explanation for that?"

"Nope."

Hargrave scribbled more notes in his book. Then he changed tactics and tried the more collegial approach.

"The investigating officer up at her apartment tells me that the guy took a .22 behind the left ear," he said. "Sound familiar?"

"Sounds like the same round and placement used by Jed's killer," I said.

"You own a .22?"

"I don't own any guns whatsoever," I said.

"My notes show that you were issued a Beretta M9."

"Your notes are correct," I said. "But that's your gun, not mine."

"How's that?"

"Aren't you a taxpayer?" I asked. The short quiz had him flustered for a moment. "That gun is property of the U.S. Navy. It is not mine and it is definitely not a .22."

He made another scribble in his notebook.

"The girl's white carpet isn't white anymore," said Hargrave. "The place looks like a slaughterhouse. I talked to her about that and asked where she would stay tonight. She tells me she's staying with you."

"Oh, no she isn't," I said.

He handed me his card. His cell phone number was pre-printed on the front.

"I don't care where she stays," he said. "It's none of my business. You two figure out her accommodations any way you like. But I need to know where to contact her and I expect you to keep me apprised of that."

He walked back to confer with the other officers again and Erica walked over to me.

"Who can you stay with tonight, Erica?" I asked.

"Have you got room at your place?" she asked.

"I don't have a place. I live on a small boat and, no, I don't have room."

It was the emphatic 'no.' The 'no' that meant 'no.' The 'no' that was specifically intended to discourage additional inquiry. Al and Monica walked up from talking to the police and stood a short distance away.

"I don't have anywhere else to stay," she said.

"There are empty motel rooms all over this county," I said.

"I am so afraid," she said. "What if the people who killed Dustin are after me?"

I turned to Monica.

"Can't she stay with you tonight?" I asked.

"I love you like a brother, Sim, but don't drag me into this."

Erica broke down in tears. It wasn't fair. Tears attack male resolve like acid. Resistance is futile. I lasted maybe ninety seconds.

"I've got a spare bunk you can use tonight but you're going to have to make a plan for tomorrow," I said.

"Oh, thank you. Thank you," she said. "I won't be any trouble at all and I could probably stay with my aunt in Moorpark tomorrow night." And then, almost without skipping a beat, "I'm starving."

Al shook his head about a half-inch in either direction.

An hour later, Erica had polished off a huge sandwich and was comfortably tucked into *Figaro*'s forward vee-berth. I wandered two slips over to have a beer with Al up on the flying bridge. Despite the late hour, there were still a few noisy weekenders having a party on one of the big power boats on I-dock. Blissfully ignorant of the drama, they were looking forward to some Sunday boating.

I didn't share their bliss.

41

I climbed up the companionway into *Figaro's* cockpit about twenty minutes after sunrise to organize and clean my fishing gear. I didn't want to wake Erica so I kept the noise to a minimum. I was putting away my gear when Jerry quietly idled his patrol boat into the feeder channel south of J-dock. He flipped one of his mooring lines over a nearby cleat, shut off the engine, and walked to the front of his boat so he could talk to me.

"I heard you lawyered up, Sim."

"You can thank Judith for that one," I said. "I guess she knows Mel Goldsmith pretty well."

"It doesn't look good for you, dude. Doesn't look good at all," he said. "Makes you look guilty as hell, in fact."

"I didn't have anything to do with Barry St. James' death, Jerry. You should know that."

"All I know is that they've got three new stiffs in the morgue right now and that a lot of the detectives at the Sheriff's office think you're to thank for it. Some of 'em think there's enough evidence to take to the prosecutor."

"Well, thanks Jerry. It's very comforting to know that so many local law enforcement personnel are complete idiots."

"C'mon, man, you and I paddle out together. I just wanted to give you a 'heads up', Sim."

He pulled out a toothpick and chewed on it.

"So if you don't have anything to do with this string of dead guys, then what the hell is going on?" he asked.

"I haven't a clue, Jerry. I'm hanging out here on my boat and just trying to do my job as a Navy cop and then, suddenly, a Category Five crap storm comes over the horizon and starts beating down on me."

He was quiet. Thinking, maybe.

"Jerry, you know I didn't do any of this," I said. "Can't you talk to Hargrave and give him a decent reason to expand his list of suspects? To keep looking for the guys who did it?"

"Ha!" he said. "You think that guy listens to me? I'm just the 'Harbor Dude,' the 'Surfer in Uniform,' or the 'Fish Cop.' That's what they call me when they want to be nice. Who knows what they say behind my back? Don't make the mistake of thinking I've got any pull with those suits."

He watched what I was doing and reached the obvious conclusion.

"You planning on going somewhere, Sim?"

"Just out to Anacapa for a quiet lunch," I said.

"Taking that cute blonde you had with you the other night? What's her name? Ashley?"

"Yes, her name is Ashley," I said. "No, I am not taking her."

He thought for a good long minute. He had something to say but couldn't decide how to say it.

"Well, just don't disappear on us," he said. "Detective Hargrave would be very upset if he found out you'd sailed off to Mexico."

"Just for the day, Jerry. I'll be back well before dark."

He smiled and nodded and walked back to the helm of his patrol boat. He slipped his mooring line off the cleat in a single professional flip of the wrist and started the boat's engine. The big outboard roared and Erica popped her head up out of the companionway as he was leaving.

"Oh," said Jerry. "A different blonde, eh? Well, have a good time, bro."

His smiled knowingly as he expertly turned the patrol boat around and moseyed back out into the main channel.

"What was he talking about?" asked Erica.

"Nothing," I said.

She needed to freshen up so I handed her the bathroom key and pointed out where the liveaboard facilities were on shore. She trotted up the dock and I went down below to rustle up some breakfast and make the boat ready for sea.

Most liveaboards don't leave the dock because it's too much bother to put away the toaster and the pillows and the dirty laundry. Even though I live simply and try to sail more often than most, I still had things to stow before casting off. Gratefully, it didn't take long.

Erica came back and ate breakfast and Al arrived a few minutes later with two bags of groceries. He helped me stow the food into *Figaro's* little refrigerator and various lockers.

"This seems like a lot of food for the two of us," I said.

"Three of us," said Al.

"No, Al. Erica's going to see her aunt or something. Isn't that right, Erica?"

Erica nodded.

"Then you'll have to drive her there. The cops came by around two in the morning and towed her car away."

"What?" said Erica. "Why would somebody tow away my car?"

I felt like I'd been kicked in the crackers.

"Forensic examination," I said. "Dustin's DNA is probably all over your car, Erica. They're now looking for mine. They want to see if there was some sort of love triangle. It's what I would do if I were in their shoes."

"But you've never even been in my car," she said.

"I've been to your apartment, though. Just a few days ago, remember?"

And the circumstantial evidence is piling higher, I thought. Mexico started to sound very appealing.

"You might as well come along with us," I said.

I started *Figaro*'s diesel, cast off the mooring lines, and motored down the main channel past the urchin boats, the harbor-side restaurants, and a long line of expensive sport fishers. I raised the mainsail as we passed the Coast Guard station and unfurled the jib when we reached the entrance channel. A car horn honked as we sailed toward the breakwater and I felt relieved to leave the land and the people and all of the noise and nonsense one finds ashore.

Once we reached the open ocean, I shut down the diesel, trimmed *Figaro*'s sails, and pointed her toward Frenchy's Cove on Anacapa Island. The sails filled with the fresh breeze and her bow lifted for each incoming swell. The harbor is safe and calm and pleasant but *Figaro* belongs in the open sea. I belonged there as well.

42

THE sky had a lot of gray in it: the typical morning scud that burns off around noon. The seas are usually calm on such days and the winds light and variable. Today was different. The swells weren't large but the wind blew a steady twelve knots straight out of the west. It had been several weeks since I last went sailing and it reminded me of how good it felt to be back at sea. On a starboard beam reach, *Figaro* lifted rapidly to each incoming swell and then raced down the other side. We made almost six knots through the water. Two hours to Frenchy's Cove.

"Would you like to take the helm, Erica? Keep us on a course of 215 degrees."

She moved over and sat behind the helm and I showed her where 215 degrees was on the compass and how to follow that course. I adjusted the traveler and sheeted in both main and jib to balance the boat. We gained a half-knot in boat speed. It's a funny thing. A half-knot means you'll cover only another thousand yards of ocean every hour but millions of dollars are spent each year among the racing crowd trying to find that next half-knot.

I sat down next to Erica on the ship's starboard side. That spot gave me a good view of the seas ahead so I could watch for traffic. Al sat directly across from me on the low side of the cockpit quietly reading a book.

"What are you reading?" I asked.

"*Nicomachean Ethics*," said Al. "Aristotle."

"Learning anything?"

"How to bring the activities of my soul into accordance with virtue," he said.

"*That* sounds like it could be a lot of work," I said.

We passed *Gina*, one of the many oil platforms dotting the Santa Barbara Channel, and I noticed that the huge mooring buoy anchored nearby was bare of seals. Some locals say it's a sign of sharks but that's pure hogwash. The sharks are always there. We kept a vigilant watch for the container ships and oil tankers that use the shipping lanes between the mainland and Anacapa Island. Those behemoths cruise along at 25 knots or more and can crush a boat like *Figaro* without their crew ever knowing they'd killed us. Several flying fish bolted out of the water in front of our bow and whizzed off to port and starboard.

"So who killed Dustin?" I asked.

"How would I know?" said Erica. "He's a lawyer, right? They make enemies."

"What kind of law did he practice?"

"All the guys there will do anything that comes through the door. Car accidents, divorces, criminal defense. If there is cash in a client's pocket, they'll take it."

"Did Dustin ever tell you he was afraid of a client?" I said.

"He had a black belt in karate or something. He wasn't afraid of anybody."

"Except for a CPA in his fifties with a knife," I said. "Except for Barry."

"Yeah," she said. "I guess so."

A half-dozen Pacific white-sided dolphins jumped at our bow as we left the shipping lanes and Erica ran forward to watch them. They stayed with us and swam in and out of our bow wave while Erica screamed in excitement. Ten minutes later, they raced off toward Santa Cruz Island as if they all had pressing engagements.

We anchored at Frenchy's Cove in twenty-five feet of water. The cove is little more than a rock-and-shell beach about a mile and a half from the west end of Anacapa. It is a small and barren spot but in the winter of 1853 it became the temporary home for over four hundred passengers who survived the wreck of the *Winfield Scott*. They huddled here for eight days waiting to be rescued. Today, there were only the three of us on *Figaro*, two guys in a small open fishing boat, and an older couple on an immaculate wooden sloop.

Some of the machinery from the *Winfield Scott* is still there thirty feet below. The water was clear that day and Al decided to snorkel over to the site and see if he could spot some of the wreckage. He went over the side like a creature born for the sea. Erica sat in the cockpit looking at the rock cliffs and listening to the cry of the gulls.

"That sun feels nice," she said. "I wonder why Barry never brought me here."

"Did you go sailing often?"

"We only left the harbor a couple of times. Barry would motor out to a big buoy and then sail along the beach for a couple of miles, I guess. Then he'd turn the boat around and we'd come back. I don't think we ever went out more than three or four hours."

"Was he much of a sailor?" I said.

"I don't know," she said. "He always talked about sailing to Mexico but I never really thought he'd do it. I guess he never will."

"I saw the boat. It seemed a little small for a long trip."

She was quiet for a minute, almost pensive, and I mistakenly thought that she was about to reveal some important information.

"Do you have a beach towel?" she asked.

"Second drawer in the locker to starboard; just forward of the head."

She had a blank look as if I'd spoken to her in Urdu.

"Up near where you slept last night," I said. "Cabinet on your right. Second drawer down."

She went below and I heard the boat's lockers being repeatedly opened and closed. Five minutes later, Erica climbed back into the cockpit wrapped in one of my thick blue and white striped beach towels.

"Is it okay if I take one of these cushions forward so I can get some sun?" she asked.

"Sure."

She wrestled one of the long cockpit cushions to the foredeck, laid the towel on it, and turned her back to the sun. She hadn't brought a swimsuit but it didn't seem to bother her. A lot of things didn't seem to bother her. She'd had two boyfriends murdered in as many weeks. She'd found the latest bleeding all over her white carpet less than twenty-four hours earlier. Today, however, was a whole new day.

A loud guttural rumbling interrupted my focus on Erica's sunbathing as a large ocean racing powerboat idled into the cove. I looked up to see three guys eyeing us as they motored by forty yards away. At first I thought it was Erica's form that drew their attention—that made perfect sense—but there was something about the looks on their faces that didn't sit well. Something deep and instinctual. I reached inside the companionway, grabbed my binoculars, and checked out the boat and its occupants as it powered away.

The boat was named *Hot N' Heavy* and it continued past us to the northwest. There was a guy in a flowered shirt and sunglasses sitting at the helm and a similarly clad fellow standing next to him. The third guy, a large black fellow in a tight yellow T-shirt, sat in a rearward facing seat. The standing guy turned around and looked over at us every half-minute. Erica was on *Figaro*'s foredeck getting the maximum sun exposure possible. I probably would have stared, too, under the circumstances.

I stepped down into the galley to fix lunch.

43

AL had the uncanny ability to sense whenever food became available. I'd often wondered how a guy in his fifties could eat so much and drink so prodigiously and still maintain a semblance of fitness. I'd no sooner finished making a half-dozen sandwiches than I heard him climbing *Figaro's* boarding ladder. I brought the sandwiches, drinks, chips, and bean dip up into the cockpit to find him toweling off and staring at Erica on the foredeck.

"God bless America," he said.

A bit of cool breeze blew through the anchorage and Erica stood up, as if on cue, and wrapped the towel around her waist. She walked back to the cockpit dragging the cushion behind her.

"The sun felt so good up there," she said. "And then the wind came up."

Al and I nodded.

"But I don't want to get too much sun anyway," she said. "Bad for the skin."

"You sure wouldn't want that," said Al.

"Is there a shower in the bathroom?" she asked.

"You turn on the faucet and pull the handset out of the sink," I said.

"Okay," she said.

"Call me if you need any, uh, help," said Al.

Erica smiled back at him as she climbed down the companionway.

"God bless America," repeated Al.

Al and I started into the sandwiches and chips and such. Erica returned a short time later showered and dressed and hungry. She grabbed a sandwich, sat down under the cockpit dodger, and tucked her feet under her. Al went back to his book. I tried to think of who might want to kill Dustin or, perhaps, who might want to kill Erica. The breeze picked up again as we finished our sandwiches and sodas.

"The Doctor is in," I said.

Erica's forehead wrinkled.

"The wind pipes up in the afternoon," I said. "Usually around one or so. It's so regular, we call it 'The Doctor.' Time to head back, I suppose."

I cleaned up the lunch mess and folded the cockpit table back up against the wheel pedestal. Al went forward to tend the anchor while I raised the main and sheeted it in. We sailed off the hook and Al pulled the chain and anchor up by hand. It was something he liked to do when he went sailing with me even though *Figaro* has a perfectly good, and newly repaired, windlass. I unfurled the jib and set a course back toward Channel Islands harbor.

"Well, I've had a nice swim, a good lunch, and some great conversation," said Al. "A perfect trifecta. I think I'll take a nap."

I tried to think of what conversation Al was referring to.

We raced across the channel at nearly seven and a half knots on a broad reach in the freshening breeze while Frenchy's Cove shrank and disappeared in her wake. The wind was strong but the ocean swells weren't large and the distance between their peaks was long. Occasionally, *Figaro* would find herself at the top of one of the bigger swells and surf down the face of it for four or five seconds. There wasn't enough wind to justify reefing the main but I let the traveler out a little to keep her from heeling too much. Still, her starboard rail dipped close to the water and every once in a while a piece of the blue Pacific would rise up and sluice down her side deck. The afternoon's breeze had blown away the overcast and the summer sun beat down in earnest. But the breeze moved the boat well and kept the heat at bay. It was fine sailing. Perfect sailing.

We were a little more than halfway back to Channel Islands Harbor, maybe two miles south of *Gina*, when I heard the roar of a big powerboat coming up on our stern. It was over a mile-and-a-half away but closing quickly and I figured it would pass us in only a few minutes.

As the big boat passed to starboard I noticed that it was *Hot N' Heavy*. I had a funny feeling about it and was about to ask Erica to wake Al when the boat slowed, crossed in front of our bow, and returned to a parallel course close on our port side.

The guy behind the speedboat's helm raised a powered megaphone to his mouth while the guy in the yellow T-shirt pulled a short-barreled shotgun from beneath the boat's gunwales and leveled it at me. There was maybe ten yards between me and the shotgun. A blind man could tear out my insides with it at that distance.

"Turn into the wind and don't make any sudden moves," said the megaphone.

I reached down to the engine controls, switched on the key, and pressed the start button. The diesel coughed into life and I pushed the throttle lever forward to engage the transmission and maintain steerage. I turned the boat into the wind and the swells. Our speed dropped to about a half-knot and I furled the jib. *Figaro*'s mainsail flogged wildly.

Hot N' Heavy pulled up close to our port side and nudged *Figaro* slightly as the third guy stepped aboard. He was thin, about six feet tall, and had dark straight hair parted in the middle. He smelled of unfiltered cigarettes. He wore khaki pants, sunglasses, and an orange and white flowered Hawaiian shirt bright enough to qualify as a navigational landmark in the fog. But this landmark carried a pistol.

"Keep the boat close and watch this guy," he said to the other two men.

"Right," said Shotgun.

The powerboat's driver kept the boat about ten feet from *Figaro*'s port side and Shotgun kept his weapon trained on me.

"You've got something we want," said the guy with the pistol as he sat down next to Erica, "and we want it now."

"Welcome aboard," I said. I tried to sound cool and sarcastic but I was actually quite concerned.

"We want what this little lady here gave you."

He waved his pistol at her as if it were an extension of his right hand. The pistol was a Glock 22. Squared-off, plain, and business-like, it carried .40 caliber bullets that weighed half-again as much as the 9mm bullets sitting uselessly in the Beretta I kept in the glove box of my Jeep. I made a mental note to keep it closer in the future. If there was a future.

"I'm not sure I know what you're talking about," I said.

"She gave you a package. We were looking for it in her apartment when her boyfriend dropped by. He told us he saw her give it to you."

"Right before you killed him?"

The guy with the pistol shrugged. I saw movement down below in the cabin and realized Al wasn't napping anymore. It occurred to me that my new guest hadn't seen Al with us while we had been anchored. Al had been snorkeling.

"You're not going to give it to him, are you?" asked Erica.

"Look, I don't want any trouble," I said to the Glock. "She gave me a box and I have no idea what's in it. It's down below under the chart table. Take the wheel and I'll get it for you."

He smiled.

"You just stay behind that wheel right there where my good friend can keep an eye on you. I'll find the box."

Then he turned to Shotgun.

"Watch this guy," he said. "I'm going below. If he moves, do him." Then, as an afterthought, "Do her, too."

From my vantage point behind the wheel, I could see down *Figaro*'s companionway into the cabin. The fellow walked down the steps and turned right toward the chart table. In only a few seconds, Al disarmed him and rendered him unconscious. A minute later our new guest was trussed up hand, foot, and mouth with the duct tape I keep in the cubby beneath the chart table. Al stuffed the limp figure against the forward bulkhead. The thumping of *Figaro*'s diesel engine and the flapping of her mainsail had covered the sound of the brief struggle. Neither Shotgun nor *Hot N' Heavy*'s driver had any idea what was coming.

Al grabbed the Glock from where it had fallen, checked the magazine and chamber, and popped up out of the companionway holding the pistol in a two-hand combat stance. Shotgun moved instinctively to swing his weapon toward the new threat and Al put two small holes in the big guy's right shoulder in a very effective double-tap. The shotgun fell to the deck and the bleeding man dropped down into a sitting position. Al moved slightly and trained the pistol on the driver.

"You move, you die," he said.

The driver froze. The big powerboat was only five or six feet away from *Figaro* and I closed the gap with a slight turn of the wheel. Al jumped aboard the powerboat, grabbed the shotgun off the deck, and aimed it at both of the guys on *Hot N' Heavy*.

"Sim, grab the duct tape, hop over here, and take the wheel."

I looked over at Erica. She stared straight ahead and shook like she was being electrocuted.

"Erica," I said. "Erica, take the wheel."

She stopped shaking long enough to ask the big question of the day.

"What's going on here?" she said. "Why is this happening?"

"Now isn't the time to lose it, Erica. Just take the wheel and do as I say."

Erica stood up to take the helm.

"I don't know anything about sailboats, Sim."

"You don't need to. The diesel is running so *Figaro* is just a big slow power boat. Nothing complicated. The wheel steers her just like a car."

I pointed a finger at San Pedro Point on Santa Cruz Island.

"Once we turn the other boat away from *Figaro*, you just turn the wheel left until you're pointed over there. That's Santa Cruz Island and it's about fifteen miles away. I'll get back to you a long time before you reach it."

"Okay," she said.

She wasn't convincing. I went below to retrieve the duct tape and noticed right away that something about our new captive didn't look right. I put my index and middle fingers in the hollow between his windpipe and the large neck muscle. There was no pulse. *Oh, well. Nothing I can do about that.* I found the duct tape and went back topside.

"You're not leaving me alone on this boat with that man, are you?"

"He's no threat to you," I said. "Trust me."

I jumped aboard *Hot N' Heavy* and wrapped duct tape around Shotgun's wrists and ankles. Blood oozed out of two holes in his shoulder but they didn't appear to be life-threatening and I didn't care all that much anyway.

"You guys are in some big trouble," said the driver.

"Noted," I said.

I pulled him from behind the wheel and sat him down beside Shotgun. He was a short guy in nice clothes. He wore a nice flowered shirt over pressed khaki slacks. Very expensive leather shoes that didn't belong on a boat less than a hundred feet long. Manicured fingernails; perfect hair. Even in the wind. I wrapped a few turns of duct tape around his wrists and ankles, too.

Then I took the big speedboat's wheel and moved it to a position about forty feet from *Figaro*. Erica looked over at me and I indicated for her to continue into the wind for the moment. I stayed parallel to her.

"You don't know who you're messing with, man," said the driver.

"Shut up, shorty," said Al. "We'll find out soon enough."

The driver said something rude and unpleasant and Al slapped him across the face.

"You think you can swim six miles?"

He shook his head.

"Then have some respect," said Al.

He handed me the Glock.

"Move us back over to your boat, Sim. I want to get that other guy over here."

"He's dead, Al."

The driver and Shotgun looked up when I said that. Al thought for a minute.

"I'll take care of it," he said. "Move us over."

I did and Al jumped aboard *Figaro* with the dexterity of a man half his age. He brought the body up on deck and heaved it onto *Hot N' Heavy* like it was a sack of potatoes. Al wasn't competing for style points on the landing and the guy's head hit the cover for the speedboat's engine compartment. He didn't feel it.

"Head toward the island, Erica. We'll be back to you in half an hour or so," I said.

Al jumped back aboard and I gave the twin throttles a jab, pulling well ahead of *Figaro*. Al picked up the shotgun and inspected it. He shucked the shells out of the magazine and examined them.

"Remington 1100 in stainless steel, 18-inch riot barrel, pistol grip stock. Eight rounds of double-ought buckshot meant for us, Sim."

"You guys are dead men," said the driver. "You just don't know it."

"Oddly, that doesn't sound particularly intimidating at the moment," said Al.

Shotgun moaned about his shoulder. Al turned to him.

"Fella, I don't like being threatened with one of these. So I will not be particularly gentle or careful in how I ask questions."

"I'm not tellin' you nothin', old man."

Al kicked him in the face with the side of his right foot and Shotgun's back hit the deck with a resounding thud. Blood poured from the man's nostrils and he struggled to breathe. Al then stepped on the man's wounded right shoulder and ground his heel into the bullet holes while the man screamed in pain.

"I'll ask again and you will answer me," said Al. "For starters, who sent you?"

"Simon hired me," said Shotgun.

"Who's Simon?"

"The guy you just killed."

"What were you looking for?"

"I dunno. Simon never told us."

"Who hired Simon?" asked Al.

Shotgun paused to take a breath. Al wasn't pleased with the pause and dug his heel into the shoulder a little harder. The man screamed.

"I don't know," he said. "Oh, man, don't do that with your foot."

"Who killed the guy last night?" I asked.

"I don't know anything about any killing, man. Simon called me up this morning and asked if I wanted to make a few bucks. It was supposed to be a quick job. Easy money."

Al stepped on the shoulder again. Shotgun screamed for about ten seconds and passed out.

"I think he might have been telling the truth," said Al. "What about you, short legs?"

"Same story. We're just day labor."

His eyes burned in hate.

Al stepped down into the speedboat's small cabin. Cabinet doors opened and slammed shut. I heard the sound of something being ripped from the boat. Al came back up with the speedboat's ship-to-shore VHF radio, a handheld VHF unit, an EPIRB, a plastic box of SOLAS signal flares, a small semi-automatic carbine, and a first aid kit. He took the first aid kit over to Shotgun, slapped him a couple times in the face, and pulled his shirt open. Shotgun came to and Al examined the two bullet holes.

"Both bullets passed through," said Al. "Still pretty nasty, though, and you'll need surgery on the shoulder but I'll fix it up good enough so that you won't have to explain it to the Coast Guard. Your employer should appreciate that."

When he finished treating the shoulder wound, Al opened up the Emergency Position Indicating Radio Beacon, pulled the battery out of the case, and threw both parts overboard.

"No sense giving the Coast Guard any idea that these guys are in trouble out here," he said.

He tossed the ship-to-shore VHF overboard.

"No reason to let them call for help, either."

"What about the handheld and the flares?" I asked.

"Spoils of war. The flares on my boat just expired and I figured you could use a handheld VHF on your boat."

He relieved our captives of their wallets, cell phones, and car keys and put them on the boat's engine cover. The driver didn't have a wallet.

"Where's your wallet, shorty?"

"I never carry one," he said.

Al examined the wallets, took the money, and tossed the rest of the stuff over the side.

"Six thousand bucks, Sim. I'm guessing that's what these guys were paid for this job. Since they didn't earn it, I'll keep it."

"Throwing the rifle overboard, too?" I asked.

"Hell no," he said. "It's a Mini-14 in stainless steel. Good shark gun. And you never know when you might run into some sharks, eh? Think I'll keep the Glock, too." He slipped the big pistol into his windbreaker pocket. "You keep the Remington. Every man needs a good shotgun."

"What are you going to do about us?" said the driver.

"We'll leave you right here," said Al. "Somebody will eventually see you and call it in to the Coast Guard. They'll come out and tow you back to port."

"What about Simon? How do I explain him?"

"Any way you like," said Al. "If you're smart, you won't bother. Doesn't this boat have an anchor and some line? You've got three or four hundred feet of water under you."

The driver's eyes lit up slightly.

"It's not the first time you've dumped a body overboard," I said.

"Don't know what you're talking about," said the driver.

"Move us back over to your boat, Sim. It's time to leave these guys."

My boat had travelled only a mile or so while all this took place and the speedboat easily made up the distance in less than two minutes. I pulled up to *Figaro*'s port side, gave Al the wheel, and hopped aboard my own boat. Erica let go of the wheel and collapsed onto the cockpit seat.

Al stayed aboard *Hot N' Heavy* and shut down the engines. We circled the boat while he opened the engine covers and ripped out electrical wiring and spark plug lines. He cut the duct tape off the driver's wrists and motioned for me to bring my boat close aboard. He jumped back onto *Figaro* and we pulled away from the disabled powerboat. I couldn't hear what the driver was saying over the sound of the flogging mainsail and the thump of her diesel but I guessed that it wasn't for polite company. Al just smiled and waved goodbye.

I turned *Figaro* back toward Oxnard and trimmed the mainsail to provide maximum speed while motor sailing. Al fished some papers out of the pocket of his windbreaker and examined them.

"Does the name Terrell Jenkins mean anything to you, Sim?"

"Never heard of him."

"The registration here says he owns that speedboat," he said. "I may have to pay him a visit."

He shoved the paperwork back into his pocket.

"I know this may be just a small detail," I said, "but what is to prevent those guys from hunting us down when they make it back to shore?"

"Already working on a plan, Sim. Head back toward Channel Islands Harbor. I'll have it all figured out in a few minutes."

Al went below. I heard him digging around in the area under my chart table. Erica sat frozen and silent on the cockpit seat. *Figaro's* diesel droned on as we hurried toward the harbor. Erica recovered from the shock of what had happened and launched into a lot of questions starting with the words 'why' and 'what.' I had no answers. But Al came back up to the cockpit with a plan and it seemed like a decent one.

44

"THESE guys didn't get what they wanted so you can't bring this tub back into Channel Islands Harbor anytime soon," said Al. "They'd spot *Figaro* in a heartbeat. And they'll be looking hard for you and the girl so you two need to hide out somewhere."

"Okay," I said. "What about you?"

"They probably don't know who I am. But they'll be watching for you and if they see me walking up and down J-dock, well, then I'm toast. I figure I got a two-hour window to grab some things off the boat, get in my truck, and see if my buddy up in Ventura has an extra room or not."

"Sorry to drag you into this, Al."

He grinned.

"No sweat," he said. "It's been a while since I've felt so, I don't know, active. Not a bad feeling, really."

I got the impression that he was comfortable in his new role.

"Put me in just south of the Mandalay," said Al. "I'll be good to go if you get me within a mile or so of the beach."

"I can do better than that," I said.

"Don't risk the boat. The swells have picked up and you're on a lee shore."

"What are you going to do?" I asked.

"I'm going to take us off their playing field," he said. "I'll get a place to hole-up while we find out who these guys are and who is paying them."

He opened up my chart book of Santa Cruz Island.

"Where can you hide this boat until we find out who we're up against?" he said.

"We?"

"It's pretty obvious these guys are connected to St. James somehow and I just killed one of them. So I'm cheeks deep in this thing. Like it or not, you got a team member."

"I think I like it," I said.

We looked at the charts and agreed that Lady's Anchorage was the best choice to hide *Figaro*. It was small but it had enough room where I could anchor bow and stern and let out plenty of scope. I'd been there dozens of times and knew it was a rough anchorage when a strong northwest swell is running but those conditions usually come in the late fall and winter. With a little extra weight on the bow and stern rodes, *Figaro* could safely ride at anchor there for two months.

I maneuvered to a spot about a half-mile offshore and Al got ready for a swim.

"Hang onto that rifle for me," he said. "I think I'd upset the suntan and sandcastle crowd if I walked out of the surf carrying a Mini-14."

"Sure," I said. "You want me to keep the pistol, too?"

"It's a Glock. It'll survive a dip," he said. "And it won't stand out too badly in my shorts."

He took off his windbreaker, T-shirt, and shoes and tossed them below onto the chart table.

"I'll come out to Lady's as soon as I can to pick you both up," he said.

"In what?" I asked.

"I'll think of something."

He shoved the Glock into his pocket and dove over the side. I watched him surface and continue swimming toward the breakers. Satisfied that he was on his way, I tacked *Figaro* through the wind and made a course for the north side of Santa Cruz Island.

The wind picked up considerably and the swells grew so I gave Erica the wheel and went forward to put a reef in the mainsail. *Figaro* was close-hauled in twenty-six knots of apparent wind. With the true wind being somewhere around five knots less, we were almost at the lower threshold of a Small Craft Advisory. I went below and plotted a course to Lady's. It was twenty-eight nautical miles away but nearly straight upwind. We would need to tack at least twice and that would add eight or ten miles to the trip. Assuming the wind held, Lady's was about six hours away and that put us in the anchorage in the dying light of sundown, my least favorite time of day to anchor.

I went topside to relieve Erica. She moved over and I took the helm.

"What do you say we wake up Kyle and let him steer?" I said.

"Who's that?"

I reached over the stern to engage *Figaro*'s wind vane self-steering gear.

"Kyle is this little contraption," I said. "He's the best crew a guy can have. He never complains, doesn't eat much, and won't steal your beer."

She made a face that reminded me of a confused German Shepherd.

"It keeps the boat pointed in the right direction so you don't have to steer it," I said.

Some of the confusion left and worry seeped back in.

"What do I do about those men who are after me?" she asked.

I thought about that. Al had the skills to hide and protect himself. The U.S. Navy had spent hundreds of thousands of dollars teaching him how to deal with 'unfriendlies.' No point worrying about him. But Erica was a legal assistant and as vulnerable as a butterfly in a wind tunnel.

"You got any place to hide?" I asked.

"I could just stay in my apartment and lock the door."

I raised my eyebrows.

"Oh, yeah," she said. "That might not work."

She thought for a minute.

"My aunt in Moorpark," she said.

"That's not going to work. Anybody farther away? Former college roommate? Somebody living in another state?"

She shook her head.

"My parents live in Chico," she said. "But we haven't spoken since I left home. I don't think I could stay there."

"You got to think of somebody who can take you in. You need to disappear for a while."

We passed *Gail*, another one of the big oil rigs, on our first tack and continued on toward the jagged cliffs of San Pedro Point. A dark mass of gulls and pelicans circled in the air and dove into the sea a mile ahead of us. Predator fish down deep were pushing a bait ball of smaller fry to the surface and the birds participated in the hunt. I grabbed my fishing pole, popped a big anchovy lure on the end of the line, and dropped it into our wake. A few minutes later the rod arced into a steep bend and the reel sang as line pulled off the spool. I disconnected Kyle, turned the boat into the wind, and landed a ten-pound bonito. Once *Figaro* was back on the desired course, I sliced up the fish and put the fillets in the fridge to stay cool. The rest of the carcass went over the side for the gulls to fight over.

We passed astern of a large container ship in the south shipping channel a few minutes before making our last tack toward Lady's. A pair of urchin diving boats blasted past us on a reciprocal course toward Channel Islands Harbor carrying hundreds of the spiny monsters closer to the sushi tables of Japan.

The seas got steeper as we sailed west through the Santa Barbara Channel but *Figaro* took it in stride, clawing up the rolling hills of blue water and racing down their backsides. A look of concern crossed Erica's face and I wondered if she was getting seasick.

"Are you all right?" I asked.

"The waves seem to be getting bigger and this is all a little scary for me."

"Don't worry," I said. "*Figaro* can handle it. We were in swells three times this size when we brought her down from the Bay area."

She did not look relieved. She sat on the cockpit bench with her back against the cabin and her legs pushed out in front of her. Her head swayed from side to side as *Figaro* first climbed a big swell and then sailed down its back. I thought of Erica being seasick and tried to remember how far down in the cockpit locker I would find my collapsible bucket.

We were a little over six miles away when the wind died and our boat speed dropped to four knots. There wasn't much more than an hour and a half of sunlight left and I didn't want to anchor in the dark. I considered falling off the wind and heading for a closer anchorage like Pelican or Fry's but I bit the bullet, started the diesel engine, and sheeted in the sails. Diesels are noisy and unnatural but I figured that I'd only have to endure it for an hour and the benefits outweighed the cost.

We had about twenty minutes of daylight left when we reached Lady's; barely enough time to get the anchors set properly. Lady's is a squarish cleft in the island; fairly deep between steep hills that drop straight into the sea. One other boat occupied the harbor and it was up against the east wall leaving the rest of the area open for maneuvering.

I turned *Figaro* into the wind, slipped the diesel into neutral, furled the jib, and dropped the mainsail. I went forward and let out four feet of chain so that the anchor barely touched the water. Going back to the cockpit, I readied my stern anchor and the nylon rode I keep in the lazarette. I slipped the engine into gear and steered toward the beach.

"Aren't you getting a little close?" asked Erica.

"The bottom here stays deep right up to the beach," I said. "Don't worry, I've done this before."

When I got to the spot I wanted I turned *Figaro* back out to sea and let the stern anchor fall. We moved slowly away from the beach while paying out nylon anchor rode. As we came close to the end of the rode, I slipped the engine back into neutral and went forward to drop the main anchor. Then came the delicate task of letting out chain from the bow while bringing in rode over the stern until *Figaro* rested in a reasonably balanced position between her two anchors.

I attached a nylon snubbing line to the anchor chain forward, threw off my shirt, and dove over the side to make sure the forward anchor was solidly buried in the sand bottom. The anchorage was nearly dark by the time I'd checked the stern anchor and got back to the boat.

Our neighbor vessel was a short double-ender with a small boomkin and an outboard rudder that hung off the stern. Faded trails of rust ran down the boat's sides from the chain plates amidships. *Sea Mouse* was written below her port rail at the stern. A short man with a full gray beard and one of those dark blue Greek fisherman's caps climbed up onto the deck, put a steadying hand on his boat's boom, and glared at us. After a minute or two of staring, he climbed back down into his cabin.

Down below, I scrounged about in the fridge and found some snap peas, mushrooms, a red pepper, two ripe tomatoes, and some Romaine lettuce. I tossed it all into a salad bowl and carried it up into the cockpit. I fired up the gas grill and oiled the grate. The bonito cooked quickly on the hot grill and Erica and I ate a fine dinner in the cockpit as the lights of Santa Barbara flickered on twenty miles away. It was quiet in the anchorage and the only other light was the warm glow emanating from our neighbor's ports. Like a lot of folk on sailboats, the boat's crew was solitary and quiet. Nothing wrong with that.

Erica agreed to wash the dishes and took them down below. She stuck her head up the companionway a few minutes later.

"Your phone is beeping," she said.

I stepped down the companionway, picked up my phone, and found that Ashley had called. I tried to call her back. She didn't pick up.

Erica pointed toward the forward stateroom.

"Am I sleeping up here again?" she asked. She seemed frightened and fragile.

"Yeah, I think that's best."

She stood up and walked toward me. She put her arms around my waist and tucked her head into my chest.

"I don't want to sleep alone, tonight," she said. "I'm too scared."

It was a significant temptation; I'd seen what I would miss. But regardless of the stupid things I'd said on Stearns Wharf two nights before, I wasn't about to discard my relationship with Ashley. Erica went forward and climbed into her berth alone.

45

THE first light of morning was still five or six hundred miles east of Lady's when I woke to clear dark skies with no wind. The brighter stars in the western sky faded as dawn approached. This was my favorite time to hunt. It's when the fish come out of hiding to get their breakfasts and I get into the water to get mine. I pulled on my wetsuit, grabbed my spear gun, and dove in.

The cold water entering my wetsuit woke me up and I kicked with vigor to warm the thin layer of seawater trapped between me and the neoprene. A sheer rock wall dropped straight into the sea east of the anchorage and it looked like a fine place for a morning hunt.

If surfing and swimming are my thinking activities, breath-hold diving is my way to relax. It's a bit of a Zen thing. You loosen your muscles and breathe slow and deep. You accept consciousness as the only reality. Relax completely and your heart rate drops. Your body shunts blood away from your extremities and the cold water becomes irrelevant. Fifty heartbeats per minute. Total relaxation. Clarity of thought.

Ocean swells, unnoticed in the protection of the anchorage, rose and fell against the rock face, stirring air bubbles into the water and ruining the visibility where cliff wall meets the sea. The water was clear twenty feet from the wall but the light wasn't yet strong enough to illuminate the area below me.

Thousands of California mussels clung to the rocks below the surface nearer the rock face. I timed my descent with the swells and dove down to break off a few handfuls of mussels and put them in my mesh bag. But these guys weren't for my breakfast. They were bait. The light grew strong enough to pierce the water and shine down into the ledges of rock that terraced down the wall below me. I couldn't see the bottom but knew that the rock terraces ended in sand around eighty feet down. But the lower terraces and the sand bottom didn't interest me. There was plenty of food within thirty feet of the surface.

The fish were out looking for breakfast. Hundreds of small damselfish, dozens of surfperch, a few copper rockfish, some blacksmith, several protected Garibaldi, and a couple dozen California sheepshead. I wanted a sheepshead. The only ones I could see, however, were smaller females. I'd have to shoot two or three to feed Erica and myself but I didn't have a place to put them for the long swim back to my boat. It would be better to get one fair-sized fish and then swim back before a blood trail could attract sharks or seals.

I grabbed a couple of mussels out of the mesh bag and broke them up with my dive knife. The knocking sound alarmed the fish at first but when I dropped the opened shells from the surface, they returned with intense interest to eat the sweet exposed meat. I took a deep breath, dropped down to a ledge about twenty feet below the surface, and left a pile of broken mussels. Then I backed away to watch the locals feed.

One of them was a big male sheepshead who stuck his nose out of a cleft in the rock face to see what all the excitement was about. He was an impressive old gent but too big for my needs. I could have fed a family of six with that one fish.

I broke up a few more of the ill-fated mussels, laid them on the rock ledge, and returned to the surface. Another male sheepshead, smaller and perfectly suited to provide a meal for two, worked his way into the crowd and drove off some of the others that dared to feed in his territory.

I took several deep breaths, clearing the carbon dioxide from my system, and dove to a spot about thirty feet away from my target. I closed in slowly and quietly while the single fish I wanted fed on broken mussels. The shot from eight feet away wasn't perfect but it was close enough for a quick kill.

The rest of the fish took off and disappeared as I surfaced with my prize and blew the water out of my snorkel. I put my hand through the fish's gills, pulled him off the spear, and swam back toward *Figaro*. It was a little over three hundred yards back to the anchorage but I was in no hurry. I kept myself streamlined; trailing my arms behind me with the dead fish in my left hand and my spear gun in my right.

46

I made it back before the sun could climb high enough to peer over the island and onto the boat. I called for Erica as I swam to the stern but she was, I presumed, still asleep. I tossed the fish into *Figaro*'s cockpit, took off my diving gear, and stacked it all on the swim step before climbing aboard.

Erica finally woke when I started cooking breakfast. She came out wrapped in one of my blankets.

"I can't believe how well I slept last night," she said.

"A ship will rock you to sleep better than your own momma could."

She saw what I was cooking and a furrow creased her brow.

"Is that all you ever eat on this boat?" she asked. "Fish?"

"Well, we didn't get much time to lay in provisions," I said. "So we eat what we have onboard combined with what we can find."

I slipped a spatula into the pan and under the fish fillet and turned it over.

"Do you even understand what's going on here?" I asked.

She sat there wide-eyed.

"It's all such a bad dream," she said.

"It's no dream," I said. "Those guys would have gladly killed you to get that box. They were probably waiting for you at your apartment when Dustin showed up. So they asked him instead. They probably guessed that he lived there with you and that he knew exactly where to find what they wanted."

Her mouth opened slowly and her brow creased again.

"He might not have known what they were talking about," I said. "And he probably acted tough with his karate training right until one of them shot him in the kneecap. Then he'd tell them anything he could to stay alive."

"But he didn't know anything," she said.

"He saw us leave your apartment together and he saw me carrying the package. Dustin told them all about it, Erica. Once they had the information they needed, they put a bullet in his head to keep him quiet and then came after us."

Her mouth opened and closed like some of the fish I'd seen that morning.

"Don't you get it?" I said. "Those guys killed Barry. They wanted that box and he wouldn't give it to them so they killed him."

"Well, let's give it to them, then. Just give them the box and they'll leave us alone."

"It doesn't work that way," I said. "They would kill us as soon as they got the box."

She sat there in silence letting it all sink in.

"We may have to hide out for a while."

"Hide out?" she said. "I don't have any place to hide out. Those men will find me and kill me."

She sat down in the small dinette and propped her elbows on the table. The blanket fell away a little bit and I couldn't help but look. It was a fine view. I bent down, reached into the fridge, and pulled out three eggs.

"Hey, look what I found," I said. "Will this make breakfast a little more tolerable?"

I pulled the fish out of the pan, cooked the eggs, and toasted some bread over the propane burners. Somebody had given me a little jar of orange marmalade the previous Christmas and I dug it out of one of the galley drawers. I arranged it all on two plates and we had a fine breakfast.

"I'm not going to work today, am I?" asked Erica. She sighed.

"Your boss is dead, Erica. Are you sure you even have any work to go to?"

A look of delayed recognition passed over her face.

She went forward to her stateroom and I cleaned up the breakfast dishes. She came back about twenty minutes later wearing one of my longer T-shirts and carrying a beach towel in one hand. Her other hand cradled a cell phone against her ear.

"I'm not making it in today, Charise," she said.

She fiddled with the towel for a moment.

"Yeah, I heard about Dustin," she said.

She walked over and sat down at the chart table while I dried and put away the last of the dishes.

"I can't talk about it, Charise . . . . . . no, I can't . . . . . . the police told me that I, like, just can't talk about it to anybody . . . . . . that has nothing to do with it . . . . . . okay, so, I won't be in, okay?"

She finished her phone call, left the phone on the chart table, and went topside. I heard a splash a half-minute later and climbed the companionway to see her swimming to the beach. The towel had been folded and left on the cockpit seat near the swim step. My T-shirt lay on the towel. She was a decent swimmer. And one of the least inhibited women I'd ever met.

I went back down into the cabin, dug out the box she had given me, and reviewed its contents again. Barry's will, some CD's, a gold ring, and a brass key in an envelope. Bartholomew's business card had been in there, too. None of it looked remotely worth killing for. I opened the CD wallet and examined each of the seven discs. They were all music discs that revealed Barry's fondness for early British invasion rock. A few, however, didn't fit in with the rest. There was something about the labels. They were poorly printed and slightly off-center.

I pulled out one of the odd looking ones and slipped it into *Figaro's* stereo but instead of hearing the opening riff to The Who's *Baba O Riley*, the disc refused to play. I tried skipping to the next song but that didn't work either. Three of the seven discs, the ones with the odd labels, wouldn't play.

I powered up my laptop and examined the discs but instead of seeing music files, I saw computer data files with names composed of random numbers. I couldn't open the files with the software on my laptop and didn't recognize any of the file extensions. The remaining discs all had music that my uncles had probably listened to on their eight-track players in the early seventies.

My cell phone rang. I recognized the caller on the screen and picked it up.

"Where are you right now, Sim?"

The smooth voice of the experienced criminal defense lawyer had a wrinkle or two in it.

"On vacation, Mel. Out for a little sail," I said.

"It might not be the best time for that, my friend. I've got a Sheriff's detective in my office right now and he is expressing some serious professional interest in where you and your boat and that blonde you're with might be. He says he'd like to know right now."

"Is he trying to arrest me?" I asked.

"No," he said. "That doesn't seem to be in the cards at the moment. He just wants to know that you're not halfway to Mexico."

"I'm not halfway to Mexico, Mel."

"While that puts me at ease, Sim, I can see that the detective here is somewhat unconvinced."

"What do you want from me?" I asked.

"I just want to know when you'll be back from your little vacation."

"What's today?" I said. "Monday?"

Mel was quiet.

"I'll be back the day after tomorrow," I said.

"You need to get back here and answer their questions, Sim. I'll be sitting right there next to you. There's nothing for you to worry about."

"Day after tomorrow," I said. "My boat is rather slow. It'll take me all day tomorrow just to get home," I lied.

"So, where are you right now?" he asked.

"See you on Wednesday, Mel."

"Wait a minute, don't..."

"Trust me, Mel."

I hung up and went back up the companionway and sat in the cockpit. Erica was walking along the beach looking at shells and rocks and whatever. I glanced over at *Sea Mouse*. The grizzled old sailor was following Erica with a pair of binoculars. Hard to blame him, I guess.

The sun was hot and Erica found an area of smooth sand away from the beach where she could work on her tan. I decided there was work to be done.

The last thing I wanted was to come back to find *Figaro* lying beam to the waves with her hull pounding against the beach so I rigged some kellets fore and aft. My soft canvas bucket, filled with rocks and tied to the midpoint of the forward anchor chain, would greatly increase the anchor's hold on the bottom. My diving weight belt, lowered down the aft anchor line, would do the same for the stern hook. I dug out two short lengths of worn-out fire hose and wrapped them around the chain forward and the line aft to prevent chafing and wear on the boat and the lines.

There was little else I could do to ensure that my boat would still be here when I got back but I had to do what I could before Al came to get us. There are other things you always do before you leave a boat, even for a few days. I turned off the propane tank, shut *Figaro*'s seacocks, and closed and dogged her hatches. I put away towels and coiled up lines. Then I grabbed a beer and my book and sat down to relax in the cockpit under the dodger.

I read about Thomas Hudson and the marlin his son David had fought all day in the hot sun of a Bahamian summer. I was enjoying the story but felt like I wasn't getting the point of it, like Hemingway was just trying to tell the reader how much Thomas

Hudson loved his three boys and regretted his divorces. Maybe that was the point. Maybe Papa was waxing autobiographical and trying to tell me something about life. Something I was missing.

The breeze blew through the cockpit and I watched small fish near the rocks on the western edge of the anchorage jump clear of the water. They were either working hard for a meal or trying not to become one. Small sea birds picked over a pile of seaweed on the shore and pecked away at the crabs that tried to hide there. I watched Erica rise from the sand, walk into the water, and swim back to *Figaro*. I looked over and saw the old sailor next door smile at me and, suffering from a flawed vision of what went on below decks, gesture with an upraised thumb. Perhaps even the most reclusive solitary sailors question their life choices.

Erica climbed onto the swim step, turned on the transom shower, and sprayed the salt off her.

"How come the water here is so much colder than it is at the beach?" she asked.

"Maybe it just seems warmer when you wear a bathing suit."

She smiled and wrapped the towel around her.

"Well, it's not like I had a lot of time to pack," she said.

She grabbed the T-shirt and went below. I went back to my book.

Hemingway had more to say about life and his boys and regrets and pain and I suddenly couldn't take it anymore. I tossed the book onto the chart table from the cockpit. It made a loud 'thwack' as it landed and Erica screamed a little in surprise. I didn't apologize and I didn't care. I took off my shirt, jumped overboard and swam out toward a long high flat rock that sat at the eastern edge of the anchorage beyond the neighboring vessel. The water didn't seem as cold as it had been before the sun came up. I pulled through the water in my best freestyle and tried to think of nothing, focusing only on the strokes and my breathing, until I reached the rock and climbed to the flat top.

It felt good to be off the boat and lying in the sun away from Erica. I watched the old guy walking around on *Sea Mouse* and I wondered why he didn't clean the rust stains off his hull below the chain plates. It was un-seamanlike. He puttered around on deck and coiled some lines and put a few things away. About a half hour later, I heard the grind of a starter motor and the flatulence of a two-cylinder diesel engine followed by the sound of cooling water splashing out of the exhaust.

The old sailor walked forward and eased his bow anchor rode and the boat drifted backwards toward the beach. After a few do zen yards, the man hardened up his bow line and walked back to retrieve his stern hook. The diesel engine coughed and sputtered as the sailor went forward again and pulled his bow line hand over hand. Old muscles pumped and sinews stretched as he pulled his boat toward the open sea and lifted the anchor to the deck. After securing the anchor, the old sailor casually walked back to the cockpit, put the engine in gear, and motored slowly toward the anchorage's entrance.

He grinned at me through his beard as he passed my rock perch. There was a tinge of envy in that smile and I got another thumbs up. The boat continued out as he went forward to the mast and raised his mainsail. The wind caught it and carried the boat east past the spot where I'd speared breakfast and out of sight behind the high cliff walls.

I swam back to *Figaro* to find Erica wrapped in a blanket and napping in her berth. Turning on the stereo would have been rude. Al didn't answer his phone so I decided to give Hemingway another chance.

He got the whole afternoon.

The last hour before sunset is magical. The sea outside Lady's became subtly darker and lumpier. The cliffs and hills turned from light brown to yellow-orange to burnt umber. Erica came up and sat on the other side of the cockpit in clothes she'd worn for two days. It had cooled considerably with the setting sun so she wore my jacket, too. She was quite a beauty in that highly altered and plastic quality that Hollywood has sold to so many men as the ultimate in feminine attractions.

She was obviously available—a fact made known in several ways—but, oddly, I had no interest in her. I was thinking of Ashley and wishing that she, instead of Erica, was aboard *Figaro* with me. I needed to reassess my fear of commitment to a wife and family. Did I truly need to sit alone with Hemingway, Conrad, London, or Steinbeck in one hand and a cold beer in the other? Or could life be fuller and more rewarding with a full-time committed partnership even if that commitment came with increased responsibilities? Was there more to life than cooking carne asada tacos for one?

I had just about decided to give it a try when the sound of a boat's engines broke my brief exercise in introspection. Erica jumped reflexively at the sound as it reverberated off the rocks and cliffs surrounding the anchorage. I looked up to see a powerboat enter the anchorage in the last rays of sunlight and reached down to pick up the shotgun. I held it below the cockpit seats, keeping it away from the view of whoever was approaching.

47

THE oncoming boat throttled down and turned toward us. It was a sleek open fishing boat about twenty-five feet long. As it turned toward us, I recognized the face behind the wheel, loosened my grip on the shotgun, and went below to get my duffel. As an afterthought, I slipped the shotgun into the duffel.

Al pulled the boat up to *Figaro* and stopped inches from her starboard side.

"You guys ready to go ashore?" he asked.

"Hell yes," said Erica.

Al smiled as he helped her into the small boat. I put a few things away, locked up *Figaro*, and double-checked her sail ties, anchor rode, and chafing gear. All seemed shipshape. I grabbed my duffel and hopped onto Al's boat. I looked back at my boat as we pulled out of the anchorage and Al gunned the engine. *Figaro* looked alone and abandoned in the dark and I felt bad for her. I hoped I wouldn't have to leave her for long.

The powerboat quickly hopped up onto a plane and accelerated to nearly thirty knots.

"Where'd you get this thing?" I yelled over the roar of the engine.

"It's a Skipjack," he said. "Friend of mine owns it."

"Where are we headed?"

"Ventura Harbor," Al yelled back. "Be there in about an hour."

Al stayed on the throttle and we pounded down the faces of the larger swells. But it was a tough boat. Tougher than most folks who buy them. Erica sat in the seat opposite Al's and hung onto a chrome steel bar fastened to the dashboard in front of her. I could see the blood draining out of her hands with the effort.

"What's happening over at Vintage Marina?" I asked.

Al grinned.

"The cops have got the place staked out pretty well," he yelled. "They're waiting for you."

"Did they grab you? Ask you any questions about me?"

He looked at me as if I'd questioned his manhood.

"What makes you think I'd let them spot me?" asked Al. "I still got some skills."

We blasted along in the dark watching for the running lights of other vessels and avoiding whatever we saw. I had to admit that dodging large commercial ships was much easier in a fast power-boat than in *Figaro*.

"What about the boys from *Hot N' Heavy?*" I asked.

"The short one came by a couple of times but he spotted the cops and kept on going. He was scoping out *In Depth*, too, so I think they've figured out who I am."

"Have you mentioned any of this to Monica?"

"I told her a little bit about what's going on and suggested she disappear for a while," said Al. "She said she might visit her sister."

I thought about how this case was affecting my fellow live-aboards and felt badly about it.

"So what's in Ventura?" I asked.

"My buddy, Don, has a house in the Keys with a dock. This is his fishing boat. He's in Europe all month. He said I could use his place; thinks I'm entertaining a woman."

"Who wouldn't?" I said.

He grinned again.

Al throttled back and cut our speed in half as we passed the flashing red light of the whistle buoy. He slowed again to about five knots as we passed the breakwater and entered the "no wake" zone of the harbor. Once inside, he maneuvered the small powerboat into the northern sector of the basin past the big resort and the public park into the first channel that served the harbor-side homes that all the locals referred to as "the Keys."

"Turn your phone off," said Al. "I'm told the cops know how to track those things."

I reached into my pocket and turned off my phone. We motored past several large sport fishers and sailboats until we reached a dock near the end of the channel. Al spun the boat around and we tied up near a stucco home with a tile roof. I helped Erica off the boat and onto the dock and Al led us both up to the house.

Erica ran off to find a bathroom and I looked around at the home's furnishings and what looked like some very expensive art on the walls. Don was doing all right.

Al produced a bag from one of the big box stores and pulled out two generic cell phones.

"Burners," he said. "No GPS chips and not traceable. Forward your cell number to it and you're invisible."

"You think of everything."

"Basic operational tactics," said Al. "Now go out into the garage and get us a couple of beers. Don keeps the good stuff in the garage fridge."

The entry into the garage was off the kitchen. I opened the door from the kitchen, looked into the garage, and saw a familiar yellow Jeep. The fridge held a generous supply of Pilsner Urquell in their lovely green bottles. Don wouldn't miss a pair.

Al grinned as I brought him a bottle and the church key. My eyebrows asked the question.

"I found the spare key you keep taped inside your front bumper," said Al. "This seemed as good a place as any to hide your Jeep."

He opened the beer and took a swig.

"Don't worry," he said. "Nobody followed me."

"You wanted it to look like I'd disappeared permanently," I said.

"Seemed like the prudent thing to do. With your boat and car both gone, they'll never figure out where you went or even how."

"*They* meaning the bad guys, right?" I asked.

Al nodded as he raised the bottle to his lips.

"Bad guys, good guys, they all get the same message," he said. "And their efforts become more geographically diluted."

"Fancy talk for an old squid," I said.

"It's the Ph.D. in me, I guess."

"Of course, this all makes me look that much more guilty."

"It ain't a perfect world, Sim."

He saw the second question coming.

"It's all right. You got a step up in the trade."

Al canted his head toward the front window and I walked over to look for myself. A silver Range Rover sat in the driveway next to a green Jaguar sedan. Al threw me the keys to the Rover.

"Take care of it," he said. "Our benefactor, while exceedingly generous, is a little picky about how his things are used."

"First thing is to get the girl out of here."

Al frowned.

"If you must," he said.

48

I wanted to put her on a train to Chico and let her make up with her parents. The Coast Starlight would get her there in fourteen hours with a reasonable level of comfort and little chance of being followed. I even offered to buy her the ticket but she wouldn't have any of it. She wanted to see her aunt.

We hopped into the Rover and I drove down the 101 to the Rice Avenue off ramp and down Los Angeles Avenue. It was late at night and most of the property we passed was farmland. There weren't a lot of streetlights and fewer signs of life. We located her aunt's house after some difficulty and I dropped her off.

My new phone rang during the return trip.

"Where have you been?" asked Ashley.

"Sailing," I said. "It's a long story."

"I'd like to see you. Are you down on your boat?" she asked.

"No. I'm staying with Al at a friend's house."

"Al's boat is still in the marina," she said. "But yours is missing. Why would Al be staying at a friend's house?"

Her voice had some edge in it.

"It's a long story," I said.

"Too long to tell me?" asked Ashley.

"I told you that I'm staying with Al at his friend's house."

"Really?" she asked. "Or are you staying with some other blonde at *her* house?"

I saw where this was going and I wasn't happy about it.

"Where are you right now, Sim?"

"I'm in a friend's car driving back to Ventura," I said.

"So who was the blonde I saw you with yesterday morning?"

"You saw me yesterday morning?" I asked.

"I drove down yesterday morning to apologize for Friday night. But when I reached the parking lot, I saw *Figaro* motoring out of the marina. I figured I'd just missed you so I drove to the end of Harbor Boulevard, parked in the lot by the main channel, and waited for you. I tried to call your phone but you wouldn't pick up."

"I had no idea you were there."

"Didn't you hear me honking?" she asked.

"No. I'm sorry."

The anger in her voice had been steadily building. There was no way out of this conversation. I didn't have a chance. The truth would have sounded so much stranger than any fiction.

"You know, Sim, you didn't really look sorry," she said. "There you were on your precious boat with that fantastically augmented blonde and she was absolutely beaming at you. It didn't take you long to find a replacement, did it?"

"It is not what it seems, Ashley."

"I was so stupid," she said. "I was thinking all day Saturday how selfish it had been for me to try and push you into something permanent, something I thought we both wanted. But now I realize that it wasn't selfish. It was foolish. It was completely and totally foolish for me to expect you to settle down. You aren't that type, Sim. You want all the benefits and none of the responsibilities. And when the girl gets hopeful or clingy or a little impatient, then you just find another one who just wants to go sailing."

"You're upset, Ashley, and you're saying things you'll only regret later."

She ended the call unpleasantly and abruptly. What she said wasn't the least bit refined or ladylike. But, given the facts she had, it was the way it had to end. She felt she'd been horribly wronged. I couldn't blame her.

The ride back to Ventura past the dark and lifeless farms was especially empty.

49

THE boat was as stiff and stationary as the *Queen Mary* moored in concrete. But she was a small fraction of its size and we were surrounded by men in speedboats. Men with guns. Long guns, short guns, shotguns, machine guns. The men boarded our boat and there was no place to hide.

I woke up nervous and sweating in the big bed and had to catch my breath. I didn't recognize the room at first but the warm glow of an orange streetlight filtered through the curtains and I realized that I was in a bed in a house on land.

The numbers on the digital bedroom alarm clock read 4:13 in the morning. Knowing that I'd never get back to sleep, I started thinking about my current situation. No girl to share my time with, no boat to sail on the ocean, a commanding officer wanting to pin my hide to his wall, local cops trying to stick me with a couple of murders, and a bunch of bad guys trying to kill me. You could say it was a low point.

I showered and dressed and walked down the hall to Don's home office. The password to his computer was on a yellow sticky note clinging to the underside of the keyboard. Security wasn't his strong point. It took me a few tries with several internet search engines but I eventually found who I was looking for. San Diego seemed like a long drive through traffic but the little voice told me that it would be worth it.

Noises from the kitchen indicated that Al, always the early riser, was making breakfast. I walked down the hall to see him cooking a pan full of eggs and drinking a beer.

"For breakfast?" I asked. "Seriously?"

"You got something against eggs?" he said.

I shook my head, scrounged a banana out of the fruit basket, and sat down at the breakfast table. The morning newspaper reported the details of Dustin's murder. As usual, they got most of the facts wrong. Gratefully, I wasn't mentioned. It was one of those articles written with neither passion nor a byline. I wondered if it was Judith's work.

Al brought the eggs, a stack of toast, two plates, and some 'fightin' gear' over to the table.

"You got a plan, buddy?" he asked.

"There were four guys who were pals on the *Enterprise* ten years ago," I said. "One is dead, another one fired me, and a third lied to me. The fourth didn't really want to talk much. There is one more fellow I need to talk to about the Big E. Do you think your friend will mind if I put a few hundred miles on his car?"

"Probably not," said Al. "Just don't scratch it and be sure to bring it back with a full tank."

I slipped two of the fried eggs onto my plate and buttered a piece of toast.

"So what do you want me to do?" asked Al.

"See if you can track down the owner of that overgrown ski boat you disabled Sunday afternoon. Odds are that it was stolen but it couldn't hurt to check out the owner."

"Seems simple enough."

He mashed his fried eggs with a corner of his toast and washed it all down with a slug of Pilsner. Philistine.

"And I've got something else I want you to figure out," I said. "There are a couple of CD's in my duffel with a bunch of odd files on them. My laptop wouldn't read them but I've got a hunch that they're what those guys were after. Do you have any computer guru buddies who can figure out that sort of thing?"

He shrugged.

"Maybe Reid does," said Al.

We ate our breakfast and Al talked about his dream diving business in the Caribbean. While I was impressed with Al's ability to compartmentalize issues and consider future plans, all I could think about was getting out of the jam I was in, patching things up with Ashley, and saving my Navy career.

Al did the dishes and I went back to my room to change into my khaki service uniform and get the CD's for Al. The sun peeked over the eastern horizon as I pulled the Range Rover out of the driveway and headed toward the freeway.

50

THE Aspen Mesa assisted living facility stood between a newer medical office building and a large strip mall only a couple miles west of Mitscher Field in San Diego. I remembered coming to Mitscher early in my naval career back when it was Naval Air Station Miramar, a.k.a. "Fightertown USA." It had been the home of TOPGUN before they moved that operation to Nevada and deeded Mitscher Field to the Marines.

Aspen Mesa covered a fairly large piece of ground with two floors of apartments, a large parking lot, and a quarter-acre of lawn on either side. A dozen ducks cruised and fed and chased each other across a small pond to the west. Elderly folk, some in wheelchairs and others on park benches, sat by the pond watching the ducks.

Wispy clouds accented the blue sky of a clear and sunny San Diego day. I parked in the lot under a large palm tree and walked across the parking lot. The main building was two-story Spanish architecture, with arched windows, stucco walls, and red-tiled roofs. In spite of the nice day, all of the windows were closed tight and air conditioners whirred noticeably. In spite of the name, there was not a single aspen tree on the property.

A pair of Marine F/A-18 fighters took off and banked to the north in a paired formation as I walked into a well-appointed lobby. The sound of the fighters' jet engines almost disappeared as the dual-pane doors closed behind me.

From the looks of the lobby, the facility could have passed for a three-and-a-half-star hotel. A grand wooden staircase leading to the second floor dominated the middle of the room. I wondered how many of the residents were ambulatory enough to use those stairs. To the left of the staircase was a formal sitting room with an ornate chess board and a large gas fire. Behind the sitting room was a ceiling-high aviary exuding the tweets and chirps of a dozen finches. The information/greeting desk was to the right of the stairs flanked by a large salt-water aquarium to one side and a door to some executive offices on the other. Johnny Mathis sang quietly through speakers hidden in the polished woodwork.

The girl at the desk noticed my uniform and smiled.

"Can I help you?" she asked. She was earnest.

"My name is Sim Greene. I'd like to visit Admiral Harker."

"Is he expecting you?"

"I believe so," I lied. "We spoke yesterday afternoon on the phone."

She bit her lower lip for a moment.

"It's unlikely that he will remember the conversation, Mr. Greene. Like many of our guests, he is suffering from some age-related memory loss."

"I understand," I said.

"For the safety of our guests with such conditions, we only allow visits from non-family in the company of a caregiver. I'll ring her and she can escort you to Mr. Harker's apartment."

I felt like correcting her—retired or not, he was still Admiral Harker—but didn't. My Mom always told me that it was rude to correct someone else's rudeness. It was the polite person's most annoying conundrum.

She punched a few numbers on her large industrial phone set and spoke a few words to the other party. I noticed an 8½" by 11" flyer on the wall that featured an ink-jet color picture of a smiling elderly lady. There was a paragraph about her life above the words

"Recently Departed." She'd passed away yesterday. The reception-ist hung up the phone and smiled at me again.

"Deborah will meet you outside Mr. Harker's apartment," she said. "He is in room number 214. Go around that corner and up the elevator and then turn right. His room is on the right side about three-quarters the way down the east hall."

I thanked her and she smiled again.

The grade of carpet changed dramatically as I left the lobby and walked around the corner into the resident area. The fabric was colored and textured in a way that any unpleasant spills could be either easily cleaned up or hidden. There was a large open area where groups of well-dressed elderly people sat at dining tables. A few of the residents sat in wheelchairs and a few more had walkers parked near or behind their seats. Waitresses in black and white uniforms brought them their meals and drinks and breadsticks. A young woman sat at a piano on a small raised stage in one corner and played softly. Except for the industrial-quality food, it had the appearance of an upscale restaurant. The residents appeared to be happy and enjoying each other's company and conversation.

I'd rather be lost at sea.

The elevator was across from the lunchroom and its wide stainless steel doors opened almost as quickly as I could punch the button. It was a large elevator suitable for wheelchairs, walkers, and gurneys headed toward an ambulance.

The upstairs hallway was lit with brass lamps and ceiling-mounted skylights. It was all light and airy with more industrial-grade carpeting that crawled up the walls for about six inches. I turned right, walked down the hall, and found a young brunette in green nurse's scrubs.

"Mr. Greene?" she asked.

I nodded.

"I'm Deborah. Admiral Harker suffers from early-onset Alz-heimer's and emphysema. He's in the beginning stages of both. His short-term memory is failing quickly and he is easily confused."

"I'm sorry to hear this," I said.

She shrugged and gave me a look indicating that such maladies were an every-day circumstance in her world.

"I just wanted to make sure you understood the situation," she said.

She pulled a key ring from the pocket of her scrubs and opened the door. Admiral Pete Harker sat in a wheelchair near an open window. He was bald except for a thin band of short gray hair that covered the back of his head from ear to ear. He was freshly shaved and dressed in dark blue sweatpants, a pair of white Adidas running shoes, and a light blue short-sleeved shirt with the two silver five-pointed stars of a Rear Admiral on each collar point. An oxygen cannula led from a small green tank at the side of his wheelchair up to his nostrils. His face was gaunt, skin drawn tight across the cheekbones. I knew from his file that he was sixty years old. He looked ninety.

"Good morning, Admiral. I am Chief Petty Officer Sim Greene."

"It's good to meet you, Chief. Please pardon me if I don't get up," he said.

The roar of another pair of F/A 18's filled the room through the open window and the Admiral raised his hand, palm toward me. The Hornets flew off, the sound diminished, and he lowered his hand.

"I love that sound," he said. "It is the most beautiful sound in the world; the sound of power and strength meeting the enemy at twelve hundred miles per hour. There is nothing else like it in the world."

He held out his hand.

"I'm retired now," he said. "You can call me Pete."

He looked from me to Deborah and back.

"Can either of you please get me a glass of ice water?"

Deborah walked over to a small kitchenette in the corner and retrieved a pair of tall glasses. She filled them halfway with ice from the refrigerator and added water.

I sat down on an overstuffed chair across from him and looked at the decorations on the walls. They included pictures of the USS *Enterprise*, various visiting Commanders-in-Chief, and an old black-and-white of a man kneeling in front of a Grumman Hellcat on the wooden deck of a World War II aircraft carrier. There was an Admiral's flag in a glass case next to a portrait-style photograph of Pete in younger days and full uniform. His hair was darker in the portrait and there was more of it. Deborah brought the glasses to us and moved to a chair against the other wall closer to the kitchenette.

"Those fighters are based at Mitscher Field," he said. "Do you know who Admiral Mitscher was?"

I nodded but it didn't matter. He was going to tell me about him anyway.

"He was a great man, Chief. He cared a helluva lot more for his men than 'accepted' naval procedure. He commanded the Hornet when Doolittle and his raiding party of B-25s paid their visit to Tokyo. He fought in the Battle of Midway when most guys his age would be planning for retirement."

He took a drink from his glass and swallowed carefully as if it took great concentration.

"My dad flew a Hellcat off the *Lexington* under Mitscher's command. One time his flight group had to come back to the Blue Ghost in total darkness. Pete ordered the flight deck lights to be turned on, totally against the rules at night during wartime, and my dad and his flight group landed safely. I was born a week after Admiral Mitscher died. That's why I was named Pete, son. Not Peter; just Pete."

He coughed and took a deep, labored breath through his cannula.

"Emphysema," he said. "My dad died two years ago. He was eighty-seven. Never sick a day in his life. Had a heart attack while playing golf. I'll be lucky if I make it to seventy."

He took another long puff of the oxygen and coughed again.

"I'd be luckier still if I died tonight," he said.

Another pair of Hornets took off and we listened to the sound of power and strength.

"But you're not here to listen to my complaints," he said. "What can I do for you, Chief?"

"I'm investigating the death of one of the officers who served under you on the USS *Enterprise*," I said. "I'd like to ask you a few questions about him if I may."

A smile spread across his face.

"The Big E," he said. "Three-quarter Mile Island. That was one fine ship, son."

He took another careful drink of water.

"Questions?" he said. "I'll do the best I can, son. The folks here tell me I've got Alzheimer's and that my memory isn't so good. I think they're nuts. After all, I can remember what Alzheimer's is, can't I?"

He smiled again.

"Do you remember a Lieutenant Barry St. James?" I asked.

There was a momentary flash of recognition in the old eyes. He picked up his glass and drank some water. The recognition dissipated.

"Do you know why they called the *Lexington* the 'Blue Ghost'?" he asked.

"Because it was blue?"

"Dark blue, no camouflage at all. And the Japanese claimed to have sunk her five times. Tokyo Rose said that the *Lexington* would go down at night with all hands and then rise back out of the sea in the morning like a blue ghost."

"You commanded the *Enterprise*, Admiral."

"Yes," he said. "Yes, I did. What did you say your name was?"

"Chief Petty Officer Greene, sir."

"Go on then, Greene."

"What can you tell me about Lieutenant St. James?"

His head moved back a fraction of an inch and his eyes took on a faraway look.

"He was our Aviation Supply Officer and he was good. The best Pork Chop I ever saw aboard ship. He had a way of getting anything the ship needed. Even stuff the Navy wasn't sure we needed. We had a surprise bachelor party one night for one of my senior officers. That guy didn't think any of us knew he was getting married in Honolulu two days later. We surprised him."

He paused a minute and his brow furrowed.

"What was your name again, son?"

"Sim Greene, sir."

He looked closely at the gold fouled-anchor collar device on my uniform and focused on the letters 'USN' near the top.

"What were we talking about, Chief?"

"You were telling me about Lieutenant St. James while you commanded the *Enterprise*," I said.

"Yes," he said. "Of course."

He took another drink of water. His brow relaxed.

"We were inbound to Pearl Harbor, probably three or four hundred miles away, and we were holding a bachelor party for one of the officers," he said. "He was going to get married. Lieutenant St. James came up with six crates of live lobsters for the party. Had 'em flown in on a Greyhound. Nobody ordered them, nobody authorized them, nobody knew anything about them. I never signed for the damned things and was never asked to. Six crates of the biggest lobsters you ever saw just appeared on my ship four hours before a party for a hundred and fifty officers. That guy was amazing, I tell you. And I liked him, too. Had a bright future in the Navy. Damned shame how it ended with that other stuff."

"Other stuff, sir?"

His brow furrowed again and he rubbed his left cheek with a bony hand. The sound of Marine aircraft filled the room once again and we listened to it.

"I'm sorry," he said. "You're going to have to remind me what we were talking about."

"Lieutenant St. James, sir. You were about to tell me about what ended his career."

He nodded toward Deborah and lowered his voice.

"I'm not going to discuss any of that with her here," he said.

I looked over at Deborah. She rolled her eyes.

"I'll step into the bedroom and clean up a little bit," she said. "Just let me know when all your classified military stuff is over with."

She stood and wagged her head from side to side as she walked into the Admiral's bedroom.

"Can we talk about Lieutenant St. James, sir, and what ended his career?" I said.

"I'd rather not get into that, son."

"Lieutenant St. James was murdered, Admiral. I'm investigating that murder and I need your full cooperation."

He looked at me with a blank face and took another drink of water.

"Go on, Chief. What do you want to know?"

"Barry St. James retired from the Navy while he was under your command," I said. "So did Lieutenant Steven Holdsworth. They were friends and they retired about the same time. Ten years ago. Can you tell me why?"

He thought for a minute and looked out the window.

"Aw hell, it's not like my hide is on the line," he said. "My career is over for good."

I waited while he put his thoughts together. He took another slow and deep breath and coughed a little.

"St. James and Holdsworth were caught smuggling," he said. "They had a footlocker full of loose gemstones they'd picked up in various ports. That thing must have weighed two hundred pounds. Sacks of sapphires and emeralds from Madagascar, rubies and something called a Tiger's Eye or some such from Thailand, and, stuffed way down in the bottom of it all, was a sack of diamonds from who knows where."

"Why weren't they court-martialed?" I asked.

"Do you remember what was going on about then, Chief? The Twin Towers had dropped into a pile of rubble not long before we found that foot locker and there was a lot of war talk going around. We'd been on full alert for a long time. Maximum readiness. More orders and classified communications than I'd ever seen come through a Comm Center."

He stopped to take another drink of water. I wondered how long he'd hold out before Deborah had to help him to the bathroom.

"Lieutenant Holdsworth's father was a three-term anti-war Senator on the Armed Services Committee. I got the word from above that his son was not about to be court-martialed in that political environment. So we worked out a 'retirement' deal for both he and St. James."

He paused and took another long, slow breath from his cannula.

"The whole thing made me sick," he said. "I wanted those two off my ship so bad, we discharged 'em at sea and flew 'em out as soon as we got close enough to Pearl. And that footlocker full of gemstones? Just in case you were wondering, it went off the taffrail in three hundred fathoms. I watched it go over the side myself just to make sure."

Deborah peeked out from behind the bedroom door.

"Are you boys done with your secret Navy talk?" she asked. "I need to help the Admiral with his shower and get him dressed and down to lunch for the next seating."

The Admiral leaned toward me a little and lowered his voice.

"She's a nice young woman," he said, "but she has no respect for rank. Maybe we should court-martial her?"

He smiled and sat back in his chair.

"I don't think I have any more questions for you, Admiral. You've been very helpful," I said.

He smiled as another pair of Hornets flew outside his window.

"Thanks, Chief. Thanks for coming to visit me."

I signed out at the front desk, walked out to the Rover, and started the long drive back to Ventura.

51

DONOVAN'S was a welcome respite from Aspen Mesa. Al sat in one of the back rooms with an order of beer-battered onion rings and a pint of Guinness.

"Terrell Jenkins lives outside Ojai," he said.

I grabbed one of his onion rings. It was exceptional.

"And who is Terrell Jenkins?" I asked.

"The guy who owns that big speedboat we met on Sunday. Funny thing, though. He never reported his boat stolen."

The waitress came to our table, opened her little order book, and took advantage of my having not eaten anything since breakfast.

"He's got a nice place up there, too, on a couple of acres," said Al. "I drove up there early this morning and scoped it out."

"So he's got a nice place, Al. That's great news."

"The garage door opened about a quarter after eight this morning and a dark blue Jaguar sedan backed out and drove down the driveway. The windows were tinted dark so I didn't get a visual on the driver. But I got a hunch and followed the Jag down Highway 33 to the 101 and on to the 126 to Santa Paula."

The waitress came back with my Smithwicks Ale. I tasted it and smiled at her. It was so worth the price.

"Do you think he saw you?" I asked.

A look of mild incredulity crossed his face.

"Sorry," I said.

"So this Jag drives into a parking structure next to a big office building. World headquarters of some outfit called 'Solavon'."

I nodded.

"It's a solar energy firm," I said. "One of Barry St. James' old Navy buddies runs it."

"Well, the Jag pulls in and parks in a spot that says it's reserved for Terrell Jenkins, Vice President. And who gets out of the dark blue Jag but our little dumb boat driver."

"He used his own boat?" I said.

"Probably planned on killing you and Erica," said Al. "No live witnesses; who cares about the boat? Didn't plan on finding me."

Reid walked into the room, spotted us, and sat down at the table. He had a thick folder of papers with him.

"You two want to tell me what the hell is going on?" he asked.

"What do you mean?" I said.

"*Figaro* is gone but you're here, cops keep dropping by to look around while trying very hard not to look like cops, and a bunch of other shady guys are watching *In Depth* like they want to repossess it. Monica tears off and disappears and the Harbor Patrol treats Vintage Marina like it's their second home."

"We're in hiding, Reid."

"From whom?" he asked. "And why?"

"Everybody but you," I said. "And the 'why' is not all that important right now."

He shrugged. The waitress came over and took his order. He didn't even look at the menu. He ordered the lamb and a single malt Scotch that was older than my Jeep.

"I'll cut right to the chase," said Reid. "There's nothing special about those CD's. They're just backup discs for a fairly common accounting system. They're from a new high-tech company that makes advanced solar panel systems. It's called Solavon. Local firm. Based in Santa Paula."

Al's eyebrows levitated slightly.

"So what is so special about them?" asked Al.

"Nothing at all, really," said Reid.

He opened up the folder and took out some pages that looked like financial statements. Reid pointed a finger at some numbers toward the bottom.

"They're losing serious money in their primary business but that's sort of expected in a new tech firm. What is surprising is that they've diversified into an area so far removed from their core competency. Even more surprising is that the subsidiary is making them tons of cash."

Al and I looked at each other.

"You want to put that in English?" asked Al.

Reid looked to the ceiling and sighed.

"Solavon's solar panel technology is losing money. The market demand is low and competition from foreign producers is brutal. They'd be declaring bankruptcy and defaulting on some govern-ment-backed loans if they hadn't branched out a couple years ago into the specialty seafood market. That is what's keeping them afloat and making them profitable."

The waitress brought our dinners and Reid's whiskey and we wasted no time. My steak and Guinness pie was superb.

"Tell me about this specialty seafood market," I said.

"Nothing fancy," said Reid. "They harvest and sell sea urchins to the Japanese. They buy the stuff we see getting unloaded right there at Channel Islands Harbor."

"That's all there is?" I asked. "Nothing weird at all on those discs?"

"Not a thing," said Reid. "It's an odd business model, if you ask me, but pretty straightforward stuff. Hey, they make money and they hire people. That's not exactly a bad thing in this economy, guys."

We ate our dinner and talked about other subjects but all the time I was wondering why Barry St. James felt it important to hide some routine file backup CD's under some odd rock n' roll labels. And why was a VP at Solavon willing to kill to recover them?

Or did he think something else was in that box?

We finished dinner, paid the checks, and walked out into the parking lot. I pulled Al aside after Reid drove away.

"I'm going to meet with that friend of Barry's over at Solavon tomorrow. Steve Holdsworth."

"You need backup?" asked Al.

"I don't think so," I said. "But if you can't find me, start looking there. And can you nose around and find out more about those urchin divers for me?"

"What do you want to know?" asked Al.

"I don't know. Everything, I guess."

"No sweat."

52

A set of three-story medical office buildings sat on the west side of South Victoria across the street from the Ventura County office complex. Their tree-studded parking lot looked like the best place to unobtrusively park an expensive Range Rover for an hour or two.

I crossed the street, walked down the sidewalk to the Sheriff's office, and turned into the lobby. My phone rang.

"It's Wednesday morning, Sim. Where are you?" asked my attorney.

"I'm in the lobby," I said.

"How'd you get past me? I'm parked out here watching for your Jeep."

"I'm not driving my Jeep."

"Well," said Mel, "I guess that explains it. I'll be in there in a minute."

He hung up and I sat down on an old brown naugahyde couch. Mel walked through the doors about two minutes later.

"Can you tell me what this is about?" I asked.

"The cops want to ask you some questions. I think cooperating with them is the best option." He thought for a moment. "Up to a point, of course."

Detective Hargrave walked out into the lobby and ushered us into a room very different from the cozy interrogation room I'd seen the previous week. This room held a large rectangular wooden table with six chairs. The fluorescent lights were bright and harsh.

Mel and I sat on one side of the table while Hargrave and an assistant sat on the other. The assistant opened a small laptop and took notes.

"You are not under arrest, Mr. Greene," said Hargrave.

"Yet," I said.

Hargrave nodded.

"So, for now, I am completely free to leave," I said.

"Of course, Mr. Greene. I need to tell you that we are recording this conversation to assist us in our investigation."

"Of course."

Hargrave paused, opened a folder, and reviewed the top sheet.

"When did you first meet Barry St. James?" asked Hargrave.

"I've never met the man. Like I told you before, I'd never laid eyes on the guy until I saw him wrapped in chains at the bottom of the harbor."

"Can you explain why your fingerprints are on his file cabinet?" he asked.

I took a deep breath.

"I was asked to investigate Lieutenant St. James' death. This investigation was a personal favor to a superior officer and I was requested to conduct it informally. As a part of that investigation, I claimed to be a client of the victim and gained access to the victim's office."

"Who asked you to conduct this 'informal' investigation?" asked Hargrave.

"I've been asked not to discuss that."

"Of course not. Because then we'd follow up with it and check out your story and find that you are feeding us another line of bull."

"Whatever you say, Detective," I said.

"Well, I have spoken to both Master Chief Joseph Richardson and Captain William Overson and neither of them seems to know anything about any investigation regarding Barry St. James. Why do you suppose that is?" asked Hargrave.

"Are you going to question my client, Detective, or merely gainsay every piece of information he provides you?" asked Mel. "If so, we can save ourselves a lot of time."

Hargrave took a breath and paged through the folder again.

"So you never met St. James before but the lawyer who worked downstairs, now conveniently deceased, told me you were one of his clients. And we found your business card in his office and your fingerprints on his empty filing cabinet."

"We're covering the same ground," I said. "I was conducting an investigation."

"And you never saw Barry St. James alive?"

"Never."

"Well, you're consistent," said Hargrave. "I'll give you that much. But you are a lousy liar."

I knew the tactics and the approach. I had used them myself. You claim to have evidence or an eye-witness or an accomplice who has implicated your suspect. But it's a lie. Standard police procedure. Perfectly legal. Hargrave knew it well.

Then he went entirely off the usual script.

He pulled a manila envelope from the folder, opened the seal, and pulled out a thin sheaf of U.S. Navy documents. He tossed it on the table.

"And I suppose you've never seen this before?" he asked.

I examined it. It was an arrest report completed in my hand. It had my signature on it. It was dated back to the time when I was a fairly new Master-at-Arms stationed at U.S. Naval Base Guam. It was almost fifteen years old. The arrested party was Barry St. James. Mel reviewed the document.

"Still no desire to change your story?" asked Hargrave.

"Detective, do you seriously expect my client to remember every drunken sailor he's arrested during the entirety of his twenty years in the Navy?" asked Mel.

"Where is your little sailboat, Mr. Greene?" asked Hargrave. "And where is your car?"

"My boat is in the shop," I lied. "Having a little work done on it. And I loaned my Jeep to a friend. He took it to Moab or Glamis or some such place."

"So how are you getting around, Mr. Greene?"

"Public transportation, mostly," I lied.

"I don't see how this line of questioning assists you in your investigation of Barry St. James' death," said Mel. "We may have come to a point where we need to terminate this interview."

Hargrave turned to Mel.

"You think this is about Barry St. James, counselor? We have four bodies, right now. Four murder victims and another person missing and every one of them has a provable relationship to your client. I don't believe in coincidence, counselor."

"Four murders?" I said. "Who in the world are you talking about?"

"When was the last time you saw Erica DeYoung, Mr. Greene?" asked Hargrave.

A shiver went down my spine as if I'd backed into an iceberg.

"Night before last," I said. "Quite late, in fact. She didn't want to go back to her apartment and she asked me to take her to her aunt's house in Moorpark. That was the last time I saw her."

"And she was with you all weekend?" Hargrave asked. "Why is that? Did you have a relationship?"

Mel held up his hand for me not to answer. I ignored him.

"Last question first: emphatic 'no.' No relationship at all. None. She had no place to stay Saturday night after her boyfriend was killed so I let her bunk on my boat. I'd already planned to go sailing on Sunday with Al Higgins and she said she wanted to come, too. Al took one look at her and was suddenly all for bringing her along. So, against my better judgment, I caved in and brought her with us. The weather was nice and we stayed the night."

Hargrave looked at me quietly.

"Are you telling me she is dead, Detective?" I asked.

Hargrave said some things but I wasn't listening. I was thinking about Erica; cute and dumb and a threat to nobody. She hadn't deserved to die so young. *How did they find her? I should have put her on the damned train.* Hargrave kept talking.

"Where were you yesterday morning, Mr. Greene?"

"On my way to San Diego. Is Erica dead?" I asked.

Hargrave nodded.

"San Diego? On public transportation?" he asked. "Must have taken you all day?"

"I borrowed a car," I said. "And you haven't answered my question."

"We found Ms. DeYoung yesterday," he said. "She had been killed early that morning. Her body was found shoved under the dock near your slip at Vintage Marina. It was tied down there with your boat's mooring lines. You tried your best to hide it but a kid fishing off the dock saw a woman's arm waving at him from under the water."

The shock was strong and I couldn't think of anything to say.

"And Judith Norton from your marina is missing, too. Didn't show up to work and doesn't answer her cell phone."

Mel's mouth dropped open.

"We have several witnesses who will testify that you had a romantic relationship with Ms. Norton several years ago. Don't try to deny that," he said.

"I won't. Judith and I were very close once but my service in the Navy got in the way."

"Don't try to hide behind that uniform, Greene. Just because you're wearing one doesn't mean you didn't kill five people," he said.

"And wearing plain clothes doesn't make you a detective," I said.

There was more than a little fire in Hargrave's eyes. I was halfway hoping he'd take a swing at me.

"Listen Greene, there are at least fifty things you've got to hide or think about or cover up when you commit a crime like this," he said. "The smartest guy on the planet will think of twenty or twenty-five of them. You aren't the smartest guy on the planet by a long shot. I'm going to find the things you didn't think of. I'll get that evidence and I will toast you."

Anger thickened the air.

"Thank you, Detective. May I have a few minutes with my client, please?" asked Mel.

"Of course," said Hargrave. "We'll leave the room."

Mel smiled.

"That's very kind of you," he said. "But I'd like to talk with my client in private with no tapes rolling, so we'll take a short walk outside. Ten minutes; fifteen, max. Unless, of course, my client is under arrest."

Hargrave shook his head.

Mel and I walked out into the courtyard between the Sheriff's station and the county courthouse. We sat on a bench in the shade of some trees. Two uniformed officers followed us out but stayed a discreet distance away.

"What's going on, here, Sim?" asked Mel. "If you had anything to do with these deaths, I need to know."

"You think I did it?" I said.

"It has nothing to do with what I think. These guys are tying a case to you, my friend, and every time you open your mouth, they slip another strand of rope around your neck."

"It was your idea to talk to them," I said.

"I didn't think you had anything to do with these murders, Sim."

"And now you do."

"I don't know what to think," said Mel. "But I do know they are stacking up a hefty pile of circumstantial evidence against you. You had a relationship with Judith Norton and it went bad. She is now missing. You wanted to have a relationship with Erica but her boyfriend interfered so you beat him up and then, the next day, you killed him. You kidnapped Erica and made her stay on your boat. She refused your sexual advances so you killed her."

"Whose side are you on?" I asked.

"Yours, Sim. But I know how prosecutors and cops think and that is what they will tell the jury. The jury of your peers. The inferences they make in court will fry you."

"So why did I kill Barry St. James and Jed?" I asked.

"Barry was angry about being arrested years ago," he said. "It ruined his Navy career or something like that and he always hated you. Later he moves to Ventura and the two of you somehow cross paths. He came after you and you killed him in haste."

"Yeah, I hastily wrapped a couple hundred pounds of chain around him and hastily tossed him into the ocean," I said. "But before that I hastily tortured him with some rare form of Chinese flesh-slicing."

Mel looked up at the sky.

"And what about Jed, Mel? Why did I kill him?"

"He saw you dump Barry's body and you didn't want a witness," said Mel.

"It all goes back to Barry St. James, Mel. Somebody tortured him slowly and then at least two guys wrapped him in chains and dropped him in the drink. The only reason I haven't been arrested is because those idiots over there cannot get past that."

"They think they have enough on you for the other three," said Mel.

"Those other killings are connected to Barry St. James and they know it," I said. "The only reason I'm here is because they think I've found something in my investigation and they want to squeeze it out of me. All this nonsense of tying me to these killings is pure bluster."

"Tell them what you know, Sim. Get them off your back and let them solve this."

I stood up and walked toward the courthouse. Mel followed.

"Where are you going?" he asked.

"I need a drink of water and there's a fountain in the court-house."

"You're a cop, Sim. How do you explain these killings?"

"I'm pretty sure that all of these murders are related to some-thing going on at a big corporation in Santa Paula," I said. "It's a company owned by a guy named Steve Holdsworth."

"Alan Holdsworth's kid?" asked Mel.

"Yeah."

"Solavon? You think Solavon has something to do with these murders?"

"Yeah, I do," I said. "I'm just not sure exactly how."

The courthouse is actually two separate buildings joined by a common foyer. It had been built between the Sheriff's headquar-ters, the central jail, and some larger county offices before the days of metal detectors and security lines. The courthouse foyer was maybe twenty yards wide with a set of glass doors on the north toward the Sheriff's headquarters and another set of glass doors on the south opening to a courtyard serving the jail and the county offices.

We reached the north doors to the courthouse and got into the security line. I looked back and saw that the uniformed cops tasked with watching us had moved toward the courthouse. I passed through the metal detector ahead of Mel and grabbed my wallet, keys, and cell phone from the little plastic tub.

"I'm getting out of here, Mel. I'm not going to stay here and let these idiots push me around and squeeze me for information just because they're lazy cops."

"Don't do this to me," said Mel. "My reputation is on the line, here."

"Sorry, dude, but I'm gone."

I jogged through the foyer toward the glass doors on the oppo-site side. Mel walked behind me. The two uniformed cops tried to jump the line and started arguing with the security guard as I

pushed through the glass doors and ran through the south courtyard and down a large circular driveway to the Victoria Avenue
entrance. The two Sheriff's deputies following me made it out of
the courthouse just in time to see me step onto a city transit bus
heading north on Victoria. I looked back to see Mel throw up his
hands in disgust.

I rode the bus for a mile and got off after it turned west on Telegraph. I jogged across the street, waited about five minutes, and
caught the return line back toward the County Government Center. Two squad cars, red and blue lights flashing madly, made the
left turn from Victoria to Telegraph as my new ride made the
right turn going the opposite direction. The bus continued its un-
hurried way south on Victoria and passed the entrance to the government center. I got off at the next stop and walked west through
the tree-lined parking lot back to where I'd left the Rover.

53

IT had been a while since I'd checked my email so there was a lot of spam and other useless junk in my inbox that needed to be discarded. It took a few minutes but the late-morning Pilsner in my hand helped me pass the time. The rest of the emails were work-related and I figured I could read those later since I was technically on leave. Navy business could wait a few more days. Or weeks.

One email stood out, though. It was a few days old and from Judith Norton. The missing Judith Norton. I opened it.

> Simba – You're right about those commercial divers. There's a good story there. These guys aren't Mensa members by any stretch but who cares? They work hard, play hard, contribute to our local economy (you'd be surprised at the $$$ they make), and they are all hunks. Every last one. And they are super friendly, too. Thanks for the lead, old friend. Kiss Kiss.

I hit the reply button, changed the subject line to 'Where the Hell Are You?', and wrote a quick message asking her to call me ASAP. I closed my email folder and took my beer out to the kitchen and made some lunch. Al must have gone shopping while I was out at the islands. There were fresh tomatoes in the refrigerator, crisp lettuce, some good whole wheat bread, and—bonus of all bonuses—bacon! I didn't realize how hungry I was until I spotted it.

About a quarter of the package went onto a plate and into the microwave. Not the best way to cook it but certainly the quickest.

I was sitting at the breakfast table eating the two BLT's I'd constructed when Al called.

"So, I checked out the urchin divers and there's nothing wrong with 'em," he said.

"What do you mean?"

"They dive for urchins, they stick 'em in baskets, and they sell 'em to the buyer from Solavon. They get paid well for their work, too."

"Nothing weird at all?" I asked.

"The boats are all pretty new and they've got some awesome diving gear. First class stuff. I figured I'd find some old surface-supply rigs for shallow-water work but all these guys have pricey mixed-gas setups."

"The urchins are that deep?"

"I don't know," said Al. "Maybe the best ones are below two hundred feet. Anyway, these guys are paid well."

I told him how my morning with Hargrave had gone. I told him about Erica and Judith.

"I should have killed all three of those guys on the boat," he said.

"Maybe so."

"So what are we going to do about it?" he asked. "What's your plan?"

"Who's got a plan?" I said. "Right now, I'd be an idiot to buy green bananas."

"I'm coming back to the house, Sim. We need to figure out a plan."

We hung up and I finished my sandwich. Then the little voice spoke up and I went back to Don's computer. I searched a little more on the internet and found the market price of sea urchins. A few pieces of my note card puzzle moved around in my head and fit together.

I went out to the garage, opened the door to my Jeep, and pulled out my blue windbreaker and my Beretta. I had a plan and I couldn't wait around for Al.

54

I got into the Rover and immediately called Ashley. Her phone went straight to voicemail.

"I know you're mad at me but I need you to do something," I said. "I need you to hide. The case I'm working on has gone sour and people close to it and me are getting killed. I don't want anything to happen to you so please, Ashley, please hole up somewhere until I get this worked out. And call me, okay?"

I drove the Rover up Victoria to the 126 and east to Santa Paula. The parking space reserved for Stephen Holdsworth, President, was empty. I hoped he was only out for an early lunch. I parked the Rover in a spot reserved for visitors, put on my windbreaker, and slipped the Beretta into the right pocket. The automatic glass entry doors opened into a spacious lobby filled with comfortable chairs and couches and large indoor plants. I picked up a copy of Solavon's latest annual report and sat in a comfortable leather chair behind a potted ficus tree that didn't quite block my view of the front doors.

A painting of a German shorthaired pointer hung on the wall across from where I sat. It reminded me of the dog I had in my teens and the good times we had hunting pheasants on my dad's farm outside Bakersfield. I remembered watching the dog picking up the scent and tracing the bird to where it held tight under a bush. The muscles in the dog's neck and shoulders would twitch with excitement and the dog's nostrils would flare.

Steve Holdsworth and an assistant walked into the building a half-hour later and I felt a little like that dog. I put my hand in the pocket of my windbreaker, wrapped my fingers around the pistol's grip, and met Holdsworth and his assistant at the elevator door. Holdsworth recognized me and turned to his assistant.

"Scott, could you please excuse us?" he said. "I'd like to talk to this gentleman in private."

Scott excused himself and walked over to speak to the receptionist as the elevator doors opened. Holdsworth and I entered the empty car.

"I'm not going to let you get away with this, Holdsworth."

"I don't know what you're talking about," he said.

"I found the records you've been searching for," I said. "The records Barry St. James took from your office."

"I truly don't have the slightest idea what you mean, Mr. Greene."

"The accounting records," I said. "The records that could destroy this company if they were made public."

"You're insane," said Holdsworth. "This company has been audited by our own accounting firm and by the Department of Energy more times than you can imagine and we have passed every one of those audits with flying colors."

"That's not what the records I have show. I couldn't care less about your company or the DOE or where you really get your money. I care about some of the people you've had killed in the last couple of days and I care about my Navy career."

"I don't know what you're talking about and neither do you," said Holdsworth.

"What do you know about sea urchins?" I asked.

"The urchin business is a sideline; a very small sideline. My vice president runs it. It is profitable but only a sideline business."

"The books I have, the real ones, show that every dime of profit comes from sea urchins."

"So what?" he asked. "Who cares?"

"It's fine," I said. "Except that you're selling too few urchins and making too much money."

"I don't know where you get that but it's all bullshit," said Holdsworth. "We make our money in leading-edge solar technology."

"Well, I am taking what I have to the feds," I said. "They'll find out which of your hired hands is out there killing people."

His eyes widened slightly and I knew I'd hit something.

"I don't know what you're talking about, sailor," said Holdsworth. "But I think you better lay off the torpedo juice."

The elevator door opened on the top floor and Steve Holdsworth stepped out.

"And I think you'd better get the hell out of this building before I call security. You may also want to go hide your head in the sand, sailor, while you still have one."

He walked toward his office and I took the stairs down two at a time.

A dark blue Jaguar with tinted windows drove into the parking structure as I left the lobby. It parked in a space marked 'Terrell Jenkins, VP.'

The guy who drove a big speedboat got out of the car and smiled at me. He held out his right hand, pointed his forefinger at me, and winked as he mimicked a trigger pull complete with recoil. And then it hit me. I'd seen the smile before in a picture on a wall in an empty apartment. The photographer had caught him standing on a sport fisher with Steve Holdsworth and Barry St. James; all three of them holding albacore they'd pulled out of the Pacific. Terrell smiled again, turned, and walked through the double glass doors into the office lobby.

I took off my windbreaker, put the Beretta in the center console of the Rover, and drove out of the parking structure straight into the bright sunlight and harm's way.

55

SOMETIMES it seems as if Southern California is filled with late-model gray or silver Toyota Camrys. And why shouldn't it be? They get good mileage and they last a long time. They are overpriced, in my opinion, but somebody with a longer commute or a bigger paycheck than mine can justify it. And not everyone is manly enough to drive an old Jeep. The Camry is a popular car in Southern California and nobody should ever be surprised to see one in his rear-view mirror.

The one I saw, however, had deeply tinted windows and had followed every turn I'd made since leaving Solavon's offices. I stayed on surface streets for a while, acted like I couldn't find the freeway on-ramp, and made several consecutive right turns to verify the Toyota's intent. I stayed in traffic and slowed down, intentionally missing a few green lights, to see if it would get close enough for me to figure out how many people sat behind those tinted windows. No luck. I decided it was better to estimate on the high side and figured that Steve and Terrell had sent two guys.

I tried to call Al, thinking we could handle this tail the same way we'd handled the fellows from Homeland Security, but he didn't answer his burner. I hung up, tried again, and achieved the same result. I was on my own.

The tail followed me onto the 126 and stayed a respectable distance behind. I got off at Wells Road, made the left turn toward Saticoy, and stopped at a gas station. It seemed smart to start a car chase with plenty of fuel so I filled the Rover's tank, walked into the convenience store, and looked through the window. I didn't see them but that didn't mean they weren't nearby.

I went to the restroom, stuffed my pockets full of toilet paper, and went back out to the cold case to check out the soft drink selection. There was an ad banner for Pepsi proclaiming that I should "Live For Now." Sounded about right. I grabbed a 20-ounce plastic bottle with a wide mouth. I also picked up a small and overpriced roll of duct tape in the short aisle where they sell light bulbs, batteries, two-gallon plastic gas cans, and under-sized jumper cables.

The tall bearded and mustachioed man behind the counter wore an orange turban and an iron bracelet on his left wrist. I remembered reading about Sikhs who had fought bravely for decades in England's wars and wondered if he'd be interested in a temp job that afternoon. He rang up the items, gave me my change, and wished me a good day like he truly meant it.

The tail picked me up again on the south side of the Saticoy bridge but didn't crowd me. There was no way to tell if they were following me so they could report my actions to higher-ups or if they were waiting for me to wander onto an empty stretch of farm road so they could blast away with a shotgun.

I drank the cola as I drove and tried to decide which battlefield would give me the best advantage. Higher ground seemed to make sense for no particular reason at all. I made a left onto Los Angeles Avenue toward Moorpark, drove about eight miles at fifteen over the limit, and turned left up a fairly wide dirt road that headed toward one of the canyons. It was a good dirt road with a few potholes and a fair amount of washboard. Exactly what I wanted. The Camry turned to follow and I punched the throttle. I was pushing seventy in Don's Rover and raising a thick cloud of dust.

The Camry wasn't visible through my dust trail but I knew it didn't have the ground clearance to follow at the speed I was traveling. They hadn't planned on any off-roading and I'd have the lead I needed when I stopped. The road ran straight for two miles past vegetable fields, orange orchards, and a large horse ranch up into an area of uninhabited hills. I stuck the empty soda bottle between my knees and shoved the toilet paper from my pockets into the wide mouth while blasting up the road and looking for the right spot.

The road narrowed as it turned into a canyon and climbed into some short hills to the north. A storm was brewing far up the canyon and the wind pushed the car from side to side in the stronger gusts. The dust blew away and I saw the Camry nearly a half-mile behind. It was time to find a good location that would increase my odds.

Avocado trees filled almost every available acre of hillside as I entered the canyon and the branches swayed in the strong wind. I found the spot I wanted and pulled off onto the gravel shoulder beyond the second turn in the road. I grabbed my Beretta, the soda bottle, and the duct tape and ran up the hill into the orchard. The lower part of the hill had been cleared some time ago of older trees and replanted with younger stock. These trees were about five feet tall and bushy. They offered fairly good cover. Sixty yards farther up the hill were older trees, spaced farther apart and with more clear space between them. I picked my spot just beyond the patch of young trees and sat down. The mouth of the soda bottle was a tight fit over the barrel of the pistol but that was a good thing. The duct tape sealed the bottle to the pistol's barrel. It would be a crude silencer that wouldn't last past the first shot but I only needed one to even the odds.

The Toyota stopped behind the Rover and idled for a few moments. An Asian fellow who didn't look old enough to drive got out of the passenger's side of the Camry and walked up to the Rover. He wore black pants and a white T-shirt. *That white shirt makes a fairly decent target*, I thought. I was glad to be wearing my khaki Navy service uniform.

The scout signaled back to the car when he realized my car was empty and pulled a balisong out of his pocket. He flipped the handles a few times the way I'd seen it done in the Philippines half a career ago and walked around the Rover with the butterfly knife's blade exposed. He spotted my boot tracks going into the orchard and yelled something back to the car in a language I didn't recognize. Two more young Asians, similarly dressed, got out of the car. I hadn't planned on fighting three of them and suddenly felt under-gunned.

The driver pulled out a small automatic pistol and walked down the road to a point about thirty yards south of my position while the guy with the knife walked up the road about thirty yards to the north. The third guy stayed by the car and cradled a fully-automatic Ingraham MAC-10 in his right hand. Their plan was clear. Knife me quietly if the first guy could, shoot me if he couldn't, indiscriminately fill me full of holes if I tried to get back to the Rover.

The first two moved up the hill in their modified pincer movement. I remembered reading in *The Art of War* how Sun Tzu had strongly advised against this maneuver as the enemy would fight all the harder instead of surrendering. Surrender was obviously not an option.

Wind blew down the canyon in strong gusts and the sound through the trees masked any noise the men made in their advance. I moved my position north toward where I thought the guy with the knife would be and, after a short time, heard him moving through the short trees. Sighting a pistol with a Pepsi bottle hanging off the front is a chancy affair but I had little choice. Where there are no alternatives, there are no problems.

The blade man's head appeared through the trees about fifteen feet down the hill from me and I pulled the trigger. He spotted me at the same time but my bullet caught him under his nose and dropped him before he could make a sound. I scrambled over to the body, took the knife from his hand, folded it, and put it in my pocket. Never leave a weapon on the battlefield. Even on a dead soldier.

My make-shift silencer had done a fair job of muffling the pistol's report but it was strictly a one-shot affair as the expanding gasses from that single shot shattered the bottle. And it did nothing to mask the sound of the action ejecting the spent shell and racking in another round. I tore the duct tape and plastic off the gun and moved south to intercept the second man.

He must have heard the sound and yelled something that sounded like a question intended for his deceased partner. He spoke louder when the question went unanswered and then yelled down to the guy by the car.

The conversation between them allowed me to pinpoint the second man's location and to close on him in the cover of the young avocados and bushes. He was working his way north so I moved down the hill behind some lower bushes, circled around behind him, and shot him twice in the back. I took his pistol and put it in my other pocket. That left me with twelve rounds in my Beretta, an unknown quantity in my newly acquired pistol, and a knife. The guy down by the car with the MAC had thirty-two rounds, though, and he could fire them all in less than two seconds.

The guy with the MAC heard the two shots I'd fired and called out several times. I found a gully south of the Camry that was choked with brush and slowly worked my way down the hill toward the road using the brush as cover. A cell phone rang north of me and I realized the third guy was trying to call his partner who had been, until recently, very good with a fancy folding knife. Moments later, a second cell phone rang where I'd dropped the second guy.

The brush ran out about twenty yards from the Camry and that was as close as I could get to the third man undetected. He paced around the car punching buttons on his cell phone. Somebody picked up on the other end and my guy stopped pacing and stood next to the rear door on the driver's side. He held the MAC in his right hand, the cell phone in his left, and carried on an excited conversation with someone while peering over the top of the car up the hill.

Twenty yards is actually quite a distance with a weapon that has a short sight radius like the Beretta. I went down on my right knee, braced my elbow on my left, and, with a two-hand grasp, centered the front sight in the notch of the rear sight with the tops of both sights level. I focused on the front sight and watched the man in the background while centering the top of the front sight on the man's head. It was a long shot and I wasn't comfortable with it but it was the best chance I would get. I took a deep breath, let out half of it, and steadily increased pressure on the trigger until the pistol fired. I pulled the trigger five more times in rapid succession worrying less about accuracy and more about getting some lead in the air.

I dropped to the ground as the man with the MAC pulled the trigger and held it. The sound of gunfire and shattering glass filled the trees and bounced off the walls of the canyon for what seemed like whole minutes.

I looked for the third man after the noise died down but couldn't see him. I didn't know if I'd hit him or if he was busy slipping another magazine into the MAC. I waited for him to pop up from behind with another thirty-two round salvo but it didn't come.

After a half-minute of silence, I moved south from behind the brush and saw the MAC-10 lying on the road behind the car's left rear tire. I walked down the hill with a pistol in each hand to find that one of my shots, probably the first, had entered the man's skull about two inches up from his left eye. He'd probably fired the MAC as a purely reflexive action. Two other shots had entered the car's back window, exited the driver's side rear window, and landed in the man's chest. There was no trace of my other three shots. If I ever get a chance to choose between my own skill and pure luck, I'll choose luck every time.

A light rain began to fall as I dragged the third man's body into the brush. The adrenaline in my system rendered him weightless. I didn't want his MAC-10 so I kicked it over to a spot near the third man. A spot where the cops were likely to find it.

Dad had been a scoutmaster and he'd taught us all to "leave no trace." That mantra seemed doubly important at a crime scene so I hiked back up into the trees and found what was left of the plastic soda bottle and the duct tape. I also hunted down the nine empty brass casings ejected from the Beretta and put them in my pocket.

The third man's cell phone lay on the ground near the car and I picked it up. Whoever had listened to all that loud gunfire had hung up. I put the phone in my pocket, got back into the Rover, and headed down the canyon shivering from the cold, the wind, the wet, and the realization that I'd just killed three men.

56

MY eyes spent a lot of time in the rear-view mirror as I drove back toward the house in the Keys. Along the way, I pulled into a stall at one of those self-serve car washes that gobbles up quarters and spits out high-pressure soap and water. I washed off all the dirt and dust and other detritus that the Rover could have picked up during my off-roading among the avocados. No sense in leaving any evidence on a vehicle.

All the time I moved about the car with the washing wand, I thought about Hargrave's warning about the fifty things a guy must do or cover up or eliminate to get away with murder.

Murder. Why was I thinking of it as murder? This was self-defense pure and simple. But I didn't feel pure and it wasn't simple. Far from it. There was an old steel drum by the stall I was using where people tossed their fast-food wrappers and foam coffee cups. I threw up in it. It wasn't the first time I'd had to kill somebody but each time before had been in the line of duty and witnesses had been there to corroborate my story. This time I'd hidden among bushes and trees and waited for men to walk into my line of fire.

The little voice inside piped up as I pulled the Rover into the driveway and parked next to the Jaguar. It was telling me that there was something I hadn't done; something I'd overlooked; something important. The house was empty when I walked in and nothing appeared to be unusual or out of place. I called for Al but he wasn't around. The four green empties he'd left on the counter the previous night stood where he'd left them as monuments to his greatness. I went into the room I was using and saw the two brass keys I'd left on the dresser. The little voice whispered to me that Barry had arranged things—"set it all up", in his words—for Suzanne "at our place in Ventura." I suddenly realized where that last missing piece of the puzzle had to be.

The Skipjack started easily and I cast off the dock lines and motored out toward the harbor mouth. The shadows lengthened across the water and I figured there was only another forty minutes of sunlight left in the day. I didn't know exactly where to look but figured it had to be close to *Rum Runner*. I motored into the south arm of the harbor and into the private boat slips.

Our Place sat alone in one of the larger slips next to a huge schooner that occupied a full end tie. I moved the Skipjack into an open slip at the far end of the dock, found a pair of binoculars in the cabin, and sat back down in the swiveling captain's chair. I looked around casually to see if anybody was watching Barry's better boat then carefully glassed the area with the binoculars. The only people paying any attention at all were an older couple admiring the big schooner from the south side of the harbor near the restaurants. I could almost hear the man telling his wife that it would be the perfect boat for them. Good luck with that one, buddy.

Nobody seemed to be paying any attention to Barry's second boat so I put away the binoculars, fished a flashlight out of the Skipjack's cabin, and walked along the dock to *Our Place* in the dark. She was a sweet forty-footer made for blue-water sailing; perfect for a long cruise. The boat looked like nobody had been aboard in weeks. Local birds had claimed the vessel as their own and had taken up residence topside. I stepped aboard and found that the second brass key, the one that was supposed to be sent to Suzanne, opened the padlock that secured the companionway hatch. Jackpot! I removed the hatch boards, placed them on the cockpit sole, and stepped below. It was dark and musty smelling;

the odor of a boat sitting idle for too many days. I didn't feel comfortable turning on the lights below so I made my examination with the flashlight.

The ship's docs were underneath the hinged chart table and they indicated that *Our Place* was Coast Guard documented and that Barry St. James was the legal owner. That explained why the state DMV reported nothing. I kicked myself for not thinking to check the federal registry.

I started my search at the bow and worked my way aft without knowing what I was looking for. The boat was well-equipped; Barry hadn't scrimped on gear. There was a ham radio, a sophisticated electronics package, radar, good ground tackle, and charts for the entire Sea of Cortez in Mexico. The usual storage places under the berths and the settees were full of canned goods and bags of rice and flour. The boat was ready for a long trip to Mexico or beyond.

I found a duffel bag under the port settee. Another small padlock tied the zipper to a chrome D-ring. The same brass key opened it. I saw the contents, quickly zipped it shut, and wasted no time looking for anything else.

The trip back to Don's house was uneventful but I took the precaution of motoring down the second entrance to the Keys and waiting at another home's dock for a few minutes to make sure I hadn't been followed. When I got back to Don's place, Al trotted down to the dock and tied off the Skipjack.

"Steve Holdsworth is our guy," I said. "He had St. James killed. Dustin and Erica, too. I'm sure of it."

I grabbed the duffel bag and brought Al up-to-date on my visits with Hargrave and Holdsworth as we walked back up to the house. I laid the duffel on the dining table, opened the padlock, and peeled back the zipper while Al watched. His jaw dropped when I pulled out the contents.

"What the hell?" he said.

He thumbed through the thick stacks of hundred dollar bills.

"Whose is this?" he asked.

"That was Barry St. James' nest egg," I said. "He was planning to take it all to Mexico in his boat."

He counted the money and let out a low whistle.

"I think it's my turn to go out to the garage and get the beers," he said as he got up.

Farther down in the bag were three manila file folders. The first folder I opened held several legal documents including a six-figure insurance policy listing Suzanne St. James as beneficiary. Still the nicest guy. The second folder was pure law enforcement pay dirt. Dates, times, distribution schedules, contact names; the whole enchilada from ICE's point of view. I picked up my phone and called Frank Bartholomew.

"I have a little gift for you," I said.

"I didn't know you felt that way about me, Greene."

"Funny," I said. "You'll like this gift a lot. What do you say you buy me breakfast in the morning and I can give it to you personally?"

"No can do, Mr. Greene. I am in Phoenix right now and I have a meeting in the morning. Can it wait a couple of days?"

I spent a few minutes reading him the contents of folder number two. I could hear his heart rate increase over the phone.

"What would you like for breakfast?" he said.

He told me where to meet him and we hung up. Al came back in with the beers and some tall glasses and we popped the tops off the green bottles.

"So what do we do with all this beautiful money, Sim?"

"I killed three people today."

Al looked like I'd claimed to be the Queen of Sheba. I told him what happened at Holdsworth's office and how I'd seen Terrell Jenkins in the parking structure. I told him about the tail, the dirt road into the avocados, and the three young men who died at my hand. Al's look changed to one of sincere appreciation. He tried to high-five me.

"You don't get it, Al. I feel sick and filthy and I want out of this whole business. People I know are dying and people I don't know are forcing me to kill them."

"What are you talking about?" he said. "Three baddies tried to kill you and you took 'em out. You helped rid the planet of some worthless crapcans. You did the world a favor, Sim."

"I'm not up to it."

I drank some of my beer and thought about it. It wouldn't be as easy for me as it was for Al. It would take a lot more thinking and a lot more time. But the beer helped.

"So what do we do with the money, Sim?"

"There is this thing called 'the law,' Al. And it's a little more complex than 'finders, keepers.'"

"You want to give it back to Barry?" he asked. "He's dead. Or maybe you think Holdsworth would be so glad to get it back that he won't send three more guys out to kill you."

For once, Al's 'spoils of war' attitude made some sense.

"Well," I said. "We should, at least, give the counterfeit stuff to our friendly feds."

"Counterfeit? What are you talking about?"

"I only checked the top bill in each stack but about two-thirds of those bills are fake. The red and blue threads are printed on instead of woven into the paper. The watermark is good and the details in the portraits are distinct. It's good quality stuff but most of those bills didn't come from the U.S. Treasury."

Al weighed the new information for a moment.

"Well, I say we keep the good stuff," said Al.

Al thumbed through some of the bills again and I opened the last file folder. Moments later I knew exactly why Captain Overson wanted his own private little investigation run by a friendly, discreet, and tame Chief Petty Officer who reported only to him.

57

FRANK had picked a nice restaurant that catered to businessmen who felt compelled to wear a suit and tie to breakfast. He fit right in. I was in shorts and a T-shirt. He wasted no time.

"Let's see it," he said.

I handed him the folder and he opened it. He read every page carefully and slowly. The waitress brought Frank's omelet and my eggs Benedict and I started to chow down. Frank sipped his coffee but otherwise ignored his meal.

"Where did you get this?" he asked.

"Does it matter?" I said.

"So it really is going down tomorrow as Barry said it would."

He leafed through the pages again.

"There's nothing here that indicates any kind of terrorist action," he said. "Just smuggling."

"Sorry to disappoint you," I said.

He smiled.

"No disappointments here, buddy. But with this little notice I'll have to give my boss some good reasons to pursue a last-minute operation. You know how it is," he said. "Can you give me some hard context for this information?"

"Barry St. James gave it to me. Posthumously."

He smiled again and waited.

"Barry's last assignment in the Navy was on the USS *Enterprise* as a Naval Aviation Supply Officer," I said. "A logistics guy. He made some close friends on the Big E. One was a guy named Steve Holdsworth."

"Alan Holdsworth's kid?" asked Frank.

I nodded.

"Daddy was on the Armed Services Committee so his kid—they called him 'the Senator'—got all kinds of special treatment from the brass. He got away with a lot of crap."

"Where are we going with this?" asked Frank.

"Holdsworth and St. James decided they wanted to bring home a little more than the Navy rate so they bought up precious stones on the cheap in Asian ports," I said. "Holdsworth was the money guy and St. James was the logistics guy. He had a handle on the Navy's shipping and receiving operations so he was in charge of getting the stones into the states where they could be sold at a profit. No customs documents, no import duties, and no shipping costs add up to much bigger profits. They got caught red-handed but the Navy didn't want to make any noise about a Senator's son so both of them quietly retired with honorable discharges."

Frank ate a bite of his omelet.

"Fast forward a few years and Holdsworth is now running a big company funded by daddy's money combined with a fat chunk of grants from daddy's former government buddies," I said. "But business isn't doing all that well in this economy so he renews some old connections in Asia. His old friend Barry comes on board to help with the logistics."

"Keep going," said Frank.

He ate some more of his omelet.

"They started small and your guys caught him early on with some of the little stuff," I said. "He gave you some minor victories along the way, counterfeit software and DVD's and such, while helping his buddy Steve get the bigger shipments past you. Some time ago, they started bringing in a highly profitable product from Korea."

I plopped the blue duffel bag onto his side of the booth and he put down his fork. He unzipped the bag, saw the stacks of hundreds, and let out a low whistle.

"Counterfeit bills," I said.

"North Korea is the leading supplier of fake C-notes worldwide," said Frank. "And they are good at the trade."

He pawed through the bills, pulled a few out, and examined them under the light.

"High quality stuff," he said. "Some think they got into counterfeiting as part of a nefarious plan to destroy confidence in the United States' dollar. I think they just need the money to buy rice."

Frank finished his breakfast and picked the folder back up to examine it a third time.

"Barry skimmed those bills off the top before it got to Holdsworth," I said.

"Honor among thieves and all that," said Frank.

"The earlier shipments were small. Proof of concept stuff. Testing and refining the system. That folder shows what's coming in tonight. And it gives you the distribution channel, every destination city, and every guy who's in charge of their downline."

"That son-of-a-gun played us pretty well, didn't he?" said Frank. "He took our money and gave us bits and pieces in return. All the time he was putting away his own little stash."

"Until his buddy Steve found out and had him killed."

"How do you know it's Holdsworth that's behind all this? There's nothing in this folder that implicates him."

I fingered the cell phone in my pocket. The one I'd picked up off a dirt road in a canyon full of avocados. It would most likely lead to Holdsworth. But I wasn't comfortable enough with Frank to give it to him. Instead, I pointed at one of the sheets in the file.

"That's a list of commercial divers who work out of Channel Islands Harbor," I said. "They supposedly dive for sea urchins but that is only a cover. There is a set of GPS coordinates next to each name. Plot those on a chart and you'll find that most of those are on a straight line a mile or so apart on the southern edge of the shipping channel off Santa Cruz Island. A big ship, probably a container vessel from South Korea or maybe a car hauler, enters the channel and sets up a course on that drop line. Somebody tips a weighted box over the side as they pass over the assigned spot and a diver moves in later to snatch it up."

Frank gave me a look of mild incredulity.

"The water is pretty deep there, isn't it?" he asked.

"Yeah, it's deep there but all the guys on that list are using mixed-gas rigs that can take them down to two or three hundred feet. They don't need that kind of advanced gear to pick urchins. They go out to sea in the early morning and come back in the early afternoon with just enough urchins to cover the weighted box."

"Barry knew all this and was holding out on me," said Frank.

"He was planning his retirement," I said. "Skimming off some cash and stashing it away while planning to give you the info on the big drop right before it happened. Then he'd sail away and disappear before the bullets started flying. Holdsworth and his guys would be in jail and you wouldn't be all that eager to grab good old Barry. He'd be anchored outside La Paz before anybody even started looking for him. That was before he was diagnosed with cancer."

Frank's eyes widened a little.

"Cancer?" he said. "I had no idea. He didn't seem to be in any pain."

"Quite the opposite, actually. His form of cancer killed a lot of his nerve response. Holdsworth's men tried to torture him, probably to get that folder. But his cancer prevented that."

"You keep talking about Holdsworth as the ring leader but I still don't see anything in here that implicates him," said Frank.

"Sorry," I said. "I always save the best until last."

I handed him another folder containing printouts of the accounting information Reid had given me.

"A subsidiary of a company named Solavon buys the urchins," I said. "It's Solavon's most profitable subsidiary by far. But I checked the market price of sea urchins and they would need to process a thousand times as many as they do to make that kind of money. The urchin division doesn't just carry out the smuggling operation; they also launder the cash."

Frank looked through the folder. His eyebrows raised when he saw the CD's.

"Those three CD's contain the raw accounting data for Solavon," I said. "You'll see every transaction. That little collection of data is the last nail in the coffin for Holdsworth."

Frank fingered the CD's and chewed on his lower lip.

"Holdsworth knows that I know about him," I said. "But I don't think he knows we have these folders."

"Then it's time for you to slip out of town, Greene."

"The cops are watching me," I said. "They think I killed Barry St. James and a few other people. Any chance you can call them off? Give me some room to hide?"

Frank shook his head.

"Nope," he said. "I can't tell anybody local about this until after it all goes down. If Holdsworth is who you say he is, then he's probably got a pet cop on his payroll. I'm not going to risk cluing him in so you are on your own for a while."

"Wonderful."

Frank paid the bill and left a hefty tip.

"Your tax dollars at work," he said.

We walked out into the parking lot toward our cars. The sun was already starting to give the asphalt some heat.

"Sneak out of town for a day or two," he said. "I'll call you with the 'all clear' after we finish grabbing everybody. Probably sometime tomorrow."

Frank stopped when he reached the door of his black car and smiled at me.

"You're pretty cagey, Greene. You slip and slide over and around things and hang onto good information for an awfully long time but when you finally put it together, it all makes sense and has real value. It would be great if a guy like you could fit in with us feds."

"But?" I said.

"You're not a team player. You're too much of an individual."

I smiled.

"Thanks," I said.

58

I got back into Don's Range Rover and tried to dial Ashley's cell phone without swerving too much. She answered on the first ring.

"What is with the weird message, Sim?"

"Look, I'm sorry about how things appeared last Sunday but there's a reason that girl went sailing with Al and me. We were trying to protect her."

Ashley was silent.

"So that is why you got the strange voice mail," I said. "This murder investigation has turned into a big bag of snakes and people are getting bit right and left. You were there when I found Barry St. James and you are close to me."

"Not so much the latter," she said.

"We'll work that out later, Ashley. Right now, you're at risk and I'm worried about you getting hurt. Al and I are going to disappear for a while and I'm recommending you do the same."

"Disappearing with that blonde, are you?" she asked.

"She's dead, Ashley. Erica is dead," I said.

I heard a sudden intake of breath.

"The bad guys got to her and they killed her. I can't tell you why all this is happening but you could be in serious danger. You need to get out of town right now."

"I'm at work," she said.

"I don't care. Walk out of there right this minute. Don't grab a briefcase or a laptop or anything. Leave now. Ask the security guard to escort you to your car. Then drive to your folks' house or pick up a girlfriend and take a road trip up the coast. Check out the wineries in Paso Robles or the Monterey Bay Aquarium or fly to New York and go shopping or something. Just go somewhere, anywhere, and lie low until I call you. Please."

There was a pause on the other side as the message sank in.

"I can't just walk out of here, Sim. I have work to do and a boss who depends on me."

"Tell him you're sick," I said. "Your co-workers probably tell that lie every time they want a day off."

There was another long pause.

"I can't protect you, Ashley. They're coming after me," I said. "I don't want them to get you."

"All right," she said. "I'm leaving. Call me tonight, okay? We need to talk."

We said our goodbyes and I dialed Reid's number.

"What's happening, Sim?"

I could hear electronic chimes and bells in the background.

"Where are you?"

"Las Vegas. Monica called and told me some stuff was going down and that I should disappear. So I have."

"Good idea. I'll let you know when things clear up."

"Don't hurry. I'm twenty thousand up and having a ball."

59

THE Skipjack started with an animalistic growl. I cast off the dock lines and we motored away from the house toward the fuel dock. We had quickly-packed duffels, empty gas jugs we'd found in the garage, and a few plastic bags of groceries we'd gathered out of the kitchen.

"How long do we need to lie low, Sim?"

"Couple of days at the most," I said.

"I don't like this," said Al. "I feel like I'm on the sidelines, like a college linebacker that grew up to be the defensive coordinator. I'd rather be in the thick of it. I'd rather be on the field."

"Well, Coach, I was out on that field yesterday and it was littered with land mines."

We arrived at the fuel dock as one of the smaller dive boats headed out for a night trip with a dozen recreational divers. It looked like a fun way to make a living and I thought about Al's offer. Still, I thought, it wasn't yet the time to buy green bananas.

Al hopped off the boat after we tied up.

"I need to get a few things," he said. "Be back in short order."

He jogged up the dock as I filled up the Skipjack's tank and the plastic fuel jugs. I paid the dock attendant with some of Barry's cash. Al came back with two white plastic grocery bags hanging from one hand and a six-pack of Coronas in the other.

"Provisions for the ride over," he said.

He started the boat and motored toward the harbor mouth. I opened one of the bags to find foam containers filled with fried fish and chips. That and the beer made the trip a lot better.

The swells weren't large that late afternoon, but we were going against them and the boat couldn't comfortably make over twenty knots. I grabbed the binoculars and glassed the other boats in the channel.

There were some private sport fishers, a few sailboats, a container ship, and a Coast Guard cutter. No urchin divers. All the vessels I spotted were headed in toward shore. The dive boat we'd seen in the harbor was out of sight, probably already on the backside of Anacapa.

There was nothing unusual in the channel. No signs of international smuggling operations taking place or of federal law enforcement efforts to bust them. Nothing of note. Just another pleasant day in the blue Pacific.

It took us an hour and a half to reach Lady's and I was anxious to see how *Figaro* had fared over the last three days. One other vessel occupied the anchorage, a very well-kept forty-footer with an older couple aboard that came topside to watch us moor the Skipjack to *Figaro's* starboard rail.

My boat had fared well and that set my heart at ease. A lot of bad things can happen in a few days. Seeing her lying where I'd left her in the condition I'd left her was a great relief.

We dug *Figaro's* dock fenders out of her lazarette and placed them between the Skipjack and *Figaro's* toerail to keep chafe and wear to a minimum. It wasn't the optimum solution but it was the best available under the circumstances.

The wind picked up about an hour before sunset and the seas outside Lady's grew taller. The swells rolled into the anchorage more heavily, rocking *Figaro* and the Skipjack from side to side. I checked the mooring lines and fenders several times but no harm was being done to either vessel. I started the diesel engine and ran it to top up her batteries and cool the little refrigerator. There is no point in having warm beer if you can avoid it.

I placed a call to Ashley to see if she was following my advice but there was no answer. I left a perfunctory message and tried to quit worrying. I failed. I wanted to know she was safe and away from Ventura County.

The sun slipped behind the rock wall to the west and the shadow cast by the top of the ridge crept steadily up the opposite wall. The male half of the couple next door came out and slapped some steak on the barbecue that hung from his boat's pushpit. Having eaten well on the way over, Al and I decided against dinner. Instead, we celebrated my having been cleared of suspicion with cold beers and lime wedges.

"You're tired of the Navy, aren't you?" said Al.

"Yeah, but...."

"But nothing," he said. "You want out."

"Sure I want out but I'm stuck," I said. "I don't have a college degree and I don't think a civilian police force would even consider hiring me now that I am a 'person of interest' in several homicides. Even if they ultimately pin them on Holdsworth and his goons, I'm still tainted."

Al finished his beer, set down one of my cockpit cushions as a pillow, and lay out under the darkening sky.

"Come to the British Virgin Islands with me and we'll open up that dive shop I keep talking about," he said. "The water is warm and the people are friendly. American tourists pay big bucks to dive among the wrecks and reefs and to hear about all that pirate history."

"I still don't have much money to put in."

"By my count," said Al, "we've racked up a fairly nice nest egg what with the dough we got from Terrell and the money you found on Barry's boat. Combine that with our monthly retirement checks and what I get from selling my boat and we might have enough to make it happen."

The sun set and the wind slacked off. I drank some of my beer. Al wasn't going to understand this.

"And there's Ashley," I said.

Al cocked his head a little.

"What?" he asked.

"Ashley."

"You're kidding me, right?" he said.

I shook my head. Al was quiet for a minute.

"So you're seriously thinking of taking a berth ashore?" he asked. "I was hoping you might be over that."

"I want to give it a shot, Al. I mean, Ashley's sharp and we get along well. She likes to sail and I like being around her. I don't really know if I can do it, but maybe marriage deserves another try."

He gave me a look of absolute disgust and shook his head again.

"Be sure to have your wedding ring put in your nose, Sim."

I finished my beer and stood up to go below.

"You want another?" I asked.

"No," he said. "Could you toss me a blanket, though? I'll sleep up here. Nice breeze tonight."

I dug a gray wool blanket out of the forward vee-berth and tossed it up to him. I stayed below and tidied up some things in the cabin while waiting for Ashley's call.

I came back up on deck about ten o'clock. Al was stretched out in the cockpit and snoring. Our neighbors in the small anchorage could have easily mistaken it for the sound of an annoyed bull elephant seal. I walked forward, sat on the cabin roof, and looked out to sea. The wind was still and the swells outside the anchorage had flattened. Myriad stars illuminated the firmament and the lights of Santa Barbara glowed from across the channel twenty miles to the north.

A large container ship appeared from behind the rocky outcropping that protected the anchorage. The ship was five miles away or more in the southernmost shipping lane. It disappeared to the west behind the cliff walls about fifteen minutes later. Another took its place twenty minutes after that. An endless stream of maritime commerce bound for the massive shipping facilities at Los Angeles/Long Beach or, to a much smaller extent, the wharves at Port Hueneme. The crew on one of those vessels was tossing sealed metal boxes into the sea at specific locations. With any luck, the feds would catch them in the act.

I checked my watch and realized that it was too late to call Ashley again. I tried anyway. No answer. I left a message, went below, dug out my book, and crawled into my berth to read while hoping she'd call me back before I fell asleep.

Thomas Hudson was now working hard at sea with volunteer undercover sailors hunting German submarines from a specially-equipped sport fishing boat. Their quarry was the crew from an abandoned German U-boat trying to escape detection and leaving a trail of carnage along the way. Innocent islanders were murdered and good men killed by Nazis trying to cover their escape. Hemingway's writing was beautiful, of course, but at some point, I couldn't handle another word of senseless death and had to close the book before drifting off to sleep.

I woke to the sound of footsteps coming down the companionway.

"You want to go spearfishing?" asked Al.

"What time is it?"

"An hour before sunrise," he said.

"I think I've only slept a few hours, Al. Count me out."

He muttered something about lazy kids and clomped around on the deck for a few minutes getting his things together. I heard the Skipjack's engine start and felt the slight shove against *Figaro* as Al motored away. Sleep reclaimed me.

Much later, the sun poured down the companionway and into my berth. I looked at my watch and decided that 9:40 in the morning was a fine time to wake up. I grabbed a bowl of cereal and turned on the weather radio to listen to the forecast. The mechanized voice of NOAA reported no gale warnings or small craft advisories. No hurricanes or tsunamis were on the horizon. All was well in the Santa Barbara Channel and the surrounding waters.

The water outside Lady's was fairly flat and I needed a long swim; I needed to think. I put on my wetsuit, dove off the bow, and swam outside the anchorage. Once beyond the rocks, I headed west to Arch Rock. I thought about Ashley, my career in the Navy, and Al's offer to blow it all off and try something new in the warm waters of the Caribbean. Warm water sounded good.

I was back at *Figaro's* swim step well before noon with no real conclusions but with the realization that I missed Ashley. She'd said she wanted something permanent and I was finally ready to talk with her about it. And, maybe, settle for a berth ashore.

Living on a boat isn't entirely fun and games. Any man-made thing left in or near the ocean will, ultimately, decay and corrode. A lot of maintenance accompanies the apparent freedom of a life at sea. I dug out some tools and set to some of the small maintenance issues that periodically plague sailboats in general and *Figaro* specifically.

It was almost two in the afternoon when Al returned from his spearfishing excursion. He tied the Skipjack to *Figaro's* starboard side and stepped over the gunwale with a large plastic shopping bag.

"You now spear fish in grocery bags?" I asked.

"I got skunked," he said. "So I blasted over to Santa Barbara and got some ribs."

"With the price of fuel, those must be the most expensive ribs ever eaten."

He held up a plastic charge card and smiled.

"Don's," he said.

We went below, ate ribs, and drank beer. It wasn't quite a Roman food orgy but it wasn't far from it, either. My burner phone rang about a quarter to three. I recognized the number.

"How did you do, Frank?"

"A noteworthy bust, my friend. Very noteworthy," he said. "You'll read about it in the papers. The Secret Service tells me this was their biggest haul of counterfeit bills ever. By a wide margin. Good quality North Korean stuff, too. They send their regards and kindest wishes."

"That's wonderful," I said. "Does this mean Hargrave will stop harassing me for killing innocent local citizens?"

"We are in the process of providing substantial amounts of evidence to Detective Hargrave and he has been taking notice. You can expect some relief there."

"Can you give me any details on the haul?" I asked. "One cop to another?"

"The info you gave us allowed us to get a rather broad GPS tracking warrant. We planted transponders on the urchin boats and watched them go to the locations you pointed out. We picked up six divers with the goods in hand and two more guys from the container ship."

"Are they talking?"

"The divers are all keeping mum," he said. "They think they're tough guys. They ask for lawyers and keep their mouths shut as if their boss will swoop down and rescue them. The guys on the ship will break, though. With any luck, we'll get some info on the outfit printing the stuff."

"What about the local boss?" I asked. "Did you get Holdsworth?"

"We went after him a little late in the game, it seems. He and his right-hand man left the country last night. But we'll find them. We're pretty good at that sort of thing."

He paused a moment.

"We discovered a few things on our own, too," he said. "Terrell Jenkins is actually 'Tony Jameson.'"

"Is that supposed to mean something to me?"

"Probably not," said Frank. "Tony Jameson is a shooter from Chicago. A pro. A very dangerous guy. We think he might have been out here on assignment from a crime syndicate to either watch Holdsworth and their investments or to protect him."

"But they're shut down?" I asked. "It's all safe, right?"

"That is a big 'affirmative,' Mr. Greene. We still have a couple of guys we need to track down but they'll be in the bag before nightfall. And we have federal agents all over that Solavon building right now. They'll be seizing hard drives and boxing evidence for weeks."

I congratulated him and hung up the phone.

"The unfriendlies are neutralized, Al. We're good to go," I said. "And we can stop using these burners."

"You want to bring your boat in tonight?" asked Al.

"I'd rather take Ashley to dinner. You mind bringing me out here tomorrow morning?"

"No," said Al. "I need to get out here to spear some fish anyway. I can't stand getting skunked."

We quickly cleaned up *Figaro* and made her ready for another night alone at anchor. I grabbed my phone and tried to call Ashley. She didn't pick up so I left a message at the beep.

"Ash, the drama is over and the coast is clear. You can come back home." I said. "Why don't you meet me for dinner at Milano's? I have some serious apologizing to do."

60

ASHLEY'S ring tone sang from Don's front room around a quarter to five and I nearly tore a ligament getting from the patio to my phone.

"Dinner sounds great," she said.

"Are you too far away?" I asked. "I don't want you to break any laws getting back here."

"I'm about to leave work. I can be at Milano's in twenty minutes."

"You didn't leave?" I asked. "I thought you were going to call in sick and disappear for a while."

"Well, I thought about it but they have excellent security here," she said. "I'm probably safer at work than at my folks' house. And you never told me exactly why I needed to 'disappear' from work in the first place."

I was quiet.

"C'mon, Sim. You're such a worrywart," she said. "Anyway, the sky must not be falling anymore if we're meeting at Milano's."

I felt like swearing at her or yelling at her but part of being a man, as my father once told me, is not always reacting to a woman in a way completely consistent with how you feel.

"Okay, I'll see you in twenty," I said. "I'll be at a table overlooking the harbor."

"All the tables overlook the harbor," she said.

"And I'll be at one looking for you."

We hung up and I went out to the Skipjack, fired it up, and motored over to the southern arm of the harbor where Barry kept his two boats. I found a guest slip in front of Milano's and walked in to get seated. It was early and I was able to grab a table for two on the sundeck close to the water. We'd split a salad and an order of seafood pasta. We'd have some wine at sunset and then take the boat over to Don's house and his hot tub on the patio. It would be a good place to discuss future plans. Plans I could try to commit to.

The waitress came and smiled at me and asked what I would like to drink and if I would care for any appetizers. I ordered their artichoke Bruschetta and two of the lemon-flavored mineral waters. I assured her that my dinner companion would be arriving any minute. The waitress smiled again and left me alone with my view of the harbor.

Ashley's ring tone sang out again and I got the sinking feeling that she was calling to apologize for being late, to tell me that her boss had a special project to discuss with her, and to suggest that we have dinner at Milano's another night.

"Hello, Mr. Greene," said the man whose real name was Tony.

I felt a stiffness in my spine and a shortness of breath.

"Who is this?" I said.

"I'm surprised you have to ask, Mr. Greene."

I listened carefully to the background noise. Tony was in a car but I couldn't tell where he was or if he was alone.

"What do you want?" I asked.

"I'd like to reunite you with your girlfriend. And I'd like to regain possession of some company property; some backup files that our former accountant copied before his recent passing. Three little compact discs."

"Sure," I said. "Bring her by and I'll give 'em to you. But how do I know you have my girlfriend?"

"Well, she's not very talkative at the moment. She's a little sleepy, in fact, but you might recognize her voice."

I heard him talking to someone from a distance. Ashley made a few noises and said some disjointed things but I recognized her voice. It was definitely her.

"Did you get that, Greene?"

I wanted to crawl through the phone and strangle him.

"Fine," I said. "Bring her by."

"No, it just isn't that simple anymore. There are folks in uniform looking for me right now. Feds and locals, as I understand it. So I need to find the right place for us to meet and I need to set this thing up properly so I'm not in any danger. I'm sure you understand, right?"

"Whatever you say, Tony. Just don't hurt her," I said.

"Hurt her?" he said. "I wouldn't think of it. She's on a little trip right now. Having the time of her life, from what it sounds like."

I wanted to tell him what a worthless human being he was, tell him that his life was over, tell him that I was going to kill him slowly and painfully. The usual emotion- and anger-induced threats. But the smart part of me knew that wouldn't help.

"I'll call you in the morning, Greene. Sleep tight," he said. "But don't even think of calling the police, okay? That would ensure that your girlfriend's little trip would end rather badly."

I said nothing.

"And don't lose those discs, okay?" he said.

He hung up the phone.

The waitress came with the bruschetta and the drinks I'd ordered. She said something that I didn't hear and I smiled back at her and nodded. I stood up, put a twenty on the table, and walked back to the Skipjack.

61

I woke up early, made some coffee, and took it out to the patio to watch the first rays of sun touch the tops of the taller masts in the harbor. I was filled with a bucket of nervous and didn't feel like eating a thing.

Al had told me the previous night to call Bartholomew. I knew he would say that. It was the same advice I would have given him had the tables been turned in that direction. It was precisely the same advice that he'd ignore, too. Exactly as I had.

A few early-rising sailors motored their boats out of the harbor. Getting an early start to the islands before the best anchorages filled for the Labor Day weekend. They'd be back Monday evening after two nights at the islands with sea stories to tell their co-workers next week over lunch. Weekend warriors.

I sat on the bench and drank my coffee. It was almost identical to the bench I'd sat Dustin on after beating him up. The same bench Erica had sat on while talking to the police hours after he'd been killed. The same bench Judith Norton used to prop her foot on while tightening the laces of her running shoes.

Two people, maybe three, who shouldn't have died so young. I thought about Ashley and realized that she had probably already met the same fate. I thought about how it could have been different; how none of it would have happened if Reid's co-ed mistress *du jour* hadn't dropped her sunglasses overboard. Or if I hadn't felt the need to show off and dive for them. I'd thought I was smart, but I'd screwed everything up and cost people their lives in the process.

More boats left the harbor as I waited for a phone call from the kidnappers. Al walked out onto the patio with his own mug of coffee.

"They are setting a trap for you right now," said Al. "They'll bring you in, get what they want, and kill both of you. That assumes, of course, that she is still alive."

"I know."

"It's not your fault," he said.

"A bunch of people who should be alive are dead," I said. "I can't help but think that I put them in danger."

"'The life of man is solitary, poor, nasty, brutish, and short,'" said Al. "'The condition of man is a condition of war of everyone against everyone.'"

"Who said that? Cicero? Socrates? Aristotle?"

"Thomas Hobbes wrote that in 1651," he said. "It was true then and it's true now."

We sat quietly for a moment drinking our coffee, watching the harbor wake up, and waiting for Tony's call.

"You going to call Bartholomew?" asked Al. "Get the feds involved in this?"

I shook my head.

"Somebody in law enforcement, either the feds or local cops, is on Holdsworth's payroll. One word from that guy and they'll kill Ashley."

"What do you want to do?"

"'It is better to fight for something than live for nothing,'" I said. "George S. Patton, Jr."

Al stood up, smiled, and raised his mug in salute.

"I'll make us some breakfast," said Al as he walked back to the house.

Three guys in a big sport fisher puttered around the corner and past Don's dock. We waved at each other for no reason at all and I watched their boat motor out toward the harbor entrance. The boat appeared to be equipped with every piece of gear that could possibly be used to catch a fish. Outriggers, bait tanks, fighting chair, a dozen expensive rods with gold-colored reels. They were ready and eager to take on their quarry.

I finished the last of my coffee and walked up to the house to eat breakfast and to wait.

The call came at noon.

62

THEY gave me less than an hour to get to their designated meeting place and I was to show up alone. They had done their homework and they'd chosen terrain that gave them the biggest tactical advantage.

I got into my Jeep, reached into the back, and pulled out the short pistol-gripped shotgun that we'd taken off the speedboat in the middle of the channel. I changed the shells. The first was buckshot with nine .32 caliber pellets in it, perfect for short-range work. The second shell was a rifled slug that would penetrate most body armor. The remaining six alternated between buck shot and slugs. I cycled the first round into the chamber, put the shotgun on the seat next to me, and covered it with an old sweatshirt.

A cool ocean breeze blew through the Ventura Keys. I shouldn't have been sweating. I checked my watch. Time to go.

I drove north to Highway 126 and then east toward Fillmore. I found the old farm silo Tony had described on the phone, turned south onto the second dirt road, and drove through a large grove of ripening Valencia oranges. In a few minutes I was driving along the sandy bottom of the Santa Clara River.

A brown station wagon of early 80's vintage sat on the sand near a sharp bend at the river's edge. I drove the last hundred yards slowly, as if they were my last, and parked thirty feet north of the station wagon. I got out of the Jeep and walked around the back to the right side.

Tony stepped out of the driver's side of the wagon. He wore a tan business suit and cordovan loafers and he held an automatic pistol in his right hand.

He walked back to the rear of the wagon and dropped the tailgate. Ashley lay motionless in the back. She was blindfolded and gagged with two strips of duct tape. Duct tape wound around her waist locking her arms to her sides. Next to her was a large, black, rolling carry-on case.

"Don't get your panties in a bunch, sailor boy. She's all right; only sleeping. She'll wake up happy and a little drunk with not much to remember. No big deal. Not even a hangover."

"Thanks, Tony," I said. "It is Tony, right?"

The short man nodded.

"Did you bring the discs?"

I smiled and nodded. I had never wanted to kill a man so badly.

"Let's make sure that's all you got, okay?"

He motioned with the pistol.

"Take off the jacket real slow and lay it on the hood of your car," he said.

A taller man stepped out of the passenger's side of the station wagon as I took off my jacket. He turned to face me. It was Steve Holdsworth. He wore an expensive navy blue suit with a white shirt and a red silk tie. Oddly, he wore a light brown cowboy hat and faded brown cowboy boots that added two inches to his height. He held a long-barreled revolver, the kind a wild-west gunfighter might have carried, in his left hand.

"Okay," said Tony. "Now take off the shirt and turn around slowly."

I removed my T-shirt and turned around so Tony could see that I didn't have a holster in my waistband or a pistol tucked into the small of my back. Holdsworth leaned against the left front fender of the wagon. They were confident. They were in complete control of the situation.

"Now lift up your pant legs to your knees one at a time," said Tony.

I did so.

"No backup pistol?" he asked. "I'm almost disappointed in you."

"Where are the discs?" asked Holdsworth.

"In my jacket," I said.

I nodded toward the Jeep's hood.

"Reach over very slowly and pull them out," said Holdsworth. "Don't pick up the jacket."

I pulled out a small, clear package of three blank CD's that I'd taken from Don's home office. Sunlight reflected off them in multiple colors like lights shining through prisms.

"Okay," said Tony. "Hold the discs in your left hand and put your right hand on your head."

He was being very careful. I did as I was told. Holdsworth walked over, took the discs, and carried them to the passenger side of the station wagon.

"You've got what you came for," I said. "Can we leave now?"

"Not quite yet, sailor boy," said Tony.

I waited by the Jeep and stood near the passenger's side.

"Where's your friend?" asked Tony. "The old guy who thinks he's got all the moves?"

"You told me to come alone," I said.

"I was kinda hoping you'd break the rules and ask him along. I feel like I owe him one."

Holdsworth got out of the car with a small laptop computer in his hand. I couldn't see the revolver. He said something to Tony that I couldn't hear and Tony shook his head. He turned back toward me and raised the pistol.

"What do you think you're pulling here?" he said. "This isn't a game, sailor."

The shotgun lay there on the seat only ten inches away. There was a shell in the chamber and the safety was off. But Tony was a shooter. He'd put three nine-millimeter holes in my chest before I'd ever touch the shotgun.

"Where are the damned discs?"

The muscles in his jaw tightened as he took up the slack in the trigger.

The truth shall set you free.

"The police have 'em," I said. "I handed them over yesterday."

Tony's nostrils flared slightly with an intake of breath. I saw the flesh of his index finger grow white with the pressure against the trigger.

"They know all about your organization," I said. "The counterfeit money, the urchin divers, and why you killed Barry St. James. They know who some of your 'investors' are, too. If you kill us they'll know you did it. If you come in and testify against your bosses, they'll give you a deal."

"No deals," said Tony. "We'll be on a private plane to Mexico before you bleed out on the sand, sailor."

I turned to reach for the shotgun knowing that I wouldn't make it in time to take out Tony and knowing that he couldn't miss me at this distance. But Tony wasn't my intended target. I heard the gunshot and instinctively looked back. Most of the left side of the short man's head fragmented and blew into the river. The automatic pistol fell from his hand and his body collapsed near the clear water.

Steve Holdsworth caught some of the blood and tissue spray on his face and chest. He dropped the little computer and reached down for Tony's pistol as my fingers closed on the grip of the shotgun. He brought the pistol up as I swung the short barrel but he was two-tenths of a second late. Nine pellets blew past his power tie and pushed him backward. A shocked look crossed his face for a half-second as another shell entered the chamber and I fired an inch-wide slug into his chest. He fell back into the river, his cowboy hat floating downstream.

Al stood up out of the brush near the dirt road two hundred yards away with his rifle. I ran to Ashley and checked her pulse. It was weak. I carried her to my Jeep, opened my pocketknife, and cut through the duct tape that bound her waist and arms.

"Don't take the tape off her eyes yet," said Al. "We don't want her to see this mess if she wakes up."

"You took your sweet time," I said. "Had me worried."

He jerked his head toward the orange orchard.

"I got sidetracked a bit up in the trees," he said. "And I had to wait until only one of them was holding a gun on you."

"Sidetracked?"

"Some tall Asian guy was waiting for me up there," he said. "He wasn't very good but I had to do it quietly, you know, with a knife. Didn't want the noise."

I strapped Ashley into the passenger's side of the Jeep, retrieved the shotgun and the two spent shell casings, and stowed them in the back.

"I'm going to take Ashley home and bring her down from whatever they pumped into her," I said. "Can you..."

"Yeah, yeah," said Al. "I'll clean up around here."

He looked around the river bank at the two bodies and the blood.

"As best I can," he said. "But you'll need to leave me the shot-gun."

Al walked over to the rear of the station wagon and opened up the carry-on bag. He let out a low whistle and I walked over to look at the largest collection of hundred dollar bills I'd ever seen in my life.

Al and I stood for a few moments without speaking. He reached into the bag and pulled out a three-inch thick stack of tightly bound bills and gently thumbed through them. He whistled again. There were at least another dozen bundles lying in the bot-tom of the bag. I examined them. They were genuine.

"I think we just doubled our seed money," said Al. He put the package back into the bag, zipped it back up, and handed it to me. "If you can figure out how to get it out of the country."

63

I drove away from the river and out of the orchard onto the 126 and turned west. I wasn't exactly sure where I could take Ashley to come down off whatever they'd doped her with but I considered my options and decided her place was best. If there were any more of Holdsworth's men running around, they probably weren't sitting outside Ashley's duplex.

The buildings of the County Government Center loomed off to the left as I exited the freeway and headed south on Victoria toward the harbor. I crossed the bridge over the Santa Clara River and wondered if I was driving over a thin stream of cold blood that I'd drawn minutes earlier.

I couldn't see anybody following me but that didn't mean they weren't there so I made a few turns and doubled back before parking in front of Ashley's duplex. I dug around for her house key, carried her inside, and made her comfortable on her bed. I went back out to the Jeep and slipped my Beretta into my pocket. Then I drove the Jeep three blocks away and parked it under a low palm tree next to a dumpster. No sense making it any easier to find us.

Ashley was still asleep when I got back. I picked up the morning paper off the porch, double-checked the locks on the doors, and lowered the window coverings. The fridge held four eggs, most of a quart of milk, and half a six-pack of Coca-Cola. I grabbed a Coke, went into the small living room, and cleaned and reloaded the Beretta. I didn't know what to expect but I was going to be ready for it.

There were three related articles on the front page of the paper. The first above the fold told how several federal agencies, including ICE and the Secret Service, had uncovered an international smuggling ring that brought in counterfeit U.S. currency from North Korea. The article was filled with superlatives like "largest" and "most intricate" and "highest dollar value." The second told the story of an up-and-coming high-tech "clean energy" corporation that had become a front for a major counterfeiting and smuggling enterprise; one that had shown no reluctance to kill. A smaller article near the bottom reported historical details of the Holdsworth family and the questionable legacy of an esteemed U.S. Senator long since retired.

All three of the articles reported that Steve Holdsworth and his trusted second-in-command, Terrell Jenkins, were now wanted by federal and state authorities and were presumed to be in hiding or to have left the country. I could have called and corrected them but it didn't seem like the smart thing to do.

My cell phone rang and I jumped from the surprise.

"How's Ashley?" asked Al.

"Still sleeping," I said. "I don't know what they drugged her with but if she doesn't start coming out of it in a half-hour or so, I'm taking her to the emergency room. Explaining it to Hargrave might be tough, though."

"Hang tight a little while," he said. "I found another bag in the wagon. It had some syringes, a couple unmarked bottles of pills, and a few vials of medicine."

"What did they shoot her up with?" I asked.

He read me the names off the vials. I only recognized one of them.

"I'm on my way back to the boat," said Al. "I'll make a few calls, check this stuff out, and call you back in an hour or so."

I agreed and we hung up.

Ashley stirred slightly a few minutes later and I tried to talk to her. She mumbled something unintelligible and fell back to sleep. Her eyes hadn't opened at all and I did not find that encouraging.

I picked up the paper and read the article about the Holdsworth family. There were file photos printed on pages four and five. He and his wife—currently unavailable for comment—had been married nearly thirty years. They had a son and a daughter. An aerial photo of the family property showed an impressive house, stables, garages, pastures, swimming pool, and a large horse arena. A few neighbors described the family as "normal," proving that people who live amid such wealth cannot properly define the term "normal."

Ashley woke up again in fits and starts. At one point, she opened her eyes and looked directly into my face.

"Daddy?" she asked.

"It's okay, Ashley. You're going to be fine."

"I want to go home," she said. "My doggy isn't well."

"Just rest," I said. "You'll be fine. Your doggy is fine."

She fell asleep again and her breathing became stronger and louder.

My phone rang.

"Okay," said Al. "It looks like they shot her up with something called ketamine. The pills are rohypnol."

I said something very inelegant about Steve Holdsworth's genealogy.

"I called a doctor I knew when I was in Bethesda and asked him about the stuff," said Al. "He said that the effects should wear off in a few hours and that when she wakes up, you'll want to give her something sugary and caffeinated. That'll accelerate her recovery. And she'll want food, too, if she hasn't eaten since yesterday."

I thought of the Cokes sitting in the fridge. They were a good start, but we'd still need food.

"What do I tell her when she wakes up?" I asked.

"I dunno, Sim. The doc says she'll probably be confused for a half day or so and probably won't remember much about what happened."

"Good thing," I said. "Is this doctor going to figure out our part in what happened this afternoon?"

"He's back East and probably won't hear two words about it," said Al. "But it wouldn't matter if he did. The guy owes me."

We hung up. I considered turning on the television, but I realized how much I appreciated the silence and went back to the newspaper instead. After reading another article about the rise and fall of Solavon, I called a local pizza shop and ordered a delivery for the unit next door.

Ashley slept loudly and I read my paper and, forty minutes later, a car pulled up to the curb and parked. The driver didn't see my M9 tucked into my belt at the small of my back but it didn't matter. He really was a pizza guy.

64

MY phone rang again. It was Al. He didn't sound pleased.

"Something's come up, Sim. I need you over here at *In Depth* right now," he said.

"What are you talking about? What's come up?" I asked. "I'm still here with Ashley and…"

"Just get down here now, Sim. Second General Order style, you got it?"

"What the hell do you mean by…."

"Now, buddy," he said. "Don't ask any questions. Don't waste any time. Just hustle on down here. Roger that?"

"Roger," I said.

I hung up my phone and wondered what sort of bug had crawled up Al's hind quarters. I reviewed my phone's contact list, found the one I needed, and pressed the dial button.

"What's up, Sim?" answered Monica.

"This is horribly presumptuous of me but are you free tonight?" I asked.

"Depends on what you have in mind."

"I need someone to watch over Ashley for a few hours," I said. "She is on some fairly strong medication at the moment and I can't leave her alone but Al just called and he's got some sort of emergency that I need to help him with."

"The things I do for you guys," she said. "Are you at her place?"

"Yeah."

"I'll be there in ten minutes."

I told her that would be fine, hung up, and looked over at Ashley. She stirred and opened her eyes wide open.

"Whuh?" she said.

"Ash," I said. "You've been on some sort of medication and you're coming out of it. You're going to be all right."

She opened her mouth but no words came out.

"Al needs me to take care of something over at his boat," I said. "Monica is coming to be with you, okay?"

She looked up at me through hazy eyes.

"I won't be gone long," I said. "It's all good. Monica will be here and you'll be fine. Just stay in bed and rest, okay?"

She nodded slightly. She looked confused and exhausted. Her head sank back into the pillow and her eyes closed.

Monica arrived and I told her very little about why Ashley needed to be watched. Monica didn't ask any embarrassing questions and didn't suggest I take her to a hospital. She lay down on the bed next to Ashley, propped her own head up with a pillow, and turned on the television.

"I got her," she said. "Go tend to Al's emergency."

I felt my pistol in my pocket and thought for a moment. I pulled it out.

"You know how to use one of these?" I asked.

She didn't even blink.

"Do you really think a lady could hang around Al for half a dozen years without learning how to shoot?" she asked.

I handed her the Beretta.

"It's not that you'll need it or anything," I said. "I'm just overly cautious these days with what's been going on around Vintage Marina."

She smiled and put the pistol on the bed next to her.

"Go do your thing," she said.

I grabbed my jacket, locked the door behind me, and walked down Mandalay Beach Road to where I'd parked the Jeep.

Something about what Al had said bothered me as I turned on-to Harbor Boulevard. What did he mean by 'Second General Order style'? I went through the mantra of the Ten General Orders I'd memorized as a recruit. The little voice spoke up when I got to the Second General Order; *To walk my post in a military manner, keeping always on the alert, and observing everything that takes place within sight or hearing.* I paid a little extra attention to my rear-view mirror and the cars around me but nobody seemed to be following me.

Instead of driving to Vintage Marina, I continued over the bridge, made a right turn onto Peninsula Road, and drove south to the park near the guest dock. It was a warm August Saturday evening and several couples sat on the grass talking and enjoying the last shreds of summer twilight.

I grabbed the small set of field glasses that I keep in the glove compartment, walked into the park, and sat down under a tree about two hundred yards southeast of and across the channel from J-dock. I focused the binoculars on *In Depth* and scanned the area. Al sat in a deck chair in the aft cockpit smoking a cigar. The red end glowed as he puffed on it. It didn't look like a dire situation requiring my immediate attention.

Then I realized there was something unusual about his behavior. Something odd about his movements, the cigar, the placement of the deck chair. My eyes grew accustomed to the dark after a few minutes and I saw another figure sitting across from him. I couldn't tell who it was in the darkness but he held something in his hand that reflected the orange beam of the overhead dock lights. I studied the reflection and realized it was a metal object. It was the glint from the stainless steel finish of a pistol.

65

I trotted back to my Jeep and dug my swimming goggles and a pair of bodysurfing fins out of the plastic tub in the back. I looked around for my swim trunks. They were thirty miles away in the dirty laundry basket aboard *Figaro*. Well, where there are no alternatives, there are no problems. I left my wallet and watch in the glove box, locked the car, hid my keys in the little open area of the front bumper, and trotted back to the park. I kept close to the trees, staying away from the park's overhead lights. Darkness was my friend.

A fairly new sport fishing boat lay tied to the guest dock but it appeared to be uninhabited. The owners were probably out for pizza and beer after a long day reeling in fish. I stepped aboard and found a short-handled fishing gaff mounted against one of the exterior bulkheads. The gaff had a big hook, maybe three or four inches between the sharp point and the shank. It was the closest thing to a weapon that I could find.

I left my clothes on the floor of the cockpit by the helm and entered the cool water of the marina channel with nothing but my fins, goggles, and the gaff. Going straight to Al's boat wasn't an option, as I would have certainly been spotted. However, it was only eighty yards directly across the channel to one of the docks south of Vintage Marina. With fins, I can swim almost a hundred yards underwater on one breath. I took a deep breath and let it out slowly. I stretched and relaxed the muscles in my legs and arms. Another deep, slow breath. A couple of late-returning boats passed through the channel. I took a few more deep breaths and ducked under the surface of the dark water.

There wasn't much to see through the goggles in the darkness below me, but I could look up and see light from the night sky above and the orange glow of dock lights. I didn't stop until a moored boat blocked the light. I surfaced behind the big ketch tethered to the end-tie at L-dock. I used the boats and floating docks between it and *In Depth* for cover as I swam silently toward the stern of Al's boat.

"He's not answering," said Al. "What more do you expect me to do?"

"Get him down here now," said a familiar voice, "or I'll wrap you in chains and sink you right here in the marina."

"What's the hurry?" asked Al.

"My boss is offering a fat bonus to whoever brings in the records you guys have. I aim to collect it."

"Your boss is dead. I saw him die."

"Bullshit," said the voice.

"Go ahead," said Al. "Give him a call. Maybe they have cell service in Hell."

"You seem pretty relaxed about dying."

"Everybody gets to do it someday," said Al. "Even you. I'm guessing I might still have a few years left, though."

"You have no good reason to think so," said the voice.

I was only three or four feet away but I was in the water below them and Al's boat had a fair amount of freeboard. I took off my fins and goggles, let them sink to the bottom, and wrapped the gaff's lanyard around my wrist. I felt around the stern of Al's boat and found some footing on the steel strut that holds up the swim step. I had to guess about the distance but, in one quick maneuver, I pulled myself up over the side of the boat, swung the gaff in a wide arc overhead, and dug its sharp steel hook into the upper arm of the man holding the pistol. I pulled hard as if I were trying to land a sixty-pound bigeye tuna.

The man screamed, the pistol fired, and the noise of it all reverberated throughout the marina. Ducks and cormorants that had been peacefully paddling about squawked and jumped up and flew off as if the end of the world were nipping at their tail feathers. The pistol hit the deck of Al's boat and Al threw a left jab at the man who had dropped it. Then Al hit him three more times. The last two punches were superfluous. He was out.

I climbed into the cockpit.

"Jerry," I said. "The happy surfing Harbor Patrolman."

"And on Holdsworth's payroll," said Al.

"Not anymore."

"You're naked," said Al. "And that water must be pretty cold." He chuckled slightly.

"I just saved your bacon, Al. You might have a little respect."

"I'll try," he said.

I went below to put on a pair of Al's shorts and to find a spare T-shirt while Al trussed up the bleeding Jerry with some extra lines. The gaff had done some damage and Jerry had lost a fair amount of blood. Al stopped the bleeding with a short length of duct tape.

"Not exactly sterile," I said.

"Like I should care."

"You want me to call the police?" I asked.

Jerry coughed as he regained consciousness.

"Not quite yet, Sim. I have a few questions I'd like to ask good old Jerry."

Jerry sat on the deck of *In Depth*'s aft cockpit and glared at me. That was okay, though. I can withstand a glare or two.

"I want to know exactly what happened to Barry St. James," said Al.

"Screw you," said Jerry.

"You know, Jerry, one of the problems with being stupid is not recognizing that old people can still be dangerous."

Al kicked him hard in the ear. Jerry fell over and whimpered. Al stepped down into his boat's cabin and returned with a small roll of blue cloth.

"I found this on that tall Asian fellow up in the orange orchard," said Al.

He unrolled the blue cloth and Jerry's eyes went wide as Al selected a thin blade of surgical steel.

"When I was in my little part of the Navy, your parents' tax dollars were spent teaching me things you law enforcement types could never even dream of."

He fingered the blade.

"I got pretty good at what we called 'advanced interrogation techniques'," he said.

He put the blade against the skin of Jerry's cheek.

"You want to answer my questions?" asked Al. "Or should I start the evening off with some meat carving?"

Jerry broke and answered all our questions. He told us a lot of things we already knew regarding counterfeiting, smuggling, sea urchins, and Solavon. We learned a few new things, too. Jerry had been the man in charge of retrieving the smuggled goods for Solavon. It had been his idea to use the urchin divers and their commercial operations as a cover. As the senior Harbor Patrolman, he could make sure they weren't bothered.

Holdsworth had told him that he suspected Barry St. James of skimming the profits and that Barry had also taken backup copies of the accounting files to use as leverage against Solavon. Holdsworth had asked his contacts in Asia for a specialist and they'd recommended a tall quiet Korean to work on Barry St. James, hoping to retrieve the accounting files and other documents. Jerry's description of the man fit the fellow Al had killed in the orange orchard earlier that day. The Korean man's methods hadn't worked, though, and Barry never broke.

Jerry told Tony about what Jed had seen and Tony killed him. Tony had killed Dustin, too. He'd also tracked down Erica and shot her. It was Jerry's idea to tie her body under the dock next to *Figaro*'s slip to implicate me. He didn't know anything about Judith.

When Jerry finished talking, Al pulled his cell phone out of his shirt pocket and pressed a button on the screen. Jerry's voice came from the cell phone in a recorded repetition of his confession. His eyes went wide as Al called the police.

66

ASHLEY was awake and feeling a lot better when I got back to her duplex. I told Monica about Jerry and Al and she went straight to *In Depth* to see how 'the old man' was doing. Ashley was glad to see me but still quite confused. I talked with her until she became drowsy and we fell asleep in her big bed while the gas fireplace flickered its blue and orange flame.

The morning brought a much more lucid Ashley and a lot of questions.

"How could it be Sunday morning?" she asked. "I left work just yesterday afternoon. That was Friday."

"What do you remember about Friday, Ashley?"

"I remember walking out of the office toward my car a little after five and seeing a guy in a cowboy hat. He asked me something. Then I remember talking to you, I think, a little bit last night but the rest is mostly a bad dream. Was I asleep?"

"You don't remember my taking care of you yesterday afternoon after I found you?" I asked.

A puzzled look crossed her face and she cried.

"They were horrible dreams," she said. "I thought that maybe I was dead."

Her voice became scratchy and I got her a glass of water.

"You're fine, now," I said.

"And there was this music that played over and over and there were things I saw that didn't make any sense at all."

"I hope it wasn't the Bee Gees," I said.

She smiled and I knew she was back.

She got drowsy again and took a short nap. I didn't think she needed a nanny anymore so I went to the store and bought some groceries to restock her vacant refrigerator. She was awake and reading the paper when I returned.

"Grocery run," I said.

"Good," she said. "I'm starving."

"Don't you ever buy groceries for yourself?" I asked.

She smiled faintly.

"I think you cook more meals here than I do," she said.

We had a Sunday brunch of French toast, bacon, and sliced cantaloupe. She ate quietly through the meal. I did the dishes while she read the paper. She seemed focused on the articles regarding the Solavon scandal.

"Let's take a walk on the beach," I suggested.

"I don't feel very well, Sim. I'm not sure what happened or where my Saturday went but I'd like you to drive me to my parents' house. Would that be okay?"

"Sure," I said.

We drove up the hill to Thousand Oaks and past the stately palm trees through the gate-guarded entrance to the country club and the Barringer home. Philip greeted us at the door and ushered us into the great room overlooking the swimming pool and the fairway. After a few minutes of perfunctory small talk, Ashley asked her parents if she could talk alone with them and the three left the room.

I looked out over the pool and onto the fairway and watched the seemingly endless train of golf carts pass by. About forty minutes of sitting alone in a house was close to my personal tolerance level. Philip walked into the room with five minutes to spare. He was carrying one of his bamboo fighting sticks.

"Did you really need to give her roofies to get what you wanted, Sim?" he asked.

"I don't know what you're talking about, Philip."

"Bullshit," he said. "You think I'm some sort of idiot? I'm a doctor, you moron. Ashley says she has no idea what happened this weekend but any fool can see that somebody doped her up. She's suffering the after-effects of any number of date rape drugs. Dissociative experiences, anterograde amnesia, lingering cognitive impairment. They're all there. Like they came straight out of a medical journal."

He approached me with the stick and I backed up to stay out of range.

"I never gave her anything," I said. "She stood me up for dinner Friday night and I found her delirious in her apartment yesterday afternoon."

He swung the bamboo sword at me and I had to dodge backward to keep from getting hit.

"What happened, sailor? Did she turn you down or something? Wouldn't put out?"

He approached me with the stick again and I moved toward the front door.

"This is really stupid, Dr. Barringer. I never gave her any drugs."

He swung again and missed me but nailed a thick glass vase on a nearby end table in his follow through. It shattered into a thousand pieces.

"Florence wants to call the police and have them arrest you," he said, "but I know what some wise-ass defense lawyer will do. He'll roll Ashley's reputation through the mud. He'll tell the jury that it wasn't rape. After all, the two of you have been dating for months. He'll tell them that it was her idea to try the drugs."

He swung again, missed me, and tore a hole in an oil painting on the wall of the entryway. The front door was open and I backed out onto the porch and down the three stairs to the driveway.

"What did you slip into her drink, asshole? Ketamine? Ativan? Rohypnol?"

"I didn't give her anything. I found her unconscious in her apartment. I swear it."

"Bullshit," he said. "You would've called 911 or taken her to the E.R."

He backed me up to my Jeep. I reached the driver's side, hopped in, and started the engine. He pounded the Jeep with the stick. I shoved the transmission into gear, let out the clutch, and left a small patch of rubber on his beautiful stamped-concrete driveway.

67

LABOR Day. The semi-official end to summer. The day for barbe-cues on the beach or eating hot dogs at Dodger Stadium. Or sail-ing.

Al and I got up early, fired up the Skipjack, and blasted out of Ventura Harbor. It seemed like I'd been spending way too much time roaring across the Santa Barbara Channel in a small fishing boat but the water was as smooth as the rippled glass in an antique bookcase and the Skipjack raced across its surface at thirty-five knots. The air was crisp and a light dusting of salt spray found our faces whenever we hit the rare oncoming ocean swell.

It was a good feeling. I was willing to endure the occasional dousing to get back to my home afloat. The din of the boat's mo-tor and the rush of the wind and spray reduced all conversation to a shouting match. We ultimately gave up and quietly thought to ourselves while the Skipjack pounded on toward Santa Cruz Island and *Figaro*.

A lot had changed in such a short time. Three weeks before, I had been living a happy life on a nice boat in a great marina sur-rounded by good friends. Surfing, swimming, spear fishing, and sailing. There was a lovely channel with fair winds and beautiful islands to explore with a fine smart and lovely young woman. I had a good reputation and a decent career in the Navy doing what I enjoyed most.

Now I found myself scanning the horizon for speedboats filled with shotgun-toting thugs and I drove my Jeep with an eye-and-a-half in the rear-view mirror looking for feds or cops or more bad guys. I no longer looked forward to driving to work through the North Mugu Road gate. Even running on the beach brought memories of dead beach bums and bodies wrapped in chains.

A few weeks ago, I was the guy at Vintage Marina that some-body would seek out to help fix something on their boat or to drink beers with in the cockpit or on the flying bridge. Now I was the guy folks would talk about under their breath. Sure, the truth would come out in dribs and drabs and folks would acknowledge my 'not guilty' status but most of the boat people would not-so-secretly wonder if it wasn't really me who had killed Jed, Dustin, Erica, and, probably, Judith.

My love life was trashed. I wasn't interested in the Jessicas and Ericas that seemed to populate so much of my beach community. As far as I was concerned, they should all be marked with a warn-ing label. And I'd had my fill of smart but spoiled doctor's daugh-ters who wanted nothing more than to wrap an anchor chain around my neck and keep me ashore. To hell with it. To hell with all of it. I was sick of the Navy, sick of Ventura County, and even sick of the Santa Barbara Channel.

Al throttled back when we reached Lady's and there was *Figaro*, just as sound and seaworthy as I'd left her. Except that she was sur-rounded by four other sailboats.

Labor Day.

"Here you go, brother," said Al.

"Coming aboard?" I asked.

"You got any cold beer?" asked Al.

"Not unless the beer fairy delivers to unoccupied sailboats."

He shook his head.

"Gotta get back to Ventura and hit the road," said Al. "I'm sup-posed to pick up Don at LAX this afternoon."

"Be sure to thank him for letting me use his Rover," I said.

"You think I asked him?"

Al maneuvered the Skipjack between the sailboats that had shoehorned their way into the anchorage. He pulled up close to *Figaro* and I climbed onto the gunwale and stepped aboard my boat.

"Let's go do that dive shop in the Caribbean," I said. "I want in."

Al's face brightened.

"You serious?" he asked.

"As serious as a man holding a pistol and getting half his head blown off into a river," I said. "As serious as a guy wrapped in chains and tossed into the harbor."

Al put the Skipjack in neutral and grabbed one of *Figaro's* lifeline stanchions.

"You know, I am really wishing you had a couple of cold beers in the fridge," he said. "Because we need to talk."

The Skipjack drifted closer to *Figaro* and Al fended it off.

"What's happened over the last few days has been pretty rough," he said. "There is no getting around it. It was hard terrain and you had to muscle your way through it. But you did it. You survived. Not everybody made it through but that isn't your fault."

A young shirtless fellow climbed up the companionway of a sailboat anchored about fifty feet away and blinked his eyes in the morning light. He looked at the two of us as if we'd woken him from a good dream.

"So you get this tub back to Vintage Marina and I'll pick up Don at LAX," said Al. "And tonight we'll sit on *In Depth's* aft deck and I'll grill a couple of thick steaks. We'll eat some rare meat, squeeze a few limes into some Coronas, and talk about it."

He reached over the lifeline and punched me on the shoulder.

"Trust me, brother," he said. "Being a survivor ain't so bad. In fact, it beats the hell out of the alternative."

Al pulled the Skipjack away from *Figaro* and, once safely out of the anchorage, gunned the engine for his forty-five minute ride back to the mainland. I set to cleaning my boat and getting her ready for the trip.

There wasn't really that much to do. I grabbed the deck brush and a bucket, scrubbed the bird crap and a few dead flying fish off the deck, and sluiced it all overboard with buckets of sea water. She'd stayed anchored in one spot long enough to gather some foliage on her undersides so I grabbed the piece of old carpet that I kept for this purpose and spent an hour scrubbing her below the waterline. I retrieved my makeshift kellets off the anchor rodes, stowed a bunch of gear, and fired up her diesel engine to charge the batteries.

My neighbors started to tidy up their boats, too. Their Labor Day weekend had started on Friday or Saturday and this was the day to sail home, put their boats away for the winter, and get ready to show up for work on Tuesday. One by one they weighed anchor and motored out of the small harbor.

By noon, I was alone.

Figaro was clean and shipshape but I was sweaty and dirty. I stripped off my clothes and dove into the sea naked as the day I was born. I swam to the beach and thought of Barry and Erica and all the people who'd abruptly died over the last few weeks because of greed and the love of money. And I thought about how so many people die slowly ashore in small increments for the same tawdry reasons.

I swam back to *Figaro* and showered off the salt water and the regrets and some of the pain. I found a clean pair of shorts, my University of Washington T-shirt, and the new L.A. Dodgers bill cap I'd bought that night with Mel Goldsmith. I fished around under the chart table and grabbed a pair of sunglasses that reminded me of the pair Jessica had dropped nearly three weeks ago.

The anchors came up without a hitch and I raised the main, unfurled the genoa, and set a course of sixty-five degrees magnetic for Channel Islands Harbor. The winds were on the light side so I let Kyle do the steering, went forward, and raised the spinnaker. *Figaro* raced along at nearly eight knots. A slightly favorable current added to our speed over the ground but winds can be fluky and currents aren't always steady. Still, I was confident that I'd be back at Vintage Marina in under four hours if the wind held.

We were about three miles south of oil platform *Grace* when my phone rang. I didn't recognize the number but it was the Naval Base exchange. I answered.

"This is Captain Overson."

"Yes, sir. How can I help you?" I said.

"Where are you right now, Chief Greene?"

"At sea, sir. It's Labor Day and I'm on leave," I said. "As you ordered, sir."

There was a pause on the other end.

"I understand that you disobeyed my orders, that you continued your investigation, and that you were also instrumental in identifying the individuals who killed Lieutenant St. James," he said.

"No, sir," I lied. "I have been at sea on my boat for over a week, sir."

There was another long pause on the other end.

"I did, however, locate some papers that had been in Lieutenant St. James' possession, sir."

"Papers?" asked Captain Overson.

"Documents kept by Lieutenant St. James, sir. I found them before I went on leave," I said. "I don't know if these are the documents you originally wanted me to locate but they may be of some interest to you, sir."

There was near silence for almost thirty seconds. I could hear the Captain breathing.

"Should I bring them in to you, sir?"

"Be in my office with those papers at eleven o'clock tomorrow morning, Chief."

"Aye, aye, Captain."

68

I'D tried to call Ashley, but she didn't answer, and she didn't respond to the text messages I sent either. I woke up early the next morning in my quarter berth with my phone in my hand. It was nearly dead.

There wasn't any food in the fridge and I was starving. But the Harbor Mart made a half-decent bacon and egg breakfast sandwich so I pulled on my shorts and my running shoes and grabbed my wallet. I locked up *Figaro* and walked up J-dock and out the card-key gate toward the parking lot.

"Where you headed, Greene?"

I turned to see Detective Hargrave sitting in a silver Toyota. It wasn't a cop car.

"I heard you and the feds found the killers," I said.

"Some of them," he said. "One of them turned out to be one of our own guys, too. Ah, but you already know about Jerry, don't you?"

"Pretty upsetting when a cop goes bad."

"You should know," he said.

"Funny," I said.

He got out of the car and reached back in to pull out a cardboard serving tray with two large green foam cups from the local high-end coffee shop. He put it on the hood of his car. He reached into the car again to retrieve two white paper sacks. He nodded toward the bench I'd sat Dustin on a long time ago.

I sat down and Hargrave handed me a cup of coffee.

"I wasn't sure how you like your coffee so I just got two the way I like them," he said.

I tasted it. He'd added too much sugar but it was still good.

"Thanks," I said.

He handed me one of the sacks and I looked inside.

"Hey, these are the good ones," I said. "From that shop up in Camarillo."

"What they say about cops and donuts is all true," he said.

I reached in and pulled out a maple bar.

"You must know," I said, "that coffee and donuts are like truth serum to a sailor."

He drank some coffee and took a bite out of an old fashioned.

"I think I know most of the truth already," he said.

"And the truth shall set you free, Detective."

He nodded and drank some more coffee.

"It puts a lot of folks in jail," he said.

I shrugged and had another bite of maple bar.

"Judith came out of hiding yesterday," he said. "She'd convinced herself that you were killing people and ran off to San Francisco."

"She must've been pretty scared."

"A lot of people have been dying around here." He paused to drink some coffee. "In fact, a couple of hikers found two dead guys near the Santa Clara River just outside an orange orchard Sunday morning."

I drank some coffee.

"The feds had been looking for the two dead guys for a couple of days," he said. "It seems that somebody tipped off Homeland Security to a delivery of counterfeit U.S. currency and these two guys were somehow implicated. I don't have all the details, yet."

"Crime doesn't pay," I said.

"One of the dead guys was a local bigwig; a real rich guy and a former Senator's son," he said. "Had a big house up near Santa Barbara; horses and stables and all that. Member of the Polo Club; pillar of the community."

I couldn't think of anything I wanted to say.

"So this rich connected guy ran some new solar energy company," he said. "The other dead guy was one of his vice presidents. As it turns out, this VP had a fairly extensive criminal record back East."

"Employers should be more thorough in their background checks," I said.

The coffee was really good. I decided that I could get used to the fancy stuff if I found myself in a position to afford it regularly.

"So it looks like the two guys killed each other in a gun fight," he said.

"Truly unfortunate," I said. "People should learn to resolve their differences peacefully."

He smiled and took another bite of donut.

"Except they didn't kill each other," he said while chewing his bite of donut. "Somebody just tried real hard to make it look like that."

"This coffee is delicious," I said. "You know, I've never felt like I could justify the money on the really high-end stuff but I now see the attraction."

He looked at me and chuckled.

"They did a fairly good job of doctoring the crime scene," he said. "They moved some bodies around, re-arranged some guns, brushed out tracks in the sand. Not a bad job, actually. But they missed an eighteen-inch long section of tire track coming into the orchard off the highway. The ground was damp there and the tire left a good impression."

"You got another donut in that bag?" I said.

He handed me the bag and I fished out a chocolate raised.

"The CSI guys decided to make a cast of that tire track. It matches the right rear tire on that yellow Jeep of yours," he said.

"It's a popular tire," I said. "There are probably five thousand sets of them in this county alone."

He shook his head slowly and gave a thin smile.

"Detective, you've been accusing me of murdering people for weeks now," I said. "What am I up to? Six victims? Seven? Or is it an even dozen, now? Give me a hand, here. A guy like me kills so many people he has a hard time keeping count."

"I was wrong about the others," he said. "We're still trying to sort it all out but Jerry has already told us about Barry St. James and some of the other victims. The feds have him now and we might never get a good chance to interrogate him. The recording Al gave us was helpful, though. It seems that Jerry worked for Steve Holdsworth and that Jerry and some other guy killed these people on Holdsworth's order."

"So I didn't kill seven people after all?" I asked. "That is mighty comforting."

"No," he said. "I think you're down to five."

I looked around and didn't see any police cars or faux plumbing vans or landscapers trying to look disinterested. Detective Hargrave was the only law enforcement in the area. I figured he was wearing a wire.

"That's all?" I said.

"We found three guys in some avocado trees off a dirt road north of Camarillo," he said. "They'd all been shot with a nine-millimeter. There was an empty MAC-10 in the bushes near one of the stiffs," he said. "It was also nine-millimeter but none of the bullets we pulled out of those guys matched the MAC."

I shrugged.

"You've got a nine, don't you, Greene?"

"It's a very popular caliber," I said.

"Yeah, probably five thousand of them in the county, too," he said.

I shrugged again. It's not hard to get good at shrugging.

Hargrave opened up the other white bag and pulled out a shard of clear plastic about three inches long and a half-inch wide. There was a small piece of Pepsi label still on it.

"You left this near one of the bodies, Greene. Our lab found a partial fingerprint on it. That fingerprint is yours."

"And yet you are not here with a phalanx of fellow law enforcement officers or even a set of handcuffs on your belt," I said. "You didn't even bring a company car."

He put the plastic back in the bag and folded the top over.

"The three guys you left cooling off in the avocado trees were baddies," he said. "Major baddies. Their fingerprints match a trio of professional killers that have been working the Northwest for nearly five years. The Seattle police have positively linked them to six contract killings and they suspect their involvement in another four. Those cops are absolutely giddy that somebody finally aced these guys."

He finished his coffee and tossed the cup into one of the marina trashcans.

"The Tacoma police have tied them to a cop killing—an ambush of one of their detectives—that happened over a year ago," he said. "Their Chief of Police wants to personally thank the guy who let the gas out of them. I figured the least I could do is buy you some coffee and donuts."

I wasn't letting my guard down.

"And they are fine donuts," I said. "Even if I don't deserve them for the reasons you may think."

He opened the little white paper sack that held the plastic shard and looked inside. He folded the top over again and looked back at me.

"Did you kill these five guys, Greene?"

By my count, I'd only killed four. Al got the credit for Simon on the boat, the tall guy in the orchard, and Tony at the river but the cops apparently hadn't found either the first or the second. So I'd killed four guys. Only four. Definitely not five. It was an important distinction.

"Of course not," I answered.

He reached into the first white bag and pulled out another donut.

"Raspberry-filled," he said. "You want it?"

"I'd be a fool not to."

I took it from him.

"Word is that you aren't planning on sticking around," he said. "That you might be transferred back East or something; might even be leaving the county for good."

"It wouldn't surprise me," I said. "The Base Commander has not been too happy with my performance, lately."

He folded up the empty donut bag, put it inside the other bag with the piece of plastic soda bottle, and dropped both bags into a nearby trashcan. He walked back to his Toyota and I walked with him.

He looked over at my Jeep when we got to his car.

"Yeah," he said. "Those are pretty common tires, I suppose."

69

TWO Navy Seahawks approached the base for landing. The rhythmic pulsing of the four-bladed rotors and the whine of twin jet engines combined to fill the Captain's office with a din that prevented any useful conversation. Late morning sun streamed through the window.

Captain Overson sat in his leather chair and glared across the desk at me until the sound dissipated. I used the time to concentrate on my heartbeat until it was the only sound I could hear. I felt my pulse slow and my breathing become deeper and more purposeful. Consciousness the only reality.

"I am told that Steve Holdsworth had Barry St. James killed," he said. "I've been told this by several sets of state and federal authorities. Civilian authorities."

"I wouldn't know, sir," I said. "I've been on leave."

"I have also been told that you may be the one who killed Steve Holdsworth," he said. "They are telling me that it might have been self-defense and some have suggested quietly and unofficially that you actually did the world a service in removing him," he said.

I remained quiet.

"We're alone, Chief. You can tell me what happened in the strictest confidence."

Captain Overson moved a short pile of folders from the middle of his desk to the right side. He leaned back in his chair and waited; as if waiting would make me nervous and talkative. He was too anxious, though. He couldn't outwait me.

"I would like to know what happened," he said.

"I was on leave, Captain. Those were your direct orders. I have no idea what these civilians are talking about."

He looked at me through half-closed eyes and waited. He could wait until Christmas as far as I was concerned.

"Okay, Chief, you mentioned some documents over the telephone. Where are they?"

I pulled the large manila envelope out of my briefcase and handed it to him. He opened the flap and looked inside. He swallowed as he pulled the papers out, laid them on his desk, and thumbed through them. He didn't read them. Didn't need to. He knew those papers.

"Did you review any of these papers?" he asked without looking up. His right hand shook slightly. He looked up at me from the letter in his hand. "I asked you if you read any of these documents."

I nodded slowly.

"I ordered you not to read them," he said. "That was a very specific order, Chief Greene."

"They're not classified documents," I said.

The pitch and volume of his voice rose slightly.

"I ordered you not to…"

"They're just some letters you wrote to Barry St. James, Captain. Letters he, apparently, wanted to keep," I said.

His eyes grew wide and his face turned red. But it wasn't the joyful hue of a Christmas tablecloth or the embarrassed pink of the shy young girl on her first date. It was the angry defensive red of a man whose most damaging secrets had been unearthed.

"Do you think you can blackmail me with these?" he asked.

"No, Sir, I don't think that at all. Those letters don't mean a damned thing. We live in a different world now, Captain. It's a completely different Navy from when you wrote those. Nobody cares anymore. Nobody will even raise an eyebrow."

"You think I'm going to let you ruin my career?"

"What are you talking about?" I asked. "Your career is safe. The 'don't ask, don't tell' policy was abolished years ago. Nobody cares about you and Barry."

His head and neck twitched involuntarily and I got the impression that something inside him had snapped and that I was no longer dealing with a rational being. He reached his right hand into the open drawer of his desk and pulled out a semi-automatic pistol. It was an M9 just like my own. From my end of it, the barrel looked as big around and as black as the inside of Al's coffee mug. He reached into the drawer with his other hand, pulled out a wicked-looking knife, and tossed it onto the desk.

"You're a maverick and a murder suspect, Chief Greene."

"You're making a big deal out of nothing, Captain."

"The Sheriff's department was closing in on you and your time was running short," he said. "You were angry with me because you thought I'd helped them and you came in here with that knife to kill me."

"You've got to be kidding me," I said.

"Pick it up, Greene. Pick up the knife."

"Not a chance," I said.

"That's an order," he said.

"That's an unlawful order, Captain, and I have no obligation to follow it."

His breathing stopped and the flesh on his index finger compressed as he took up the slack in the trigger.

"Copies of those letters are being held by two friends of mine," I said.

His eyes grew wide at the news and his index finger relaxed. He took a deep breath.

"You son of a bitch," he said.

"Whatever you say, Captain. But if anything happens to me, anything at all, one of my friends will send his copies to the newspapers and the other will mail his copies to the Pentagon. They'll know why you killed me."

He held the gun on me, the barrel pointed directly at my chest.

"Captain, I've had a lot of guns pulled on me during the last couple of weeks and I'm pretty damned tired of it," I said. "I think you'd better put yours away."

His tongue snaked out of his mouth and he licked his upper lip.

"How much money do you want?" he asked.

"None."

"I don't believe you."

"I don't care," I said. And then, as an afterthought, "Sir."

A gallon of tension drained from his face. He let out a breath and put the gun back into his desk drawer. He picked up the knife, folded the blade, and put it next to the pistol in the drawer.

"What do you want?" he asked.

"All I want, Captain, is to get the hell out of the Navy. I want an honorable discharge with full retirement pay."

"That's all?" he asked.

"I want the paperwork expedited and completed this week," I said. "I want you to have the docs drafted this afternoon and sent via courier this evening. And I want you to personally make the phone calls and secure the approvals and get me out of this uniform by Friday."

His mouth opened slightly as he realized his good fortune.

"You're serious?" he asked.

I nodded and his mouth closed into a silly and stupid grin. He closed his desk drawer without a sound.

"Done," he said.

70

THE beam from the Pt. Loma light flashed a millimeter above the horizon as *Figaro* passed west of San Diego. The skies were clear in the wee hours of the morning and the glow from the city lit up the eastern horizon before the sun would get its chance. A quick review of my chart revealed that the Coronado Islands were still over three hours away and that our current course would take us at least five miles west of them as we crossed the imaginary boundary into Mexico. It would be light by then and I'd be able to avoid those rocky islands with no difficulty.

Figaro had slipped out of Channel Islands Harbor just after midnight the previous day and I had been awake for almost twenty-eight hours straight. I didn't sneak out under the cover of darkness because I thought the police might be after me—it is hard to run away at only six knots—or because I feared retribution from any surviving member of Holdsworth's organization. I figured those guys were preoccupied with hiring lawyers or staying under ICE's radar. I left when nobody was looking because I wanted to get out quietly.

So I made my escape in the dark of night with no fanfare, no announcement, and no discussion. Captain Overson had handed me my DD-214 and other discharge papers at two o'clock Friday afternoon and *Figaro* and I motored away from Vintage Marina less than twelve hours later.

We'd already covered about a hundred and sixty miles since then and the two of us had eight hundred and fifty miles more before we could put in at Cabo San Lucas. Two of us. *Figaro* and me.

There was no reason to stick around once my retirement had been approved. There were plenty of reasons to leave. Ashley wouldn't return my phone calls and, after a while, I stopped calling. Master Chief Joe, the only one of my co-workers who didn't treat me as if I were radioactive, took me out for a burrito on my last day of service. Some retirement party. Detective Hargrave made it a point to drop by every once in a while and tell me how amazed he was that I was still in the area. Even Judith avoided me.

Any bridges that I'd had with the Navy, the Sheriff's Department, the Harbor Patrol, and Ashley had all been burnt to the waterline. There was nothing and nobody left in Southern California for me. I wasn't exactly wanted. It was time to make wake.

Two days before I left, a fellow that Al thought was only a tire kicker walked down the dock, pulled out his checkbook, and paid him the full asking price for *In Depth*. Al wired the proceeds to a bank in the British Virgin Islands. Gil bought my Jeep at a deep discount due to the dents caused by an angry doctor's bamboo fighting staff.

Reid came out of the adventure okay, though. He'd paid attention to the financial statements we'd uncovered and realized that bad things were going to happen to Solavon. So he made a few bets in the stock market.

It was merely local news when Frank Bartholomew and his colleagues busted the smuggling operation. Initially, it only made the county paper and got a little play on a few radio stations. But when Homeland Security descended onto Solavon's offices like a black cloud of uniformed accountants, every hard news outlet from the *Washington Post* and the *Wall Street Journal* to *Modern Dog* magazine laid out the story of governmental corruption, smuggling, lobbying, influence peddling, counterfeiting, murder, and money laundering in excruciating detail.

Solavon's stock became as worthless as a bald tire in a snow storm and good old Reid made another fortune out of the chaos. He was grateful enough for the inside info to buy Al and me dinner. Such a friend.

Al and I decided to keep the non-counterfeit dough Barry St. James had skimmed from Solavon, as well as the stacks of bills we'd found in the back of Holdsworth's station wagon. We were certain those guys wouldn't miss it and we figured that it would go a long way toward buying and outfitting a first-class diving operation in the British Virgin Islands.

The trick, of course, would be getting it there without having to explain it to governmental agencies and customs inspectors. Such explanations can be embarrassing, so I hid all that lovely money on *Figaro* before casting off and slipping away from J-dock.

And I'm not telling where.

AN EXCERT FROM

BROAD REACH

Another Sim Greene/*Figaro* Mystery

1

ISLANDS rise from the sea as you approach them. A smudge on the horizon becomes a greenish lump then an island with trees. In the Caribbean, the fragrant smell of frangipani blossoms hits you about the same time you see the white sandy beaches.

The water turns progressively lighter, too. The deepest blue becomes dark green then jade. When you reach a good anchorage in pale turquoise water you can see the hard dark green and tan coral heads sticking up from the floury sand below.

And it is good that you can see them.

St. John rose in the early light of a clear Sunday morning and I was glad to see it. I knew I would—I'd seen that island on my chart for days—but there is far more comfort in sighting land after a long sail than there is in watching your position advance toward it on paper.

I'd spent three months sailing my thirty-nine-foot boat from California; most of it with fair winds and favorable seas. The last two weeks, however, had been tough. After six days on a comfortable broad reach, the wind clocked around and dealt me eight solid days of beating into a stiff wind that never quite turned into a gale. I was bone-weary, sleep deprived, and eager to see Al.

Al is a well-educated, barely house-trained, short brown bear of a fellow. He is generally quiet and moderately principled. My friend and new business partner, he'd flown to the British Virgin Islands three months earlier to find a dive shop for us to buy. It was the dream job he'd always talked about. The dream he'd talked me into.

Tortola began its steady rise from the sea an hour after St. John. By the time Norman Island appeared on the horizon, I'd already reviewed the cruising guide and prepared *Figaro* for landfall. The Customs and Immigration office would be closed so I could either pay the exorbitant after-hours fee or anchor out in the harbor and sit in my cabin until a customs officer came in on Monday morning.

After fourteen solid days and nights at sea, I was ready for some human contact and looking forward to a long swim and some solid ground. But the Scotsman in me wasn't about to pay an onerous after-hours fee. I chose the third, somewhat less legal, option of ignoring Customs and turned ten degrees to port.

With over twelve-hundred nautical miles under my keel since leaving Panama, another five to Jost Van Dyke wouldn't kill me. Keep quiet, stay under the radar, and blend in with the hundreds of chartered sailboats that ply the local waters. Nobody would be the wiser.

An hour later I dropped the sails, fired up the diesel engine, and powered the last few hundred yards into White Bay. The bay nestles up to a narrow scimitar of pure white sand wedged between blue Caribbean waters and steep green hills covered in manchioneel trees and coconut palms. A shallow reef protects the anchorage. Safe and comfortable, a guy could spend days there just relaxing. I needed one night and a cold beer.

I slipped *Figaro* in behind the reef on the east side and set her anchor in hard sand below eight feet of water. I tucked a few bills into the front pocket of my swim trunks and dove in.

It was a couple hundred yards to the beach in front of Henry's Good-Time Bar and Restaurant and I let the long steady strokes unwind the muscles in my shoulders and back while I reflected on the trip behind me. The last stretch of solo sailing in a three-month long escape from California was over and it felt good to have my boat at anchor and my body in the water.

Two weeks at sea had ruined my land-legs, but the fine warm beach sand felt good under my feet as I walked unsteadily past the coconut palms and sea-grape trees to the little restaurant. Henry's was constructed of rough boards that somebody had painted a vivid shade of turquoise and then covered with sea shells arranged into unusual shapes. Artful.

A barefoot middle-aged black man in faded brown shorts and a sparkling white linen shirt sat on a bench in front of the bar reading a newspaper. He looked up from the paper and smiled as I walked up.

"I'm Henry. We've got fresh grouper and conch fritters tonight for dinner. Best on de island."

"No, thanks," I said. "Just something cold to drink."

He gave the sigh of the disappointed entrepreneur.

"It's an honor bar, mon. If you can make it, you can drink it. Just write it down on de bar tab and pay before you go."

"Got any cold beer?"

"In de fridge, mon."

He turned back to his paper. Dried palm fronds hung above the door to the bar. I had to duck to get in. Nautical flags and yacht club burgees hung from the ceiling. Seashells, license plates from a dozen countries, and old T-shirts signed by their former owners covered the walls. A few pictures of lesser celebrities smiling with Henry hung behind the bar. A newer sign advertised free wireless internet access.

The room itself wasn't much larger than my old office at the naval base but, with one older couple and two very cute girls occupying the only tables, it was considerably more crowded. One of the girls was a brunette on the short side of twenty with large glossy brown eyes. The other was a younger bleached blonde with a tattoo in the small of her back. Depending on the observer's philosophical point of view, the tattoo could have been either some sort of tribal design or a bull's-eye. She was barely legal and wore a barely legal swimsuit. She could have kept a spare in her cell phone case.

"Like what you see?" said the blonde. She wasn't angry.

"What's not to like?" I said.

"What can't you see?" said her friend.

The blonde's jaw dropped and the two giggled in faux shock.

Whether it's biological compulsion or nautical tradition, sailors fresh from the sea tend to lose all reason when they find themselves near the opposite sex. The girls probably expected me to shake like a dog and roll over on my back. I almost did.

But gentlemen have their limits. So do I. At my age, I limit myself to women. Girls bring the complications that accompany inexperience and youth. And I'm too old for giggling.

I kept a cool head and refused to rise to the bait. Instead, I grabbed an ice-cold Carib from the back of the fridge, pulled off the cap with the church key that hung from the wall, and put a couple of bucks in the cigar box that sat on the bar. I smiled at the girls and went back outside to talk to Henry.

Henry's newspaper lay folded on the bench next to him. He sat at a small wooden table with a top made from four large white ceramic tiles. Several brightly colored cards lay face up on the tiles. Henry studied them.

I sat down on a chair nearby, dug my toes into the warm sand, and pulled a fine long drink from the bottle. The cold liquid washed away some of the salt from my throat and a few hundred miles off the trip.

"Henry, there is nothing like that first taste of beer."

"Yeah," he said. "Nothing like de cold beer after a long trip, eh?"

"Long trip?" I asked.

Henry studied the cards some more. He pointed at a card in the middle of the table. A man poled a small wooden boat through dark water. A half-dozen steel swords pierced the boat's bow.

"You've been on a long lonely journey, mon." He said it with conviction as he stroked his right temple with a long index finger. "And you've come here to get away from something painful or difficult. Maybe something dangerous, eh?"

I took another swallow from the bottle. It was almost as good as the first.

"Oh c'mon, Henry. You saw me bring that sailboat into this bay and anchor it by myself. And you can see I've had too much sun and wind, that I need a shave, and that walking straight on land is a bit of a challenge. It's not hard to guess that I just finished a long sail."

"You don't believe de Tarot." It was not a question. His smile was wide but not happy.

"I believe you've learned to size up the tourists pretty well over the years," I said.

He shook his head from side to side. "You're no tourist," he said.

He got up to greet two middle-aged couples coming from the beach. He reeled them in, told them about the daily special, and ushered them to a table at the restaurant side of the building. I pushed my toes deeper into the sand and took another pull at the bottle. The liquid smoothed a few more of the rough edges off my trip as the sun dropped below the palm trees and fizzled into a postcard-beautiful Caribbean. I finished my beer.

The girls walked out of the bar.

"We're going over to the Soggy Dollar," said the blonde. She shifted her weight from one foot to the other and then back with an effective and well-practiced bit of hip-wiggle. "There's gonna be a dance on the beach around nine," she said. "See you there?"

As tempted as I was, they were both younger than my lower limit.

"Sorry, not tonight," I said. "Henry tells me I've had a long and dangerous trip and that I need my rest."

The brunette laughed. The blonde looked puzzled at first but then smiled. I smiled back. The smile from the fish that gets away. They walked west along the beach and my eyes followed. I thought how nice it would be to dance with the blonde I'd left in California.

Melancholy pressed for another beer so I went to the fridge, grabbed Carib number two, and put a couple more bucks in the cigar box. The older couple had left the bar so I sat down at one of the now-empty tables. Henry came in and checked the contents of the cigar box. He smiled, grabbed a beer for himself, and sat down across from me.

"Nobody drinks alone in my place," he said.

He tipped back his beer and then dealt two more cards onto the table with a third one below the first two. The last card pictured five guys fighting with long sticks. Henry's eyes narrowed a bit and his voice lowered.

"Oh, you got big troubles coming, mon."

I leaned back in the chair and looked up at the ceiling.

"All God's children gots troubles, Henry."

He pointed at the five guys with the long sticks and poked the card several times with his long index finger. "There is great strife and hard times ahead for you," he said. He poked the card as I drank some more beer. "It's right there in front of you, mon."

This was my first conversation with another human in two weeks. I'd hoped for small talk with a tourist or maybe some local wisdom from a seasoned islander. Instead, this guy threw me the evil eye. He dealt two more cards.

"You carry a big anchor for such a small boat."

"It's forty pounds or so," I said. "Seems about right."

Like this guy had something to teach me about sailing?

"A heavy weight in de soul with a long chain."

I drank some more beer. "That sign over there says 'Henry's Good-Time Bar' and here you sit trying to scare away paying customers? It doesn't seem like a very sound business practice."

He put the cards back in his pocket, cocked his head a little to one side, and lowered his voice.

"Man come here to dis island—he no tourist, he no charter—he come alone on his own boat to the BVI. Man your size wearin' nothin' but swim trunks, a tanned hide, and a broken nose? Man looks like he take care of himself, too." He leaned back in his chair. "Alone in dese islands," he said, "that man will find real trouble soon."

"Thanks for the warning, Henry. I'm just here to relax and have a good time. Broken or not, I'll keep my nose clean." I finished the beer and stepped outside onto the beach.

Henry spoke up as I left. "You try to be de good boy, eh?"

I walked back down to the bay shaking my head and wondering why I always ran into the local crackpots. I swam back to *Figaro* through the dark water, showered off the salt, and went below to click on the anchor light. It was seven o'clock and too early for bed so I dug my laptop out from under the chart table and logged onto Henry's Good-Time free wireless internet service.

There were only a handful of emails worth reading. A short terse note from the blonde in California shared her many frustrations with me and indicated no small degree of finality to our relationship. It wasn't exactly unexpected but the words still stung.

Another, nearly a week old, was from Al. He'd been granted his government work permit, talked with a few diving operators, and worked out a deal with a guy who was looking to retire. He'd even made a down payment. All he needed to seal the deal was for me to show up with the rest of the money.

I threw a high five to nobody in particular.

The last email, two days old, made me want to throw my laptop against a bulkhead or punch a hole through a door. Al's girlfriend,

Liv, reported that he'd been arrested and charged with murder for killing a tourist. Henry's prophecy had some nasty yellow teeth. *Great strife. Big trouble in the islands, mon.* Thanks for the welcome, brother.

I sent Liv a reply and told her to find the best attorney on Tortola, to make an appointment with him, and to meet me at the West End ferry terminal at nine the next morning.

Tired and worn out, I crawled into *Figaro's* quarter berth, listened to the rhythmic hiss of ocean swells as they washed across the reef, and tried to fall asleep. For two solid weeks, I'd sailed *Figaro* alone and non-stop making do with forty-minute catnaps. Now at anchor, I should have hit my berth like a felled tree.

But a fortune teller's warning overpowered sleep. How did he know about Al or why I'd spent three months escaping the problems in California?

He didn't, I reasoned. *Cards couldn't tell him that.*

You can find out more about BROAD REACH, the next
Sim Greene / *Figaro* mystery, at **www.robavery.com**.

ACKNOWLEDGEMENTS

There are too many people who have helped me during this project for me to adequately thank them all. But I'll list a few anyway (in no particular order): Jeff and Cheri Earl, Wes and Cari Clark, Gordon and Frances Smith, Dean and Deanna Sonnenberg, Brett Boulton, Jay Allen, John Arthur Taylor, my family (Emily, Cameron and Allison, Jay, Frances, and Henry), and my agent and friend, Jacques de Spoelberch. I could not have finished this book without their encouragement and advice.

ABOUT THE AUTHOR

Rob Avery was born and raised in Burbank, California, but spent as much time as he could at the beach or in the Pacific Ocean. He is a criminal defense lawyer by profession and has a passion for sailing. His writing combines the two. Rob also hates referring to himself in the third person but can do so when pressed.